WITHDRAWN

The NATIVE STAR

M. K. HOBSON

SPECTRA

BALLANTINE BOOKS • NEW YORK

A Spectra Mass Market Original

Copyright © 2010 by Mary Hobson
All rights reserved.

Published in the United States by Spectra, an imprint of The Random House Publishing Group, a division of Random House, Inc., New York.

SPECTRA and the portrayal of a boxed "s" are trademarks of Random House, Inc.

978-0-553-59265-8

Printed in the United States of America

www.ballantinebooks.com

9 8 7 6 5 4 3 2

For Nora

ACKNOWLEDGMENTS

A book is like a pearl. The author supplies the grit in the middle, but it is friends and colleagues who add the thin bright layers that make it shine.

(Following this metaphor through, one might suppose they do this because they find the author and her grit so damned irritating—but let's leave such hobgoblinish consistency to littler minds, shall we?)

There are many writers who have given freely of their time (and nacre) to help me make this book smooth and fine, including Sara Mueller, David D. Levine, Sandi Gray, Robin Catesby, Jim Fiscus, Douglas Watson, John Bunnell, Denny Bershaw, Simone Cooper, Francine Taylor, George Walker, and the late Chris Bunch. To these comrades-in-arms, I offer my humble thanks.

Thanks as well to my fierce and fabulous agent, Ginger Clark, who contributed at least three layers of opalescence before she even took me on as a client. Thanks to the splendid Juliet Ulman (who picked up the book) and the creative team at Spectra (who ran with it): my brilliant editor, Anne Groell, copy editor Faren Bachelis, David Pomerico, and everyone else whose names I either don't know, can't spell, or am afraid to say three times out loud.

Additionally, I am deeply grateful to the kindred spirits who have bolstered my sanity or encouraged my insanity at critical moments: Douglas Lain, Ellen Datlow, Shawna McCarthy, Jessica Reisman, A. M. Dellamonica, Camille Alexa, Heidi Lampietti (and Kiri), Madeleine Robins, Nancy Jane Moore,

Serge Maillioux, Karen Berry, and the entire graduating class of Clarion West 2005.

And finally, of course, thanks to my family: Dan and Nora, Mom and Dad, Rachel and Albert. It's from them that I got the grit to begin with.

It is a beauteous evening, calm and free,
The holy time is quiet as a Nun
Breathless with adoration; the broad sun
Is sinking down in its tranquillity;
The gentleness of heaven broods o'er the Sea:
Listen! the mighty Being is awake,
And doth with his eternal motion make
A sound like thunder—everlastingly.
Dear Child! dear Girl! that walkest with me here,
If thou appear untouched by solemn thought,
Thy nature is not therefore less divine:
Thou liest in Abraham's bosom all the year;
And worship'st at the Temple's inner shrine,
God being with thee when we know it not.

—WILLIAM WORDSWORTH

Prologue

Five loud, hard, sharp crashes. Someone was knocking—no, not knocking, rather *pounding*—at the door of Mr. Everdene Baugh's house on Church Street.

It was well past midnight. A violent tempest of bird-shot rain and screaming wind—the biggest storm to hit Charleston in a decade—was raging outside. *Anarchy and insolence,* Baugh fumed as he fumbled his way down the dark, narrow stairs, wool-stockinged feet sliding on bare wood. Every day he was unpleasantly surprised at how much closer to savagery the world had drifted.

Baugh threw open his door with the intention of telling the pounders to go to Hell and exactly how to get there. But when he saw that it was a detachment of Union soldiers on his doorstep, their rifles gleaming, the words froze in his mouth. Before the soldiers stood a hulking officer with dripping muttonchops, who seemed hardly to notice the rain sluicing down on him from the broken gutters above.

"Captain John Caul," the man introduced himself curtly, not bothering to touch the brim of his hat. "You're Baugh, of E. W. Baugh and Company?"

Baugh clutched the edge of the door, knuckles white. Sherman's bloody march was only a few months in the past. The ashes of Columbia had barely cooled, and the once-fertile fields of South Carolina were barren, ruined by the despoiling

northern Warlock squadrons who had sown every field with
black sorcerer's salt. And since Lincoln's assassination, the
Yankee garrisons had been itching for blood.

Baugh prayed they weren't here for his.

"Your firm operated a warehouse before the recent conflicts," Caul said. His voice was strangely flat, as if he was
attempting to make each word balance precisely with the
next. "I have been informed that you might be willing to
let it. I've come on behalf of an associate who wishes a
viewing."

"You want me to take you 'round to see the warehouse?"
Baugh blinked in astonishment. "But . . . but it's . . ."

" . . . *haunted*," Caul finished for him, with a distinct sneer.
"Yes. I know all about that. Get dressed. My associate is waiting."

The walk to the warehouse was brief but no less unpleasant
for being so. The driving rain was cold and stinging, and Baugh
had to lean forward against the hard wind to make headway.
Better, though, to lean forward into the wind than back against
the rifle that one of Caul's men was jabbing between his shoulder blades.

When they reached the warehouse, Baugh saw a black carriage waiting in the street. Caul's associate.

"It'll be just a moment," Baugh said apologetically as he
went to the great rusting padlock. He unlocked it carefully;
then, when no one was looking, he placed his hand on the
door's wooden frame.

"Ghost," he whispered. "It's me."

There was a soft, cool exhalation from within the building,
a distant moaning of recognition.

Feeling the presence of his ghost cheered Baugh immeasur-
ably. The ghost was the most useful sorcellement he'd ever purchased. During the recent unpleasantness, its talent for striking
terror into the hearts of the living had been the only thing that
kept the Union armies from commandeering his warehouse.
Baugh glanced back at the ruffians in blue who'd escorted him
here. It would be awfully satisfying to instruct the ghost to send
them packing, too.

However, Captain Caul had used the word "let." And the

word "let" implied money. And Baugh, like every other hungry Confederate son, very much needed money.

"Your services won't be required," he whispered, patting the door frame tenderly. "Not yet, anyway. But stand ready in case I need you." A creaking sound of understanding and compliance came in reply.

If these Yankees wanted to let his warehouse, he'd take their money. Otherwise he'd call his haunt down on them quicker than rain off a tin roof.

Baugh made a great show of removing the padlock, as if he'd been fiddling with it the whole time. Only when the doors of the warehouse were opened did Caul's associate, a man in a shining beaver top hat, suffer himself to be handed down from his carriage by a soggy sergeant.

And it was not until they were inside, and one of Caul's soldiers had kindled a lamp, that Baugh got a good look at the mysterious stranger. The man's limbs seemed to have been molded precisely to fit his elegantly tailored chamois trousers and fashionably cut coat. His fingers sparkled with gem-set gold rings, he wore a neat Vandyke, and his eyes were an alarming shade of peacock blue.

"Monsieur Rene," Caul said. "Comte d'Artaud"

"Pleased to meet you," Baugh said. Artaud didn't even look in his direction. Instead, the Frenchman walked around the building slowly, hands loosely clasped behind his back. He looked up at the cobwebbed rafters, then at the dirty windows. He squinted at a sudden flash of lightning.

"How large is this warehouse?" he asked, his accent pleasantly elliptical.

Baugh threw out his chest proudly. "Why, it's the only warehouse hereabouts rigged up with an extradimensional enchantment . . . I had it done before the war. The warehouse is five thousand square feet on the outside, eighty thousand on the inside. I paid dearly for that . . ." He paused. "Not that I'd pass the cost along—"

"A very useful enchantment," came a voice from behind him. Baugh startled. Caul was standing right at his shoulder. How had the big man crept up on him like that? The captain was staring down at him, eyes flat and still as those of a corpse.

"Very . . . very useful." Baugh licked his lips. "The Warlock who sold it to me was a traveling fellow, from Boston." How he wanted to get out from under those horrible eyes! "He . . . sold me quite a few little witcheries."

"Yes," Caul said. "I've heard."

"Here, Captain." Artaud was pointing to a spot on the floor. Caul snapped fingers at his men, and two of them hurried out into the storm. They returned carrying a huge iron-banded chest, which they set near the place Artaud had indicated. One of them handed Caul a crowbar.

Before Baugh could say a word, Caul thrust one end of the bar between two floorboards, prying them up with a creak of iron nails and a scream of pine. Caul set the boards aside, and he and the Frenchman peered down into darkness, where the building's foundations were sunk in the murky swamp of the delta.

"What are you doing!" Baugh cried. But neither Caul nor Artaud answered, and since no further destruction seemed forthcoming, Baugh said nothing more. He did, however, move closer for a better look.

Artaud opened the iron-banded chest and withdrew a narrow cherrywood box, the kind that might hold a billiard cue. Within it, seated in velvet, lay five long tubes of silver, gradating from the circumference of a child's wrist to that of a lady's pinkie. Four were designed to telescope out into longer sections; the Frenchman pulled these out and began screwing them together.

While Artaud did this, the captain reached into the iron-banded chest and strained to remove a final object, wide as a washtub and tall as a tea table. Caul kicked the chest closed and set the object on top of it. It was a machine of polished steel and glass. On each side it had a large flywheel with a bulbous wooden crank handle.

Artaud had finished connecting the silver tubes, and now had a long, flexible pole. He threaded this through the hole in the floor thin-end first, letting it slide through his fingers until it hit the mud with a distant *plip*. He twisted the pole until it was well seated. Then he took the fifth piece from the cherrywood box and fitted it onto the pole's end. This piece was different from the others; it was a kind of cap, with a long, cloth-wrapped cord sprouting from its terminating end. Artaud connected the cord to the machine, then gestured to two of Caul's soldiers, who began vigorously cranking the machine. The machine came alive with a warbling hum—a slightly irregular sound that rose and fell with the minutely varying speed of the men's exertions.

"What are you . . ."

The Frenchman threw his hand up curtly, stopping the words in Baugh's mouth. He was peering at an enameled gauge that was domed with blown glass and inscribed with beautifully scrolled French indicators. He stared at it for some time before making a sound of disgust.

"It is hopeless!" he muttered, glaring at Caul. "Your Boston man said the readings were unprecedented!"

"So they must have been," Caul said. "Try again."

"Non," Artaud snapped. "Your scout was an idiot. There is nothing here."

He seized the pole as if he meant to wrench it out of the ground. But the instant his skin touched the metal, a flash of ice-blue light crackled like a thousand tiny Chinese firecrackers, knocking him across the room. He landed with a thud. He did not move for a moment, but then he groaned and stirred.

Horrified, Baugh rushed to help Artaud to his feet. A thick lock of brilliantined hair flopped across his forehead and his cheek was streaked with grime—but oddly enough, the Frenchman was grinning broadly.

"What could have happened?" Baugh stammered, brushing dust from Artaud's coat. "Some kind of lightning bolt, perhaps? These storms— "

"No, no," Artaud said, waving away Baugh's fussings. He smoothed back his hair, then straightened his collar. "Thank you, my dear sir. We've seen all we need to see."

Baugh's heart sunk at the finality with which the words were spoken.

"Then you won't be wanting the place?"

Artaud fixed his gaze on Baugh, and Baugh almost screamed. The Frenchman's eyes had gone completely black from iris to lid. It was like looking into an open grave. Fumbling backward, Baugh found that Caul was right behind him. The big man grabbed him, held him.

"On the contrary." Artaud's black eyes were dull as wells of tar. "We'll take it immediately."

"Ghost!" Baugh choked. "Ghost, help me!"

Before the words had left his lips, a spectral form began to coalesce. Greasy ectoplasm dripped from the walls—a miasma that made the warehouse glow with a sickly yellow light. It grew until it was a vast figure, vaguely human in form, with a distended head and long spindly limbs. It opened its black mouth and began to shriek—a sound that was the pure distillation of death and torture, terror and misery, sorrow and despair.

Even Baugh, who owned the ghost, found it terrifying.

Caul, however, did not. Shoving Baugh toward one of his men, he strode toward the atrocity. His impassive face was illuminated by the haunt's shifting yellow glow. Pulling a two-chambered glass pendant from beneath his collar, Caul thrust it toward the ghost. He began speaking in guttural cadences that resounded against the walls, beating against the howling of the ghost like a base drum contending with a steam siren. He spoke louder, and knives of light shone in the air, threads and wires of gleaming red and black that tangled around the ghost, slicing it into shining blobs of ectoplasm that fell from the air to sizzle and quiver on the floor like spat mucus. The ghost's shrieks grew fainter and fainter. Finally, they faded away entirely.

"Ghost?" Baugh called softly.

"It has served its purpose." Caul turned to look at Baugh. "The Warlock from Boston—the one who sold you the ghost— he was one of mine. He put down wards against fire and flood, too." Caul paused. "We commandeered this warehouse long before the war, Baugh. You just never knew it."

Caul walked slowly toward him, his hand going to his belt.

"Now, one final sacrifice is required of you." He drew a long silver knife that gleamed in the half-light of the lanterns. "To exorcise the haunt completely, I must have the blood of its master."

Caul gave him no chance to scream. The knife's cold edge flashed up, then down. His own blood, spraying cherry-red in a flash of lightning, was the last thing Baugh saw.

CHAPTER ONE

Ashes of Amour

Lost Pine, California
Wednesday, April 23, 1876

When the sun's first rays touched the tops of the pines in the creek hollow, Emily Edwards shivered as if thin pink and gold fingers were creeping stealthily up her spine.

She hid for a moment under her quilt, chewing on her lip. The instructions in Pap's grimoire said the words had to be spoken at first light. No use dawdling over it.

Snatching the little blue and red calico spell bag from the pine table beside her bed, she squeezed her eyes shut and whispered:

"My decision is firm,
My will is strong,
Let this spell bind him
All his life long."

It was done. The Ashes of Amour were finished.

Emily threw off her covers, sending a pair of raggedy cats into grumpy flight. The chill morning air had a crisp, pitchy smell that mingled with the fragrance of the dried flowers and herbs that hung from the rafters. She tucked the little bag of ashes into a pouch she wore around her neck then dressed quickly, gray wool over scratchy underwear, thick knitted socks over icy toes. Then it was time to face the not-inconsiderable task of brushing and braiding her hair.

Emily's chestnut-colored hair was thick and shiny as silk floss—an extraordinary female endowment. But like most female endowments, it was generally more trouble than it was worth. In particular, it possessed a prodigious ability to tangle—a perverse genius that could be thwarted only by keeping it tightly braided at all times.

But the grimoire had indicated that the Witch must wear nothing knotted or tied or sewn or fastened while working the spell. That meant unbraided and naked. At midnight. In April. In the Sierra Nevada mountains.

She had built a small fire, over which she'd burned the ingredients in a small brass cauldron, but the spell's directions hadn't allowed her to linger by it; she had to complete an intricate series of steps and turns and rhymes around the fire as the ingredients crumbled to a potent ash guaranteed to compel the eternal love of anyone who touched it. By the time she'd gotten back to the cabin, she'd been so cold that all she could do was dive under her quilt and hope that some tonsorial miracle would greet her on the morrow.

Sighing her regret that no such miracle had occurred, she picked up her boxwood comb and began picking the snarls out from the ends.

This was not a good start to what was supposed to be the happiest day of her life.

By the time her accustomed plaits were tickling the backs of her knees, the sun was well up. She climbed down from the attic loft quietly so as not to wake Pap, who was snoring in the iron bedstead by the banked fire, blanketed by a half dozen purring cats. Pap had been her adoptive father for twenty years and Lost Pine's charm maker for twice that, and all of those years had been filled with hard work. Since fever took his eyesight last summer, the work that had been Pap's livelihood—gathering plants, compounding salves, charming buildings, reading fortunes—had fallen to Emily. She was glad to do it.

She went to the table where items were collected in a willow basket: brushes and pots of milk paint, sticks of charcoal and a platter-size slab of white oak. The oak had been edged and planed by Dag Hansen, the most prosperous lumberman in Lost Pine, who had commissioned a protective hex plaque for the topmost eave of his big new timber shed. Taking the basket, she stole quietly from the cabin.

Her foot was on the threshold when a vivid flash of rust-red caught her eye. A robin, the first of spring, flew from where it had been perched on the sill of the small front window. She watched it vanish into the top of a blue spruce.

A robin on the windowsill—an omen of true love. That seemed encouraging. But less so the question it begged: true love for whom?

Not you. The robin's call drifted down from the spruce's crown. *Not you.*

Tucking the basket under her arm, Emily walked quickly, as if she could outrun the sound. But it followed her, high and piercing:

Not you.

On a grassy swale overlooking the main road from Dutch Flat to Lost Pine, where the rapidly rising sun was bright and hot in the cloudless sky, Emily set herself down to work

She laid the slab of oak on her lap and looked at it for a long time. It showed the signs of Dag Hansen's strong, industrious hands. He was a good man. A good, kind, trusting man. He'd make a wonderful husband.

She opened the pots of milk paint. Reaching into the silk pouch she wore around her neck, she took out the little bag of ashes. She put a generous pinch into each pot.

Then she dipped a horsehair brush into the yellow and began dabbing carefully at the oak, muttering rhyming incantations as she laid the bright color onto the wood. She focused her intentions, concentrating on prosperity and happiness, goodwill and success, love and (Heaven help her) fertility.

She focused closely on her work, so deeply engrossed that when an echoing "Hey there" came up from the road, she almost knocked over the pot of red. Shading her eyes with a paint-stained hand, she noticed how high the sun had climbed.

"Hey, Em Edwards!"

On the road, a pair of heavy bays stood in front of a stout buckboard. It was Mr. Orta, the delivery agent for the Wells, Fargo & Company express office in Dutch Flat. She waved, set her work aside, and hurried down, glad to stretch her stiff legs.

"I thought it was you," he said, pushing his cap back. "What are you up to?"

"I'm painting a hex for Dag Hansen's new shed." Emily was aware of a high, tense note in her voice. For goodness' sake, it sounded like she was confessing to a shooting! She licked her lips and continued. "They're putting it up this afternoon."

"Folks say he'll have the narrow-gauge track laid into Dutch Flat before summer, and you folks won't have to wait for me to haul deliveries up to you." He gave her a sly look. "I suppose there'll be a dance later?"

"I suppose," Emily said, not wanting to talk about Dag and dancing. She craned her neck to see what Mr. Orta had in his buckboard. Two huge crates, half covered with canvas.

"Who are *those* for?" She pointed.

"Curiosity killed the cat," he chuckled. "But I guess it can't do no harm to a sturdy young Witch like you. One's for that easterner, that fellow Stanton. The other's a bunch of separate deliveries from Baugh's Patent Magicks—an order in it for almost everyone up here, it seems."

Emily looked at the crates more closely. Sure enough, one was marked with the distinctive blue logo of Baugh's Patent Magicks—a saucy genie rising out of a bottle in a cloud of smoke.

A whole crate of Baugh's. Emily felt like spitting in the dust.

"I don't suppose I could talk you into dumping that crate into a ditch and pretending it never came?" Emily gave Mr. Orta a winsome, slightly desperate smile.

Mr. Orta chuckled awkwardly. They were, after all, joking about her livelihood.

"Sorry, Em." He scratched the back of his head. "I guess times change. Anyway, you need a ride? I can get you closer to Hansen's place than you are now."

"No, *thank* you," she said, entertaining the dramatic notion that she'd rather walk than ride in a buckboard with a crate of Baugh's Patent Magicks. "I have to go see about Pap's lunch."

Mr. Orta slapped the lines and clucked to the horses. Whistling, he disappeared beyond the bend, and Emily climbed the hill to gather up her paints. The hex she'd painted had dried nicely in the warm sun. She ran her fingers over the bright rough surface. She'd done it up neat, but the plaque was . . . *rustic*. Not shiny and precise like a hex of baked enamel from Baugh's Patent Magicks would be.

Damn that Baugh, whoever he was! After looking to make sure Mr. Orta was gone, she *did* spit in the dust, and muttered a curse, too. But her curses seemed to be of little avail when it came to Baugh's.

Over the past year, more and more folks had taken to buying patent magic from Baugh's. Advertised in colorful chromolithographed catalogues, the products came in shiny pasteboard boxes stamped with gold foil and lined with blood-red tissue paper. They made Emily's hand-sewn charm bundles and home-brewed potions look shoddy and questionable by comparison. And business had suffered for it.

The past winter had been the worst. Paying Pap's doctor had left them short on cash-money, and as the hungry snow months had closed around them, Emily had watched Pap's cheeks grow hollow, his collarbones grow sharp, and his spirit grow tired. She'd gotten them through on mangy possums and stringy jackrabbits, but having to watch him starve . . . starve! After forty years of hard, honest work! It wasn't fair. Something had to be done.

And that something was Dag Hansen.

It seemed the perfect solution. All she had to do was get him to marry her, and Pap could live in comfort and plenty. And she was no cheat; she'd take on the job of being a pleasant and loyal wife just as she'd taken on Pap's magical work. It was just trading one job for another.

But how to catch the prosperous lumberman? Her twenty-fifth birthday was a half year gone, which made her a pretty shelf-worn item. So she'd turned to Pap's grimoire for help, and she'd gone to the Hanging Oak, and she'd danced naked in the light of the full moon, and she'd made the Ashes of Amour.

Tucking her paints away, she put the hex plaque in the willow basket and didn't look at it again.

"I only want what's best for everyone," she muttered to herself. "And if you're going to make an omelette, you have to break a few eggs . . ."

Then she stopped and pressed her lips together, resolving not to think about what she'd have to break to make a marriage.

She climbed back up Moody Ridge to Pap's cabin, walking as fast as she could, making her legs burn. The exertion felt good. Loose wisps of hair tangled around her lips and ears; she pushed them back with annoyance. The chickens in the front yard welcomed her with low chuckles; she scattered the lazy biddies with a swing of the basket.

Inside, brightly colored bottles shone on the windowsills, and the bones of powerful animals dangled from braids of dyed red string. Scrolls of old vellum and parchment were rolled in stacks, ready to have spells writ upon them with eagle quills in ink of blood red or black gall. Pap's most important tools hung above the stone fireplace: the ceremonial dagger that he called an *athame,* and his purple charm cap. Pap himself sat in front of a hugely roaring fire, wrapped in a bright wool trade blanket. As usual, he was surrounded by cats. Most regarded Emily with boredom, but one or two bumped their soft heads against her legs as she came in.

"Em's back!" Pap smiled a greeting. A barn fire in Pap's youth had left the right side of his face a cobweb of shining pink scars. When he smiled, his face crumpled like crepe fabric.

There was the sound of movement in the cooking part of the room (while it was screened by a sheet hung from the ceiling, it could hardly be called a kitchen), and Mrs. Lyman poked her head out.

"I made your pap some lunch, and brought some fresh cornbread and a dried-apple pie." Mrs. Lyman, a mining widow with no fewer than ten grown children, lived on the place about a mile over. Pap had once cured her of recurrent warts on her hands, and she had been devoted to the old man ever since. "I thought you'd go straight over to Dag Hansen's. I reckon he's the only man in Lost Pine can make you forget about your poor ol' pap."

Emily flushed, and not just from the heat of the room.

"There's not any man in the world who could make me forget Pap." Emily gave his shoulder a squeeze as she carried her paintbrushes to the table to wash. She poured water into a bowl and began working the almost-dried color from the horsehair. "But if you've already eaten . . ."

"I've eaten," Pap said. "And Mrs. Lyman's going to stay and read to me."

"From *Ladies' Repository,*" Mrs. Lyman added, her tone suggesting that Emily was missing a treat. She had settled into a chair by the fire and already had the magazine spread across her lap.

Emily, however, was heartily glad that she would miss a night of *Ladies' Repository*. It was a magazine that jumbled articles of an improving nature (often subtitled, quite annoyingly, "A Warning to Young Ladies") with sickly sweet tales of love and romance. Emily much preferred it when Mrs. Lyman read from one of her mail-order subscription novels; at least they could be counted on to feature a clever mystery-solving Witch or the grand magical doings of eminent European Warlocks.

"Go on to your dance, Em." Pap's voice was gentle. "You deserve a little fun."

"Or you can stay and listen for a while." Mrs. Lyman tapped a luridly colored illustration on cheap newsprint. "Listen to this one I been saving out . . . a real *juicy* one! *'Her Tragic Mistake'* . . ."

"No thanks," Emily blurted, letting the brushes drop with a clatter. "I guess I *had* better get a move on."

After bolting up the ladder to her garret, Emily sat on the edge of her bed for a moment, closing her eyes and trying to swallow down her hard-thudding heart. Then, flinging open her trunk, she dragged out a vibrant spring calico that had been packed away since fall. She gave it a hard, mean shake. She debated whether to forego her long underwear; the dress would look better without the red flannel showing at the ankles and wrists. But if she shed the flannels, Mrs. Lyman would certainly notice and nag poor Pap about it all night. And after all, what did it matter? Dag was going to fall in love with her anyway.

What a depressing thought.

Well, at least she could spare Pap the aggravation. She left the flannels on, then slid the dress over her head and did up the blackened bone buttons. Smoothing the fabric over her hips, she then bent to retrieve an embossed morocco case from under her bed. From it, she withdrew two long, heavy hair sticks of beautifully engraved silver—one of the few inheritances from her mother. She twisted her heavy braids on top of her head and stabbed them through with the sticks. Regarding herself in her bit of cracked mirror, she rubbed stray streaks of paint from her face with a wetted thumb, then nodded soberly. At the very least, falling in love with her would not be a downright embarrassment.

Since she'd be walking home late, and she knew from recent experience just how cold April nights in the Sierras could get, she threw on her big buffalo coat before shinnying down the loft ladder.

She took Pap's big leather charm satchel from its place next to the door and slung it over her shoulder. When Pap had been younger, he'd carried it with him everywhere like a badge of office—and since she'd assumed most of his responsibilities, she never went without it either. She tucked Dag's painted hex into the satchel and pulled down the flap.

Mrs. Lyman wagged a finger at Emily. "Now, if it gets too late, you stay in town at Annie Bargett's, or walk home with one of my girls." She leaned toward Pap conspiratorially. "Things just aren't safe anymore! Why, I heard tell of the most awful spate of Aberrancies outside of Sacramento. Mrs. Foster's boy, Harlan, he was just telling me the other day . . ."

Emily slipped out of the cabin quietly, smiling to herself. Mrs. Lyman loved to talk about the Aberrancies—"the horrible, slavering monstrosities that roamed the wilderness in vast numbers; terrifying beasts of native legend that beggared description and made strong men blanch and tremble" (in the words of a true-to-life account from *Men's Adventure Monthly*). In fact, Emily felt certain that Mrs. Lyman would be positively tickled if she could actually encounter one of the semimythical terrors. But while Emily had often heard talk about the Aberrancies that bothered the trains, she'd never seen one, and would be willing to swear that she never would.

You never will now, anyway, she told herself. *For you've set yourself to become a good wife. And good wives don't have much to do with slavering monstrosities.*

Emily was surprised at how disappointing this thought was, but she lifted her chin resolutely. She'd take disappointment over starvation any day.

Following the well-worn trail that led from the cabin, Emily headed down the ridge toward Lost Pine, Dag Hansen, and her future.

Dag Hansen's new timber shed was being raised near the planned terminus of the narrow-gauge railroad tracks he was having laid into Dutch Flat. He'd managed to build half of the side line the past summer. This year he intended to finish the job and bring prosperity to Lost Pine. The way he said "prosperity," with such delicious anticipation and pride, made it seem as though he were talking about an actual person: a big jolly fellow with luxurious face whiskers and gold-capped teeth.

Over the past decade, prosperity had been no stranger to Dag Hansen. He'd made good money selling his timber to the railroad companies. The new side line would allow him to send moss-covered logs down from the slopes of Moody Ridge to the mills in Dutch Flat year-round.

Emily followed the ringing of hammers and the rasping of saws. There wasn't much to Lost Pine—a small saloon, a smaller general store, a few diminutive homes, and the silver-gray buildings of the old timber camp. The shed was being raised at the edge of the settlement, in a big sunny clearing. The smell of fresh-cut fir hung in the air, and the clean new wood gleamed golden in the warm afternoon light. The walls had been raised already, and Dag and his men were nailing up stout crossbeams.

Dag was large and sturdy, with cornsilk hair and elk-brown

eyes, a deeply tanned face and a strong brown throat. He'd un-
buttoned his shirt against the heat of the day, and the sweat
filming his bare arms and powerful chest made him seem to
glisten. All in all, he wasn't exceptionally difficult to look at.
A perfect target for a designing Witch.

She'd known him since they were children. He had been a
unique specimen of boyhood—one who did not find it great
fun to do painful things to her long braids—and had grown
into a stalwart, kindhearted man. Not an overly deep thinker,
but an excellent lumberman.

When Dag saw her, he laid down his hammer and hurried
over.

"Hey, Em!" he said, slightly breathless. He gestured to the
shed proudly. "What do you think? We've made some
progress, eh?"

Emily made herself smile.

"I painted your hex," she said. With trembling hands, she
drew the oak plaque from the satchel. Dag pushed his hat back
with his thumb and smiled broadly—a smile of real pleasure.
A good, kind, honest smile.

The smile almost made Emily lose her nerve. She couldn't
go through with it, she just couldn't!

Then what happens next winter? a hard, determined part
of her whispered. *What happens next time Pap gets sick and
there's no money for medicine?*

Swallowing the lump in her throat, Emily thrust the hex
plaque at Dag. He took it in his big dirt-stained hands, bringing it up to admire it.

"That *is* fine!" he said. "Much nicer than one of those tin
jobs from Baugh's . . ." Then he paused, scrutinizing her work
more closely, as if he'd found a flaw. A strange look came over
his face—an abrupt, yawning discontent. He blinked in slight
confusion. He looked at Emily, and there was something ex-
pectant in his eyes, as if he'd suddenly remembered that she
had come to tell him a secret, or deliver a large sum of money.

"That'll keep your lumber safe from wandering spirits,
baneful curses, fire, and most varieties of . . . rot." Emily
choked over the last word, her throat suddenly dry. But Dag
didn't say anything, just looked at her with odd expectancy.

"You sure look pretty today," he murmured. "Is that a new dress?"

"I put away my winter clothes." Emily felt strangely shy. "I figured it was warm enough."

"You look fine," Dag said. "Really . . . fine. You . . . ah . . . stayin' for the dance later?"

"I guess," she said.

"You know . . . you know, ah . . ." Dag's stammering made Emily wince. Usually, he was as direct as a hammer. "This is . . . ah . . . this is just the beginning. Once the track is completed, then Lost Pine will really be on the map." He twisted the oak around in his hands. "What I mean to say is, I plan to make real things happen here. I'll be doing more building . . . probably a new house. A big house, nothing but the best."

"Oh?" Emily felt slightly dizzy, as if her entire torso had been inflated with cold air.

"A *family* house." He blushed and looked away. "Anyhow, the thing is . . . I'll need more hex paintings like this one here." He looked at it. "Such a pretty job. You're so—" he stopped. "Anyway, maybe tonight, we could go off walking and . . . and talk. Talk about . . ."

"Sure, Dag." Emily gave him a bright smile. She punched down the feeling of sickness in her stomach and covered it with steely resolve. She wasn't about to lead him on a coy chase. She'd made her bed, and now she'd . . . well, maybe that wasn't the right metaphor.

Or maybe it was exactly the right one.

She took Dag's hand and gave it an encouraging squeeze.

"I'll look forward to it," she said.

Dag's eyes widened with elation. He took two dizzy steps backward, grabbed his hammer with a fumbling hand, and shinnied up the skeleton of a wall, all the way up to the roof eaves. He nailed the plaque to the topmost beam, then gave a loud whoop that echoed off the mountains high above.

Dag's men shouted at him and laughed. Emily turned away quickly, blushing. She hurried off along the granite-bouldered main road toward the timber-camp kitchen to help the women with the food. It seemed the thing to do.

The rest of the afternoon passed in a blur of biscuit rolling, china washing, chicken frying, and child chasing. By the time the platters of steaming food had been carried down to the new shed and set out on a long trestle table and the lanterns had been lit and someone had pulled out an accordion to commence the dancing, Emily was exhausted and slightly numb.

Stars glittered down through the fresh-hewn beams of the yet-unfinished roof. The night air held winter's frosty memory, but the lively music and the large bonfire in the yard—not to mention the mugs of hard cider and the frequent nips of whiskey—kept everyone pleasantly warm.

Dag wasn't about to let anyone else dance with Emily, so she was in his arms all the way from the waltz to the schottische and on past that to the cheat-and-swing. He kept pulling her closer. After a couple of hours of his hands resting heavy on her back, his chest pressed against hers, his lips getting closer and closer to her face, Emily felt flushed and anxious. Pushing itching wisps of hair back behind her ears, she evaded Dag's invitation to jig-and-reel and slipped out the back in search of calmer air.

Outside, she paused under the hanging lantern, leaned against the fragrant new wood, and closed her eyes. Through the siding boards she could feel the pulse of noise and conversation, and it was like another heartbeat. A new heartbeat that would become her own, over time. She'd seen the robin on her windowsill, the omen of true love. She liked Dag Hansen an awful lot. She'd get used to his hands. She'd fall in love with him eventually, sure as spring followed winter. Pap would be provided for, time would pass, and this would become her life.

And it would be just fine.

She was still trying to convince herself of this when she heard the soft clanking of metal on metal coming from a ways off in the darkness. Reaching up, she unhooked the lantern and held it before her as she took a few steps forward.

"Who's there?" But then, the lantern's light illuminated the clatter, and an answer became unnecessary.

He was an angular gentleman, tall and extremely lank, hardly more than a wired-together aggregation of very large bones. He wore a dark suit of a cut too fine to have come from

Lost Pine, or Dutch Flat, or even Sacramento for that matter. His name was Dreadnought Stanton.

Emily let out a sigh and prepared to be annoyed. For when it came to being annoying, Dreadnought Stanton never disappointed.

He was a Warlock, and the manner in which he typically declared this left the distinct impression that the word must be spelled in strictly capital letters. He was a Warlock, a member of a lofty brotherhood whose kind ran factories, advised ancient monarchs, and were appointed to cabinet posts in Washington, D.C.; doers of great deeds who turned the tides of war and vanquished monsters; superior men who shored up the underpinnings of reality and other extremely splendid and eye-popping things.

Dreadnought Stanton was a Warlock, and during his tenure in Lost Pine, he seemed never to tire of reminding people of that fact.

Emily was similarly fond of wondering (aloud) what such a fabulously powerful being was doing in a backwater like Lost Pine. The answer? Having studied at a prestigious institute in New York, he was on some kind of humanitarian mission to bring the light of modern magical methods to the nation's dimmest corners. And because Pap and Emily were the only ones in this particular dim corner with any interest in magic, he'd focused his attentions on them.

The first time Stanton had ridden up the ridge on his black horse, she'd thought he was a tax collector. Or a census taker, maybe. Someone from as far away from Lost Pine as it was possible to be, at any rate. She'd stared at him until he was close enough to stare back, examining her as one would a peculiar exhibit at the zoo. Only then did she remember that it was the middle of wash day, and she was wearing one of Pap's shirts soaked to the sleeves, old pants tied at the waist with a rope, and boots crusted with mud.

It was right then that Emily decided she despised him.

Obligingly, Stanton had gone on to give her ample reason to continue doing so. That first visit, he ended up stealing hours of Pap's valuable nap time with a derisive lecture on how the methods the old man had used for more than four decades were ludicrously outmoded.

As if Pap needed teaching from a puffed-up pedant with a head too big for his black felt bowler. It made her blood boil. After that, Emily had been downright inhospitable, turning the Warlock away whenever he came riding up on one of his pair of expensive black horses. Then, winter snows had made the cabin nearly inaccessible, and though she and Pap had endured awful hardships, at least they'd been blissfully Warlock-free for almost five months. Now, however, with spring's return, Mr. Stanton had shown every indication of resuming his assault on Pap's outdatedness. He'd ridden up to the cabin once already while Emily was out, and had managed to corner Pap with a lecture on something called "new herbalism." Pap had found it fascinating, and Emily had thought him rather a traitor for thinking so.

"Exactly what are you doing, Mr. Stanton?" Emily asked. The question hardly needed answering, for it was clear that Stanton was rummaging through the tools that the laborers had laid aside.

Stanton glanced up, and even though Emily wore her nicest clothes, he gave her the exact same look he had that first day, when her boots were muddy and her belt made of rope.

"Oh, it's you," he said. He returned to his rummaging. "I *do* hope I haven't interrupted your hoeing-down."

"These tools aren't yours." Stanton didn't seem to notice how haughty and disapproving she was trying to sound. He straightened, a hammer in one hand and a crowbar in the other. He gave each a momentary appraisal, then threw back the hammer.

"I received an important shipment today." He stepped over the tools and pushed past her. "From New York. And I have no means of opening the crate."

For a moment, Emily considered whistling for Dag and his men and leaving Stanton to his fate. But she'd had enough of toying with men's fates for one evening.

"Well, I don't know how things are done in New York," Emily said, "but in Lost Pine, it's considered polite to ask before running off with someone else's things."

Stanton sighed, and even in the darkness she could see him rolling his eyes.

"Then will you be so kind as to direct me to the owner of this *excellent* and *valuable* crowbar, so that I might request the privilege of its usage?" His intonation was extravagant. "Formally, I mean."

She showed him into the shed, and with a sharp motion, pointed a finger at Dag, who was towering among a group of friends, laughing in a huge voice.

Emily snuck a sideways glance at Stanton, hoping to revel in his discomfiture, but he was already halfway across the room, moving with long, purposeful strides. If only Dag would fly off in an uncharacteristic rage and send the pompous Warlock scurrying! But Dag was singularly unobliging. His men were clustered around him, clapping him on the back and yelling congratulations. Dag looked over at Emily, letting his eyes linger on her for a long time. Emily blushed furiously, heat rising up her throat. At the very least he could have gotten a yes before he started telling everyone!

In his transport of excitement and joviality, Dag didn't even notice the Warlock standing behind him. Stanton's throat-clearings went from quietly polite to aggressively cathartic, but were of no avail. He shifted idly from one foot to the other until he was distracted by the sight of women bringing in fresh platters of food. His nostrils twitched as he eyed the piles of fried chicken, the heaps of steaming biscuits, the mounded beef cutlets cloaked in cream gravy. Without another look at Dag, he tucked the crowbar under his arm and followed a steaming apple crisp over to the table. Emily watched with indignation as he took a plate and began to pile it high.

She was about to set the Warlock straight when someone raised a cry: "Besim!"

The call was taken up by dozens of voices: "Besim, Besim!" until finally a scrawny old man with scraggly black hair and skin the color of rawhide allowed himself to be pushed to the center of the dirt floor.

"It's Besim!"

"Hey, Besim!"

"Do us a Cassandra!"

The request echoed, rippling in dozens of different voices: "A Cassandra, a Cassandra!"

Smiling toothlessly, Besim motioned to a young man standing nearby, who had obtained a pint bottle of whiskey and was holding it with eager anticipation. The young man leaped forward, proffering the bottle to Besim.

Besim drained it in one protracted guzzle.

The room exploded in congratulatory cheers. Coins rained down on Besim, thrown by the men in the crowd. Besim scrambled for these, thrusting them deep into his pockets.

"Regrettably, your lumberman is in no mood to discuss crowbars." The voice came at Emily's elbow. It was that insufferable Stanton, crowbar still under his arm and a brimming plate of food in his hand. He used a chicken leg to gesture at Besim. "So who's this?"

"That's Besim," Emily said. She eyed the chicken leg meaningfully. "He's one of those varmints who show up whenever there's free food and liquor to be had."

Stanton chewed thoughtfully as he watched Besim begin to spin. The old man gained speed as he rotated; bystanders pushed him back to the center whenever he threatened to topple over.

"What the devil is he *doing*?"

"He's doing a Cassandra," Emily muttered. She hated Besim's Cassandras. The old man had once been a charm maker in Dutch Flat, and in his better days he'd been Pap's biggest rival for custom. But the rivalry had faded as Besim slid into drunkenness and its concomitant poverty. These days, the only money he got was from his impromptu liquor-lubricated prognostications. These were doubly embarrassing to one of her profession in that while they tended toward the ridiculous, they proved right about half of the time—which was about the same success Pap had with his scrying.

"Fascinating," Stanton said. "He's a dervish."

"What are you talking about?" Emily asked. "Pap always said Besim did Indian magic."

"Rubbish. That man's no more an Indian than I am. He's a Turk. He was a Sufi holy man once, or he studied with one." Stanton pointed to Besim's hands. "See how his right palm is turned upward and his left is turned down? Power comes down from Heaven into the right hand and returns down to the earth from the left. All that energy rushing through the dervish's body supposedly endows him with supernaturally clear insight into the true nature of all existence—past, present, and future." He took another bite of the chicken leg. "I must say, though, the addition of a pint of whiskey tends to undercut the rite's spiritual element."

At that moment, Besim fell with a great crash in the middle of the floor, and lay moaning and writhing, holding his gut. Words began slurring out of his mouth.

"Emily . . . Emily *Lyakhov*." Emily froze. Besim wasn't going to Cassandra about her, was he? She didn't recognize the name Lyakhov, but she didn't have time to think about it before Besim spoke again. "Emily, you have been doing bad magic."

A few people turned to look at Emily curiously. She wished she could sink through the floor, except there wasn't any floor, just dirt. *Shut up, Besim,* she whispered to herself, clenching her hands tight.

"You have bewitched someone for your own good. Someone who has not asked for it." Besim spoke with the slurry slyness of a very drunk man, waggling a finger. "You have woven a fine little net, Emily. But it will not catch you what you want . . ."

Dag stepped forward, his hands balled into fists.

"You quit talking about . . . You just *shut up,* Besim!" There was odd, hesitant anger in his voice—anger that didn't know where it came from. "Miss Emily wouldn't do anything like that, and you know it! That's not the kind of Cassandra-in' we want."

"You get the Cassandra you get, you cow-eyed fool!" Besim flared back. But drunk as he was, he knew which side his bread was buttered on. He fell silent for a moment, staring into space, apparently searching for a more satisfactory message from the ether. When the next message came, however, it was worse than the first.

"The Corpse Switch!" Besim shrieked, his face contorting with sudden horror. "The Corpse Switch up at Old China has *failed*! The dead . . . the dead will rise from beneath the earth!"

There was a storm of muttering. Emily stared at him, confused and appalled. Besim's Cassandras were usually light-
hearted revelations about which young scapegrace had stolen
a pie from which matron's windowsill. They were never this
dire. Corpse Switches controlled the zombie miners that the
mine owners bought to work their most dangerous mines—
the ones that live men wouldn't work in for any money. The
zombie workers had been paupers, criminals, and other dangerous and unsavory types. Certainly not the sorts one wanted
roaming the mountains without the control of a properly sor-
celled Corpse Switch.

As if that weren't bad enough, Besim was crawling across
the floor toward Emily. He stopped, kneeling in front of her,
clutching the hem of her dress and pressing it to his tear-
slicked face.

"The dead have been driven mad, *büyüleyici kadin*. Driven
mad by a blue star." He looked up at her, eyes glowing like embers. "You must stop them. It is not right . . . that the dead . . .
should walk the earth . . ."

Each successive word dropped from Besim's lips more
slowly, and after the last one he slumped at her feet, still and
silent. Emily snatched her skirt away and stepped back, aware
of dozens of silent eyes appraising her. She flushed from
throat to scalp.

"What a pile of nonsense," Stanton said loudly. "A Corpse
Switch can't *fail*. They're made with multiple redundancies at
a licensed necromantic factory in Chicago. Which I've toured,
by the way. They have an unblemished performance record."

Even this pronouncement did not completely satisfy the
unsettled crowd. Dozens of worried eyes turned toward Dag,
waiting for his verdict on the matter.

"You think there's anything in it, Dag?" someone shouted
from the back of the room.

"Aw, hell no!" Dag nudged Besim with the toe of his boot.
The dervish released a loud, muttering snore. "Besim's thrown
bunk Cassandras before, but that was the bunkest! A blue star
in a mine? Not in a blue moon!"

There was uneasy laughter at this weak attempt at humor;
Dag clapped the accordion player on the back.

"Let's have a real cheerful one!" As the music resumed, Dag called over it: "You all heard Mr. Stanton. Corpse Switches don't fail! So let's get back to dancing. And for God's sake, someone drag Besim someplace he can sleep it off!"

A couple of men stepped forward to oblige, and Dag came to Emily's side, taking her arm and drawing her close. He'd had more than a few cups of apple brandy; she could smell it on his breath as he put his face close to hers.

"I don't know what got into that old faker tonight," he said. He wrapped his arms around her waist and gave her a squeeze. "Let's get out of here. Let's go have that walk we were talking about."

"Listen, Dag . . ." Emily pushed back against his embrace. "What if he's right? What if the Corpse Switch *has* failed?"

Dag grinned. "C'mon, Emily. Besim's just never got used to the idea of zombies. He's been jumpy as a cat since Old China brought 'em in. His imagination just ran away, that's all."

"But shouldn't we go up and check?"

Dag blinked in astonishment.

"Go to Old China *now*? Five miles straight up? On *Besim's* say-so? You must be kidding!"

"No, I'm not." She tried to speak quietly, but the cheery tune had gotten everyone laughing and talking even louder than before. "If there's any chance what he's saying is true—"

"There isn't." Dag smiled indulgently. "I mean, he said you'd been doing bad magic, too. There wasn't no truth in that, was there?"

"That's not the same," Emily whispered fiercely, pushing herself from his arms. Dag looked confused. He lifted his big hand in a gesture of dismissal.

"It's all the same, all hooey." Dag suddenly looked extremely tired, as if all the drink and dancing had caught up with him at once. "I wish some of these people would clear out so we could go for that walk."

She chewed on her lip, nervousness making her stomach flutter. Finally, she took a deep breath and smiled.

"You're right, Dag," she said. "Listen, I'm going to go help wash up. I'll come find you later, all right? And we'll have a walk."

"Yeah," Dag said. And then, right there in the middle of everyone, he gave Emily a kiss on the cheek. She shivered, feeling eyes on them all around. She knew this should please her. If they weren't engaged before, they were as good as now.

But she didn't feel victorious. She felt nothing but dread, dark and sickening.

Retrieving Pap's leather pouch from where she had stowed it, she slung it over her shoulder, clinging to the strap like a lifeline.

The fluttering nervousness in her stomach had congealed into sour apprehension. Besim hadn't thrown a bunk Cassandra. She *had* been doing bad magic—or at least, *he'd* think it was bad magic. And if he was right about that . . .

She considered her options. She could tell Dag the truth, that she *had* bewitched someone, and that by "someone" she meant him. That'd be the end of her professional credibility. She and Pap could be horsewhipped out of Lost Pine, or Dag could bring law against her. Baugh's Patent Magicks were bad for business, but a turn in the county jail would be an awful lot worse.

Or she could go up to Old China and sort the mess out for herself.

She walked away quickly, the cheerful notes of "Sweet, Sweet Spring" chasing her into the darkness.

CHAPTER TWO

The Corpse Switch

Emily walked briskly up to the Old China Mine, jumping from rock to rock along the narrow pony path that wound alongside the darkly rushing You Bet Creek. The night had grown bitterly cold, and patches of snow glowed blue in the moonlight. She pulled her buffalo coat tighter around herself, glad now that she hadn't put her winter flannels away too soon.

Besim's Cassandra puzzled her. How could the Corpse Switch have failed, and what was a blue star doing in a mine? But the part she kept coming back to was the part of least immediate interest: the name Lyakhov. The name seemed so familiar. Could Besim have stumbled across something useful? Something about her mother?

Of her mother, Emily remembered nothing. It was not that her memories were sketchy or vague—they simply did not exist. She remembered when she'd first come to Pap's cabin. But before that, nothing. A clear demarcation—a horizon beyond which stretched only shadow.

All Emily's efforts to find out more had been thwarted. Her mother had left so little behind. Emily reached up, feeling for her hair sticks, reassuring herself that they were still there.

She'd made Pap tell her the story a hundred times. How her mother had staggered into Lost Pine on an icy black night twenty years ago, just after the first snows had fallen in the highest passes, frostbit from her toes to her blue fingertips. Five-year-old Emily was clinging to her chest, a man's woolen coat pulled tight around them both.

The timber camp workers had gotten her inside, bundled her

up in front of a blazing fire. She had made only one impenetrable utterance before losing consciousness:

"We must get to the Cynic Mirror."

Pap had been called. He'd piled counterpanes and quilts over the delirious woman, coaxed powerful herbal tisanes down her throat. He spoke spell-words over her, remonstrated with her departing spirit, but nothing was any use. She died within days.

Lyakhov. Could it have been her mother's name? Then that would make her Emily Lyakhov, as Besim had called her. She'd heard names like that, names ending in -itch and -ov, among the thick-bearded Russians who drove cattle through the passes. They sometimes stopped to ask Pap for charms to ward against curses and the evil eye. They always asked for hot tea to drink, and jam to put in it.

Deep in thought, she hardly noticed when the moon slid behind the clouds and darkness fell like a blanket. Having roamed the mountains most of her life, she had no difficulty keeping to the path, and was not unnerved by the scrapings, squeaks, and hoots that surrounded her. But when there was a huge pop and a flash of dazzling white light, her heart stopped in her chest. She spun, balling her fists.

"Dag?" she called. "Is that you?"

"Of course it isn't." A man's voice, irritable. A spare form held up a pine stick that glowed with magical incandescence. "He was asleep in a corner when I left. Your absence took the steam out of him. Make your love spells pretty harsh, don't you?"

"Mr. Stanton?" Her voice was high with disbelief, then a ferocious whisper. "What are you talking about? Love spells?"

"Oh, please. I was riding back from Dutch Flat last night, and I saw—" He stopped abruptly, evidently reconsidering his words. "Well, it was obvious at the dance tonight. Your lumberman smelled like a French whorehouse just burned down. Ashes of Amour, I take it? You used far too much lavender."

"You . . . *saw* me?" Emily hissed. "Under the Hanging Oak?"

"I haven't the faintest idea what you're talking about."

"But I was . . ." Emily choked on the words: *naked as a beggar's toes*.

"All right, so I may have *glimpsed* you," Stanton said. "Briefly. But with your hair all undone, I certainly couldn't see . . ." He paused. "Anyway, I rode on immediately. I certainly had no wish to watch you lay a trap for some poor male to blunder into."

"You dirty spy!" Emily was hot with embarrassment.

"I make no judgments." Stanton's tone implied that he didn't have to, that judgment had already been passed by eons of respectability and decency. "Of course, it represents an egregious breach of professional ethics, but he *is* the richest man in Lost Pine, and not missing any limbs or digits, so I can understand—"

"Oh, yes, I'm sure you understand *completely*," Emily snarled. "You're so all-fired insightful. See if you can guess what I'm thinking right now."

Stanton didn't venture. Rather, he picked up another stick from the ground and said, *"Lux."* The branch flared to light with a loud *pop*—the same sound that had startled her a few minutes earlier. He handed it to Emily. To her surprise (and slight regret, for her fingers were stiff with cold) she found it gave off no heat, and rather glowed as if illuminated from within.

"Thank you," she said. "What are you doing here?"

"I guessed you'd take it upon yourself to check on things at the Old China Mine. And not knowing the way to get there, I decided that following you would be the best way for me to get there, too."

"Why do you want to go up to Old China?"

"Isn't it obvious? I can't let a female with such dangerously antique notions about magic—not to mention such a questionable code of ethics—face a pack of zombie miners alone." He paused. "Pap couldn't go, and none of those drunken sots back there would be any help."

"Then you believe Besim was telling the truth?"

"Of course," he said. "Half of Besim's Cassandra, the half about you casting spells on people without their knowledge and being a *büyüleyici kadin*—that translates as 'bad Witch,' in case your colloquial Turkish has gotten rusty—was entirely accurate. Knowing that, I have every reason to believe the other half. Or at least to believe that *he* believes the other half. I still maintain that Corpse Switches do not fail."

"Well, I don't want company," she snapped, turning on her heel. *Especially not your company.*

"You may not want my company, but you need my help." Stanton's long legs easily matched even her most rapid strides on the rough path. "I have studied with professionals who have done years of necromantic research. You haven't the least exposure to modern theories of revivification or devivification—subjects with which I have practical experience."

"This is my job," Emily said. "Besides, you've got a whole new crate from New York to open. Why dirty your hands with real magic?"

"And what would you know about *real* magic?" The scorn in his voice made her want to punch him. "Lives may be at stake. Perhaps you could curb your pride and think about that?"

Emily clenched her teeth. Insufferable.

"Suit yourself," she hissed.

Emily and Stanton reached Old China two hours past midnight.

Shacks and mine gear glowed stark white in cold moonlight, and everything was graveyard-still. In a mining camp that used live labor, this would not be unusual at two in the morning. But zombies didn't sleep. The whole point was their ability to work continuously, for months on end, until they literally fell apart.

And indeed, there were signs that work had just recently come to a halt. Flickering coal-oil lanterns still burned along the hundred-foot board sluice that stretched like a dark road up to the mouth of the mine. A thin trickle of black water ran off the sluice into a muddy pit that snaked down to rejoin You Bet Creek below.

The foreman's cabin, crooked and leaning, shone silver-gray in the moonlight. Dark shadows under its eaves made it look angry. Stanton used his foot to carefully ease open the door.

"No one inside." He disappeared through the door and Emily followed.

The cramped foreman's cabin was packed with mining paraphernalia—crates marked "California Powder Works" spilling drifts of wood shavings, spools of timing fuse, rope and drills, and broken headlamps waiting to be mended. But it was an enormous machine, huge as the upright piano in Mrs. Bargett's boarding house, that dominated the space.

It was a behemoth of gleaming brass and polished mahogany, ornamented with a great deal of machine-engraved scrollwork. Here and there, lights flickered under blown-glass buttons. Emily squinted to read the enameled plaque:

Vivification Control Switch, D. J. Conway and Company, Chicago, Ill., Pat. Pend. 1862.

"This is the Corpse Switch?" Emily asked, but Stanton didn't answer. He was twisting a dial and looking closely at one of the needle indicators.

"It seems to be working just fine."

"You sure? Maybe touring the factory doesn't make you as much of an expert as you'd like to think."

He glared over his shoulder. "Corpse Switches are really very simple, even though they do a complex job. If one were to fail, it would be immediately apparent."

"All right. If the Corpse Switch is working, then where are all the corpses?"

At that moment, a distant, piercing scream sliced the night air. It came from the entrance of the mine where iron tracks vanished into the blackness.

They rushed out of the shack and up the hill to the heavy-timbered mouth of the mine. From deep within they could hear the amplified echoes of an incoherent shriek of pain and terror. The sound was like a cold steel rod rubbed against Emily's spine.

Stanton grabbed the satchel from Emily's shoulder and threw it open, ignoring her cry of outrage. He pawed through bottles and leather pouches, peering at labels.

"*Chelidonium majus, inula helenium, hyssopus officinalis, viscum album* . . . house-magic basics. Oh, and black storax! That will help immensely. At least you're well prepared." He poured garlic and salt and cayenne onto a flat rock, then, using a smoothly rounded piece of granite as a pestle, he ground them together with a few of the other herbs, finally adding the storax. He muttered charms in low cadent Latin.

"You're not rhyming," she snapped. "You have to rhyme!"

"There isn't time for that nonsense," he said. "This is an extremely simple devivification powder, the kind a schoolboy might compound as an amusement on a rainy Sunday." He scooped two handfuls and put them in his pockets. He gestured to Emily to do the same.

"Throw it at anything that moves," he said. "It's not strong enough to hold them off long, so don't let your guard down."

They crept into the mine, holding their brands before them. The bright white light cast harsh flickering shadows against the rough-hewn pine supports, made the mining-car tracks seem as sharp as if they'd been honed on a whetstone. A thin trickle of muddy cocoa-colored water ran down the middle of the tracks, smelling of iron or, perhaps, Emily thought as they got closer to the anguished screams, blood.

They followed the screams to the end of a shallow test tunnel off the main line. There, they found him—Mr. Hart, the foreman, the mine's only live employee. He was buried under huge, mud-slick boulders and crumbling earth. Only his head and shoulders and arms protruded. His breathing was choked, constricted by the immense weight pressing down on his chest. Blood trickled from the corner of his mouth, black in the half-light.

"Em Edwards, thank God you've come." He raised a shaking arm to clutch at her hand. His skin was freezing cold, waxy and gritty with dirt. "Thank God . . ."

Emily brushed mud from his face. "I won't leave you."

"Light . . ." The man's voice was small and terrified. "Don't let the light go out . . ."

"How is he?" Stanton called. Emily came close to Stanton's side, dropped her voice low.

"He's still alive, but he's under a ton of rock. I don't know how we can get him out."

"Do whatever you can . . . quickly." Stanton was looking down into the frigid gloom of the main tunnel. Deep in the darkness, Emily could hear shuffling and grunts and small groans, and now and again she saw something glitter. Eyes.

"They're holding off for the moment," Stanton said. He threw one of the brands down the tunnel. In the sudden flare of light, Emily caught her first glimpse of the zombies. Crouching half bent, in filthy shredded rags, they pulled back from the light, but not far.

Emily hurried back to Hart's side and looked at the rocks that covered him. They were far too big to move.

"They . . . they went crazy." Hart's voice was thin and distant. "The diggings were . . . Everything was normal. Until they found . . ."

The man's leather-gloved hand fell open, and a warm glow filled the side tunnel. In his palm lay some kind of gemstone, rich blue threaded with glowing filaments of white. It shimmered from within, as if suffused with remembered sunlight. Emily brought her light down to examine it.

"The blue star," she murmured.

"They were afraid of it. I picked it up to look . . . and they went crazy. Turned on me. Not supposed to do that, not with the Switch. They . . . wanted to bury me, bury it forever . . ."

The effort of the last word made the man splutter and choke. An agonized cough racked him, and with it came a bubbling gush of black blood.

"Miss Edwards . . ." Stanton's voice was tense.

"He's dead," Emily said softly. The sudden presence of real death among all the half-death suddenly made everything seem heavier and slower. "There's nothing we can—"

But her words were lost. As if by some silent signal, the zombie miners swept forward in a wave of rags and rot, trampling Stanton and the light as they crowded down the side tunnel.

Emily shrieked, scrambling backward until her back was against cold rock. She felt for the devivification powder in her pocket, but it was too late. The miners were upon her, reeking of mud and rust and decay. In the flickering half-light she saw the face of a man, swollen and brutish and slack with the stupidity of death, his cheek a mass of black mold.

The thing got a slimy icy hand around her throat. The

bones of the skeletal fingers dug into her windpipe, pressing hard against the wall. The close blackness of the tunnel spun around her. She struggled for breath as the corpse pushed her back . . .

"Mort statim!"

The words made the rocks and earth around them shudder. Stanton's lanky form was outlined in blue flame, and there was a colossal flash. The zombies were harshly outlined in sudden daylight brilliance, then dissolved into sparking clouds that glittered like gold dust.

Darkness fell abruptly as the magical brightness faded.

"Lux," Stanton snapped, and his pine brand flared once again, weak and wavering. The radiance of the attack had seared vibrating black spots onto Emily's eyeballs. She tried to blink them away, but they stubbornly refused to vanish, and in a moment, Emily realized that they were not black spots at all, but two corpses that had not fallen in Stanton's attack. They were lumbering toward her. One had a pick in his crumbling hand, and was looking at Emily as if she had a vein of gold in her forehead.

"Don't just stand there!" Stanton was slumped against the rock, breathing hard. She reached out, trying to squeeze past her zombie attackers, but the one with the pick clutched at the loose end of one of her long braids. It yanked her back hard, forcing her to her knees. The pick gleamed above her.

Desperately, she grasped for anything she could strike out with. A gleam caught her eye. She lunged for it, and her hand fell upon the blue gemstone.

The moment her fingers touched it, everything changed. She could perceive everything with complete clarity. The texture of the walls. The sound of Stanton's breathing. The bright metal head of the pick soaring down to split her skull. Faster than thought, she rolled to one side as the pick struck sparks on the rock by her ear. Dumb and dizzy, she grabbed one of the zombie's leather-dry legs. If she could just knock it off balance . . .

. . . and in an instant, the thing collapsed to the ground, the pick clattering against rock, the end of her braid still clenched in its bony fist. She struggled to free herself, but the second corpse gave her no chance; it clawed at her arm, but the moment its dead flesh touched hers, it shuddered and stilled, falling across her in a slimy heap.

Then, all was silent but for the sound of Emily's tattered breath and the roaring of her heart in her ears. The next thing she knew, Stanton had shoved aside the no-longer undead and was slapping her cheeks, even though she thought it perfectly obvious that she was completely awake.

"Stop it," she snapped, pushing him away. "I'm . . . I'm fine. What happened?"

"I couldn't get them all." Stanton's voice was distant and hollow. "How did you manage to . . ."

"I don't know," Emily said. "They just . . . fell down."

She felt funny, drifting and warm and oddly light. She lifted a hand to brush a dirty lock of hair from her face and noticed that the strange blue stone seemed to have become stuck to her palm.

No, Emily thought, "stuck to" wasn't right. "Embedded in" was a more precise description. The stone had somehow worked its way entirely through her hand, a roundish lump protruding from her palm. She looked at it quizzically, turning her hand over slowly; the gem protruded from the back of her hand as well. She held her hand up to Stanton's torch. The light glowed through the stone as if it were a piece of cobalt glass. The thin threads of white shimmered.

"My word!" Stanton's brow wrinkled. He put down the torch and took Emily's hand, touching the stone with both thumbs. "Does it hurt?"

"It does with you pawing at it like that!" Emily jerked her hand away. Then she noticed Stanton staring at her face.

"What?" she asked.

"Your eyes," Stanton murmured. "They've gone all black."

But there was no time for further discussion of Emily's eyes, for there was a skin-crawling shriek from the mine's depths, and then another—long protracted shrieks that were coming closer with alarming rapidity.

"There are more of them down there?" Stanton said.

"Last I heard, Old China had well over a hundred zombies," Emily said.

"Let's not stay to count."

In a sudden flash of panic, Emily reached to feel the back of her head. Her mother's hair sticks were gone. Scrabbling on her hands and knees, she ran her hands over the dark mine floor, pushing aside corpses, groping around underneath them.

"What are you *doing*?"

"My hair sticks!"

Stanton reached down and grabbed her arm. He tried to pull her to her feet, but she jerked away from him, and in that instant she saw the sticks glimmer in the light of his torch. Grabbing them, she caught Stanton's sleeve and they raced up the tunnel. The shrieks of the undead were louder now. The corpses were moving fast, but she could smell fresh, cold air up ahead.

"We have to block the entrance!" Emily said as they emerged into icy moonlight. She pointed at the rocks over the mine entrance. "Magic those rocks down!"

Stanton stumbled to a stop, his eyebrows knit mournfully.

"Miss Edwards, I just mortified two dozen rampaging zombies. I am in no position to magic anything right at the moment."

"If we don't get this opening blocked, there'll be dozens more in Lost Pine before dawn!" But even as Emily said it, she knew what to do. Running to the foreman's cabin, she threw open the door. In an open crate, sticks of dynamite lay buried in wood shavings. She grabbed a stick and reached for the spool of fuse cord.

Running back up the hill, she heard the shrieks of the undead echoing against the black forested hillside; they had reached the mine entrance. Stanton had picked up a heavy mossy branch and was holding them back as best he could, swinging the branch wildly at a clot of zombies that seemed to find this action extremely annoying.

The man could even annoy the undead! Despite herself, Emily found this rather impressive.

Digging into her pockets, Emily came up with two handfuls of devivification powder. She flung it at the zombies, but they continued to shriek and scrabble, unaffected. Emily drew back behind Stanton.

"See, I told you you needed to rhyme." She held up the dynamite. "Can you light this?"

"Flamma." Stanton glanced back, snapping his fingers.

Nothing happened. He looked confused as he snapped his fingers again.

"Oh, forget it!" Emily threw the stick of dynamite to the ground. She was about to rummage around in Pap's satchel for the flint and steel he always kept there, but the instant she dropped the stick of dynamite, the fuse exploded in a shower of brilliant sparks.

"Ten seconds of fuse!" Emily yelled, kicking the dynamite against the timber brace that framed the mine's opening. Then she dove under the board sluice, clasping her hands over her head. Stanton, however, remained at the mine opening, apparently determined to keep the corpses at bay.

"Get clear!" she screamed at him.

At that very moment, Stanton threw down the branch and gave an exceptional leap—a leap given far greater distance by the energy from the flash and roar of the explosion at his heels.

After the roar subsided and the last chunks of muddy rock and splintered timber had clattered to still silence on the ground around her, Emily rolled out from under the board sluice.

The mine entrance was gone, replaced by a sundered wreckage of tumbled rock and twisted trees. Emily listened for the sound of the undead shrieks, but all she heard was her own breathing, heavy and irregular.

"Mr. Stanton, are you alive?" she called.

Her answer was a groan from a clump of blackberries a good fifteen feet distant from where the mine entrance had once been.

"Showing off like that, you deserved to get blown to kingdom come." She scraped heavy handfuls of red-clay mud from the back of her skirt as she spoke.

"I'm fine, thank you for inquiring." Stanton straightened unsteadily. "And yes, I did do quite a fine job of keeping the undead from escaping before the dynamite blew. Thank you for mentioning that, too."

Emily leaned against the rough wood of the board sluice as

he limped up beside her. One side of his hair stood up like an exclamation point, and his broad forehead was streaked with soot.

"How are my eyes?" she asked. He squinted at her face in the moonlight.

"Still black," he said. "And your hand?"

"Still got a rock in it." Emily lifted her hand with fingers spread, then flexed them experimentally. It didn't hurt, precisely; her fingers felt clumsy and stiff, but her hand felt warm. She held the stone up to the moonlight; it glowed clear through. She could see no bones, no muscles, no tendons . . .

She closed her hand over the stone. "So, you're the great Warlock. Explain what this is."

Stanton rubbed the back of his head.

"Well," he averred finally, "I'd hate to jump to any hasty conclusions."

"Mr. Hart said that the zombies were afraid of it." Emily said. "They were trying to rebury it and he got in the way."

"Horrible," Stanton said.

"Will it hurt me, do you think?" She struggled to keep fear out of her voice.

Stanton shrugged with his customary dismissiveness. "Well, you're not dead yet," he said.

Here, she thought, *is where I treat this tactless lout to a snappy retort.* But suddenly, she didn't feel like doing much of anything snappy at all. Instead, she looked back over her shoulder toward the mouth of the mine. She thought of the man who would remain buried there forever. She clenched her fist around the stone, as tightly as she could.

"I'm going home," she said.

CHAPTER THREE

The Rule of Three

By the time Emily got home and was able to get a look at herself in the mirror, her eyes had returned to normal. Her hand . . . now, that was a different story. Nothing would shift the glimmering blue stone from where it was embedded in her right palm. No amount of distracted fiddling, pressing, or pushing helped in the least. The gem remained firmly and stubbornly imposed.

She and Stanton had parted at the bottom of Moody Ridge. Emily, turning up the path that led to Pap's cabin, had been more than willing to forgo the niceties of a good night, but Stanton had stopped her.

"Listen, the crate that came for me today is a shipment of periodicals and collected journals. I've been waiting for them all winter. I'll look through them and see if I can find reference to such a singular occurrence."

Early morning sunlight, pale and peach-colored, peeked through the back windows as Emily went to kindle the stove. While the water was heating, she climbed to the attic loft and changed out of her mud-caked calico dress. She frowned at the stains. They'd never come out. Spoiling her best dress would have seemed an utter tragedy twenty-four hours ago, but now it seemed a pretty trifling thing.

When the water boiled, she made a pot of fresh coffee (clumsily, for she wasn't used to working with a hand half crippled) and set out some of the cornbread that Mrs. Lyman had left. Then, as she waited for Pap to wake up, she sat staring quietly at the stone, watching the shifting light of morning cast smoky blue shadows through it onto the white tablecloth. When Pap finally stirred, scattering cats, she said simply: "You'll never guess what happened to me last night."

After pouring him a strong cup of coffee, Emily told Pap about her trip to the Old China Mine. She kept the story simple, leaving out the more distressing elements. No need to alarm Pap about trivialities when the main issue was sure to trouble him enough.

When she came to the part about the stone, she laid her hand on the table, palm up, as if inviting him to read her fortune. He felt the stone in her hand with his rough thumbs, his sightless eyes straining to remember how to see.

"Well, if that don't beat all . . . It's a stone, you say? A blue-colored stone?"

"Yes." Emily leaned forward. "You know something about it?"

"Nope." Pap shook his head. "But it feels powerful, whatever it is. It's got something in it, I can't quite feel what. It doesn't really feel like magic or power, or anything, really. More like . . . I don't know, like something that isn't yet, but might be. Like light from a star."

Emily was slightly surprised. Pap was rarely given to such poetic abstraction. She shook her head with impatience.

"Well, anyway, can you get it *out*?"

Pap was silent for a long time, his thumbs stroking Emily's palm.

"I can't see as there's any way to medicine it out without cutting," Pap said. The thought made Emily cringe. "And no way I can see that you wouldn't lose all the use of that hand."

"That's my writing hand," she said. "I couldn't do charms or anything without that hand."

"Your other hand would learn, in time," Pap said distantly. "But, Em, I don't know if we should make any decision too quick. It's not doing any harm where it is . . . none we know of anyway. And we know taking it out would do harm. So maybe leaving it in—"

"Leave a rock in my hand?" Emily said. "It's not natural!"

Pap chuckled. The sparkle in his eyes made Emily almost think that he could see her.

"Ain't much that's more natural than a piece of rock," he said.

"Not a piece of rock that's stuck in my hand!" Emily wailed. "There's got to be more to it."

"I'm sure there is," he soothed. "But, Em, there are bigger magics in this world than I know about. An old Kentucky goomer doctor like me don't have any call to meddle with things like that, so I never set myself to learn about them." Pap stroked his grizzled chin. "But maybe that educated young Warlock feller, Mr. Stanton—"

Emily snatched her hand away. She was about to give Pap a piece of her mind about Dreadnought Stanton (who had cashed in his small store of goodwill by lecturing her all the way down the mountain about how a woman her age should know better than to grab willy-nilly at mysteriously glowing objects) when a knock came at the door. Emily threw the door open and was not pleased to see that it was the very Mr. Stanton of whom they had been speaking. One of his pair of fine black horses was hitched to a nearby tree. He carried a saddlebag over his shoulder and sported a richly variegated black eye.

"Good morning, Mr. Stanton." She stared at him coolly. "What happened to you?"

"Well, someone had to alert the town about what happened up at the mine. I explained the situation to Mr. Cunningham at the general store— I thought he might be able to get word to the mine's owner. Mr. Hansen happened by, heard that we'd gone up to Old China together. One thing led to another."

Dag! Emily put her hand over her mouth, as if to hold in a groan. She'd forgotten all about Dag.

Stanton took a seat at the table across from Pap. Absently, he filched a piece of Pap's cornbread and devoured it in three large bites.

"What's wrong with Dag?" Pap asked.

Stanton dusted cornmeal from his hands. "Your girl makes her love spells too strong," he said. "Too much lavender."

"Love spells?" Pap's brow knit. "Em, what's he talking about?"

"Ashes of Amour," Emily murmured hesitantly. Then she

pressed her lips together and was silent for a long time—a silence Pap interpreted with terrible accuracy. His face fell.

"Oh, Em . . . you didn't."

"I thought if . . ." She paused. "It's been so hard. He would have . . . helped."

Pap sighed. "Emily, I'm ashamed. Sore ashamed." These five words were the entirety of Pap's remonstration, but Pap's remonstrations didn't get much harder than that. The deep disappointment in his voice and the tired slump of his shoulders made hot tears sting her eyes.

She turned abruptly and went into the screened cooking area. Pap wasn't able to see her tears, but she'd be hanged if she would embarrass herself in front of Stanton. Angrily, she dashed a drop from her cheek.

Poor Dag! She'd promised to meet him for a walk and instead ended up going off with another man. That it was to battle a pack of rampaging zombies wouldn't make a bit of difference. He'd be hurt and furious.

She got out herbs from earthenware pots on the windowsill, thinking absently of Stanton's bruised eye, wanting mostly to give her hands something to do. She put a clean piece of white cheesecloth into a blue-enameled bowl, and on the cloth she sprinkled willow bark, nettle, thistle, and a good deal of black tea. Then she poured warm water into the bowl and let it all steep, watching the herbs swirl in the water. They were turning widdershins. A bad sign.

"Perhaps this is a punishment," Emily said, softly. "Besim called me a bad Witch. Bad magic always gets its comeuppance."

"Ever mind the Rule of Three . . . Three times what thou givest returns to thee." Emily heard the ruefulness in Pap's voice as he quoted the old rede to her. He did not elaborate—he did not need to.

"Can we please take one problem at a time?" Stanton said. "Your lumberman is the least of our worries. I told you I'd look in my journals and see if I could discover anything about the stone. Well, discover something I did."

Emily lifted the cloth from the bowl, wringing out the extra water, then she turned in the corners of the cloth so they enfolded the dampened herbs. She handed the poultice to Stanton. She tried to conceal the fact that the hand offering it—the hand with the stone in it—was trembling slightly.

"That will take down the swelling," she said. He placed it over his eye, gingerly. "What did you find out?"

"Something I began to suspect last night. The Corpse Switch didn't fail. The miners did."

"How, exactly, does a zombie fail?"

"Let me tell you what a Corpse Switch actually does." Stanton leaned back in his chair, and assumed an infuriatingly pedantic air. "Zombies are soulless creatures, and being soulless has been empirically proven to result in an unpleasant disposition. The Corpse Switch provides them with an artificial soul."

"You don't say?" Pap leaned forward, fascinated. "How does it do that?"

"The Corpse Switch stands in for the traditional control of a *bokor* or voodoo sorcerer." Stanton also leaned forward, obviously pleased to find a receptive audience. "It generates a very large magical aura—a signal which penetrates the minds of the undead. It gives them memories. Not real memories, of course—the mine owners make them up whole cloth. Happy memories featuring picks and shovels and holes in the ground."

"My, my!" Pap's milky eyes glistened. "What will they think of next?"

"The Switch pushes the terror of their half-life into abeyance. It comforts them, makes them placid and tractable."

"But you've already said the Switch didn't fail," Emily said.

"It didn't. It was producing the aura just fine. It was the stone that interfered with the zombies receiving it."

With a dramatic flourish, Stanton reached down to open the flap of his saddlebag. He pulled out a huge leather-bound book, very new looking, with the words *Journal of Recent Thaumaturgical Advancements—Volume CDLXXVI* pressed upon it in gold. He opened the book to a slender bookmark of carved ivory, then gestured to Emily. "Read that."

Emily read the rather grandiose title of the article, which was "Prominent Mysteries in the Occult Sciences: Frontiers

That Remain Unexplored, Presenting Various Intriguing Fields of Study for the Warlocks of Future Decades."

She followed Stanton's finger down past a paragraph subtitled "Can the Mantic Anastomosis Be Cleansed Through Human Intervention?" and another subtitled "Geochole—A Resource for Future Exploitation?" When Stanton's finger came to rest, she began to read aloud, for Pap's benefit:

"What Is the Native Star?

"This blue-white mineral of unknown properties is a preternatural mystery of the first water. The only known specimen, hardly the size of a lady's shoe button, currently resides in the British Museum, returned there after discovery in 1820 in a Canadian gold mine by native laborers, who claimed it was a piece of the evening star.

"The stone shows every evidence of possessing a great quantity of inchoate energy, which is exceptional in that it refutes the common understanding that only organic materials are capable of storing and holding magical power.

"The gemlike mineral has the appearance of the clearest cobalt glass threaded with filaments of crystalline white. The stone immediately absorbs and nullifies any magical energy that is exerted in its vicinity. It is theorized that examples of Native Star may represent actual fragments of the Mantic Anastomosis. Further study is warranted to completely understand the properties of this singular mineral."

That was all. Emily looked up at Stanton.

"Native Star?"

"Found in a gold mine," he said. "Cobalt blue, crystalline white filaments. Absorbs magical energy."

Emily contemplated the stone in her hand as Stanton continued.

"When you touched those zombies they fell down instantly. The stone in your hand must have absorbed all the magical force animating them."

"That's all well and good," Pap said, "but none of it answers why the stone worked its way into Em's palm in the first place."

"Or how to get it out," Emily added.

"That will require further research. Research which cannot be performed in Lost Pine." Stanton closed the book. "Miss Edwards must consent to be examined by professionals."

"What?" Emily didn't like the word "examined," or even "professionals" for that matter.

"I have no doubt that the professors at the Mirabilis Institute would be extremely eager to study this case," Stanton said.

"I most certainly am not a *case*!"

"The Mirabilis Institute—that fancy institute you studied at?" Pap frowned. "You can't mean she'd have to go all the way to New York?"

"Not at all," Stanton said. "There's an extension office in San Francisco—that's less than a week's ride. The Institute would assume all expenses of the journey, of course—"

"San Francisco?" Emily said. "Are you kidding? I can't go to San Francisco!"

"With that stone in your hand, you can't do anything else." Stanton looked at her. "You certainly can't do magic."

He paused, absorbing Emily's glare with equanimity.

"Remember last night, when we were trying to light the dynamite?" Emily saw Pap's eyebrows rise. She hadn't mentioned the dynamite part to him. "I should have been able to light the fuse easily. *Flamma*." He snapped, and a little tongue of flame dazzled at the point where his thumb and forefinger met. He spread his fingers and the flame disappeared. "But while you were holding it, the spell did not work. It did not work, in fact, until you threw the stick of dynamite to the ground."

"You said yourself that you'd just blown two dozen zombies into gold dust and were too drained to do anything else," Emily countered.

"I certainly wasn't too drained to produce a tiny flame." Stanton was scornful. "If I had been that incapacitated, I wouldn't have been able to hold off the undead at the mouth of the mine so that you could throw the dynamite at them."

"You were throwing *dynamite*?" Pap's eyes followed their voices back and forth.

"Look, I didn't want to put such a fine point on it, but you've left me no choice." Stanton did not take his eyes off Emily as he spoke in Pap's direction. "Mr. Edwards, you can still cast a levitation, can't you?"

Pap blinked, apparently still trying to get past the dynamite. Finally he nodded.

"Haven't done one in years. Ain't much use in 'em when you've got two good strong arms. But I reckon I still can, if required."

"Will you do one for me now?"

Pap rolled up his sleeves. "Em, get me my things."

Emily was turning to comply when Stanton got up quickly, reaching past her.

"You'd better let me," he said. He gathered Pap's athame and charm cap from where they hung above the fireplace and placed them before the old man. Then he took down a green glass bottle from the windowsill and placed it on the table.

"Miss Edwards, hold his hand while he attempts to levitate that bottle."

"Oh, honestly!" Emily sniffed, but she sat down next to Pap anyway, taking his light, dry hand in hers and giving it a squeeze.

First, Pap took up his charm cap—a jaunty affair constructed of purple velvet, covered with glittering bric-a-brac, feathers, and small bird bones—and placed it on his white hair at a rakish angle. Then, using the tip of his athame, Pap traced a shaky circle around the bottle, clearly and carefully speaking the rhyme as he did this:

"Air, mist, wind, sky,
Lighter than all, fly, fly, fly!
Breezes, breaths, fogs, skies,
Rise up to join them, rise, rise, rise!"

The bottle did not so much as wriggle.

"That bottle must be to the ceiling by now." Pap smiled, a pleased look on his face. "I feel the power working on it."

No, you feel the power going into the stone in my hand, Emily thought, for she, too, felt the tingling of power, threading around her hand like streams of warm water. But she didn't want to give Stanton the satisfaction of hearing her say it. She let go of Pap's hand and stood up from the table abruptly, moving to the other side of the room and crossing her arms.

The moment she did, the bottle rocked, lifting into the air with a zipping *whoosh* and coming to a twisting dangle in midair.

"There certainly seems to be a distance correlation," Stanton said. His fingers looked as if they itched to write down the finding. Having neither paper nor pen, he shoved his hands into his pockets and looked at Emily.

"I take it you are convinced?" Stanton said. "So, as long as you stay well away from your pap, avoid handling any of his magical objects, and allow him to do all the charm work—including deliveries, for you won't be able to touch anything magical that he produces—well, then I suppose you'll be fine."

"So what?" Emily was seized by a sudden defiance. "There's plenty of things I can do that don't have anything to do with magic. Gathering herbs, making poultices . . ." She picked up the poultice that Stanton had laid aside and threw it at him. Obviously he was expecting something of the sort, for he caught it easily.

"All things that any woman can do," Stanton said, as he replaced the cloth over his eye. "They are not magic."

"People pay us for the things they *can't* do, Em," Pap said soberly. "They pay us for the charms and potions. The herbs they take because they're our neighbors."

Emily sank into her chair, her thumb caressing her palm.

"The stone in your hand is exceptionally valuable." Stanton spoke slowly, as if trying to impress something important on a willful child. "It is my duty and responsibility to escort you to a place of research where the stone can be removed and preserved for study. You want the stone removed, don't you?"

"Of course I do," Emily said.

"And there is no organization better suited to help accomplish that goal than the Mirabilis Institute of the Credomantic Arts." Stanton paused thoughtfully. "You know, the Institute is extremely well funded. I'm sure it would pay awfully well to secure such a rare and unique specimen."

Emily narrowed her eyes at him. "How much?"

"A hundred dollars. That'll more than defray Pap's cost of losing you while you travel to San Francisco." Stanton frowned at one of Pap's scruffy cats as it leapt onto his lap; he removed the offending animal and made a great show of brushing his trousers. "And let's say another hundred at the end, for your return to Lost Pine."

Two hundred dollars! Emily bit the inside of her lip to keep from blurting out her astonishment. It was a vast sum. Two hundred dollars was more cash-money than they'd ever made for anything . . .

"The trip won't take more than a week, maybe two," Stanton continued. "I can assure you, there will be no greater claim upon your time than is strictly necessary."

"What do you think?" Emily murmured to Pap.

"I don't like the thought of you going so far from home," Pap murmured back, "but I'll manage. And I don't know what else we can do."

"Well?" Stanton removed the poultice from his eye. The swelling had gone down substantially. She could still do something right, at least. "All your expenses will be paid, of course. And I should be surprised if you didn't find yourself—however briefly—the toast of the San Francisco magical community. I would think that might appeal to a girl of your station."

Emily opened her mouth, about to use some words that were even more appropriate to the station in which Dreadnought Stanton imagined her, when someone rushed in the front door. It was one of the boys from the timber camp, a young jobber named Nate.

"Miss Emily! Thank goodness you're here. You have to hurry! There's trouble in town. It's Mr. Hansen. He's . . . Miss Emily, hurry!"

"He says he's done with it!" young Nate said, as he and Emily raced down Moody Ridge toward Lost Pine. "He says he's done with it all! Damn the tracks, damn the lumber, damn it all . . . pardoning my French, Miss Emily."

Emily didn't give a damn about Nate's French. Her skin crawled with foreboding. The icy unpleasant feeling only became stronger when she and Nate finally arrived in Lost Pine about a half hour later and found a small crowd of worried onlookers gathered to watch Dag Hansen. He was working furiously on his timber shed—but he was not adding to it. He was using a hammer to methodically knock it apart, board by board.

"Dag?" Emily pushed her way through to him. "Dag, what are you doing?"

"I won't have it." His voice was carefully restrained—the kind of restraint that hinted at fury smoldering beneath. "I won't have anything on my land that reminds me of *you*."

Emily's brow knit, but she made her voice calm and reasonable. "This shed is for your timber. For your business. For the town. It's not—"

"I built this *all* for you!" He shouted, waving his muscular arm in a gesture that encompassed all of Lost Pine. "All of it was supposed to be for you. The rail line, everything! But I don't want any of it anymore."

"Dag, it wasn't for me," Emily said. *At least it wasn't before last night*.

"Why would I care about growing this town unless it was to make it a better place for my wife? For the family I wanted to have?"

She started to say something, but then he looked at her, and she couldn't remember what she was going to say. She couldn't remember what words were at all for a moment. His eyes were belligerent, pleading, furious. In them, hatred and love tumbled, slippery and shining, like oil and rainwater shaken in a jar.

"You made a fool of me last night, Emily." His voice was low and brutal. "To think that I was strutting around, telling everyone that you and I—" He stopped short, closing his eyes and opening them again, as if that might make the world look right again. "I wanted you to be my wife. I wanted to . . . give you things. Mahogany furniture and . . . I would have made you the queen of Lost Pine. But you snuck off last night with that . . . that . . ."

"Don't be ridiculous." Fear made heat creep into her voice. "We only went to the mine, and the only reason he came was because Besim said the zombies had gotten loose. And they *were* loose, and if he hadn't been there—"

"Stop it!" Dag roared, throwing down the hammer with a shed-rattling crash. "I don't want to hear another word about how wonderful your *Warlock* is. I don't care if zombies stampeded through Sacramento! We would have had our *walk*!"

Emily let out a long, tremulous breath. Stanton said she'd made the love spell too strong, but she was sure she hadn't made it *this* strong. How could the spell have miscarried so completely?

This was not love. This was misery and anguish and despair. And it would rankle Dag until there was nothing left of him—nothing but bitter, unalloyed hate. If the hatred were directed at her and her alone, she deserved that. But it would pollute him, poison his life, his business, the town . . .

She had to get the love spell off him. No one else could. She had bound him, and she had to release him. And it wouldn't be hard. A little backpedaling under a full moon, some rhymes of regret and dismissal . . .

. . . but she couldn't do even that.

With the stone in her hand, she couldn't do magic at all.

But the stone could draw off magic. It had with the miners, anyway. Moving closer to him, she raised a desperate hand to touch his face, to touch the stone against his cheek . . .

Dag saw her movement, grabbed her wrist, wrenched it painfully aside. He thrust his face close to hers.

"If that's all I wanted," he growled, "I would have gotten myself a whore."

She swallowed hard, willing herself not to tremble.

"Let go of my hand, Dag," she whispered.

Dag clenched his teeth, and squeezed harder. Emily gasped in pain, wondering if he would break the bone. Fear gave way to real anger and she bared her teeth in a fierce snarl.

"I said, *let go*!"

The words were like a slap; Dag pulled back, blinking surprise. The edge of murder in his eyes dulled. He released her then, shoving her backward. She fell, landing hard on the sawdust-strewn ground.

"Get out of my sight." Dag turned away from her. Bending to pick up his hammer, he clenched it in a white-knuckled fist. "This is *my* town. You're not welcome in it."

Emily climbed to her feet slowly, cradling her aching wrist against her chest. All around her, men and women crowded, frowning. She was surrounded by small angry noises, terse unflattering words . . . Shoving her way through the muttering mob, she launched into a flat run for home, her head spinning with shame.

Oh, Dag, what have I done?

She ran until she was well away from the town. When she came to the Hanging Oak she collapsed against it, pounding her stone-hand against the rough bark, screaming frustration at the top of her lungs. This did nothing but make her hand ache and her throat sore. Finally, she stopped. She wiped tears from her eyes, raked wisps of hair from her face, and took a deep breath.

She would go to San Francisco. If the professors at Stanton's institute couldn't figure out how to remove it, she'd cut the damn thing out herself. Then she could return to Lost Pine and fix everything.

It was the only way.

CHAPTER FOUR

The Flight of the Guilty

When Emily returned to the cabin, Stanton had already gone, leaving word that he would return that afternoon for her answer. Emily swore under her breath—even someone as nettlesome as Dreadnought Stanton deserved to be warned of the prevailing mood in town.

Well, he's the great Warlock, Emily thought bitterly. *He'll just have to take care of himself.*

She began to worry, however, as warm afternoon mellowed into blue evening and the Warlock did not return. No one came to call, not even Mrs. Lyman, and there was no news to be had. Emily slept fitfully, dreaming of nooses and hammers and the eyes of a man eating himself from within in great ravenous bites.

It was not until early the next morning that Stanton rode into the clearing, whistling casually, his second horse saddled and in tow.

Emily dropped the breakfast dishes and ran to watch him ride up. One glance at his saddlebags told her that he was packed and ready to leave. Her relief at seeing him unharmed and seemingly cheerful filled her with the perverse urge to tell him to go straight to the devil. She'd had entirely enough of everything to do with eastern Warlocks, and his whistling made her want to slap him down from atop his prancing black horse. She stalked out of the cabin and looked up at him, planting her hands on her hips.

"Well, I suppose you can guess my answer. I'll go to San

Francisco with you if it means I can get this rotten thing out of my hand."

"I'm afraid neither of us has a choice about leaving now," Stanton said. "But I suppose it's nicer to pretend that it's of our own volition, as opposed to being chased out of town."

Emily's throat tightened.

"As bad as that?" she asked.

Stanton nodded, sliding down from the saddle. "I had a rather unsettled time of it last night. Two dozen of Hansen's timbermen, in varying stages of inebriation, were brandishing torches and discussing various means of stringing me up." He hitched his horses to a tree, lashing leather over leather with a fierce movement. "I save their town from zombies, and they want to lynch me. Provincials."

"So how did you get away?"

"A few of them—representing, I am sure, the cream of Lost Pine's intelligentsia—realized that the joy of burning down the boarding house with me in it would also have deprived poor Mrs. Bargett of her livelihood. I settled my bill before dawn— with a generous gratuity—and snuck out while they were still sleeping it off." He looked at Emily. "If we get going right away, we'll be in Dutch Flat by nightfall, and to San Francisco that much quicker. Are you ready?"

Emily said nothing for a moment, but eyed the huge black horses warily.

"I don't know how to ride," she said.

Stanton blinked. "What do you mean, you don't know how to ride? We're in the middle of California! Everyone knows how to ride."

"Do you see any horses around here?" Emily gestured broadly. "Unlike some people, we can't afford one horse, let alone two. I have ridden Mrs. Lyman's burro once or twice, for a lark." But Stanton's beasts were a darn sight larger and livelier than that stubby little animal. "I don't suppose it's the same."

"Not quite." Stanton looked ruefully at his horse, as if to offer it a silent apology. "Well, nothing like being thrown into the water to learn how to swim."

Emily didn't like the sound of that at all.

"Go get your things. I'd like to be well away from Lost Pine before Hansen's men start waking up. I hardly think the mood of last night will be improved by their hangovers."

Emily went into the house and up to her loft. Taking out her canvas traveling bag, she threw it onto the bed. She'd already thought out in detail what she would take. She'd started to pack half a dozen times, and had stopped herself every time, dizzy with a mix of apprehension, resignation, and—though she hardly wanted to admit it to herself—excitement. She had to go. The stone had to be removed from her hand, and as quickly as possible. But the rational comprehension of this fact did nothing to calm her nerves. Everything was tumbling around her so unexpectedly. Packing for a hasty trip to San Francisco, as good as run out of town . . . She thought she had problems before. If only she could trade them back for the ones she had now!

She pressed her hands to her hot cheeks and breathed in deeply. Pap's words echoed: *Three times what thou givest returns to thee.* She let the breath out slowly and began stuffing the traveling bag. Then she turned her attention to the clothes she was wearing.

If she was going to be riding, she'd need something to go under her gray wool dress. She pulled on an old pair of Pap's pants that she'd commandeered for wood chopping and other hard chores. She tied on her largest apron. Over everything, she pulled on her buffalo coat. It would be hot during the day, but it would keep rain off and could serve as a blanket at need. Then she twisted up her braids, plopped an old hat over them, and skewered the straw with her silver hair sticks.

She didn't need to glance in her mirror to know she looked like the biggest rube in all creation. But she was comfortable, and if she could horrify Dreadnought Stanton into the bargain, so much the better.

Before she went down, she pulled out the silk pouch she always wore next to her skin. It still contained the calico spell bag with the Ashes of Amour in it. She considered leaving the spell bag behind—in fact, she longed to throw it out the damn window—but she decided against it. The little bag of ashes was a reminder of the wrong she'd done—and a reminder of her promise to undo it. She would keep it until Dag was free.

There was something else she couldn't leave behind either. Reaching into her morocco case, she retrieved two delicate earrings of gold and amethyst. Another precious inheritance from her mother, and she liked to keep them close. Emily had worn the gems only once or twice; they were far too delicate and beautiful to dangle from her usually dirty ears. She admired their glint and sparkle, then put them into the silk pouch and tucked it down her collar.

Downstairs, Pap and Stanton were sitting by the fire. Stanton was apparently making an eleventh-hour attempt to convince Pap that urine was not the best medium for a tincture to cure baldness. That, in fact, urine was not a particularly good medium for any tincture.

"I'm ready," she interrupted curtly, hoisting the canvas bag over her shoulder.

To her disappointment, Stanton didn't seem to notice her outfit. At least if he did, he didn't comment.

"Where's my money?" she asked, more churlishly than she might have if he'd given her the slight satisfaction of a raised eyebrow or a tugged collar. "A hundred in advance."

Stanton reached into his pocket and withdrew a small pouch that seemed to be black silk. It hardly seemed large enough to contain the ten gold eagles that Stanton withdrew from it.

"Give the money to Pap," Emily said. She squeezed the old man's shoulder and put her head close to his. "I'm leaving the money with you. Mr. Stanton says he's going to pay the expenses, and I intend to hold him to it."

Stanton was laying the money in Pap's gnarled hand when Mrs. Lyman stormed in. She had obviously come 'cross lots in a great hurry, and her face glowed with purpose and indignation.

"Ignatius Edwards!" she bellowed upon entering, "I want to know exactly what that girl of yours thinks she's—"

The woman stopped short, taking in the scene with astonished eyes.

The gold being passed from hand to hand, traveling clothes and packed bags, the horses saddled outside . . .

The Flight of the Guilty, the inscription under the tableau would read, were it an engraving.

"And just *what* is going on here?" Mrs. Lyman bawled.

"Em's going down to San Francisco with Mr. Stanton," Pap answered mildly, dropping the money into his pocket with a clink.

"What?"

"I'm going to San Francisco with Mr. Stanton," Emily repeated matter-of-factly, pretending that Mrs. Lyman had simply failed to hear.

Mrs. Lyman seized Emily's arm, jerked her roughly to the back of the cabin, where—ostensibly—the men could not hear.

"Emily Edwards, just what do you think you're doing? Do you know what they're saying in town? You're not going to stop those rumors by . . . by riding off on a horse with a *traveling Warlock*! And certainly not to San Francisco! *Sin* Francisco, they should call it!"

"I'm a grown woman, Mrs. Lyman. Everyone's got it all wrong. I'm going with Mr. Stanton for business reasons."

Mrs. Lyman raised her eyebrows in alarm.

"*Magic* business," Emily felt compelled to clarify.

"Listen, I've read enough *Ladies' Repository* to know just what's going on here. You're a nice girl, an *innocent* girl. You don't know the kind of . . . Well, the kind of troubles one can get into!"

Emily stared at Mrs. Lyman. Her head was beginning to ache.

"There's no question of that," she said.

"There's never any question of that until—*boom*!" Mrs. Lyman's emphasis made the relinquishing of one's virtue sound like the firing of a cannon. "You're ruined, a drunkard, and working at a house of ill repute in Stockton."

"I'm not going to end up in a house of ill repute in Stockton!" Emily had never raised her voice to Mrs. Lyman before, and doing so now made the old woman stare at her with blank amazement. Emily took a deep breath and lowered her voice.

"Dag needs my help. I can't explain it right now, but if I go with Mr. Stanton, I can help Dag."

Mrs. Lyman looked at her for a long time. Then she let out a protracted sigh, her hand pressed to her cheek in anxious resignation.

"Emily, listen. Your pap has sheltered you quite a bit."

"Not *that* much."

"No, no . . . not just about that. About Witches and War-locks. What people think about them. In Lost Pine, we live and let live, because, Lord knows, we're all sinners under the skin. But there are other places, other people—godly people." She shook her head. "It's a dangerous world, Emily. You don't understand how dangerous."

"You've got to stop reading so many pulp novels," Emily said. "The world isn't all rampaging Aberrancies and evil blood sorcerers. In fact, I am certain that the world in general is much the same as it is in Lost Pine, except with more people and better amenities."

Mrs. Lyman stared at Emily sadly. Then, with a wail, she drew Emily into her arms, crushing her against her broad bosom. She sniffled in Emily's ear, patted her back with a large hand, then pushed her back to arm's length.

"All right, listen. If he gives you anything to drink, for heaven's sake, don't drink it!" She wagged a finger in Emily's face, her voice low and conspiratorial. "For that matter, don't eat anything either. Don't take your buffalo coat off for any-thing . . . and you make him pay for separate rooms!"

After all, Emily was rather glad for Mrs. Lyman's arrival on the scene, for it made a long, awkward good-bye out of the question. And while Emily wanted nothing more than to put a dozen miles between herself and the sounds of sobbing coming from within the cabin (Mrs. Lyman had settled her-self in and was carrying on like a paid mourner at a Chinese funeral), she did pause on the doorstep outside the cabin to give Pap a long hug.

"I'm sorry I've caused so much trouble," she murmured in his ear. "I'll make it better, honest I will."

"It's too bad you have to start a trip on a Friday." Pap stroked her arm as he used to when she was young and scared. Then he reached into his pocket and pulled out a sprig of dried comfrey, which he tucked into the folds of her buffalo coat.

"Nothing like comfrey to protect the traveler," he said, and for a moment it seemed as if he would leave it at that. But instead of turning away, he shifted nervously on both feet. She knew that anxious little dance; it always presaged something important he didn't want to say. She waited for him to speak. He scratched vaguely at the shiny web of scars on the side of his face.

"Well, after all, Mrs. Lyman says I ought to mention it . . . I never wanted to bother you with such things. But she's had a hand in raising you, too, so I reckon she's got a right . . ." He fell silent for a moment, breathing in to help gather his scattered thoughts. When he spoke again, his words rang low and clear.

"I never told you why I left my gramp's place in Kentucky, back in the forties. Why I come to California."

"That was more than thirty years ago," Emily said. "What does that—"

"I got run out, Emily." Pap interrupted softly. "A group of godly folks, they despised me for being a Warlock. They burnt me almost to death. These scars . . . they weren't from no barn fire."

Emily blinked at him.

"There's not time to tell the tale, and even if there was, I wouldn't want to. I lived, and then I come to California, where I guessed a man could start out fresh."

"And you've been practicing magic all this time, all out in the open, without a breath of difficulty." Emily was furious with Mrs. Lyman for digging up trials and troubles that belonged in the past. Oh, she would give the old busybody a nice piece of her mind when she got back from San Francisco! "Witches and Warlocks are all over the place now, even in the big cities. Why, Mr. Stanton comes from a whole institute of them!"

Pap nodded. "I guess times is different now. And them books Mrs. Lyman reads me, the ones about Witches and Warlocks and all the grand adventures they have. They never have anything in them about when they put the wood around your feet, and the black smoke starts curling up . . ." Pap's voice trailed off, and he stared at the ground, transfixed.

"Miss Edwards." Stanton's voice was impatient.

"Listen, never you mind what Mrs. Lyman says," Emily said to Pap. "She just likes to think the world's mixed up and complicated. It makes a better story. But these are modern times. I'll be perfectly safe."

"It *was* a long time ago. But please, Em. If you run into anyone who despises you for being a Witch, well . . ." His voice became a low, harsh whisper and he clutched her arm hard, milky eyes shining. "You *run*. That's all, Em. You just *run*."

"Miss Edwards!" Stanton repeated, louder.

"Just a minute!" she yelled back at him, before putting her lips next to Pap's ear. "I won't even let them burn Mr. Stanton, though it might take him down a peg or two."

Pap nodded, as if finally satisfied.

"He's a good sort," Pap said. "Mostly."

Then he turned away abruptly, vanishing into the cabin and closing the door behind himself. Pap never said good-byes.

So it was that Emily was left to stare at the huge black horse in front of her.

"His name is Romulus," Stanton said, so formally that Emily expected the animal to lift a hoof and shake her hand. "He's very valuable, so please handle him with care."

"*Me* handle *him* with care?" Emily muttered, as Stanton gave her a leg up. "How exactly you reckon I'm going to damage your horse?"

Stanton did not favor her with a precise answer. And over the next several hours, it became clear that such precision would have been impossible, in that he felt there was a veritable galaxy of ways she could damage his horse. He spent the better part of the morning defending the poor tender lamb against her abominable ignorance.

"Look, you may have never ridden anything but a burro, but even a burro would plot homicide if you kept jerking his reins like that. Don't touch the reins at all. Just sit there like a good girl. He knows what he's doing."

Emily let the reins fall slack. The horse tossed its huge head gaily and gave a little caper that made Emily hunch forward in terror. The ground seemed to be a million miles away, and the black beast kept dancing from side to side most unaccountably. With her good hand, she clutched the pommel for dear life. She found that doing so made her feel better. The pommel really was quite a handy thing.

"Why is this creature so all-fired lively?" she asked, aware of a quaver in her voice.

"Romulus and Remus are a carriage-matched pair of Morgans," Stanton said. "I'd be most concerned if they weren't quick and lively."

"I can't think why you brought horses like this out to California. Aren't many carriages in Lost Pine."

"No, as I discovered, Sunday turns around the park aren't quite the thing," Stanton said. "Now, see that steep place in the trail up ahead? Lean forward in the saddle; don't just slump like a sack of flour."

Once the steep place had been successfully negotiated, Emily sat back in the saddle and looked at Stanton thoughtfully.

"How did you end up in Lost Pine, anyhow?" Emily asked. "I mean, it couldn't have been by choice."

To his credit, Stanton bit back his immediate response, which Emily supposed was something along the lines of "Good Lord, no!" Instead, he said something that sounded like a memorized recitation:

"As the holder of a Jefferson Chair, it was my duty to accept a placement wherever the Institute deemed fit."

"A Jefferson Chair? What's that?"

"It's a system of regional positions endowed by a gentleman named Harmon Jefferson. There are more than two dozen chair holders throughout the United States and Europe."

Emily *hmm*ed thoughtfully. "So where's yours?"

"My what?"

"Your chair. Where do you keep it? You don't have to drag it around, do you? Sounds awful inconvenient."

The thought of this amused Stanton vastly, or at least she supposed it did; he gave a small, dry chuckle.

"No, the chair itself is pure abstraction." He held up a hand. On his finger there was a gold ring with a crest on it. "This is the only physical representation of the office."

"And you fellows do what, exactly? Annoy small-town charm makers who just want to be left alone?"

"We research local magical customs and anomalies and bring modern practices to the rural and unenlightened."

"Six of one, half a dozen of the other," Emily said. "And in Lost Pine, the rural and unenlightened were me and Pap. What a waste of all your talent! Why would your institute send you someplace so small?"

"I have no doubt Professor Mirabilis sent me where he thought my talents would be best utilized," Stanton said.

"Professor Mirabilis. Of the Mirabilis Institute?"

"The same," Stanton said. And then, as if to protect the idea of the professor from disrespect, he added seriously, "A very fine man."

Emily would have said something more, but at that moment Romulus stumbled and her heart lodged behind her windpipe and pounded there for some moments.

"Are we really going to ride all the way to San Francisco? You said your institute had plenty of money—why don't we take the train from Dutch Flat? It would be quicker and a whole lot more comfortable."

Stanton waved a hand as if the idea didn't even bear considering. "Where I go, my horses go. They're the most valuable things I own."

"Seems like they own you, more like," Emily grumbled. "Look, there are at least a dozen stables in Dutch Flat that would take good care of your horses. We could be to San Francisco and back in a few days instead of a couple of weeks. And your horses would be spared the trip."

"All excellent points. But they don't take into account one fact. I don't want to have to come back to get my horses because I don't intend to return."

The curt proclamation caught Emily off guard, but of course, it made perfect sense—Stanton would never be welcome again in Lost Pine, even if Emily was successful in returning to remove the love spell from Dag. And, she thought

with a sinking heart, even if she could remove the sorcellement, what promise was there that she would ever be welcome again either? She shook the thoughts from her head.

"Won't your institute be upset with you for getting run out
of town?"

"It was hardly *my* fault that I was run out of town," Stanton
reminded her. "And anyway, Lost Pine does not need a Jefferson Chair. You and Pap don't need or want any help. The
Institute must find me a placement that is more suitable, or
else . . ."

He fell silent. Emily waited for the other shoe to drop.

"Or else?" she prompted.

"Or else I *quit*. I'll put my horses on a steamer at San Francisco and go home to New York."

Emily was taken aback by the vehemence of feeling behind the Warlock's words. She raised an eyebrow.

"You can't just give up," Emily said.

"Ah, the spirit of the great American pioneer," he said, in a
tone that suggested said spirit was vastly overrated. "Well, it
is similarly my right as an American to give up whenever I
please."

"You'd give up being a Warlock?"

"Don't be ridiculous. I've invested far too much in the de-
velopment of my talents. But there are always opportunities
for trained Warlocks. Situations where the sacrifices a man
has made for his craft are appropriately valued."

"Maybe the necromantic factory in Chicago is hiring,"
Emily said.

Stanton frowned, but did not comment.

"Well, perhaps your institute will see things differently
when they see this." Emily held up her hand. The blue stone
glittered in the warming light of afternoon.

"I hope so," Stanton said. Then a note of distance returned
to his voice as if he'd suddenly remembered to whom he was
speaking. His next words were condescendingly smooth. "I
imagine the idea of seeing San Francisco must be quite a
thrilling prospect for someone like you. You've never been,
of course?"

Annoyance surged in Emily's chest. Reaching down for

the reins, she pulled on them hard. Romulus danced backward, chin to chest.

"Let's get one thing straight." Emily glared at Stanton. "I'm not going to San Francisco because I want to gawp at the gaslights and the tall buildings. And I'm not going because I want to be the toast—however briefly—of the magical community of San Francisco. I'm going because I made an awful mistake, and I have to fix it, and I can't fix it with this . . . *thing* in my hand. I am going because Dag needs my help. That clear, Mr. Stanton?"

Stanton stared at her with distaste, as if her outburst came with an unpleasant smell attached.

"As window glass, Miss Edwards," he said. Then he tapped his heels against Remus' side. "We'd better hurry if we want to reach Dutch Flat by nightfall."

The main street of Dutch Flat ran up a steep hill from a desolate white field of mine tailings; long purple shadows of dusk stretched across dessicated mounds of white granite gravel like stripes on an exotic sleeping tiger. The road from Lost Pine to Dutch Flat had been frequently pockmarked with such abrasions—places where entire hillsides had been blasted away by diamond-hard jets of water.

False business fronts loomed along either side of the main street, and they all bustled with end-of-day activity. A shop clerk was bringing in wares that had been displayed on the sidewalk. A large man with an apron and a bushy mustache was sweeping a slab doorstep of uneven granite. A girl in a dirty pinafore was washing the bakery's front windows. All along the road, hitched horses pawed impatiently, eager to head home.

They came to a stop in front of a large store, built of heavy blocks of rough-hewn serpentine. Stanton swung down and looped Remus' reins around the hitching rail.

"If you'd be so good as to wait a moment . . ." Emily liked to think he was saying it to her, but she got the distinct impression that he was speaking to the horse. When Stanton emerged, he held out a pair of white kid gloves. She frowned at them.

"Don't want to attract attention, do we?" he prompted innocently, giving the gloves a little shake. She snatched them.

Of course it wouldn't do to have folks staring at the glowing rock in her hand. But he didn't have to get her something so damn *dainty*. So this was his version of a tugged collar, eh? She jerked the gloves on, resolving to get them dirty as quick as she could.

Riding on a little farther up the street, they came to a hotel proudly dubbed the Nonpareil. At the polished oak reception desk, Stanton pulled out the small black silk purse Emily had seen before, again withdrawing coins to pay the clerk. He signed the ledger in a jagged angular script: "Mr. Dreadnought Stanton and sister."

"That's it? Sister?" Emily limped up the carpeted stairs on legs that had somehow turned to jelly during the course of the day's ride. "Would it have killed you to come up with a name?"

"I have three sisters, Miss Edwards. I didn't think you'd appreciate being burdened with any of their names."

"Try me," Emily said.

"Euphemia, Ophidia, and Hortense."

Emily wrinkled her nose. "What fool did the naming in your family?"

"My father is the fool in question. He is a man who feels the need to publicly memorialize his esoteric and obsessive passions—passions which have included the later history of Rome, reptiles, eighteenth-century Flemish aristocracy, and clipper ships." Pointing to a door, he handed Emily a key. "Early start in the morning. Downstairs by seven."

Downstairs by seven, Emily mouthed in a snotty voice as she let herself into her room. It was small but trim, with a cheery pot of gardenias on the windowsill. The bed looked soft and inviting, and Emily would have gladly fallen right into it, but travel was a grimy business. On her way to fetch some hot water, chipped china pitcher in hand, she passed two women. Their heads were held close together in intense, private conversation. She caught a snippet as they passed:

". . . at least, that's what the men downstairs were saying."

"To think we were going to take that very road! But the train will be able to get through, won't it?"

"They say the train is the only safe route to Sacramento until the government troops arrive . . ."

And then the women passed out of earshot, and Emily was left to stare after them. She was still thinking about their conversation as she carried her pitcher of hot water back up to her room and washed her hands and face in the basin. She smoothed her hair, and then she went and knocked on Stanton's door. He opened it a parsimonious crack, eyeing her warily.

"Take me down to dinner," she said.

"Allow me to acquaint you with the word 'please.' It's all the rage in the better social circles. And if you're hungry, have dinner brought up to your room."

"There's news afoot. Something about the roads not being safe, and government troops being dispatched. I want to know what's going on."

"I'll ask around later," Stanton said.

"Come on, Dreadnought *dear*." Emily attempted to mimic a sisterly wheedle. When that failed, she tried to push the door open. Stanton pushed back with surprising force. After a moment, Emily gave up with a stomp of her foot. "Listen, I won't be treated like luggage. You can't just stow me in a room and forget about me. I want to know what's going on! If we're going to ride through Sacramento on those beasts of yours, I want to know what's wrong with the roads."

"Fine," Stanton sighed. "I *am* a bit peckish. But please remember, Miss Edwards—you're supposed to be impersonating my sister. So far we must seem about as fraternally matched as the cuckoo and the nightingale."

"I've always thought the cuckoo a rather clever bird," Emily said thoughtfully, as she led the way downstairs. "I mean, they know how to get things done, don't they?"

Stanton did not answer, but busied himself with straightening his tie.

Downstairs, they were given a place at the common dining table. Men were drinking by the fire, talking low among themselves. A woman brought them plates of food, and Emily was surprised to find that Stanton was "a bit peckish" kind of like the Pacific Ocean was a neat little puddle. She watched him eat a whole roasted chicken, a serving bowl of buttered potatoes, a jar of pickles, and a dozen biscuits with butter and jam.

"Travel takes it out of you, I see," she commented, as she watched him pour a pint of heavy cream over half an apple pie.

"A Warlock has to maintain his reserves of energy."

"Where do you put it all? You're skinny as a rail!"

He gave her a look that indicated he deemed such discussion presumptuous. He'd already given Emily that look exactly eleven times that day. She'd kept count.

"I have an unusual metabolism," he said, but Emily had already lost interest in Stanton's metabolism. She was watching the men by the fire. Their discussion had become intense, with the words "roads" and "military" rising above the din.

"Go find out what they're talking about!" she whispered fiercely, elbowing Stanton in the ribs. He frowned down at her.

"I'm digesting," he said, shifting a little farther away from her.

"Digest faster," Emily said. "Unless you want your sister wading into the middle of a bunch of ruffians!"

He was clearly appalled, though he tried unsuccessfully to hide it. She seized the advantage.

"Or how'd you like it if 'Euphemia' called out for a shot of whiskey, neat?"

Stanton rubbed his eyes. "Forgive me," he said. "I'm trying to eradicate the image of my eldest sister bolting a shot of whiskey. I'm sure the headache will clear presently."

"Then for the sake of your aching head, I won't ask you to imagine Euphemia climbing up on the table to sing the one about 'Madcap Molly, Maid of the Million-Dollar Mine.' "

Stanton shuddered. He dropped his napkin on the table. "All right. I'll go and glean whatever limited information they might possess. Just finish your dinner and *please* stay quiet."

Over her coffee, Emily watched as Stanton went to the bar. He purchased a cigar, then installed himself by the fire, busying himself with the little movements of smoking: clipping the cigar end, piercing it, lighting it (with a lucifer from the box on the mantel, Emily noticed; no finger-snap flames here among strangers). He smoked contemplatively, adding nothing to the conversation but listening with extravagant casualness, as if the men were trading choice stock tips.

When Stanton had finished smoking, he strolled back to where Emily was sitting.

"Well?" she said.

"Wasn't a bad cigar for a nickel."

"You know what I mean."

"Come along, then." He offered her his arm. She stood and took it, then startled. He was astonishingly hot, as if burning up with fever. She looked at him, scrutinized his face.

"Are you sick?" She yanked the glove from her hand, touched his cheek. He pulled back as if alarmed.

"You're hot as the bottom of a kettle!" It was as if he'd been sitting in the fireplace, instead of standing next to it.

"I'm fine," he said, curtly. "I told you, I have an unusual metabolism. Now, if you don't mind?"

Pulling her glove back on, she took his arm again and they went upstairs toward the rooms.

"All right, here's the big news. *Aberrancies*." Stanton spoke as if the word itself was tedious. "Apparently there's a spate coming from a pit mine close by the main road to Sacramento. Causing trouble for some of the travelers here. There's talk of government troops being dispatched to clear the trouble."

Emily stopped short. "*Aberrancies*?"

"Hardly unusual. Incidents involving Aberrancies have been increasing steadily over the past twenty years. Especially out here in the West."

"Why would we have more Aberrancies?"

"Their appearance is correlated with certain geological irregularities. Mining—pit mining especially—often exposes these irregularities."

"Aberrancies are caused by mining?"

"No, Aberrancies are not *caused* by mining." He sighed as they came to the door of her room. "Rather, they are an unfortunate by-product. It's all rather complicated—"

"Explain it to me." Emily leaned against the wall next to her door.

"Not in the hallway of a public hotel." As if pretending to be her brother gave him the right to talk to her like one! "It's just too common."

"Not as common as having your mad sister pound on your door until you tell her what she wants to know." Emily narrowed her eyes. "I think you can guess, Mr. Stanton, just how common I am willing to be."

Stanton glared at her. Emily smiled sweetly.

"Your comfort with extortion is an extremely ugly personality trait," he said. Then he sighed. "I'll make it as simple as possible. Deep within the earth lies the Mantic Anastomosis. In layman's terms, it is a vast interconnected web, like a filigree over the whole globe. This web is made of a special type of mineral—a mineral almost never seen aboveground."

"Native Star," Emily said, her thumb stroking her palm. Stanton nodded.

"According to accepted theory, this mineral web is part of the cycle by which magic is absorbed, purified, and released. The Mantic Anastomosis exudes magic slowly, and the magic is knitted into all living things. When those things die, the magic returns to the earth and the cycle begins anew."

"Yes, I know all about the cycle of magic. Pap taught me," Emily said. "But everyone knows magic can't be held within things that never lived. So how can it be stored in a rock?"

"It is theorized that magic binds to the mineral structure of the web, is attracted to it by some kind of magnetism. Therefore the power is not actually within the mineral itself, but held close to it." He paused, suddenly looking exasperated. "But see here, you wanted to know about Aberrancies. If you're after a broad-based tutorial on magical theory, we'll be here all night."

"All right," Emily said somewhat reluctantly, for she did like to learn despite her general resistance to being taught. "Aberrancies."

"Humans have been developing techniques to concentrate and extract magic since the dawn of history. But it is only in the past two hundred years—since most civilized people stopped burning Witches and Warlocks wholesale—that any large-scale, modern application of magic has been developed.

Over the past century, research has begun to suggest a correlation between the use of magic in ever-more concentrated forms and an increase in the harmful toxic residuals in the Mantic Anastomosis."

"So humans working magic dirties up the rock web somehow?"

"Close enough," Stanton said. "Aberrancies are understood to be the result of the Mantic Anastomosis cleansing itself of these toxic residuals. By some process not entirely understood, the web segregates this highly unstable material. It is called geochole—Bile of the Earth."

"Black Exunge." That was the skin-shivering term always used in Mrs. Lyman's pulp novels.

"Yes, I believe that's what it's called *popularly,*" Stanton said. "When large boluses form, it works its way out through thin places in the earth."

"Like mines," Emily said.

Stanton nodded approvingly. "The foul substance binds to any living thing that comes into contact with it. The result is horrible mutations, both physical and spiritual."

"What about people?" Emily looked at Stanton. "They work in mines. Has a human ever been . . ."

"There was a famous case in Ohio before the war. A young man encountered quite a large black bolus and did not have the sense to know that it was something that should not be touched." He paused, and Emily wondered if he was going to give her another lecture about grabbing things willy-nilly. "He terrorized an entire county before a detachment of military Warlocks was able to put him down."

"He couldn't be cured?"

Stanton shook his head gravely. "Death is the only cure—preferably a quick and merciful one. There is a period of vulnerability during the mutation. They're easier to kill if you catch them early."

"This man in Ohio . . . They didn't catch him early?"

"He grew to fifty feet tall and smashed an entire township with his bare hands," Stanton said. "Fortunately, such cases are extremely rare. Most Aberrancies are nothing more than a small animal, or insect, that has the misfortune to be present when a black bolus is expelled. In such instances, large-caliber silver bullets are typically sufficient." Stanton cocked his head and looked at her. "You certainly are interested in Aberrancies."

"Aren't you?" Emily countered. "Oh, well, of course I suppose you've seen a hundred Aberrancies and dismissed them with a snap of your fingers."

"It takes more than a finger snap," Stanton said. "But forewarned is forearmed. We'll ride well south of Sacramento, and avoid the area in which the Aberrancies have been reported."

"I still think we should take the train," Emily grumbled. "You won't win any points with your professors if I get eaten by an Aberrancy."

"You will not be eaten by an Aberrancy," Stanton said. "Besides, the train does not stop everywhere we need to go."

Emily registered the cryptic comment about going places the train didn't, but decided she'd harassed Dreadnought Stanton enough for one evening. She smiled brightly at him and extended a hand. "All right then, you may retire. Downstairs by seven!"

He took her hand and gave it a wan shake.

"Good night, Miss . . . Euphemia," he said.

"Good night, Dreadnought *dear*!" she chirped.

CHAPTER FIVE

The Aberrancy

The next morning after breakfast, Stanton made a trip to the general store, and when he returned the horses were loaded with supplies—mostly foodstuffs, Emily guessed—for the ride to San Francisco. The next leg of their journey would take them down the North Fork of the American River, high and wild with fresh snowmelt, down to where the rich Sacramento Valley spread like a green tablecloth. The morning was cool, and though a haze filmed the horizon, the pink-streaked sky held the promise of another warm, clear day.

"We should make good time today." Stanton's pleased tone suggested that making good time was a virtue right up there with Justice, Courage, Wisdom, and Moderation.

But the joke was on him, Emily thought, because there was no way anyone—especially not a clock-watching Warlock—was going to persuade her to remount that equine rack of torture. And in her constellation of aches and pains was one bright glowing sun of discomfort that she preferred, for obvious reasons, not to discuss. She simply insisted on walking the first few miles to stretch her legs.

As she limped before Stanton and his plodding horses, she imagined a smirk against her back. A couple of times she spun, trying to catch the Warlock out, but his face was always set with a placidity that suggested the deep contemplation of the noble virtues previously mentioned. She made a note of it; this Dreadnought Stanton was far sneakier than she'd given him credit for.

Finally, she could stand it no longer. Sore or not, she wasn't

going to be licked. Jerking the reins from where they were
hitched to Stanton's saddle, she muddled her way up onto Romulus' back. This was not accomplished without considerable
awkwardness and indignity. Finally, though, she sat stiffly, her
back staff-straight, teeth clenched.

"I take it your legs are sufficiently stretched?" Stanton asked.

In reply, Emily used those legs to give Romulus a petulant
nudge in the ribs and held onto the pommel for dear life as
the animal leapt forward in a lively canter.

It was not until they stopped to eat lunch that Emily decided
to speak to Stanton again. She doubted that her silence represented any kind of a punishment, but it certainly suited her
better. Just outside Colfax, off the main road to Auburn, they
came across a pleasant meadow where the horses could graze
on juicy new spring grass. Leaving Romulus with Stanton,
Emily wandered off to answer the call of necessity. Following
the sound of rushing water, she discovered a lively little creek
at the foot of a timbered hill. She knelt for a drink.

Tucking her gloves into the pocket of her buffalo coat, she
felt the rasp of the comfrey Pap had given her, and something
else, something cool and smooth. It was a coin, one of the gold
eagles Stanton had paid over. Emily clutched it in her hand, a
wave of affection for the old man warming her whole body.
Swiftly, she transferred the coin into the silk pouch around her
neck for safekeeping.

"I'm going to make it right, Pap," she murmured. "I promise."

When she came back, she saw that Stanton was no longer
alone. He was speaking with three men by the side of the
road. They were all dressed in solemn, dusty black and were
mounted on skinny rib-sided nags that swished their tails with
boredom and annoyance. The only words Emily caught were
Stanton's:

"I'm afraid not. But I'll keep it in mind."

"Good day to you, brother." The man who had been speaking looked down at Emily, and tipped his hat. He had a thin
face, with prominent, knifelike cheekbones. "Sister."

When they had ridden off, Emily finally broke her self-
imposed silence.

"Who were they, and what did they want?"

"No one, and nothing." Stanton watched after the men until they were well down the road.

Then, Stanton unpacked food from the saddlebags, and Emily spread her skirt over the grass, stretching out her stiff legs. The farther they traveled down the flanks of the great Sierras, the warmer and more fragrant the air grew. It felt very much like spring now; everything around them smelled of juice and sap and growth. In Lost Pine, on days like this, she would be out gathering fresh herbs for charm work. They were under a Taurus moon now, good for collecting items to be used in spells that required fortitude—potions against drunkenness, nostrums to ease the pains of childbirth, elixirs for those who had difficult journeys to undertake . . . She sighed, feeling homesick already.

She watched as Stanton poured cold coffee from a flask into a tin cup. He waved his fingers over the cup and the liquid warmed to steaming.

"Is it really worth dirtying the Mantic Anastomosis to have hot coffee?"

"Don't nag," he said.

"But you said yourself that the increased use of magic is harmful, and causes Aberrancies. So shouldn't people stop doing so much magic?"

"I said that was one *theory*," Stanton clarified. He poured sugar into his coffee from a waxed-paper bag. "But magic is building this country, Miss Edwards. Will you ask the government to surrender its military Warlocks? The police to do without their Warlock investigators? And what would industrialists do without fashionable Warlock secretaries to light their cigars?"

Stanton swirled the coffee in his cup, took a sip. Grimacing, he added more sugar until the liquid took on the consistency of molasses.

"Useful things will be used," Stanton said. "Advancements come with costs. No one ever said manifesting a nation's destiny wouldn't hurt a bit."

"Well, the kind of magic Pap and I do doesn't hurt anyone," Emily said.

"Except poor stupid lumbermen."

Emily glared, and contemplated saying something cutting. But how could she? Stanton was right. She stared at her hand, at the stone glittering in the sunlight.

"Poor Dag," she whispered. "Before we left Lost Pine I touched him. I touched his face. Why didn't it help? Why wasn't the magic extracted, like it was with the zombies?"

"The zombies were animated entirely by magic." Stanton chewed on a thick piece of bread, which he'd buttered and topped with even more sugar. "The stone absorbed the magical energy that drove them. But it seems not to affect magic that has already worked its way into a living creature's life force."

"That's a shame," Emily said.

"Not really. If the stone worked like that, you'd most likely be dead."

"Instead of on a road to San Francisco, trying to rescue a man who loves me so much he hates me?"

Stanton looked at her as he tore another hunk from the now-ravaged loaf. "Still feeling guilty, are we? I'd have thought you'd be over that by now."

"I have a nettlesome little thing called a conscience," Emily hissed. "Ever hear of it?"

"They're out of fashion in New York," Stanton said, and though she guessed he was joking, he didn't sound humorous. "Listen, you'll be back in a fortnight, and you can smooth everything over. That love spell was strong enough for ten men. A few tears, some nice little endearments, a lighter hand with the lavender . . . he'll marry you in a heartbeat."

The thought made Emily shudder.

"No, it was a stupid idea to begin with," she said. "I just want to take the spell off and—" She fell suddenly silent. And then what? Return to her life in Lost Pine? She'd be right back where she started. An aging spinster—now complete with an unsavory history—trying to compete against shiny mail-order spells in gilt-paper boxes. She and Pap would be two hundred dollars richer, but when that money ran out, then what?

"What happened to that pioneer spirit?" Stanton chided. "You can't just give up, can you?"

Emily said nothing.

"Well, I must say I don't get you, Miss Edwards." Stanton brushed crumbs from his trousers and began replacing things in the saddlebags. "You must love the man, otherwise what's all this nonsense about love spells? And the minute you get him to love you back, all you want is for him to stop loving you? I don't—"

"You wouldn't understand, Mr. Stanton." Emily interrupted him. "Don't bother trying. There are limits even to your superior intelligence."

"I hardly think it's a question of limited intelligence. At least not on *my* part," Stanton said, tossing the dregs of his coffee onto the ground.

By nightfall they had reached Auburn, where they stopped at a small hotel. But if there was any talk of Aberrancies, Emily didn't hear it, for the exertions of the past two days caught up with her all at once. She went directly to bed and slept for twelve hours straight.

Stanton knocked at her door before dawn the next morning, saying he wanted to make up the time they'd lost the day before. And so they found themselves atop the last foothill of the Sierra just after sunrise, overlooking the broad fertile dish of the Sacramento Valley. The sun looming over the towering black mountains behind them cast long shadows of lustrous peach and velvet blue over a seemingly endless checkerboard of green and buff. In the clean fresh light of dawn, everything seemed to glow with supernatural clarity.

"That's one pretty valley." Emily stared in awe at the beauty before her. "I've never been this far down the hills before."

"It is quite pretty this morning," Stanton agreed. Then he pointed to the western horizon, where heavy black clouds massed over the hazy coast range in the far distance. "I believe we'll have rain later, though."

"April showers bring May flowers," Emily said cheerfully, clucking to Romulus.

April showers indeed!
Emily huddled under her buffalo coat, but it did little

good. Rivers of rain were dripping from the edge of her sodden straw hat and pouring down the back of her neck. No matter how she tried to pull the coat tight around her, there was some place that the cold rain lashed at her.

Beneath her, Romulus was just as grumpy, plodding heavily in the sticky mud, head down and ears back. Every now and again he gave a fussy shake, throwing off additional sheets of spray to further soak Emily.

It was midday—though one could hardly tell because the sun had not managed to emerge from behind the clotted black clouds since morning—and they were riding well south of Sacramento, making for Suisun City. From there, Stanton said, it was one day's hard ride to Oakland and the ferry that would take them into San Francisco.

Emily squinted through the driving rain to look at Stanton. From somewhere in his pack he'd produced a bright red oilskin poncho that was wide enough at the hem to cover his horse's shoulders and withers. It made him look like a geometric proof wearing a black felt bowler. Despite the fact that Emily had always hated math, she decided that the minute they got to Suisun City, the Institute was going to buy her one of those red ponchos. And a new hat, too. He'd told her the Institute would pay expenses, and by God, she was going to hold him to it!

They were riding through a glade of ghostly white birches, along a muddy freshet that twisted down toward the Sacramento River. The trail was overgrown and hard to follow, and Emily was about ask Stanton if he was sure they were going the right way (which she didn't relish doing, for she'd asked that particular question a dozen times already and Stanton's replies kept getting curter) when a horrible sound rent the air. It was loud and eldritch—a cluttering shriek that echoed against the trees. Emily had never heard anything like it before.

She jerked the reins, pulling Romulus up short, pushing her hat back to look around. The surrounding forest was gloomy and dripping. She wiped water from her forehead, then slowly urged her horse forward to stand next to Stanton's. Stanton had also drawn his horse to a halt and was listening, stock-still.

"What was that?" she whispered.

But Stanton said nothing; he was staring into the darkest part of the trees, where the undergrowth was thick and tangled. Remus danced nervously beneath him.

It was hard to tell, but Emily thought she saw something move. Something large and dark. She furrowed her brow, squinting, trying to peer through the murk.

Then, suddenly, with a rushing sound of tearing foliage and snapping branches, a huge black and gray thing leaped into their path, landing with a chittering snarl and a flick of its bushy striped tail. The thing was huge—huge as a house, huge as two houses, it seemed to Emily. Its glowing red eyes, embedded deeply in a coal-black mask, were on a level with hers on horse top—that would make the thing ten feet high at least. Its fur was matted and lank, dripping with black oily slime, and it exuded the most horrific smell, like the decaying corpses of a hundred skunks. In an instant she realized what it was . . . or what it had been.

"Raccoon!" Emily screeched, and Romulus plunged and wheeled. Emily dug her heels into the horse's side, urging the beast to run, but then, from behind her, a single barked command—"Romulus, *placidus*!"—made her horse stop dead in its tracks.

"For God's sake, don't run," Stanton shouted. "It'll chase you!"

"Better than being eaten here!"

Underneath her, Romulus was dancing backward, trying to put as much space as it could between itself and the slavering creature. She developed an instant appreciation for the horse's good sense and excellent judgment.

Stanton stood up in his stirrups and raised both hands.

"Contra procyon lotor!" he said, bringing both hands together in a loud thunderclap.

The effect was spectacular. A ball of white magic gathered around Stanton's clasped hands, and with a cry, he hurled it at the raccoon. But the instant he did, an invisible force grabbed the wrist of Emily's right hand, forcing it up. The ball of magic swerved like an iron filing toward a powerful magnet. She felt her hand drawn to the magic, pulling her almost off the horse. Luckily, Romulus planted his feet and she was able to brace herself against her old friend, the pommel. The brilliant white flash broke against her palm, jolting her hard, then a pleasant warmth flooded through her.

Stanton glared at her. She glared back.

"Well, *you're* the one who said not to run!"

The monster made chuckling sounds deep in its throat. It took two steps toward Stanton, lifting its dripping black hand to swat at him. Stanton leaned sideways in his saddle to dodge the blow. Remus had the same idea, except in the opposite direction. Unbalanced, Stanton flailed. The next instant he was on the muddy ground and Remus was bolting off at a flat run. The horse's movement attracted the Aberrancy, and it followed Remus, fat black tongue slobbering greedily. Panicked, the horse floundered up a steep embankment of salal, reins tangling around a dead tree limb. The horse screamed, throwing its head back and trying to tear itself free, but it was no use; the Aberrancy was closing in.

"Hurry!" Emily gestured to Stanton, reaching down to offer him her hand. But though Stanton leapt to his feet quickly, he didn't even look in Emily's direction, much less accept her offer of aid. Instead, he strode toward the monster, throwing his poncho back over his shoulders to free his arms. Reaching inside his coat, he brought out what looked like a cigar case, silver-etched and cylindrical. He held it firmly in one hand, and with a flick of his wrist, unfurled a long slender blade that telescoped out of the silver handle with a hissing *snick-snick-snick*.

Emily fought the urge to put her hands over her eyes.

"Hey! Hey, you raccoon!" Stanton bellowed. The monster pulled back, blinked in Stanton's direction, and cocked its huge head curiously. Distracted from trying to eat the poor thrashing Remus, it sidled over, sniffing at Stanton. Sharp yellow teeth gleamed as it curled back matted-fur lips. It snapped at Stanton. Stanton jumped back, boot heel sliding in the mud.

Then, with an astonishingly quick movement, Stanton brought the blade up and drove it toward one of the monster's burning red eyes.

It was an elegant attack. Which made it even more of a shame when the monster swept Stanton aside like a cat playing with a ball of string. Stanton sprawled into a nearby bramble of blackberries. He did not move for an agonizing moment, but then he stirred, pulling himself up onto his hands and knees. The telescoping blade was still in his hands, but the demon raccoon was shambling toward him quickly, making its terrible chuckling noises, sniffing and licking its greasy chops.

Fire surged in Emily's gut. With a high, full-throated whoop, she slammed her heels into Romulus' side. The horse surged forward. Screaming at the top of her lungs, waving the hand she wasn't using to hold onto the pommel, she rode straight at the demon raccoon. Instinctively, the monster lumbered back with a squeal and a hiss.

In the confusion, Emily didn't see Stanton get up, but a moment later he was by Remus, using his blade to slash the reins free. He swung himself up into the saddle and wheeled his horse alongside Emily's. His face was pale under the thick globs of mud and dirt, and there were ugly welting scratches across his throat from where the brambles had torn into his flesh.

"I guess you were right about the running," Stanton breathed, reaching over to give Romulus a smart slap on the haunches. "Romulus, Remus . . . *race!*"

The horses sprang like bullets from a gun. But Emily could feel the enraged beast behind them, the irregular *thump-thump, thump-thump* of its huge strides, the crashing sound of tearing undergrowth.

"We'll never make it," she said under her breath. She glanced to her left, where Stanton rode almost at her side; his hands, desperately clutching the horse's mane, were white with tension.

And then there was the sound of screaming. Not their own screaming, as Emily had supposed she'd hear next, but echoing whoops and ringing staccato cries.

The sound of dozens of rifle shots rang through the air.

All at once, Emily could feel the monster falling away. There was a grunting roar from the beast, then a series of little chitters, and then silence.

Emily would have been more than happy to keep running without looking back, but Stanton pulled up and vanished from her side. She kept riding for a moment, but Romulus didn't want to leave Remus behind, so he slowed to a balky trot, tossing his head backward.

Grudgingly, Emily let the horse turn.

The monster lay on its back, dead, black claws curled against its chest. There were Indians all around, some in fringed buckskin trousers, some in flannels and denim. All held rifles. And Stanton was trotting toward them, one hand raised.

Out of the frying pan, into the fire! Emily thought furiously. *Avoid getting eaten just to get yourself scalped?*

But the Indians were utterly nonplussed by Stanton's arrival. Stanton rode into their midst and slid down from the saddle, laying a hand on his horse's lathered neck. He stood with the men, exchanging a few words, looking over the enormous dead raccoon.

She rode forward slowly until she was in earshot of Stanton.

"You know these . . . men?" she called from a safe distance.

Stanton looked up at her, as placidly as if he and the Indians were just looking over a curiously formed tree root.

"They were just trying to understand why, while I was trying to save one horse, you were doing your best to kill the other."

"I was trying to keep the beast from sinking its huge teeth into your pompous backside!" Emily snapped. "It works with bears. Usually."

"An Aberrancy is not a bear," Stanton said. "But, shrill and foolhardy as it was, you certainly did provide a distraction. Thank you."

"That's the first time you've ever thanked me for anything," Emily said. Her heart was still pounding, and it made her feel awfully cross. "And if you only thank me when I save your life, I guess it'll be the last."

"These men are of the Miwok tribe," Stanton said, ignoring the barb and gesturing to the umber-hued men who gaped at her, open mouthed.

"What are they staring at?" Emily growled, gathering her buffalo coat around herself tightly. "I'm sure they've seen a white woman before."

"Not with black eyeballs, they haven't," Stanton said.

"My eyes?"

"I'm beginning to think that the color shift must be the result of an altered energy state within the stone, or perhaps an alteration of the stone's interaction with your physical person—"

"Spare me," Emily hissed. Her pique amused the Indian men vastly. One of them clapped Stanton on the shoulder and said something Emily doubted was entirely polite.

"So they're friendly, at least?"

"If they weren't, we'd be in the belly of that ugly beast right now," Stanton said. "I've had dealings with this tribe before. Native magics are an expanding field of inquiry in my profession. I was a guest of their *Maien*—their Holy Woman—last spring, before my arrival in Lost Pine."

"They let you *study* them?"

"It's a simple matter of professional courtesy."

"Professional courtesy?" Emily lowered her voice to a whisper. *"They're savages!"*

"Savages who just saved your life, and who have invited us back to their camp for rest and food." Stanton frowned at her. "But if you'd rather sleep on the ground and hope that there aren't other Aberrancies roaming the area . . ."

"No, no." Emily stared at the massive corpse of the demon raccoon around which the Indians were circling, long knives drawn. "That's quite all right."

CHAPTER SIX

Lawa

Most of the Indians remained behind to skin the massive raccoon, but one—a man with a licorice-colored braid that snaked from under a black felt hat—took them back to the Miwok camp. He and Stanton chatted as they walked ahead together along the overgrown path; Emily hung well back, brushing dripping foliage away from her face.

She followed them to a wide clearing on the shores of the slow Sacramento River. It was ringed with oaks and shaggy cottonwoods, and within it stood several round dugouts, domed with willow and tree bark. Campfire smoke drifted against the gray afternoon sky. Children chased one another, making high hooting sounds; dogs nipped at their heels. Women chatted over stone mortars, clay pipes clamped between black-stained teeth.

When they stopped, Emily slid down from her saddle. The man in the black felt hat took both horses' reins; without a word, he led the animals away.

"Hope you see your horses again," Emily muttered, watching as a group of young boys clustered around the animals, laying light brown hands on their warm glossy sides.

"Spoken with all the broad-mindedness and generosity of spirit I've come to expect from you, Miss Edwards," Stanton said. "He's taking them to food and water. Come along . . . Komé will be waiting."

"Komé?"

"Komé is the tribe's Maien, of whom I spoke earlier. She's

a very powerful practitioner. I want to get her opinion on the stone in your hand."

"So you meant to ride down here all the time?" Emily said. "You could have told me."

"And listen to you complain about it all the way from Dutch Flat?" Stanton looked at her sidelong.

They stopped before a long low house, much larger than the other dugouts. They stood outside and waited for what seemed quite a long time. Long enough for the rain to pick up again. Emily pulled her hat down and peered at Stanton from under the brim.

"Well? Shouldn't you knock or something?"

"She knows we're here," Stanton said.

And indeed, a few moments later, an old woman came out of the longhouse, ducking underneath the low door. She leaned heavily on a feather-tipped staff. She was followed by a large dog, wrapped in a brightly colored blanket . . . but no, Emily thought, it was not a dog. It was a girl who couldn't be more than fourteen, whose back was bent so drastically that she could not stand, only creep along in a painful shuffle. She kept her balance with one hand on the ground, her long black braids dragging in the dirt as she hitched herself along. When she looked up at Stanton and Emily, her eyes narrowed suspiciously. Emily knew it was rude to stare, but she could not take her eyes off the girl, who came to rest by the old woman's feet.

"Hiti weychin, Komé," Stanton said, raising a hand.

The Holy Woman was cheerful and chubby, with bright white teeth. Her skin was a rich russet, and black tattoos ran from the bottom of her lower lip over her chin and down her throat, disappearing into the collar of her soft doeskin tunic. Her ears were pierced with thick cylinders of blackened, polished bone, and beads glittered from where they had been woven into her salt-and-pepper hair. Even the cut-glass beads, however, could not match the sparkle of her eyes as she looked at Stanton and Emily. She smiled broadly, as if they'd both done something vastly amusing.

"Komé, Miss Emily Edwards. Miss Edwards, Komé." The

introduction was spoken so formally, Emily wasn't sure whether to curtsy or bow or shake hands, so she did a bit of each and ended up looking silly. Stanton began speaking haltingly in Miwok. It was clear he was no expert in the language, but the woman bobbed her head indulgently, as if listening to a favorite grandchild.

"Show her your hand," Stanton said.

Emily pulled off her glove. Then she stretched her arm to extend her hand, not wanting to step any closer to the girl at Komé's feet, having gotten the distinct feeling that she might get bitten. The stone winked dully in the heavy gray light of late afternoon. The old woman glanced at it, but it didn't appear to interest her. Emily's face, on the other hand, she seemed to find fascinating. She searched it, muttering as she pinched Emily's cheek. She then held Emily at arm's length and looked her up and down, appraisingly. She squinted at Emily's ankles, her waist, her hair. All the while, she talked under her breath in a creaking monotone.

"Sizing me up for the cook pot, no doubt," Emily muttered.

Indeed, even Stanton seemed frustrated with Komé's unwillingness to get to the point. He shook his head and said something that cut her mutterings short. The Maien looked at him, shocked, then gave a big boisterous laugh. She hit Stanton fondly, punching him in the arm with her little gnarled fist.

"What is she saying?" Emily whispered furiously. Stanton paid no attention to her, but rubbed his arm as he spoke to the old woman again, separating each word carefully. With a smile, the woman took Emily's hand again and looked at the stone more carefully. The twisted girl shuffled closer, too, reaching up to put both her hands on Emily's arm. Her eyes were turbulent pools. There was a question in those eyes, a question that Emily wished she knew how to answer. A question she wished she understood.

The strange moment was broken when the Maien threw up her hands and waved Emily and Stanton away, peppering them with a rapid verbal staccato. She turned back toward her longhouse, and the girl shuffled after her without a backward glance.

"She's got no more time for us tonight," he said to Emily, taking her elbow. "She and Lawa have to get ready."

"Lawa? That bent girl?"

"Her daughter," Stanton said.

"She gave me the shivers." Emily looked up at Stanton. "So what was all that about? She went on and on."

"When speaking to Komé, threshing the grain from the chaff can be a taxing pursuit."

"What did she say?"

"She congratulated me," Stanton said. Emily knit her brow at him.

"Congratulated you? For what? You haven't done anything."

"The congratulations were part of the chaff," he said. "The grain, on the other hand, was her insistence that the stone is watching us."

"Watching us?"

"Watching over us. Protecting us."

"That's the most ridiculous thing I've ever heard," Emily snorted. "If the stone was watching over us, it certainly wouldn't have sucked up all that magic you tried to throw at the raccoon. Indeed, given the evidence, it seems more likely that the stone would like nothing better than to see us in our graves."

"She said that the stone was trying desperately to speak to us. *But it cannot,* she said, *for it does not have the tongue to speak and you do not have the ears to hear.*"

Emily looked at him.

"It's a mineral, Mr. Stanton."

"As I said, she can be somewhat abstract in her expression. The point is that she speaks of the stone as if it were . . . alive."

"Min-er-al." Emily emphasized each syllable.

"A few magical theorists have pursued the question of whether the Mantic Anastomosis possesses a kind of nonhuman consciousness." Stanton rubbed his chin thoughtfully. "They've all been dismissed as crackpots. But that's understandable, because to believe that it does implies that we might have some sort of responsibility to it. And no one likes responsibility."

"Leaving magical theory aside . . ." Emily stroked the stone with her thumb. "What if it does have some kind of consciousness? What would that mean to us?"

"I can't answer that," Stanton said. "But it would be interesting to know what it was trying to tell us, wouldn't it?" Then, sniffing the air, on which a succulent and meaty odor wafted delicately, his eyes closed with pleasant anticipation.

"Finally," he said. "Dinner is served."

Faced with the dinner offered by the Indians, Emily would much rather have eaten soggy bread and cheese from the horses' saddlebags. But, for the sake of politeness, Stanton insisted that she at least sample the Indians' feast.

"What's this?" she asked, pointing to a pile of mush that had been presented to her on a broad, flat oak leaf.

"*Maskala*. Acorn bread." Stanton was shoveling his down like a sailor who hadn't seen port in a week. "Acorns are a staple of their diet."

Emily tasted it gingerly; it was bland and slightly bitter, like cornmeal soaked in water and seasoned with black tea. Emily forced down a couple of bites and deemed politeness more than served. Stanton, however, helped himself to seconds. The Indians seemed to find feeding him a challenging entertainment. The women brought dish after dish and he worked valiantly to keep up the pace. Finally, they brought a great wooden platter of steaming meat. Emily took a whiff, recognizing it immediately.

"Raccoon!" She looked at Stanton suspiciously. "Don't tell me—"

"Waste not, want not," Stanton said taking a piece of meat with his fingers.

"Is it safe to eat?"

Stanton took a big bite.

"The Indians have been feasting on Aberrancies for years," he said, licking a thumb. "They call them 'tragic gifts of the earth.' "

Emily took a piece of tragic gift meat and tasted it. It was aggressively gamey—a flavor that reminded her unpleasantly of the hard winter just passed. She wondered what Pap was doing. What was he eating? *Was* he eating? Mrs. Lyman would see to it that he got his meals, wouldn't she? The old busybody wouldn't abandon Pap just because everyone in town thought that his foster daughter had run off with a traveling Warlock . . . would she?

Emily's worried thoughts were interrupted by a general mumbling from the people around them. Komé came into the middle of the circle. She was followed by Lawa—limping, shuffling, and bent. In her hands, the girl clutched her mother's staff.

Komé was magnificently arrayed in a skirt of iridescent magpie feathers and a hat of flicker plumes. She wore a tunic and leggings of white deerskin, fringed and beaded. Taking the staff from the bent girl, Komé began to chant, a sibilant song that resonated with gravity and meaning. All around her, the feasters stilled in respectful silence.

Stanton used a handkerchief to wipe his hands, then leaned close to murmur in Emily's ear:

"You might find this interesting. Komé will lead a spirit dance tonight to pray for the soul of the dead raccoon. It's a fascinating magical ceremony, with roots in the most ancient traditions on the North American continent."

"Then I'd better get as far away from it as possible." Emily thought of how Stanton's magic had been sucked into the rock in her hand. She certainly didn't want to do anything that would interfere with the satisfactory disposition of the spirit of the evil raccoon. Besides that, thinking of Pap had left her feeling somewhat low-spirited and weary. "I think I'll just go to sleep."

One of the women showed Emily to a hut that was used for storing food. It was dry and tidy, full of finely woven baskets brimming with acorns and dried meats. Herbs hung from the ceiling, and Emily looked them over with a professional eye. Balsam and purple milkweed, black nightshade and mountain misery, rattlesnake weed and monkey-root—even desert lavender. She crumbled some in her hand, sprinkled it all around herself, wishing she could empower it with a rhyme of general protection. But since she couldn't, she satisfied herself with the relaxing odor.

On the floor had been laid a massive pelt, large as the fancy carpet in Mrs. Bargett's reception parlor. Emily felt the fur between her fingers. Beaver, the largest beaver one could imagine. Another "tragic gift," no doubt. She wondered how one went about cleaning black slime off a pelt that size.

Wearily, Emily curled up under her soggy buffalo coat, the smell of which did battle with the lavender and won handily. She did not sleep. The Maien's slow rhythmic chanting made the darkness vibrate. It made Emily's nerves jangle and her muscles tense, and even when it started to rain again, the soft pitter-pats on the leaves overhead did nothing to soothe her. After what seemed an eternity of frozen wakefulness, there was a noise at the door. She felt for the heavy rock she'd hidden beside her. She lifted it, ready to brain any redskin who came looking for trouble, but it was just Stanton. He came in, shaking water off his coat.

"I'm sorry, Miss Edwards, but we'll have to share. It's a foul night, and I have no intention of sleeping outside after the day I've had."

"Suit yourself." Emily made her voice diffident, certainly not wanting to reveal her relief that Stanton would be nearby. "I can't sleep anyway."

"Then you won't mind a little light?" Stanton took a small spirit lantern from his saddlebag. She heard him snap his fingers and mutter, *"Flamma."*

The wick of the spirit lantern burst into brilliant flame. He shook his head, his eyes narrowing with thought.

"You were yards away from me today, and the stone sucked up the magic like a sponge. But here you are not two feet from me, and I can summon flames."

"Something forced my hand up to catch the magic. I couldn't have stopped it if I'd tried."

"I have a theory as to why," Stanton said.

"Of course you do." Emily sat up and wrapped her arms around her knees.

"Remember I said there was a distance correlation? That is, the farther away you are from the source of the magic, the less likely the stone is to grab onto it? I believe there's also a force correlation. The greater the force of the magic, the more the stone seeks to absorb it."

"So, the more powerful the spell, the more likely the stone is to suck it up?" Emily said.

"Evidence seems to support it," Stanton said. As he spoke, he took out the telescoping blade he had used earlier in the day. The segmented blade, when fully extended, was about three feet long and brilliantly shiny. Using his handkerchief, Stanton began cleaning it.

"Nice little knife," she said. "Carry it around to peel apples, do you?"

"It's called a misprision blade," Stanton said, squinting along its edge. "Useful for many things. But you can't let them get dirty. They might fail to open at an inopportune time."

There was a pause in the chanting outside. Emily relished the sweet sound of rain echoing in silence. But within moments the chanting resumed, now to the accompaniment of drums.

"They're *still* dancing?" Emily said, sounding more snappish than she would have liked. "In the rain?"

"They've moved into the earth lodge." Stanton wiped a speck from the bright metal. "You really are afraid of these people, aren't you?"

"Why shouldn't I be?" Emily said.

"I would think you might have some sympathy for them. Driven from place to place to make room for wheat and sheep. Doesn't that strike you as a bit unfair?"

"Well, what use are they making of the land?" Emily said. "They don't farm, or ranch."

"Sometimes I wonder if everything must always have a use," Stanton said.

"Well, as far as I can see, Indians don't."

"Is that your considered opinion, Miss Edwards?" Stanton's tone was chilly. "I suppose you agree with President Grant, that the Indians should be relocated and reeducated? Dressed in suits and made to be useful?" He gave the blade a fierce swipe with the cloth. "Or perhaps your opinions run closer to those of Little Phil Sheridan, who only likes Indians when they're dead?"

"Spoken like a sanctimonious easterner," she hissed. "I'm perfectly aware that you think everyone on this side of the Great Divide is ignorant and unfair and reckless to boot. But your 'friends' have shown themselves perfectly capable of giving as bad as they get. I'm sure you've never seen that side of them, Mr. Stanton."

"And you have?" Stanton's voice was derisive.

"Yes," Emily spat fiercely, "I have."

Then she was silent for a long moment, confused by her own sudden vehemence.

Why on earth had she said that?

Surprising as an easterner like Stanton would probably find it, Emily hadn't seen many Indians in her life in Lost Pine. And the handful she had encountered, she'd given a wide berth to. She'd certainly never been harmed or even threatened by an Indian. And yet . . . there was something in the back of her mind, calling insistently to her, demanding to be remembered.

It was like watching a strange glimmer of light move in a well of complete blackness. She was silent, watching the distant brilliance as it grew and expanded into a memory—a memory she'd never had before.

"Miss Edwards?" Stanton's voice prompted, but she hardly heard it. She was staring at the rough dirt floor, but she wasn't looking at it. She was looking through it at the memories welling up behind her eyes . . .

A late summer night.

The plains, brooding dark beyond borders of moonlight. Sleeping next to her mother's warm body under a heavy wool coat. The sound of calls—Indian calls, urgent and terrifying. The clop of unshod hooves on hard-packed clay soil. Her mother scrambling to her feet, screaming. Running.

"My mother," Emily said in a monotone, narrating the strange images as they bloomed within her brain. "I was with my mother. We were traveling across the country. I was very young, and they chased us. Braves in paint. They were yelling at her, calling her names. They were angry at her."

Emily held onto the memory, clung to it tightly. She looked at her mother's face, trying to fix an image of it, but for some reason, all she could see were her mother's eyes, glowing and glossy with fear.

"She was terrified," Emily whispered. "We got away from them, but I don't know how. They had horses. They could have caught us and killed us if they wanted to. Maybe they just wanted us to go away." She paused, the sting of remembered tears making her eyes ache. "They didn't have any call to scare her like that."

Stanton collapsed the misprision blade. The soft click of it broke Emily's concentration. The images scattered like blown leaves.

"I'm sorry about your mother," Stanton said. He tucked the knife away, and was silent for a moment before speaking again. "But why in heaven's name was she traveling across the country with a child, alone?"

Emily shrugged, shaking her head.

"I don't know," she said. She had only the mysterious words her mother had spoken to the timber-camp workers . . .

She wrinkled her brow, looked at Stanton.

"Have *you* ever heard of something called the Cynic Mirror?"

"The Cynic Mirror?"

"They were the last words my mother ever spoke. She said, 'We must get to the Cynic Mirror.' "

"I've never heard of an item by that name," Stanton said. "But there are many arcane objects for which no records are kept."

"Oh," Emily said, her brows knit.

"If you'd like, once our business in San Francisco is completed, I could take you around to the public Hall of Records. Perhaps you might be able to find out more about the name Lyakhov, or this 'Cynic Mirror' you're looking for."

Emily looked at him, unexpected hope rising in her chest.

"You think I might be able to find something?"

"The city maintains excellent records," he said. "I've been meaning to stop there anyway. They recently installed a clever new information storage system that uses tiny interdimensional windows to store records safely off-site. Very useful for a city that manages to go up in flames every ten years or so. At least it would be worth a look."

"Yes." Emily sat up straight. "That sounds like a wonderful idea. Thank you, Mr. Stanton."

"Least I can do," he said as he wrapped himself in his blanket. Then he blew out the spirit lamp, and darkness enfolded them—a darkness heavy with the sounds of chanting and rain.

The next morning the clouds had parted and brilliant sunshine illuminated a perfect blue sky. The horses were brought, saddled and frisky. Despite Emily's suspicions of the day before, the animals were in good working order; the man in the black felt hat had even repaired Stanton's slashed reins with clever knots.

Before riding out, they went to pay parting respects to Komé. And indeed, when they came to the longhouse, Komé was standing before it to watch them go. But this was a Komé terribly changed. Gone was the cheerful, vibrant, animated Maien; this old, old woman swayed unsteadily, even though she was clutching her feather-tipped staff with one hand and leaning on Lawa with the other. Her skin was a haggard yellow-pale, the tattoos dark and drastic. There were harsh purple smudges beneath her eyes.

"She must have overexerted herself last night," Stanton said, his voice low. Emily wondered if the tormented spirit of the raccoon had been worth it.

Stanton lifted a salutational hand as they rode past, and it was clear that he expected that formal gesture to serve as a farewell. He looked somewhat surprised, therefore, when Komé called out to him, a guttural croak, and began hobbling toward them with a jerk and a stagger, as if her feet could not find the ground. Stanton pulled his horse up quickly, as if he was afraid the large animal might trample the small, suddenly fragile-seeming old woman.

The Maien came to Emily's side, looked up at her for a long time. Emily stared down at her. Her eyes, once glittering as topaz, now seemed dull and distant. Dull and distant and *empty*.

Strange images played through Emily's mind. Hollow bowls, husks, blown eggshells . . .

Emily shook her head as the Maien took her right hand, the

hand with the stone in it. The old woman held Emily's hand tight and, pressing her forehead against the stone, closed her eyes.

"Tenkiju, ososolyeh," she rasped.

Then, opening her eyes, the Maien pressed something small and hard into Emily's hand. She closed Emily's fingers around it. Then she looked around herself, her gaze encompassing the trees, the rising smoke, the growing brightness of morning. She breathed a deep breath in through her nose, seeming to relish it as if it were her last. She smiled. Looking up at Stanton, she reached over and swatted him on the knee fondly. Stanton reached down and clasped the Maien's hand.

"Josum, Komé," he said.

"Josum?" The Maien's face crumpled in a strange smile, and she released a soft laugh, weak and kittenish. *"Mi, jose!"* Then she turned and staggered back to her hut, casting no shadow, her feet making no sound.

Lawa, Emily noticed, did not follow her. Instead, the girl stared after them, her eyes hard and unshifting.

"What did you say to her that was so all-fired amusing?" Emily asked, once they were well away from the camp.

"I just said good-bye," he said. *"Josum* means good-bye, and she said, 'Oh, yes! Go!' I can't say I get the joke either."

"She gave me an acorn." Emily held up the small hard nut that Komé had pressed into her hand. "She called it *tenkiju* . . . is that the word for acorn?"

"No," Stanton said. "Acorn is *muyu.*"

"Then what does *tenkiju* mean?"

"Well, that's an interesting question. You see, the Miwok have no word in their language for 'thank you.' I suppose it's because they believe that thanking someone implies that there is a need for thanks, which implies—"

"Oh, skip it!" Emily sighed, exasperated. "You know, you may get tired of explaining things to me, but not half so tired as I get listening."

"Tenkiju. Sound it out. It's a phonetic approximation of the English words 'thank you.'"

"What was she thanking me for?"

"I don't think she was thanking *you*. I think she was thanking the stone. She said *tenkiju ososolyeh*. She was thanking the evening star."

Emily looked at him.

"The evening star?"

"*Ososolyeh* translates as evening star. She called the stone that before, in fact, when she first saw it."

"In the journal you showed me, it said that the Indians who found the specimen that's in the British Museum also thought it was a piece of the evening star!"

"Exactly so," Stanton said.

"Acorns and evening stars," Emily said contemplatively, holding up the nut. Then, with a dismissive gesture, she threw the acorn over her shoulder. Stanton gave a cry and pulled Remus up short. Jumping down from the horse, he felt around in the leaf mold until he found the acorn. He wiped mud from it and tucked it back into Emily's hand.

"*Never* throw away something a holy woman gives you."

Emily looked at him.

"I'm supposed to carry a nut around, just because some old Indian Witch handed it to me?"

"Humor me, Miss Edwards."

Emily sighed. Pulling the silk pouch out from under her collar, she tucked the nut inside, then returned the pouch to its habitual hiding place.

CHAPTER SEVEN

San Francisco

It was a hard day's ride to Oakland, where they would board the ferry for San Francisco, but the bright spring sunshine warmed their backs and heartened the horses. They cantered along one of the broad wagon-roads that connected the Sacramento Valley with the prosperous markets along the Pacific Coast. All along the way, farmers were plowing the fields with their heavy teams. The sound of birdsong and the vivid smell of loamy black earth was everywhere, and Emily felt the return of her normal good spirits.

It wasn't just the beautiful weather that cheered her. She had gained a memory of her mother. She didn't know why, or how . . . but it was a memory, and it was new, and it was precious. She kept going back to it, dark and murky as it was, trying to tease out additional details. She couldn't remember her mother's face, but she could remember the shape of her nose in the shadows, the smooth parting of her hair. It was a memory, the first she'd ever had. It buoyed her and made her feel bright as new-shined brass.

The sight of Oakland sprawling on the horizon gave Emily's spirits an additional boost. Oakland was by no means lovely, but it meant they were almost to San Francisco.

As they came into the town proper, the main road narrowed to a crowded swath of hard-packed dirt flanked by thriving industry: livestock pens and machinery works and woodlots. Romulus and Remus shied at rumbling drayage carts and the shouts of the heavy men who drove them. The road ended at the waterfront, where dozens of wooden warehouses crowded onto San Francisco Bay, cantilevered over the water on spindly stilts.

It was late in the day, but they found they could still make the last ferry. As Stanton purchased tickets, Emily stood on the wharf, holding the horses and looking out over the bay. It was the largest expanse of water she'd ever seen. Flat and gray, it reflected the shifting color of the sky. There were clouds moving swiftly in from the ocean, fat white clouds that promised rain farther inland. Through the clouds, shafts of sunlight cut down and made places on the water shine with a silver dollar's brilliance.

"Come along, ferry's this way." Stanton came up behind her, tickets in hand. He took the reins and clucked to the horses to follow; their hooves were a hollow drumbeat on the wooden pier.

The ferry's interior was lush, with heavily varnished woodwork and shiny brass fittings. They passed the area at the back of the boat where the Chinese rode; Emily glimpsed blue coats and braided queues. In the boat's main passenger area there were only white faces—farmers holding battered hats in their rough, dirt-stained hands; miners chewing tobacco, arms crossed; flashily dressed men and women in fabulous colors, laughing too loudly.

Stanton led her right through the parlor room into another room, one filled with tables.

"Hungry?" he asked. She shook her head. "It is suppertime; you've eaten hardly anything since we left Auburn. You have to keep your strength up, you know."

She shook her head again. She'd never thought of it before, but the very idea of food was absurd. How ridiculous eating was. For some reason, it seemed she remembered another way, an older and more satisfying way, pulling sustenance from a hot hidden core within herself, through veins that pulsed with fire . . .

She toyed idly with these strange thoughts as she watched Stanton place an order with a passing waiter. Again, he paid from the black silk purse.

"How does that work?" Emily asked, cradling her chin in

her palm, glad for the distraction. "It's always got money in it, but I never see you put any in."

"It's a Warlock's Purse." Stanton showed it to her but didn't let her touch it. It was indeed empty.

"It's a service offered by some of the larger banks in the East." Stanton tucked it back into his pocket. "It's directly connected to my account in New York. I am able to withdraw the money I need, yet there is never any loose gold in it to tempt pickpockets. If a thief were to get ahold of it, he would not be able to access any of my funds."

The waiter delivered Stanton's order—two large roast beef sandwiches, a piece of thickly frosted chocolate cake, a cup of hot coffee, and a glass of cold milk. Stanton pushed the milk to Emily.

"Here," he said. "Milk is very restorative."

"I didn't know I needed restoring," Emily said, taking the glass.

Stanton reached for the cake; as he did so, his sleeve brushed the fork off the plate and it clattered to the floor. Out of habit, Emily muttered, "A man will come to visit."

"What?"

"If a fork do fall, a man will call."

Stanton smiled to himself as he reached down to retrieve the fork.

"Well, that's what it means!" she said hotly.

"Yes, I'm familiar with the superstition." Stanton wiped the fork with his napkin. "Rhyming house-magic is just so quaint, that's all."

"What do you have against rhymes, anyway?" Emily leaned forward. She very much did not like being called quaint.

"Not a thing," Stanton said, sinking his fork into the cake.

"I'm sure you prefer Latin, so you can sound educated and sophisticated."

"There happen to be several very good reasons for casting spells in Latin," Stanton said.

"Why? I suppose it's some fabulously powerful language?"

"Ask a man on the street what a spell is supposed to sound like, and he will either make up a rhyme or babble some imaginary version of Latin at you." He raised a finger. "But ask that man which spell he believes to be more powerful, and he will choose the spell in Latin. The stereotype has become ingrained in the Western consciousness over many hundreds of years. Thanks largely to the Roman Catholic Church, ironically enough . . ."

"Who cares what some man on the street thinks? It's the spell part that's important."

"Ah, that's where you're wrong. The magic isn't in the *words*." Stanton paused for a bite of cake, letting this provocative statement hang while he licked frosting from the silver. "The magic is in the effect the words have upon the listener—or, indeed, upon the speaker himself. At its root, magic relies on human cooperation and expectation, both conscious and unconscious. It has its basis in what humans believe. That is the fundamental precept of credomancy."

"Credomancy?"

"The magic of faith, the tradition of magic I have chosen to specialize in. Credomancy draws its power from the human perception of reality. For example, you know that it takes a silver bullet to stop a werewolf, right?"

"That's what they say," Emily said. "I've never tested it."

"Well, if you ever come up against a werewolf, I hope you have a silver bullet handy."

"So a silver bullet will kill a werewolf not because it's magic, but because everyone *believes* that it's magic?"

"Precisely."

Emily leaned her elbows on the table, looking sideways out the open window. The ferry had gotten under way, and they were gliding across the bay. The keen smell of brine and churning water was surprisingly pleasant.

"But which came first?" Emily said. "The belief or the power? I mean, wasn't there a time before people knew about werewolves and silver bullets? What would have killed a werewolf then?"

"An excellent question," he said. "No one really knows. The prevailing wisdom is that belief and power evolve together."

Emily pondered this for a moment.

"What if everyone stopped believing?"

"Then credomancers like myself would have no more power," Stanton said. "Indeed, it is one of the weaknesses of the credomantic practitioner. People can stop believing, or forget their beliefs. That is why we credomancers have to continually popularize the beliefs upon which our power is based."

"Popularize? How?"

"Well, you've seen those subscription novels, haven't you? The ones printed on horrible pulp paper, with titles like *Secrets of a Warlock* or *The Mystical Jebez*?"

Emily nodded, thinking of Mrs. Lyman and her fondness for such thrilling accounts of derring-do.

"Mystic Truth Publishers in New York puts those out. Mystic Truth is owned by the Credomantic Foundation, which was started by a man named Benedictus Zeno over a hundred and fifty years ago." Stanton paused for a sip of coffee. "The books are designed to have the broadest possible appeal. The more people read those books, the more they believe. The more they believe, the more power we credomancers have."

Emily snapped her fingers. "Then *that's* why everyone was buying Baugh's!"

"Baugh's? You mean those patent charms sold by mail? The ones with the garish boxes?"

"Everyone in Lost Pine believed they were more modern, more up-to-date, more effective. And if people believed they were more effective . . ."

". . . then they were," Stanton finished for her.

Emily sat back in her seat, crossed her arms over her chest.

"Well, thanks for nothing," she said. "That kind of magic, all flash and gold leaf and tissue paper . . . it's putting Pap and me out of business."

"For heaven's sake, don't dismiss your training that quickly," Stanton said. "There are three grand magical traditions—animancy, sangrimancy, and credomancy. Spirit magic, blood magic, and faith magic. There are hundreds of kinds of magical practice, each of which blend elements from these traditions in various proportions. You've been mostly trained in animancy."

"Animancy." Emily experimented with the word.

"It's the practice of working with the life essences that

animate living things. In herbalism, for example, you take the unique life essences of individual plants and use them to perform works. I'm sure you did similar magic with animal bones and wood and such."

"So that means I'm an animancer, and I never even knew it." Emily shook her head. "My word, such fine airs I could have given myself!"

"Which shows why you should have paid more attention to me in Lost Pine, instead of always chasing me off." The words were spoken with an insufferable tone of conclusion.

"It's all right," she purred. "Lost Pine suffered no lack of fine airs regardless."

Stanton swapped the empty cake plate with the full sandwich plate, directing his attention to a stray morsel of roast beef.

"Komé is an animancer, too." He speared the meat with his fork. "But not all animancers are Indian holy women or backwoods Witches. It might interest you to know that in the Slavic regions, Russia especially, animancy is an old and refined art, and animantic practitioners are extremely powerful."

Emily narrowed her eyes. The name Lyakhov popped into her head. A Russian name.

"Fascinating," she said.

It was nearly ten when they arrived in San Francisco, but Emily was so excited she didn't feel tired at all. After retrieving the horses, they rode out from the wharves and into the largest aggregation of buildings Emily had ever seen. Structures towered above her—behemoths of brick and stone and wood, rising story upon story into the dark night sky. Gas streetlights cast a warm tawny glow over everything. Even at that late hour, the streets were alive with activity: hansom cabs and brewery carts, groups of men walking fast and talking loud. Romulus' and Remus' hooves clattered smartly against the street's smoothly rounded cobblestones.

They rode to a hotel on Kearny Street. It was an extremely splendid hotel and made the other hotels they'd stayed in seem unforgivably shabby. Where other hotels had flashy red-lettered placards pushing their names, this hotel had only a small, refined sign of etched brass: *Excelsior*.

The lobby was huge, high ceilinged, with marble columns around which palms in celadon pots were decoratively arranged. Acres of extravagantly flowered carpeting stretched from wall to mahogany-paneled wall. The richly colored expanse was dotted with velvet-covered circular couches and plush overstuffed banquettes, islands in a baroque sea. The coved ceiling was encrusted with gilt plaster. Gaslight blazed from cut-crystal chandeliers.

Emily was suddenly acutely aware of how ridiculous she looked. Pap's old denim pants peeked from beneath the hem of her skirt, her buffalo coat was matted and ripe from the soaking it had received two days before, and her white kid gloves had come to resemble the skin of a month-old corpse. Blushing, she thrust her hands deep into her pockets, trying to ignore the people in the lobby who were doing their best to stare without staring.

She hung back while Stanton arranged for rooms. After making sure Emily had a bellman to see her up, Stanton went to arrange the stabling of the horses.

"Doesn't the hotel have stables?" Emily asked him.

"It certainly does," Stanton said, tipping his hat to her. And then he was gone.

Throwing her saddlebags over her shoulder, Emily prepared to follow the neatly dressed bellman up to her room. But the fellow just stood there, looking uncomfortable. He had to clear his throat twice before she figured it out. She let the bags slide to the floor, and the bellman seized them happily.

Of course, she scolded herself, as she followed him up. *That's what they're for. Toting bags and carrying notes and busting in on guilty lovers and such.* Emily cast her mind back over all the stories from *Ladies' Repository* in which bellmen had played a part.

The room was nice enough, with a lovely view of the bay, but it was the lavatory that fascinated Emily—right in the room itself! Emily had rarely seen water on tap, much less *hot* water. Fragrant soaps wrapped like little gifts sat on a side table and huge white towels were folded neatly on a nickel-plated rack above the steam register.

After some fiddling, she managed to run herself a hot bath. Sliding into the claw-footed tub, she unbraided her long hair and let it float around her. The hot water, the warmth of the steam registers, and the lilac scent of the soap all conspired to make her feel extremely sleepy.

She held up her right hand, lazily watching the light from the flickering gas jet shine through the stone. Strangely, the color of the stone seemed to have changed. She remembered it being as clear as a piece of blue glass, but now it seemed milkier, yellower, and it was flecked with little dark inclusions. She remembered Komé's words . . . *the stone is trying to speak to you, but you do not have the ears to hear, and it does not have the tongue to speak.*

She stared at the stone hard, trying to feel the message it contained, trying to feel if there was really a message at all. Finally she gave up, plunging her hand into the soapy water.

After her bath she could have folded herself into the crisp white bed immediately, but she couldn't let a whole tub of good hot water go to waste. She washed her chemise, petticoat, and stockings, hanging the items to dry over the steam register. When she was finished, she turned down the gas and slid between the smooth sheets, stark naked save for the silk pouch she always wore. She pulled the covers up around her chin, remembering what Stanton said about San Francisco burning down every ten years. She sincerely hoped the city wasn't due for another big conflagration; being cast naked into the street would be almost as embarrassing as walking through the lobby of the Excelsior in a buffalo coat.

At nine the next morning, Emily waited for Stanton in the palm-fronded lobby. Wearing her best poplin dress—which Mrs. Lyman had sewed for a trip Emily and Pap had taken to the Nevada State Fair a couple of years back, and which had sustained the rigors of travel admirably in the bottom of Emily's canvas bag—she felt able to hold her chin up to all the finery that surrounded her. The dress had a tight bodice that buttoned up the front with jet-black buttons, close-fitting sleeves that terminated in little pleats of black satin at the wrists, and a narrowish, simple skirt. Flounces draped across the rump were Lost Pine's nod to the bustle, which, according to *Ladies' Repository,* "Dame fashion decreed as de rigueur for the well-turned-out miss."

When she finally saw Stanton walking toward her, she noticed that he, too, had shed his coating of trail dust. He was freshly barbered, and his suit had been neatly brushed and pressed. The black eye that Dag had given him back in Lost Pine had already faded to a pale streak of yellow that stretched across the top of his right cheekbone. He looked astonishingly stiff and sturdy, as if he were cut from pasteboard.

"You look like a banker who never says yes to a loan," she said.

"And you look like a schoolmarm who never says yes to anything," Stanton replied, offering her his arm. "Shall we?"

They walked out of the hotel onto Kearny Street. It teemed with activity, carriages parading up and down the cobblestoned street and horses shouldering their way along the thoroughfare. On both sides of the street, vast shimmering seas of plate glass framed unimaginable commercial glories. It was all Emily could do not to stop every five feet to stare at some novel treasure. One window, draped with velvets and satins, displayed an array of hats. Another window held a half dozen chalk heads, on which were arranged huge masses of gleaming hair. The window of Grandmother Myrna's Mystic Emporium featured fabulously colored magical charms and talismans, including a swag of tiny lights, each no larger than Emily's pinkie nail, sparkling in shifting colors of blue and gold and red. As Emily paused to stare at the charms in the window, the tiny lights dimmed and flickered, going dead as embers drenched in a bucket.

Stanton put a hand firmly on her elbow and impelled her forward.

"Come along, or we'll have Grandmother Myrna to answer to," he said. "Goodness knows how many magical applecarts you might knock over, walking through a commercial district with that stone in your hand."

They took a horsecar to California Street—a broad avenue

of imposing commercial buildings, monuments of shining white stone decorated with fluted colonnades, plaster ornaments, and heroic statuary. The building they stopped in front of was stark by comparison; its face was of smooth black marble, and only a collection of small, raised gold letters gave any indication of what a visitor might find behind its bright red door:

Mirabilis Institute of the Credomantic Arts, San Francisco Extension Office.

The lobby of the building was as simple and stylish as the exterior. High ceilinged, red walled, its only decoration was a long row of gold-framed portraits of sober-looking gentlemen. Emily looked at each of the dour faces as they passed. The sound of her heels clicking on the highly polished black marble floor seemed an insult to their collective dignity.

They came to a small reception area, where a pale thin clerk sat hunched over a ledger book, making careful notes with an ink pen. When he heard Emily and Stanton approach, he looked up with odd apprehension.

"Good morning." Stanton presented a crisp white card, making sure the gold of his ring flashed in the young man's face. "My name is Dreadnought Stanton. I am a Jefferson Chair, assigned to the eastern region of the state. I must see Professor Quincy on urgent business."

"I'm . . . I'm terribly sorry, but the professor is not in today." The young clerk looked anxiously between Emily and Stanton. "Perhaps, Mr. Stanton, if you'd like to make an appointment to call early next week . . ."

"Next week?" Stanton fixed the man with an imperious glare. Emily appreciated seeing it fixed on someone other than herself. "Next week is completely unacceptable."

"I'm sorry, Mr. Stanton," the clerk stammered, "but Professor Quincy is not available."

"Indeed." Stanton narrowed his eyes. "Urgent business on the coast, I take it?"

The clerk looked miserable. He straightened his skinny black tie and glanced at Emily.

"Mr. Stanton, *really*."

"Well?" Stanton pressed, his voice curt and impatient.

"Yes." The young man whispered. "I'm afraid you're correct."

Stanton *hmph*ed disapprovingly and plopped his hat on his head. Then he took Emily's arm and hurried her back along the hall through which they'd come. The staunch men in the portraits seemed to find their hasty retreat as unsatisfactory as their arrival.

"What are we going to do?" Emily asked.

"*I'm* going to find Professor Quincy." Stanton opened the door onto the brightness of the street. "*You're* going back to the hotel."

"Excuse me?"

Stanton gave her a weary look.

"Professor Quincy has an unfortunate predilection for faro. There are several establishments offering such diversions between Washington and Dupont streets, in the section of town commonly known as the Barbary Coast."

"I'm coming with you."

"No, you most certainly are *not*."

"I am!"

"It's the worst sort of neighborhood. It's no place for . . ."

Emily set her jaw. "I told you before, I'm not luggage you can put on a shelf whenever you feel like it. I've been pawed by zombies and chased by an Aberrant raccoon. I can take anything that San Francisco has to dish out."

Stanton pressed his fingers to the bridge of his nose and shut his eyes. Without opening them, he said, in a clipped tone, "Nice ladies don't visit the Barbary Coast."

She looked at him for a moment, folding her arms. "Mr. Stanton, you should know by now that I am anything but a nice lady."

"Miss Edwards, you are a much nicer lady than you like to pretend. All things considered."

"All things considered?" The persnickety little qualifier made Emily's blood boil. "You're insufferable, Mr. Stanton. I'm coming, and that's that. Don't make me get common."

"All right." Stanton threw up his hands, looking furtively up and down the quiet street. It was obvious that he did not relish the thought of Emily getting common in front of his institute.

When he spoke again, his voice was an annoyed hiss. "Forgive me for imagining you might want to preserve some shred of feminine reticence and delicacy. Come if you want. But don't complain to me when you get some unflattering offers."

He hailed a cab and gave the driver an address in a low voice. Emily and Stanton rode for a great while in huffy silence, neither looking at the other.

After a while they came to a neighborhood that did look exceedingly dubious. Clusters of rough-looking men clotted around corners, throwing dice or drinking from bottles. Threadbare old vagrants lay in muddy gutters, passed out or worse. Chinese porters hurried purposefully down dark alleyways, balancing heavy cloth-covered baskets on the ends of pliant bamboo poles. Emily caught sight of two fabulously dressed women walking along the sidewalk arm in arm. One was clad in a blue satin gown of extravagant cut and tailoring; the other wore a dress of deepest green, embroidered with sprays of pink and white cherry blossoms. As they walked they held their heads together in close conversation, smiling now and again, showing white teeth. Emily thought they looked very free and pleased with themselves.

"Don't stare at the prostitutes," Stanton said curtly.

"Oh, quit sulking." Emily settled back in the seat. "If I didn't have a well-developed spirit of adventure, I would never have gone up to the mine that night. You wouldn't have this wonderful stone to present to your professors, and you probably would have been eaten by that raccoon."

"I shall endeavor to count my blessings," Stanton sniffed.

They rounded a corner, and Emily caught a glimpse of a scuffle. Two policemen were pushing four men into a large, box-shaped black carriage. The policemen wore gray uniforms with brass buttons, and on their chests gleamed brightly polished silver stars.

She pressed her nose to the carriage window. Gesturing to Stanton, she pointed at the huge black carriage.

"What's that?" she asked.

"That's a Black Maria," Stanton said. "In New York we call them paddy wagons. Keep your eyes open, you're sure to see plenty of them where we're going."

The cab turned up Washington Street, then came to an abrupt halt.

"This is as far as I go, mister," the driver called back. Stanton paid him and handed Emily down into a swarming mass of debased humanity. There were shouts and catcalls, snatches of riotous song, girls offering to sell flowers or themselves without apparent preference.

"We'll try the Bull's Run first. It's just up the street." They had to pick their way over a couple of exceedingly drunk veterans in tattered blue uniforms. One of them grabbed at Emily's ankle, trying to feel up to her knee. She kicked him smartly and he laughed nastily at her.

They passed a squat brick building, on which hung a half dozen large, inexpertly painted signs. They bore messages like: "Free meals for the hungry" and "Let all who want be fed" and "The Lord wants you to be happy." Outside the door of the building there was a man in sober black standing on a wooden crate with a Bible in his hand. Emily could hear his words as they approached.

". . . foul sons of Baal and daughters of Lucifer the fallen! Witches and Warlocks, enchanters and sorcerers walk freely among our streets, thinking they can mock the Lord our God. But the Lord is *not* mocked, brothers, His swift judgment will be visited upon them. For are we not commanded, *Thou shalt not suffer a Witch to live!* And does not the prophet Isaiah say, *Woe to them that call evil good, and good evil; that put darkness for light, and light for darkness; that put bitter for sweet, and sweet for bitter* . . . step inside, brother, step inside and be fed . . ."

The last words were addressed to a grubby, emaciated man in tattered clothes. Emily's interest was piqued. She wanted to hear more, but Stanton gave the street preacher a wide berth.

"Did you hear that?" she murmured to Stanton. "Did you hear what he was saying?"

"That is one of Brother Scharfe's soup kitchens," Stanton replied, under his breath. "And one of his street preachers to go with it. You can recognize them by the red crosses they wear around their necks. Stay away from them."

"Why? Who is Brother Scharfe?"

"Brother Scharfe used to be a Baptist minister, but they were too free-thinking for his taste. He started his own sect, commonly called the Scharfians, and now enjoys quite a bit of national fame. He's a ceaseless tourer of lecture circuits and revival meetings. He has established soup kitchens for the poor all over the United States."

"Well, that's nice of him," Emily said. Stanton grunted.

"He uses them as stumping posts for the expounding of his radical theology. The Scharfians advocate a return to the good old days when sons of Baal and daughters of Lucifer were burned at the stake." Stanton cast a furtive look back at the street preacher. "Scharfe has a great deal of support in many regions. A man can hardly declare himself a Warlock in parts of the South without fear of retribution."

Emily felt suddenly cold, remembering Mrs. Lyman's words. She remembered the peculiar way that the scar tissue on Pap's face looked like a honeycomb. She imagined the wood piled around his feet, the terror he must have felt. The thought made her feel ill.

"But magic is perfectly natural!" Emily said. "Everyone knows there's nothing evil about it. You said it yourself . . . magic is building America! What would the governments and businesses do without Warlocks?"

"Hire Scharfians, I suppose," Stanton said. "Ah, here we are. The Bull's Run."

The Bull's Run had a garish sign over the door (depicting an improbably endowed red bull in a state of arousal that *was* somewhat unsettling), but it was hardly the foul den of iniquity that Emily had expected. Rather, it was a neat, snug saloon with red velvet draperies and a variety of men at the bar who seemed, if not complete gentlemen, men to whom behaving gentlemanly at least remained an option. These men hardly looked up as Stanton and Emily walked in, and Stanton gave them no time to look; he hurried Emily through the saloon toward an unobtrusive door at the rear. On the door hung a small card that read "Club Room." A man sat stiffly on a chair near the door, chewing on an unlit cigar, watching them approach.

"Games running?" Stanton was brisk.

The man's eyes narrowed, and then glanced inquiringly toward Emily.

"Bring your sister for luck?"

Stanton frowned at him. He slid an arm around Emily's waist, jerked her close in a gesture that was apparently intended to suggest some form of pleasant intimacy. As Stanton's was the lesser of the two insults, Emily took up the ruse. She licked her lips and let her eyelids droop suggestively.

"Looks like she needs a nap." The doorman continued to chew lazily on his cigar. With a grumble, Stanton rummaged in his pocket for a gold eagle. He flipped it at the man scornfully.

"Swindled without even placing a bet," he said as the doorman caught the gold in one hand and opened the door with the other.

Descending a flight of narrow steps, they came into a low, hot room. Lit brilliantly with gas, it was furnished with dozens of long tables covered in green baize. The air was close and sticky, and the smell rank. There were perhaps two hundred men in the room, but there was little conversation, only the sound of clinking coin and the voices of the dealers, calling out the action of the games. Now and again there was a cry of despair or a shout of excitement. The cries of despair, Emily noticed, seemed more frequent in her general vicinity. The stone in her hand was probably upsetting money-luck spells right and left.

"Monte, rouge et noir, diana, chuck-a-luck, poker dice . . ." Stanton pointed out the games to her in an undertone as he guided her through the room. "Professor Quincy used to stick to the more respectable casinos on Montgomery Street, but there was the matter of some unpaid debts. Now these are the only places that will admit her."

"Her?" Emily turned, her eyes wide. "It's a *her*?"

"Ah, there are the faro spreads. And there's Professor Quincy." Stanton gestured to a sharp, bony woman in a black silk dress that was encrusted in glimmering beadwork of cut jet. She wore black gloves and a small hat with a heavy veil that entirely covered her face. "Mrs. Henrietta Quincy. A somewhat unpleasant individual. I recommend you don't talk much."

Stanton touched Mrs. Quincy on the shoulder. The woman jerked around angrily and lifted her veil. Her elderly face was pinched and papery, and she had thin, suspicious lips.

The instant Emily saw the old woman's face, something strange happened. She heard chanting. Very distant, as if it were coming from outside the building somewhere, but chanting . . . the kind she'd heard in the Miwok village. Emily's heart leapt unpleasantly, and she turned her head from side to side, trying to locate the sound. But as soon as she moved, the chanting was gone. She shuddered, blinked. It was probably all the cigar smoke.

"Dreadnought Stanton?" Mrs. Quincy was saying. "For pity's sake, I thought you were off in the mountains somewhere. Good place for you, too. Nice and cool."

"I have returned, ma'am." He examined the bets she had on the table. "You're spread rather thin."

"Leave the gambling to experts," Mrs. Quincy snapped, and turned to push in another bet, very obviously for spite. The action of the game moved quickly, and within a moment, the money was swept away. With an unpleasant sniff, she rose and jerked her bead-fringed black shawl around her shoulders. She walked away from the table, leaving Stanton and Emily to follow in her wake.

"Well, make it quick, young man. Why are you here?"

"I have come across a very interesting anomaly," Stanton said as they trotted to keep up. "I wanted to bring it to the Institute's attention immediately."

Mrs. Quincy tossed a glare in Emily's direction.

"Who is she?"

"Miss Emily Edwards. She is the anomaly."

Mrs. Quincy stopped short and looked Emily up and down. "How nice for her."

Mrs. Quincy gestured them to a small withdrawing cove off the main room. Sitting, she opened a black lace fan and waved it vigorously beneath her chin, muttering ill-temperedly.

"Just when my luck was about to turn, too." She jabbed the fan at Stanton. "Boy, this better be good, or by my dead husband's ears I swear I'll—"

"Show her, Miss Edwards."

Emily drew the soiled kid glove from her right hand and held out her palm to Mrs. Quincy. Mrs. Quincy blinked, fan stilling. She leaned forward, her eyes wide. The arrangement of her face when astonished was particularly unattractive.

"Unbelievable," she whispered. She looked up at Emily, and then at Stanton.

"I believe it's a specimen of Native Star," Stanton said, summarizing their adventures with admirable brevity. While he spoke, Mrs. Quincy held Emily's hand and turned it over and again in the flickering half-light.

"Well done, Mr. Stanton," she murmured when Stanton had finished his précis. "Maybe you *will* come to something, burned and all." Emily noticed a flicker of distaste pass over Stanton's face when Mrs. Quincy used the word "burned."

"I'll have my carriage take you back to my house." Mrs. Quincy gestured a houseman to call for her driver. "The mysteries of this stone must be explored."

"That's very generous," Stanton said, "but won't you come with us?"

"I'll be along later," Mrs. Quincy said. "I have a few more things to see to here." Her eyes were already drifting back to the faro tables.

"Things to see to indeed," Stanton muttered later as they were riding in Mrs. Quincy's splendid barouche. "Incorrigible."

"What did she mean, 'burned'?"

"Never mind," Stanton said sharply. "The important thing is that we've made it." He stretched, leaning back against the plush seat of the carriage. "Believe it or not, it's a load off my mind. Now, at least, I have the full structure of the Institute to help me."

"Help you what?"

"Help me deal with *you*." He put a great deal more emphasis on the word than Emily thought strictly necessary. She contemplated sticking her tongue out at him, but refrained. Then she, too, leaned back, enjoying the comfortable softness of the seats. "Why would anyone gamble with a Witch, anyway?"

"Did you see how much she was losing? They line up to take her money."

"But she's a Witch! Why does she let them win?"

"Well, aside from the fact that using magic to win at cards would be *cheating* . . ." Stanton gave Emily an all-too-familiar look of reproach, "Witches and Warlocks have no advantage in casinos like that. Everyone's got a luck charm or a money spell or a something to hamper his opponents. The mantic atmosphere gets so cluttered that everything cancels everything else out."

Emily glanced out the window, saw that they were passing the street preacher they'd seen earlier. She could not hear his words, but his mouth was moving vehemently.

"Oh, and by the way," Stanton said, "don't call her a Witch. Most female practitioners prefer the more delicate *sorcière*."

"Everyone always just called me a Witch," Emily said.

Stanton did not comment.

CHAPTER EIGHT

A Man Calls

Mrs. Quincy's house was built into the side of a steep hill. It was an imposing structure, tall and square and butter yellow, frosted on every surface with decorative scrolls and fretwork. The inside of the house, into which they were shown by a maid in starched black and white, was as fussy as the outside. The sitting room was crammed with knickknacks and whatnots, shells and painted fans and brightly colored paper umbrellas and dozens of enameled pots containing a small jungle of trailing plants.

"Now what are we supposed to do?" Emily asked, feeling stifled by the politeness of clutter.

"We behave like civilized people." Stanton sank into a leather wingback with a contented sigh.

Emily sat on a slippery horsehair couch, trying not to disarrange the embroidered pillows or the carefully draped antimacassars. Stanton took up a newspaper that bore the ornate scrolling masthead, *Practitioners' Daily*, and unfolded it across his lap. A box full of cigars sat next to his chair; he took one and gave it an appreciative sniff before lighting it.

"I thought gentlemen weren't supposed to smoke in front of ladies," Emily said.

Stanton choked, coughing heartily.

"I want to smoke a cigar, and suddenly you're a lady?" He snapped his newspaper at her quite meaningfully. "If you wish me to refrain from smoking in your presence, Miss Edwards, you'll have to come up with a better reason than your frail femininity."

With a sniff, Emily let her eyes drift aimlessly around the room. On the marble mantelpiece, lustrous purple and blue peacock feathers sprouted from an alabaster vase. Pretty, but everyone knew peacock feathers inside a house drew bad luck. Her eyes traveled over pictures of foreign lands in polished silver frames, loudly ticking clocks (who needed five clocks in one room?), and everywhere doilies. Just being in a room with all those doilies made Emily tired.

On the wall was an important-looking picture. The frame was adorned with draped bunting and decoratively cut silver paper. The important-looking picture was of an important-looking man. Emily scrutinized him. He was stiff and unsmiling. He had wide staring eyes and looked rather crazy. At first, Emily thought that it must be the late Mr. Quincy, but then she saw that he wore the high stiff collar of a priest.

"Who's that?"

Stanton did not even glance up from behind his paper. "That is a picture of Benedictus Zeno, the father of modern credomancy."

"A priest?"

"Excommunicated," Stanton said. "Rome was not pleased."

Emily looked at Benedictus Zeno's face for another moment, then stood up. She went to stand directly before Stanton. With her gloved hand, she delicately folded down the top of his paper.

"So. What's your plan?" She peered down at him. "I mean, is Mrs. Quincy going to get this thing out of my hand, or what?"

Stanton looked up at her.

"That may not be within her range of abilities," he said. "But if she will consent, I hope she will contact Professor Mirabilis and ask him to pay us a visit."

"But isn't he all the way back in New York? That would be weeks waiting here. She didn't seem *that* hospitable."

"No, it wouldn't be weeks," Stanton said. "Mrs. Quincy has a Haälbeck door."

"A what?"

Stanton gestured to a door that Emily had taken, at a glance, for a closet. On closer examination, however, she realized that it was far too fancy to lead to a musty room full of moth-balls. It was extravagantly inlaid from panel to frame.

"This door?" Emily went over to it.

"Don't touch it!" Stanton leapt to his feet. "There's no telling what that stone in your hand would do to Mr. Haälbeck."

Stepping past her, he touched the frame of the wood, closing his eyes. Under his breath, he murmured, "Greetings, Herr Haälbeck," and then grasped the ornate wrought silver handle and opened the door. It opened onto a papered wall.

"Locked," he said. "Just as I expected."

Emily looked at him. She let out a long sigh that suggested oceans of abused patience.

"Haälbeck doors have terminal points in many different locations. If it weren't for the stone in your hand—and the fact that Mrs. Quincy very wisely keeps the door locked—we could walk through this one right now and be in New York. Or Chicago, or London, or Bombay, or any one of hundreds of different locations."

"Really?" Emily said. That did sound quite useful, "But that doesn't explain why you were so concerned that I might do harm to whoever this Mr. Haälbeck is."

"Have a look at the wood of the frame," Stanton said.

Emily did, not quite understanding what the door frame had to do with the mysterious Mr. Haälbeck, but resigned to the fact that Stanton was going to explain it to her, probably exhaustively. The wood was a strange color—gold with a bluish tinge, like oak that had been stained with huckleberry juice.

"It is uchawi wood. It comes from Africa. It has an extremely high capacity for storing mantic energy. Each of the Haälbeck doors is made from this wood, and the frame of each door contains a small piece of the wood in which the spirit of a German Warlock named Haälbeck resides." Stanton pointed to a place on the upper left-hand corner of the door frame, where a small piece of old-looking wood had been inlaid as part of a pretty star pattern. "There's the piece that contains Mr. Haälbeck."

Emily wrinkled her nose.

"You're telling me that that little piece of wood contains his whole spirit?"

"Spirit, essence, soul, whatever you prefer to call it. And no, his spirit is not just in that little piece of wood. It's spread out among all the other little pieces of wood that were taken from the Haälbeck timber to make Haälbeck doors."

Emily settled herself back onto the horsehair couch.

"All right, what is the Haälbeck timber?"

"The year was 1789." Stanton clasped his hands behind his back and assumed a professorial stance. "Herr Gustav Haälbeck, a Warlock with a mercantilist bent, was determined to make his fortune by creating a teleportational portal through which items could be shipped over great distances. Traditional magical teleportation requires a very large amount of mantic energy, and he was working with a large trunk of uchawi wood, trying to find a way to make it hold enough energy to fuel a stable portal.

"His preliminary experiments were unsuccessful. Even uchawi wood could not hold sufficient quantities of mantic energy. So Haälbeck began to experiment with the structure of the wood itself, altering it to make it more mantically attractive, so that more power could be stuffed into it, so to speak."

"And he succeeded?"

"All too well. He imbued the wood with too much attractive force, which resulted in a violent and involuntary metempsychosis . . ." Stanton paused at the look of bewilderment on Emily's face. "Put simply, it sucked his soul right into it, much against his will."

Emily stared at Stanton, wide-eyed. "His soul got sucked into the wood?"

"Yes," Stanton said. "And that piece of wood became known as the Haälbeck timber."

"How . . . unfortunate!"

"Well, every cloud has a silver lining. Haälbeck's spirit imbued the Haälbeck timber with an immense amount of power—more power than anyone has ever since been able to contain within any material. Because of this, we have the ability to make Haälbeck doors from it."

"And what happened to Mr. Haälbeck?"

"Pardon?" Stanton said, even though Emily knew he'd heard the question just fine.

"Is he alive, or dead, or what? His soul is in the wood of all these doors . . . what does that mean for him?"

"He can still communicate with the people who use the doors—you heard me greet him just now. But I'm afraid that he hasn't much to talk about. He complains about rusty hinges and badly oiled locks. The years have left him much more like a door and much less like a human."

Emily shuddered. "That sounds like a terrible fate for someone's soul."

"There are worse ones," Stanton said. Emily would have asked him to elaborate on that comment, but at that moment the maid, in her crisp black and white, appeared at the door to show Emily up to her room.

"I unpacked your things from the hotel, but I'm not sure they sent everything." The maid sounded worried. Emily peeked into the open closet where her things had been hung. Buffalo coat, wrinkled gray dress, apron, straw hat, Pap's old pants . . .

"They sent everything," Emily said. She did wish that she'd thought to tuck a few cakes of that beautifully wrapped soap into her saddlebag.

"Oh . . . good!" The maid brightened. "Well, my name is Dinah. Mrs. Quincy sent word that dinner is to be served at eight. I'll be happy to help you dress or do your hair, if you require."

"I don't think I'll need help."

"That's a shame. You have such pretty hair, I'd be pleased to do it for you," Dinah said. "I can tell that it's all real. So many women wear false hair these days."

"False hair?" Emily said.

"Oh, yes. Lots of hair is the fashion, of course, so women without much will pay to get more. Poor girls sell their hair down at the shops on Mason Street." Dinah eyed Emily's hair approvingly. "You'd get a pretty penny for all that hair of yours."

"I think I'll hold on to it, thanks." Emily smiled as she pulled off her kid gloves and laid them on the bureau. Dinah reached for them with a little frown.

"Oh, miss, what have you done to these?"

"Rode a hundred miles on a big black horse," Emily said. "It's murder on the gloves."

"Oh," Dinah said vaguely, as if Emily had just quoted some impenetrable scripture in Tibetan. "Well, I can clean them for you, if you'd like. Get some of the stains out, maybe . . ." She did not sound optimistic. Clutching the battered gloves, she paused with her hand on the doorknob.

"If you don't mind my saying it, miss . . . you certainly don't seem like most of Mrs. Quincy's friends. Meaning no disrespect, of course."

"No," Emily said drily. "I doubt very much I'm like any of Mrs. Quincy's friends."

At eight o'clock precisely, Emily was dressed and ready for dinner. Dinah had restored the kid gloves to some of their former softness by rubbing them with lanolin, but there was nothing to be done about the stains.

"I don't know why ladies have to wear white gloves anyway, miss. Nothing but heartache, if you catch my meaning."

Emily did indeed.

Mrs. Quincy had returned at half past six, and in a foul mood, too, if the harassed look on Dinah's face was any indication. Emily had consented to let Dinah arrange her hair, but Mrs. Quincy seemed quite put out by the fact that she was not the sole focus of Dinah's attention. Emily had given up on her entirely and was twisting her hair up into a simple bun when Dinah finally hurried into her room.

"I'm so sorry, miss! I can see to you properly now. Mrs. Quincy is finished and has locked herself in the parlor."

Emily raised an eyebrow as the girl came to stand behind her, taking an ivory-backed brush and running it through Emily's hair with quick neat strokes.

"Locked herself in the parlor?"

"Oh, she does that every night," Dinah said. She bent closer to Emily. "I think she likes to take a dram or two."

Within a quarter hour, Emily was dressed and coifed. As a concession to the grandness of the home, Emily put her mother's gold and amethyst earrings through her ears, where they winked and sparkled.

When she came downstairs, she found that Mrs. Quincy had unlocked the doors of her sanctum to admit Stanton (the dram apparently having been drunk prior to his arrival), and the two of them were sitting in the parlor engaged in a close and heated conversation. Emily caught Stanton's last sentence: "I honestly can't say I understand your reluctance . . ." and then they parted, both frowning, as she came into the room.

"Well, good evening, my dear Miss Edwards!" Mrs. Quincy rose, extending her hands to Emily. Her aspect was entirely changed. Though still dressed in unbroken glittering black, her brusqueness and unpleasantness had vanished, and she was now surprisingly jocund. "I trust you were able to rest a bit after your long journey? Mr. Stanton has been telling me more about your amazing adventures."

"I feel very rested, thank you," Emily said.

"What charming earbobs," Mrs. Quincy purred, lifting her index finger to touch one of Emily's earrings. "The purple amethysts match the dewy violet of your eyes so nicely."

Emily glanced at Stanton, unsure of what to make of such a comment. He shrugged almost imperceptibly.

"Thank you," Emily said finally, sitting down and folding her hands in her lap.

Then, before any other words could be spoken, there was a rapping from behind the ornate Haälbeck door. Stanton gave Mrs. Quincy an inquiring glance.

"We shall have a fourth for dinner." Mrs. Quincy smiled. "I telegraphed him this afternoon. He graciously consented to join us this evening."

She laid a hand on the frame of the door, muttering a few unintelligible words. Then, reaching for the carved doorknob, she opened the magic door. Emily blinked. It no longer opened onto a papered wall, but onto a hazy room. The features of the room were mostly indistinct, but Emily could see a large chair of brown leather on which was draped a black-fringed shawl.

The features of the half-seen room faded in a blaze of bluish-pink light as a man in a brown suit stepped through the door, hat in hand. He was an imposing figure. Well past middle age, he retained the straight back and bulkiness of what must have been an extremely powerful youth. He wore his iron-gray hair close-clipped, as if to balance the excessively voluminous, white-streaked muttonchops that flared from his cheeks.

"Ah, Mr. Cruickshank," Mrs. Quincy said. "How wonderful of you to come. Mr. Andrew Cruickshank, this is Mr. Dreadnought Stanton. He's one of the Institute's Jefferson Chairs. And this is Miss Emily Edwards, the girl I mentioned in the telegram."

Cruickshank shook Stanton's hand briskly and nodded to Emily.

"Mr. Cruickshank is an occult geologist," Mrs. Quincy said. "He is currently working with some large mining concerns in Panama City. I thought he might be able to shed some light on this anomaly."

"If I might see the object in question?" he asked. Pulling off the glove, Emily laid her right hand in Cruickshank's massive palm. His hand was warm and strong and surprisingly smooth for a man who worked for a mining concern in Panama City. He turned Emily's hand over, examining how the stone protruded from both sides.

"Incredible," he said in a voice so flat that Emily wondered if he was being sarcastic. She was about to ask him what an occult geologist was when Dinah came into the room and murmured something in Mrs. Quincy's ear.

"Ah, dinner is ready," Mrs. Quincy said. "Shall we go in?"

Emily had never had such a dinner. The board was laden to groaning with roast beef, fresh fish, chicken, and veal. There were three kinds of potatoes and two varieties of raised bread; there was fresh asparagus in hollandaise sauce and new lettuce dressed with vinegar and sugar. Stanton tucked in with zeal, but Emily hardly got a chance to eat a mouthful, as she was occupied answering a barrage of rapid-fire questions from Mrs. Quincy and Mr. Cruickshank. Mr. Cruickshank was particularly interested in Besim's Cassandra. He kept returning to it with uncomfortable questions.

"How did you know that this Besim fellow was telling the truth? Not a very reliable source. It seems strange that you would go up to a mine in the middle of the night because some drunk dervish told you to."

"Miss Edwards is a Witch," Stanton interjected, spooning more potatoes onto his plate. "And a very capable one. She is perfectly able to tell the difference between a false prognostication and a real one."

Emily gave Stanton a grateful look, but he was far too interested in his potatoes to notice it.

"You're a Witch?" Mrs. Quincy's eyes widened and she glared at Stanton. "But why didn't you tell us? That's likely to be important!" She looked at Emily. "What kind of magic do you practice, my dear?"

Emily shrugged. "It's just the magic my pap taught me. Charms and horoscopes and elixirs."

Mrs. Quincy and Cruickshank exchanged glances.

"Miss Edwards and her adoptive father practice standard Ozark herbalism, overlaid with elements of old Scottish Wicca." Stanton looked hard at both Mrs. Quincy and Cruickshank. "Their practice is quite respectable."

"Of course it is," Mrs. Quincy purred, but Emily caught her smiling into her glass. Just what was so funny? And what in blazes did Stanton mean, their practice is "respectable"? She looked down at her plate, her cheeks suddenly hot.

"At any rate, I'm sure Professor Mirabilis will be able to clear all this up." Stanton picked up a fork for a renewed attack on his food. "I hope we shall be contacting him after dinner, as we discussed?"

"We will be contacting him if I deem it fit, Mr. Stanton." Mrs. Quincy's earlier harshness was back. "Do you know what time it is in New York?"

"I am perfectly aware of the time." Stanton set his fork down with a loud clank. "Which is why it seems reasonable that we might contact him before the hour grows much later."

And then, again, suddenly . . .

Chanting.

It was the same chanting Emily had heard in the casino, but louder now. This time, Emily had no doubt that it was the voice of the Maien from the Miwok camp, her raggedy rough voice eliding and dipping, long notes wavering in the distance. Emily looked around furtively. Where was the sound coming from?

Something was terribly wrong, but she didn't know what. She couldn't stand the awful chanting—it was unsettling, enervating. Her eyes darted between Mrs. Quincy and Stanton, and suddenly she felt dizzy. She swayed slightly, looking down at her plate to keep from swooning, concentrating hard on the half-eaten spear of asparagus swimming in the fatty yellow sauce. Looking at it made her feel sick. Putting a hand over her mouth, she closed her eyes.

In the distance, she heard a voice chanting words she did not understand. Urgent words.

And then, although her eyes were squeezed shut tightly, she saw something. She saw it as clearly as if her eyes were open . . .

. . . Mrs. Quincy and Mr. Cruikshank. In a room.

It was the room she'd glimpsed through the Haälbeck door; there was the large brown leather chair. And there was the shawl she'd seen draped over it, but the shawl was now around Mrs. Quincy's shoulders—the black bead-fringed shawl she'd first seen the old woman wearing in the gambling house.

"I don't like it, Captain Caul, I don't like it at all!" Mrs. Quincy clutched the shawl around her throat, paper-white hand trembling. "No one will care about the girl . . . But Dreadnought Stanton! He was sent to California to stay out of trouble like this. Mirabilis wanted him placed where he was least likely to encounter any kind of . . . excitement. I was supposed to see to it!"

"Your incompetence is not my concern," Cruikshank—or was it Caul?—said.

"But can't you just take her? You know who Dreadnought Stanton's father is, don't you? Argus Stanton. Senator Argus Stanton. The stupid boy left his card at the extension office when he called today! My clerk saw them."

"I want them both," Caul said. *"My men and I will take care of everything. Don't forget who we are."*

"I know exactly who you are, and that's why I'm worried," Mrs. Quincy blazed. *"The Maelstroms have never been known for their delicacy. I won't have a scandal in my house!"*

"If it's scandal you're worried about, take the money we're paying you and settle your gambling debts," Caul said. *"From what I hear, that is far more likely to damage your reputation—to say nothing of your health—than having two unexceptional individuals disappear from your house."*

The room in which Mrs. Quincy and Caul stood began to spin, melting into a wash of colors and sounds, and then the chanting became louder, drowning out the sound of their voices . . .

Emily snapped her eyes open, looked wildly around the table. Stanton and Mrs. Quincy were still bickering about Professor Mirabilis, and had not noticed a thing. But Cruikshank was looking at her. Staring at her, his eyes dull as slate. Emily's heart leapt into her throat.

"Will you excuse me, please?" Emily mumbled, standing abruptly. In her haste, she knocked her leg against the table, making the china rattle. Stanton looked up at her, his brows knitted.

"Are you all right?" he asked.

She rushed from the table without answering.

She went into the parlor, threw open a window, leaned her head out. She drank in the fresh air greedily, as if she were parched and it was purest water. Everything was still and silent, the chanting of the Maien in her ears fading into an elusive memory. Gradually, her heart slowed a little—that is, until she saw the police wagon in the street below.

It was a Black Maria, the kind she'd seen the wrongdoers pushed into that morning. Two heavy dray horses stamped impatiently in front of it, one giving a shake under its bulky harness. The clatter of its steel trappings echoed through the still street.

There was a noise behind her. Emily spun. But it was only

Dinah, her small form looking even smaller as she stood huddled by the door.

"Are you all right, miss?"

Emily gestured her to the window and pointed down into the street at the Black Maria.

"Is there any reason for that to be there?"

"A police wagon? In a nice neighborhood? No, miss!"

Emily's heart was beating hard again as she took Dinah by both shoulders and turned the girl to face her.

"Listen, Dinah, I need your help. Tell Mr. Stanton I need him, but without all sorts of fuss. Just calm-like. Can you do that?"

Dinah said nothing. She was staring at Emily, openmouthed. Emily gave her a little shake.

"Dinah, do you hear me? Can you do that?"

"Of . . . of course, miss." Dinah turned on her heel and ran from the room.

A few minutes later, Stanton made a dignified entrance, as if he were coming to retrieve a book on mathematics.

"Took your time, didn't you?" she snapped.

"It's just like with the Aberrancy," Stanton said. "Never invite unpleasant things to chase you. Now let me have a look." He took her chin in his hand and turned her face toward him. She pulled back.

"What are you doing?"

"You gave that girl quite a turn," Stanton said. "But she's right. Your eyes have gone all black again."

"I . . . I saw something. Had a Cassandra." The words tumbled out of her mouth too quickly. "Mr. Cruikshank . . . she called him Captain. And his name isn't Cruikshank, it's Caul . . . and he was looking at me . . ."

"Slow down," Stanton said.

". . . And look outside!" she said. Stanton went to the window, looked down into the street. "He wants us both, he said. Mrs. Quincy arranged it all! To pay off her gambling debts—"

"Custody?" Stanton said, whispering now. "But we haven't done anything wrong!"

"Listen, it's all true, and there isn't much time." She waved a desperate hand, trying to remember what else Mrs. Quincy and

Caul had talked about. She snapped her fingers and pointed at Stanton. "Mrs. Quincy doesn't want him to take you because your father's a senator and she doesn't want any scandal."

He looked at her through narrowed eyes, brow knit.

"Who told you that?"

"*Nobody* told me. Mrs. Quincy told Cruikshank . . . Caul. I saw it . . . I just started to feel sick, and I heard chanting . . . I heard Komé chanting. She was there with me, I think."

Stanton stood for a moment. Then he went to the window at the opposite corner of the room and threw up the sill. He grabbed the braided satin rope that held back the massively draped curtains. It was looped multiple times, creating attractive swags, and when unhooked it represented quite a length. He made one end fast and threw the rest out the window.

"I can't climb down a rope one-handed!" Emily held up her right hand, wiggling her fingers slightly to remind Stanton of its near-immobility.

"I'll go first and break your fall," he offered, without apparent irony. He swung out of the window and disappeared into the darkness outside.

Emily leaned out over the windowsill, watching him clamber down the wall. It was a good thirty feet to the ground.

"I can't, Mr. Stanton. I just can't!" she whispered furiously.

"Miss Edwards, I have complete faith in your ability to do anything in a pinch." Stanton called up urgently. "Hurry, now!"

Emily took a deep breath. Sitting on the windowsill, she swung her legs out, then turned awkwardly onto her belly. She was just beginning to let herself down when the parlor door opened and Caul walked in.

Startled, Emily slid. Scrabbling with her feet, she managed to catch herself against the house's ornate clapboard siding, halfway down.

Caul thrust his head out of the window above her. He fumbled at his collar, pulling out a two-chambered glass pendant on a silver chain. Holding it in a clenched fist, he thrust it toward Emily with a booming cry. There was a smell of rotting flesh and a tormented wail and a dazzling flash, and Emily lost her grip and slid down the rope, landing heavily on Stanton.

The blast of magic enveloped them both, and Emily felt

the stone absorbing it. The magic couldn't hurt her, but it could disable Stanton. Was that what Caul had in mind? She grabbed for Stanton's hand. Let the stone protect them both.

"Come on, run!" Stanton said when the dazzle had faded. He pulled her to her feet. They tore through Mrs. Quincy's garden, leaping over a low white fence into a neighboring backyard.

From behind them, from Mrs. Quincy's house, came the high piercing sound of a whistle, and Caul's roared shout: "They're on the run! Get after them!"

Emily tried to keep up, but even with Stanton pulling her along, she felt terribly ill. Her stomach roiled and turned, and there was a horrible taste in her mouth—the taste of congealing blood. She gagged, coughing, choking on bitter bile that forced itself up her throat and into the back of her mouth.

From behind them came the sounds of men shouting to one another and a multiplicity of high shrieking whistles. Emily and Stanton kept running downhill, through gardens and flower beds. The whistles echoed behind them, but they grew fainter and fainter. They left gardens behind, trading them for backways and empty lots overgrown with tall grass. Finally, they came to a quiet street. It was lined with closed-up shops and a few warehouses. Turning down a narrow alley, they crouched behind a tall tower of empty wooden packing crates. Stanton was breathing heavily, watching down the way for pursuers.

Emily's stomach was churning violently, spasming against her hard-beating heart. Leaning with a hand against the cold ragged brick, she vomited.

When she was finished, she wiped her mouth with the back of her trembling hand. Stanton was still watching down the alleyway, his shoulders rising and falling.

"Are you all right?" he asked, looking back at her.

"No," Emily said. "I don't think either of us are anymore."

CHAPTER NINE

Mason Street

It was well after midnight by the time Emily and Stanton felt safe enough to emerge from the shadows and walk slowly along the narrow gaslit street. The light, however, did nothing to improve either one's appearance or attitude. They were both covered in mud and scratches from their mad tear across lots, and they were both thoroughly dismayed and disheartened. When they came upon an all-night chophouse offering "Eastern Oysters—All Styles" they went inside and took a table in the darkest corner farthest from the door.

Stanton ordered coffee and sticky buns and a hot cup of chamomile tea to soothe Emily's still-fluttering stomach. The tea was served with a little almond cookie, but Emily couldn't even think of eating. Her whole body felt shaky and sick and cold, and even her good hand was trembling so violently that she could hardly lift the cup to her lips.

"Well, Mr. Stanton, it was a pleasure getting to know your colleagues."

"I couldn't understand why she was so hesitant to contact Professor Mirabilis." Stanton popped a glazed walnut from atop one of the buns into his mouth. "Now it all makes sense."

"If it all makes sense, explain it to me," Emily said. "Explain why I heard Komé chanting in my head, or why I saw Mrs. Quincy and Captain Caul talking, or why I tasted blood . . ."

"The last one is the easiest," Stanton said. "Caul is a sangrimancer—a blood sorcerer. You could tell from the alembic he used to cast his spell. The stone absorbed the spell he threw at you, and that must have made you feel ill."

Emily shuddered, taking a sip of the chamomile tea to wash away the sickening memory.

"You've told me about credomancers and animancers, but you left sangrimancers out."

"They're not a pleasant topic of conversation," Stanton said. "Sangrimancy is the most powerful of the great magical traditions. But a sangrimancer's power comes at a terrible moral cost. He must obtain it by extracting it from the blood of living creatures."

"Like . . . animals?"

Stanton inclined his head slightly. "Some branches of sangrimancy use animal blood, but its potency is minimal." He paused. "Remember when I said that magic wasn't in words, but rather in how words act upon the human mind? Likewise, it's not the blood itself that provides the sangrimancer with his power—it's the emotions bound within that blood. *Human* emotions. Hate, love, anguish, despair—these are his weapons. To obtain them, he must have human blood, taken by force, seasoned with pain."

"Seasoned?"

"The greatest concentrations of power are found in humans who are slaughtered in a state of extreme physical or emotional distress. Which means sangrimancers are usually accomplished torturers as well." Stanton flexed his hands in a strange way, as if he could flick the thought of sangrimancers off his fingers like drops of water. "The practice of blood magic has been illegal for the past fifty years, but laws won't stop people from taking advantage of such power."

Emily stared at him for a long time. Then she remembered something else from her vision. "Mrs. Quincy said Captain Caul was a Maelstrom."

Stanton blinked at her.

"What did you say?"

"A Maelstrom. She said the Maelstroms don't care about propriety."

Stanton took a deep breath, then let it out in a long hiss.

"They most certainly don't." He looked down at the table.

"You know them?"

"The Maelstroms are a special branch of President Grant's

Secret Service. The units are commanded by old military War-locks who served in the war—Caul could certainly fit that bill."

"Then they're all old men?" Emily asked.

"No, they continue to actively recruit . . ." Stanton paused as if momentarily lost in a maze of thought. Then he shook his head. "They have a special dispensation to practice sangri-mancy, supposedly for the public good. They are deployed in situations that need to be resolved quickly, quietly, and with-out bothering with that troublesome little thing called the Con-stitution. If the Maelstroms are after us"—he let out another long breath—"then we really are in trouble."

At that precise instant the little bell above the door tinkled merrily. Both Emily and Stanton startled; Emily saw Stan-ton's hand go to the inside pocket of his coat as his eyes darted to the door. There was the sound of heavy, irregular footsteps and a loud, drunken demand for a steak to be prepared, dou-ble quick. Stanton withdrew his hand, lifting it reassuringly, but Emily did not relax.

"Why should the Maelstroms be after us?" Emily whis-pered. "If the government needs the stone for the public good, why didn't they just ask?"

"Maelstroms don't ask." Stanton shook his head. "Honestly, I knew the stone in your hand was an incredible discovery, but I never anticipated—"

Stanton stopped speaking as the drunk man who had called for the steak lumbered by their table, giving Emily a good hard leer as he passed them. She sank down in her seat, lowering her eyes while the man moved past.

"Are my eyes still black?" she whispered to Stanton.

"No, they're returning to their customary 'dewy violet,' though it looks as though the garden has suffered a recent bout of frost." Stanton dipped one corner of his cloth napkin into his glass of water and gestured to her. She leaned forward, and he wiped dirt off her cheek.

"And what about Komé? Why was she in my head chant-ing?"

"That's a more difficult question. I imagine it has something to do with the acorn she gave you."

"The acorn? You think I'm having visions because of a magical acorn?"

"Do you have a better explanation?"

Emily sighed. Of course she didn't. "Well, what are we going to do?"

"We have several problems." Stanton reached into his pocket and pulled out a few small coins and laid them on the table. "Problem number one. That's all the money I have."

"What about your Warlock's Purse?"

"I'm afraid I left it sitting safely with all my other things, on a chair in Mrs. Quincy's spare bedroom," Stanton said. "Shall we go back and ask for it?"

Emily stared at him. "You left it in the spare bedroom?" She said each word slowly.

"We were just going downstairs for dinner! How was I to know we would end up exiting through the parlor window?"

"All right," Emily sighed heavily. "That's problem number one."

"Problem number two. We have to get out of town, and quickly."

"And the minute you go back for your horses, Captain Caul is certain to be waiting."

"Actually, that is not a problem." Stanton looked smug, and for once, Emily found it very comforting. "Mrs. Quincy does not know where my horses are stabled, nor did I divulge that information to the proprietor of the Excelsior Hotel. I took them to my customary stabler near the waterfront to get them reshod. It should be quite safe to retrieve them. But that brings us back to problem number one. I don't know what I'll tell them when it comes time to settle the bill."

Emily reached into her collar and pulled out the silk pouch. From it she withdrew the ten-dollar gold coin that Pap had tucked into her pocket when she'd departed Lost Pine.

"Will this be enough?"

He took the coin from her, looked at it with astonishment.

"I guess Pap thought I should have something in case of emergency," she said.

"Your pap is an astute old gentleman." Stanton tucked the

money into his pocket. "All right, that'll get us the horses back."

"That's a mercy," Emily sighed. "So when we get out of San Francisco—if we get out of San Francisco—what then?"

"We have to go to New York," Stanton said finally. "We have to get to Professor Mirabilis."

"New York!" Emily stared at him. "That's . . . that's thousands of miles away! We can't go to New York!"

"Name me an alternative," Stanton said. "Stay in San Francisco and wait for Caul to find us? Go back to Lost Pine and wait for Caul to find you there? Mrs. Quincy was my only connection to the Institute on this side of the continent. Now that she's betrayed us, I won't trust anyone but Professor Mirabilis himself."

"And how, exactly, are we supposed to get to New York without any money?"

"I'll have to sell my horses," Stanton said.

"Oh, no!" Emily blurted, for she had grown surprisingly attached to Romulus. "I'm sure Pap still has the money you gave him, and that's enough to get us a pair of tickets to New York. Maybe we could sneak back to Lost Pine and—"

"Lost Pine is the last place we should go. The Maelstroms will be looking for us there, after everything we told Caul."

"But your poor horses!"

"Better them than us." To his credit, it sounded as if he mostly meant it. "But I don't think we should sell them in San Francisco. It'll take too much time, and the Maelstroms will be on the lookout. Besides, it just so happens that luck is on our side. You remember when we were riding out of Dutch Flat, and we stopped near Colfax for lunch? I talked to a small group of men."

"I remember. You didn't tell me what they wanted."

"They wanted to buy my horses," Stanton said. "They were from a place called New Bethel, about ten miles east of Dutch Flat."

"Dag goes to New Bethel to buy hay for his teams every week." She paused, the memory of Dag giving her a twinge. "But Pap never let me go there. He said it wasn't wholesome."

Stanton *hmph*ed grimly.

"Well, we've been through quite a number of unwholesome experiences already; I suppose one more won't hurt."

Emily sighed in frustration. The thought of selling Stanton's regal horses to those sour-looking men made her angry.

"Isn't there any other way to contact Professor Mirabilis? What about those Haälbeck doors? Can't we get to one and . . . well, you could go through anyway, and bring Professor Mirabilis back!"

"Magical society in San Francisco is small and close-knit. There are only two Haälbeck doors in San Francisco, one of which is in Mrs. Quincy's house. The other is at the Calacacara, a club for gentlemen Warlocks. I am not a member, and even if I were, Caul will have surely posted someone to watch it. The Maelstroms know that flight is our only recourse. I'm sure they're doing everything they can to cut off our avenues of escape, magical or otherwise."

"How about a telegraph? Couldn't we telegraph the professor and tell him that he must come to San Francisco?"

Stanton thought about this, stroking his chin.

"Professor Mirabilis, your presence San Francisco required. Stop. Urgent. Stop. Professor Quincy untrustworthy. Stop. Maelstroms hot on our heels. Stop. Look for me lobby of Excelsior Hotel, wearing red carnation. Stop. Signed, Dreadnought Stanton, the man of whom you thought so highly that you banished him to the most pathetic little town in California." Stanton gave her a look.

Emily gave him his look right back and then some, but said nothing.

"Besides," Stanton continued, "there is no way to know who might intercept such a message. Mrs. Quincy is a highly placed member of the faculty. The fact that she betrayed us makes me worry that there might be others. A telegraph could be easily intercepted and a misleading reply composed that would send us directly into a trap. No, I won't be satisfied until we're standing in front of Professor Mirabilis himself."

Emily was silent, biting her thumbnail thoughtfully.

"Your father," she said, after a moment. "He's a senator, right? Isn't there some way—"

"Entirely out of the question." Stanton said curtly. "I prefer not to involve him in such matters."

"Well, I prefer not to run around San Francisco with blood sorcerers chasing me and no money!"

"No, Miss Edwards." Stanton's voice was firm. "My father is a . . . blunt instrument. Contacting him wouldn't make things better. It would very likely make things worse. Trust me."

Emily pondered this. Then she let out a breath.

"All right. We sell your horses. We take the money and catch the train. We can board at one of the smaller stops above New Bethel—the Maelstroms can't watch them all."

Stanton nodded. It was clear that he was thinking hard. His green eyes were lustrous with concentration. His long forefinger tapped a rhythm on the tabletop as he whistled softly to himself. He stopped abruptly, looking up.

"Yes, it seems a reasonable plan," he said. "Which leaves only my immediate concerns to be addressed."

"Immediate concerns?"

"After I pay for the shoeing and stabling of the horses, we'll have less than five dollars. That's hardly enough to feed us past Walnut Creek, much less all the way back to New Bethel."

"We're running for our lives, and you're worrying about whether you'll get your regular breakfast?" Emily was incredulous. "Going without a few meals will hardly kill you."

"No, I'm afraid you're wrong there," Stanton said. He pushed his coffee cup around on the saucer. He opened his mouth to say something then closed it. When he opened it again, he spoke in a quick, clipped tone.

"You recall that Mrs. Quincy made a disparaging remark at the casino—she referred to me as burned. That is the crude colloquial term for an impairment, a defect from which I suffer. *Exussum cruorsis*." He paused, centering the cup on the saucer with more precision than the action really required. "You see, practitioners are supposed to be like Swiss cheese—full of holes through which mantic energy can be funneled and directed. Much of a Warlock's formal training consists of manipulating these pathways, the *viae manticum*. While the *viae manticum* are open, they represent a great drain on the physical system. In most cases, they are only opened while a Warlock is actively working a spell and can be closed at will." He paused again. "In my case, however, I am unable to close them. They remain constantly open, and I am like a lamp that is always kept lit. It's quite draining. If I don't keep well fed, I'll be worse than useless to you."

Emily absorbed this strange flood of information, blinking.

"Are there many Warlocks with this . . . condition?"

"It is extremely uncommon," Stanton said.

"And there's nothing you can do? There's no cure, or . . ."

"No," Stanton said. "There's no cure."

Emily leaned back, crossed her arms, and looked at him.

"Well, I must say I feel sorry for whoever it is decides to marry you. You'll have her cooking all hours of the day and night." She paused. "It's not catching, is it?"

"It's a defect, not chicken pox." Stanton frowned. "Training as a Warlock aggravates it substantially. In most cases, the burned relinquish all aspirations to a magical career. If training is discontinued swiftly enough after the discovery of the defect, the opening of the *viae manticum* can be reversed, and the individual can return to his original state of health."

"But you continued your training," Emily said.

"Most mantic institutions refuse to train students who are burned, citing a mealymouthed concern with the ethics of it." Stanton lifted his chin proudly. "But Professor Mirabilis perceived profound advantages in having me attend the Institute. And so I did."

She shook her head. "But there other perfectly acceptable professions in the world. Why on earth did you go on with magic?"

He looked at her as if he could not fathom the source of such a question. "Because it was what I wanted to do," he said.

There was a long silence between them.

"Anyway, there's always Brother Scharfe's soup kitchens," Stanton said, raising an ironic eyebrow.

Emily picked up her cup of tea. She placed it on the table. Then she pushed the plate with the little almond cookie on it toward him.

"My pap has a word for men like you, Mr. Stanton," she said. "Mulish."

To her surprise, he smiled at her. To her even greater surprise, she realized that he had quite a nice smile.

"Let's hope that's the worst word your pap can ever apply to me." He took the cookie and ate it in one bite. "I'll go retrieve the horses. You wait here."

"Wait here?"

"For once, Miss Edwards, please do as I ask." He dusted almond crumbs from his hands. "It is safer for you here than on the streets. I doubt even the Maelstroms have the manpower to search every chophouse in San Francisco. Here. I want you to keep this while I'm gone." He pulled the Jefferson Chair ring from his finger and dropped it into her outstretched hand. "If we find ourselves separated, it will be useful."

"What would I do, pawn it?"

"You wouldn't get much. It's index metal—gold alloyed with iron. The iron comes from a special mine and contains a rare mineral called diabolite. The chemical makeup of each ring is unique. Anyone wearing a ring of index metal can be found by a simple magical search for the ring's particular alloy. If you keep it with you, I can always find you."

Emily looked at the ring, suddenly wary.

"What about Caul? Can he find us by searching for the ring?"

"Professor Mirabilis is the only man who knows the chemical signatures of all the Jefferson Chair rings," Stanton said. "If the Maelstroms are able to find us using that ring, then all hope really is lost."

"So this will help you find me if I go missing." Emily slid the ring onto her thumb. "But it hardly helps me if Caul spots you riding around San Francisco."

"If I'm not back in three hours, you'll have to find a way to get to New York on your own," Stanton said. "Get to the Institute and tell Professor Mirabilis everything."

"Get to New York? On my own?"

"You'd find some way," Stanton said. "You're very resourceful, and you've shown that you can be entirely ruthless if required."

When he was gone, Emily toyed nervously with the gold ring. Sliding it off her thumb, she examined it. A phrase in

Latin was inscribed on the inside of the band. *Ex fide fortis*. From faith, strength. She looked down at the cookie crumbs on the saucer. Stanton had to keep fed, at least until they got to New Bethel and got some money in their pockets. She reached up and felt the hair sticks, the smooth cold weight of them.

Ruthless. Yes, she thought, she could be ruthless.

She went to the man behind the counter.

"How far is Mason Street from here?" she asked.

Stanton returned to the chophouse two and a half hours later. An expression of alarm crossed his face when he didn't see her waiting for him, even though she was sitting in exactly the same spot. He looked around for a moment, rubbing his chin. She stepped forward and thrust her hand out to shake his.

"Good evening to you, sir," she said, in a lowish voice.

He blinked at her. She watched the wariness in his eyes transmute into horror, and knew that her disguise was completely successful.

"Miss Edwards?" he fairly choked on the words. "My God, what have you done to yourself?"

After Stanton had gone, Emily had ascertained that Mason Street was not a far walk, and she'd hurried down there, keeping to the shadows along the way. Mason Street was garishly lit and bustling, even at three in the morning, and Emily had no difficulty finding a buyer for her extraordinary hair. She had squeezed her eyes shut as the large scissors flashed over her ears, snicking cleanly through her thick braids. Afterward, the man offered her another sawbuck for her silver hair sticks and the amethyst earrings, but she declined. The hair she could grow back. The inheritances from her mother could not be replaced.

Her next stop was a small, untidy secondhand shop. After prolonged fingering of the material and exceedingly close scrutiny of Mrs. Lyman's handiwork, the pockmarked old rag merchant said he'd take her poplin dress in trade for a suit of men's clothing. Unfortunately, the only suit small enough to fit her was made of a screamingly loud plaid that mingled the colors of cherry red, peacock blue, and apple green in a way they had no business being mingled.

The rag merchant told her she could change in the back room, pointing to it with his thumb in a bored way as if women changed into men's suits in his back room every hour of the day. Perhaps they did; on her way back he handed her a folded length of wide white linen.

"You'll need this," he said.

She could not imagine why he thought she'd need the fabric until she discovered exactly how narrow the jacket was through the chest. Using the white linen to subdue her remaining female endowments wasn't easy or pleasant, but eventually she succeeded in molding her torso to fit the garment. When she came out of the back room, the rag merchant presented her with a pair of brown gloves in a brown felt hat.

She wedged the hair sticks securely up into the tall crown of the hat for safekeeping, then fitted the hat onto her head. Jauntily, she touched the brim to the man as she walked out into the cool night.

She felt exceptionally pleased with herself as she strolled back to the chophouse to wait for Stanton. Indeed, she felt quite manly and direct. *Ruthless,* that had been Stanton's word. She felt keen and ruthless. She felt like buying a cigar and smoking it with one thumb tucked under her suspender. Instead she tucked her hand into the jacket pocket and found, to her surprise, that the suit's previous owner had left a fine linen handkerchief there. She pulled it out, examined it. It was embroidered with the letter "M." For Mike probably.

Ruthless Mike, that's what they'd call her.

Now, however, standing in front of Stanton she felt somewhat less ruthless and somewhat more ridiculous. She reached into the pocket of her vest and pulled out a folded wad of greenbacks.

"Twenty dollars for the hair," she said. "That'll feed you to New Bethel, at least."

"Your . . . hair?"

"I'd appreciate a thank-you." She frowned at him. "You needn't look so shocked."

Stanton said nothing. His eyes were trying to negotiate a peace with the suit, with no apparent success. He gestured to it hesitantly.

"And this?"

"I couldn't ride in a dress," Emily said. "And you have to admit, it's a perfect disguise. The Maelstroms will be looking for a man and a woman, not a man and a—"

"Tablecloth?"

Emily crossed her arms and looked at him coldly.

"I know I'm hardly a plate of fashion," she said, "but one must be ruthless when exceptional odds are arrayed against one. You said it yourself."

Stanton took a deep breath, then let out a heavy sigh. He took the wad of greenbacks between thumb and forefinger as if they were soiled.

"At least they could have paid you in gold," he muttered. Then he fell silent, shaking his head. There was a look on his face, a look that was both sad and amused. It was a look that she didn't quite understand and didn't particularly like.

"What?" Emily snapped, uncrossing her arms.

He was silent for a long time before he spoke. Then he fished in his pocket and pulled out the ten-dollar coin she had given him. He pressed it into her hand.

"Your hair was very pretty," he said, finally.

CHAPTER TEN

Basket of Secrets

They wasted no time riding out. Dawn was approaching and they wanted to squeeze whatever advantage they could out of the cover of darkness. They did not, however, ride down to the ferry terminal at the end of Market Street. Instead they rode along Second Street until they reached the silent, jagged wharves. Full-bearded, heavy-bodied men arriving for their day's work regarded them curiously.

"One of the men at my stables has a brother who's a steve-dore on China Basin," Stanton explained in a low voice. "He has made arrangements for us to cross tonight on a freight barge."

They led the horses down an old, rickety-looking pier, where the aforementioned brother hailed Stanton, his sub-dued call sounding abrupt and out of place in the predawn silence.

They and the horses were loaded onto a flat black scow that brooded on the dark water. Grunting, monosyllabic men pointed them to a cargo hold, where Emily and Stanton were left to make themselves comfortable among piles of burlap bags and rough wooden crates. Romulus and Remus whuffed discontentedly, nosing at the sawdust that covered the floor.

"All right, I'm ready for an explanation," Emily said. "Somehow you managed to save my money, which means you didn't pay your stabler. But he was still willing to ask his brother to smuggle us aboard a barge?"

"Oh, I paid him," Stanton said. "You'll never guess what he wanted."

"What?"

"Apparently, there's a certain young lady who works in a shop up the street from his stables. He asked if I could fashion a charm that might help win her affections."

Emily squealed with sudden laughter, and despite the tightness of her linen bindings, it felt surprisingly good. "You mean he wanted you, Dreadnought Stanton, the great Warlock, to make him a love charm? So what did you do?"

"I braided together a straw poppet for him to give to her. I imbued it with some general powers of attraction. I was careful not to make it too strong."

Emily thought of Dag, and sobered abruptly. This unhappy turn of events meant that it would be weeks—at best—before she could return and remove the spell. And what if the worst happened? What if they were captured or waylaid or betrayed again? What if, by some horrible machination, she was never able to return to Lost Pine? Contemplating the sad fate this would mean for Dag, she came to an abrupt understanding of the sad fate it would mean for *her*. Coldness suffused her. What if the man . . . or men . . . who were after them were willing to *kill* to get the stone?

She swallowed hard, aware of an unpleasant lump in her throat. Stanton would help her. He'd protect her, and . . .

. . . and what if he gets hurt, or even killed? There's another man's fate on your conscience.

Three times what thou givest returns to thee.

She was hardly aware of her hand plucking at the frayed edge of some sacking, until she saw that it was trembling. Stanton must have noticed it, too, for he clapped her on the shoulder in a particularly manly way.

"Buck up, Elmer," he said. "Always darkest before the dawn."

Whether it got darker or not Emily could not confirm, for she drifted off into an uneasy sleep and when she woke, the sky over the misty wharves of Oakland was bruised purple and orange. After retrieving the horses, they rode about an hour into the little town of Walnut Creek, where they stopped to purchase supplies. To Emily's dismay, she found that her money bought less than she had hoped it would.

"If we ride hard, we can make it back to the Miwok settlement by nightfall," Stanton said, slicing himself a chunk of dry sausage to eat in the saddle. "I'm sure Komé will give us shelter and allow us to rest the horses."

Emily nodded. "And I have a few questions to ask her regarding acorns."

Emily was glad when they finally glimpsed the smoke from the Miwok camp. She wanted nothing more than a place to stretch out and sleep—the cramped dugout now seemed a paradise of luxury, and a bowl of stewed raccoon meat didn't sound half-bad either.

But as they dismounted and led their horses into the camp, her eager anticipation of food and rest was buried under a sense of gathering dread. Everything was different. There were no children or dogs playing now, no sounds of industry or amusement. A leaden pall seemed to have quenched every hearth fire. The air smelled of tears. No one greeted them; in fact, most stared with dark belligerence. The man in the black felt hat, the one who had cared for Stanton's horses, spat at Stanton's boots as he passed.

In front of Komé's longhouse, they found a large group of women clustered together, slumped. The women rocked, moaning softly; their heads were powdered with fine white ash.

They sat in a loose circle around a jumbled bed of mesquite tinder. On the unlit pyre was laid a small human form, bound tightly in deerskin.

Lawa knelt before the swaddled body, carefully arranging charms, chanting in a broken voice. Emily's legs trembled, and she had to catch herself against Romulus' side to keep from falling to her knees.

"Mother," she whispered, the word passing from her lips involuntarily.

Lawa's eyes jerked up, glittering.

"How dare you come back here, devil?" She fairly spat the last word.

"I am . . . I am sorry . . . we were . . . not knowing . . ." Stanton's stumbling grammar grated on Emily's ears. But Stanton was not speaking English. He was speaking Miwok.

"Komé is dead?" The words rolled from Emily's tongue in clear Miwok. Stanton blinked at her, but Lawa's lips twisted in a bitter mockery of amusement.

"Yes, you can speak now, can't you? Now that you have taken my mother's tongue."

"I . . . I didn't take anything," Emily said.

"You took her spirit," Lawa keened, her voice echoing. She wrapped her hand around the smooth wood of her mother's feather-tipped staff, pulled herself up its length. Thus supported, she was able to stand almost upright. "And a body cannot live long without a spirit."

"The acorn," Stanton muttered in English. "She must have done the same thing that Haälbeck did with his doors. Metempsychosis. Spirit transfer."

But Emily didn't need Stanton to tell her. The terrible truth of it was clear. She stepped forward, into the circle of mourners, coming to stand face-to-face with the girl.

"Why did she do it?" Emily had to force herself to stare into Lawa's eyes, to remain upright against the hatred in them. "Why didn't she tell me?"

"Ask her yourself," Lawa hissed, shooting out a hand and striking Emily a hard blow on the chest, where the acorn rested in the silken pouch. "She said nothing to me, her true daughter. She left me with nothing more than a body to burn."

"I'm sorry," Emily whispered.

A small, bitter smile twisted Lawa's lips.

"You will be sorrier, Basket of Secrets," she said, her voice exultant and despising. "Sorrier than you can possibly imagine."

Emily and Stanton did not speak for a long time after they rode out of the Miwok camp. They rode in silence as sunset gilded the flanks of the high, jagged Sierra and the waning half-smile of the moon crept slowly up the northern horizon. As night gathered, Stanton rode a little ahead, kindling a magical brand to light the way. She heard him whistling absently to himself.

After midnight they stopped in a sheltered copse well away from the main road. It was cold, and Emily sorely missed her buffalo coat. It wasn't safe to light a fire, so all she could do was wrap her arms around her knees and shiver.

"Here." Stanton dug into his saddlebag. He unscrewed the top from a small silver flask and handed it to her. Sniffing it, she discovered it contained whiskey.

"Strictly medicinal," Stanton said. "It will help keep the chill off."

Emily lifted the bottle to her lips and took a drink. It burned like hell going down, but it was a better class of spirit than she'd tasted before. It warmed her from the inside out and blunted the edge of her weariness.

"Not too much." Stanton took the flask from her when she went to raise it again. "Medicinal, remember?"

He tipped the flask to his own lips, then returned it to the saddlebag. Then, taking one of the horse blankets, he came to sit down next to her, his side pressing against hers. He wrapped the blanket around them both. She basked in his warmth, ignoring the fact that the horse blanket smelled, without a doubt, far worse than the buffalo coat ever had.

"Not exactly proper," he said. "But propriety won't do us much good if we freeze to death."

Emily suddenly remembered Mrs. Lyman's words about not drinking anything Stanton gave her. And Mrs. Lyman certainly wouldn't have approved of Emily cozying up under a horse blanket with him. Emily blushed at the thought. She was suddenly very aware of the feeling of his body against hers. It wasn't an unpleasant feeling. All in all, more pleasant than she would have expected. She put her arm through his and curled closer. Just to avoid freezing to death.

Stanton cleared his throat, but made no move to remove her arm from his. "Well. Let's review. You are in possession of an acorn into which a Miwok holy woman has transferred her spirit. You've also gained a complete mastery of the Miwok language, which almost certainly is not coincidental."

"Indeed, it is one useful little nut," Emily said. The whiskey and Stanton's warmth were already working in tandem, making her head heavy with sleep. Her hand drifted to the silk pouch around her neck, to touch the hardness of the acorn there. How could something as large as a soul be encompassed in such an infinitesimal place? "Do you really think that Komé's spirit is . . . here? With us?"

"I don't think Lawa was being metaphorical," Stanton said, after some consideration.

"But she was alive when we left," Emily said.

"Bodies and souls are surprisingly autonomous things," Stanton said. "Some men can live a long and healthy life without any soul at all."

Emily pondered this, then discarded it as not particularly pertinent.

"How long can she stay in there?" Emily said.

"The acorn is alive," Stanton said. "The tiniest spark of life, but life nonetheless. She can live as long as the acorn lives. A few months, a year perhaps. But the human spirit, especially the spirit of a powerful practitioner like Komé, is far too large to fit inside an acorn for long."

"And then what?"

"Then she dies," Stanton said.

"But couldn't she go to another acorn?" Emily asked. "Or into a flower or a tree or something?"

"She could," Stanton said, "but it is dangerous magic. Repeated metempsychosis results in terrible degradation, both intellectual and moral. The more times a spirit is transferred between vessels, the more of itself it loses."

Emily stared at him blankly. He rubbed a thoughtful thumb against his lower lip and tried again.

"Once a spirit is emancipated from the body to which it was originally bound, it loses much of its sense of . . . well, of responsibility, I suppose. The commonplace morals and ethics that guide us in our human lives become meaningless. In the most extreme cases, an emancipated spirit may lose all sense of right and wrong and become a Manipulator."

"A what?"

"A Manipulator is an emancipated spirit that transfers itself from body to body, heedless of the damage it causes to the vessels it inhabits. They are the worst kind of criminals. They are, thankfully, quite rare."

"So Komé is stuck in an acorn," Emily said, "because leaving it could cause her to lose her humanity?"

"Close enough," Stanton said.

Emily sighed. "Since we've dispensed with propriety for the moment, why don't you dig that whiskey back out?" If her head was going to be addled anyway, at least the addling could be of a more pleasant variety.

"I don't think we've dispensed with propriety quite that far." Stanton looked down at her. "Sleep will help more. And you might be able to do that more comfortably if you put your head on my shoulder."

Emily doubted the offer would be extended twice, so she laid her head on his shoulder and closed her eyes.

"Sangrimancers willing to kill us to get the stone," she said. "Indian holy women willing to die for it. I'm beginning to think, Mr. Stanton, that this stupid mineral is more important than either of us guessed."

"I believe you're right, Miss Edwards." Stanton leaned his head back against the tree and tilted his hat down over his brow. But he did not close his eyes, not until long after.

When Emily woke again, the first thing she was aware of was how cold she was. Her cheek was pillowed against the rough horse blanket. Stanton was sitting on a broad shelf of granite a little ways off.

He had put handfuls of grain into his hat and was watching Romulus and Remus nose each other aside trying to get at it. She had never imagined he could look so sad. She did not move, afraid of making the moment worse by intruding on it.

But then his gaze stole over to where she lay. When he saw that she was awake, his face hardened with familiar guard.

"Good morning," he said briskly. "Sleep well?"

"I dreamed about acorns and sangrimancers all night," Emily yawned, as if she'd just opened her eyes. She stretched her stiff muscles. "I rather wish you'd let me have the whiskey instead."

"Before we get on the road, I want to try something. I want to try to contact Komé." He paused. "We'll conduct a séance."

"We can't do a séance," Emily said. "The stone won't let us."

"A séance is very small magic, and we know that the stone is less likely to absorb small magic. Furthermore, Komé seems to have the ability to mitigate the stone's interference—after all, she sent you the vision about Caul and Mrs. Quincy. If we reach out, maybe she'll reach back."

Emily was silent. There were so many questions she wanted answers to, it was worth a try. Wiping her hands on the back of her trousers, she came to sit across from Stanton, who shifted to make space.

"I've never done a séance before," Emily said.

"And I don't suppose you've ever done any power work either . . ." He caught himself and softened his tone. "Have you?"

"I don't know," she said.

"Well, it's simple. Put your hands over mine, without touching." He extended his hands toward her palm-side up. Emily let her fingertips hover a few inches above his, felt the warmth radiating up from his skin. "The aim is to run the power in a circuit between your hands and mine."

"Oh, healing hands!" Emily said. "We used healing hands to knit broken bones and such."

Stanton nodded. "But instead of directing your will to knit a broken bone, concentrate on your memories of Komé . . . the way she looked, the way she moved. Concentrate on making her absolutely real in your mind."

"All right," Emily said. She remembered Komé's small plump body, her face like a dried apple, the tattoos on her chin, her luminous sparkling eyes.

A glow started around Stanton's fingers, and the stone in her hand tingled with warmth. And almost instantly, Emily could hear the Maien's cracking-old voice, chanting low and cadent.

Emotion washed over her. Flashing memories of Komé's life splashed on her skin like warm raindrops, each drop a moment of the woman's existence. Smoke and mud, laughing children, laboring women. Death and anger, happiness and despair. And love. Love for the broken child whose feet had been set on such a difficult path. Her daughter. Emily and Komé, each a reflection of the other—a daughter who had lost a mother, and a mother who had lost a daughter. Their sadnesses interlocked as precisely as two halves of a broken bowl.

Releasing a trembling thread of breath, closing her eyes, Emily surrendered herself to the washing sounds of distant song. Fingers of power threaded around her body, trickling over her skin. She felt as if she were floating, warm breezes from below buoying her up.

In the center of her mind Emily saw the form of the Maien, kneeling, radiant. The old woman had something in her arms, and she was wrestling with it. Sometimes it looked like a baby, sometimes like a wildcat. The Maien crooned to it soothingly, but still it struggled ferociously against her.

"Komé?" Emily whispered.

The Maien's head came up quickly, her eyes black as pitch. And Emily suddenly saw the thing she was holding. It was a huge ball of blackness, writhing and foul, bubbling and boiling and churning. It wanted to swallow her, Emily realized with horror. She could not hold it for long . . .

Emily shrieked, forced her eyes open, jerked her hands back. They stung as if they'd been dipped in acid. She pressed them flat against the cool granite. Stanton, too, shook his hands as if his fingers had been singed.

Breathing hard, Emily stared at him for a long, silent moment, before blurting: "What was that?"

"She was fighting with something, did you see? Something fierce. Something terrible."

"Is that the stone?" Emily said. "The consciousness of it?"

"I don't know. But it's dangerous, whatever it is. And she's protecting you against it."

Emily looked at her hand, at the stone glimmering in it. A chill chased down her spine.

"I always figured it was powerful," she said, "but I never thought it was dangerous."

"The two often go together," Stanton said.

There was a moment of silent contemplation, which Emily

broke with a sudden peal of laughter. Stanton's eyes focused on her with a spark of annoyance.

"What's so funny?"

"I've never heard you say the words 'I don't know' before." Emily cocked her head. "They suit you."

Stanton stood, brushing dirt from the knees of his trousers. "I think you'll find they lose their charm over time," he said.

CHAPTER ELEVEN

The Wages of Sin

They rode hard all day, the horses trudging back up the Sierra's steep flanks. They skirted Auburn, stopping only for a few hours' sleep in the darkest part of the night before pushing on toward Dutch Flat. When they reached it, they rode well around, the horses picking their way along a cow trail on the ridge above town. Suppertime smells drifted up from the houses below, making Emily's stomach rumble.

"I don't suppose we could sneak down for a hot meal?"

Stanton shook his head, though it was clear the suggestion was tempting.

"I'm sure the Maelstroms headed for Lost Pine the minute we gave them the slip. Dutch Flat is the closest train station to Lost Pine. We don't want to show our faces anywhere the Maelstroms might have been."

The settlement of New Bethel was about ten miles east of Dutch Flat, nestled in a wide, swampy valley between two high ridges that enfolded it like greedy arms. The town was perched on the edge of a dismal marsh that was tall with winter hay. Emily had never been to New Bethel, and her first impression was how odd it was that the town just seemed to . . . start. It had no outskirts. Other towns had seedy establishments crowding the edges—rowdy saloons, gambling dens with faded signs in Chinese, rickety buildings that could be counted on as whorehouses.

But in New Bethel, the first building on the main road was a tidy little bank, built of buff stone. Which led to Emily's second distinct impression of New Bethel: it was so strangely clean. Every building looked freshly painted. No litter on the street, no sloppy piles of firewood, no broken-down wagons in need of repair. Everything was neatly stacked, arranged, and organized. And it wasn't just disorder that seemed to be banished from the town. Ornamentation, decoration, superfluity of any kind was also completely absent. There were no milk pots planted with gardenias, no lace curtains at the windows. It was as though the town had been ordered from a catalogue and assembled by someone with a gun to his head.

The streets were dead still. This was, Emily supposed, not unusual in a small town at suppertime. But as they came around a bend, she was surprised to see a half dozen men chatting quietly outside a boxy white church. She knitted her brow. It wasn't Sunday, was it? She was under the impression that it was a Friday. She wondered how she could have lost track so quickly.

Stanton stopped at the general store to inquire after the gentleman he'd met outside Colfax. Emily waited outside, thumbs hitched in the pockets of her vest. There wasn't any traffic to watch, so when a man came driving an empty buckboard up the road, he was an object of scrutiny by default. The driver was stocky, with a particular hunched way of sitting that suggested both weariness and extreme physical power at the same time . . . dark tanned skin, cornsilk blond hair . . .

She put her hand over her mouth.

Dag!

Coming to New Bethel to purchase hay . . . on today of all days! She stepped back into the shadows of the overhanging porch, wondering where she could hide, but then remembered that he wouldn't recognize her anyway in her hideous man's suit. She pulled her hat down over her eyes and watched him from under the brim. He rode past her, up the main street to a feed store at the far end of town.

Quickly she ducked into the store where Stanton was speaking to the counterman.

"Elijah Furness?" the counterman was saying. "Why, sure." He pointed in the direction of the whitewashed church they'd passed. "Preparing for Friday evening service, I imagine."

"He never misses them?" Stanton said.

"Never misses 'em?" The man smiled slightly, and for some reason it struck Emily that it was probably one of the man's most riotous expressions of amusement. "Why, it would be a shame if he did, given he's the preacher and all."

Stanton thanked the man and went to the door. Emily followed him onto the porch.

Stanton looked down the street at the church, at the people gathered in front of it. His jaw rippled, and he sighed heavily.

"Did you see the church?" Stanton said, low. "More to the point, did you see the red cross on the church?"

Red cross? Emily wasn't entirely sure what Stanton meant, until it came back to her in a flash. The street preacher they'd seen in San Francisco, the one outside the soup kitchen . . .

"It's a *Scharfian* church?"

Stanton nodded grimly.

"Not just a Scharfian church, a whole Scharfian community. And the man who's offered to buy my horses is the town preacher."

"We have another problem," Emily said. "I saw Dag."

"Your lumberman?" Stanton's brow knit. "Where?"

"He was riding up to the feed store, probably to buy a load of hay for his teams." She paused. "Listen, let's not risk it. Let's take the horses and ride out of here. This all just feels . . . wrong."

"And go where?" Stanton said. "With what money? With what supplies?" He put his head closer to hers, spoke lower. "We need what Furness is offering to pay for train tickets to New York. We'd have to ride all the way back to Sacramento to get the price he said he'd pay, and that would give the Maelstroms time to catch up with us."

Emily chewed her lip, looked in the direction of the church.

"Well, he doesn't have to know you're a Warlock, right?" Emily said.

"Right," Stanton said. He took a deep breath and let it out. "You stay by the horses here. I want to get Furness as far away from his church as possible. Keep your hat down. And for God's sake, don't say anything. You're entirely unconvincing as a man."

Stepping down from the porch, he paused by the horses,

laying a silent hand on each glossy neck before striding across the dusty road to where the people stood before the white church. He hailed one of them. Emily leaned against the wall of the store and watched.

Stanton removed his hat and held it in his hands as he spoke to a white-bearded deacon. The deacon nodded and called inside the church. After a moment, the knife-faced man she remembered emerged, now in the clothes of a preacher: long black frock coat and a high white collar. A large red cross rested on his chest. Tucked under his arm was a massive Bible bound in black leather. The preacher looked at Stanton, and then toward the store, at the horses. He gestured a few of his parishioners to follow him.

"Been to Sacramento, eh?" Emily heard him saying as they approached. "I just saw you near Colfax a few days back. You were riding with a woman, I recall."

Emily pulled her hat down over her face, crossed her arms, cleared her throat gruffly.

"That was my sister. I was seeing her to Sacramento to visit friends," Stanton said. He didn't even look in Emily's direction; apparently he believed that if he ignored her entirely her presence would go unnoticed. "I'm afraid that my financial circumstances took a turn for the worse in that city."

"Gambling, I suppose." Taking the Bible out from under his arm, Furness handed it to one of his parishioners. The man took it with great reverence, laying a protective hand on the cover. "Maybe having to sell your nice horses will remind you what the book says about the wages of sin."

Stanton lowered his eyes soberly. "You may rest assured that it will."

Furness took a moment to run his hands over Remus' feet and ankles. Then he grabbed Romulus' bridle and jerked the horse's head over. He pressed his thumbs in the corner of the horse's mouth to look at the teeth.

"Well, they seem sound withal," Furness admitted. "Fine animals, to make it to San Francisco and back so quick-like."

Emily's heart thumped.

"You must have misheard me, sir," Stanton said. "We only went to Sacramento."

"Ah," Furness said. "I guess you're right, I guess I misheard you." He gave Stanton a dagger-slash grin. "They're fine horses in any case. Join us for evening service. You can come to supper after and I'll see to your payment."

"I am in a hurry," Stanton said. "I would like to make arrangements quickly."

"Is there a problem stepping inside a church, Mr. Stanton?"

Stanton said nothing, but Emily was certain he wouldn't have given the preacher his real name. She pushed her hat up slightly. The men that Furness had brought with them were pressing in closer, their hands flexing in preparation for violence. Emily's heart pounded harder.

"We had a lawman named Caul through here earlier today," Furness said. "He was handing out these."

He pulled a folded piece of paper from inside his coat and held it before Stanton's eyes. There were two pictures on it. Their own pictures, quickly and crudely rendered, above the words "Dead or Alive."

"Says here the man is a Warlock, a servant of Baal. And the other"—he looked up at Emily, and she suddenly felt the piercing sharpness of his eyes—"is a woman."

One of the men leapt onto the porch, strode to where Emily was standing. She flinched as he snatched the hat from her head. The hair sticks clattered to the ground. Indignantly, she bent to retrieve them, glaring up at the man.

"There's been a mistake." Stanton looked at the men closing in around him.

"Really?" Furness said. "Then I want to see you go into my church."

"What does that have to do with anything?" Emily said, her voice sounding too loud.

"The Lord will not suffer a sorcerer in his house," Furness looked up at her. "If he's no sorcerer, then he should have no difficulty coming to stand under the sight of God."

Emily took a step closer to Stanton. She spoke in an anxious whisper: "What are you waiting for? Go into the church!"

Stanton was silent for a long time, staring at Furness. His jaw was held tightly.

"I can't," he said, finally.

The instant the words left Stanton's mouth, the preacher's men swarmed over him. Emily lunged forward, trying to reach him, but a heavy hand fell on her shoulder and the man who had snatched her hat jerked her backward. She stumbled against the threshold of the porch, falling hard.

Hands spread, Stanton barked words in Latin to defend himself. But Furness' voice rose quickly to an apocalyptic level, drowning him with sound: *"Diviner, enchanter, witch, charmer, consulter with familiar spirits, wizard, necromancer! For all that do these things are an abomination unto the Lord: and because of these abominations the Lord thy God doth drive them out from before thee!"*

Tearing his Bible from the hands of the man he had given it to, Furness pressed it against Stanton's forehead and held it there. With an unearthly shriek, Stanton fell backward, clawing at his face.

"Stop it!" Emily screamed. She scrambled to her feet, but the man behind her clamped his arms around her waist. She kicked out as he pulled her up onto the porch. "Leave him alone!"

"The lawman told us he'd ensorcelled you." Furness looked up at her, his eyes lingering on her ugly man's suit and shorn hair.

"No one has ensorcelled me!" Emily hissed. "And Caul is a Warlock himself. A blood sorcerer, a murderer! You should have asked *him* to go into your church."

"Captain Caul walked into that very church this morning." Furness' sharp eyes cut through her. "He took his hat off in front of the tabernacle and delivered his warning to godly people. He is no sorcerer."

Caul could enter a church but Stanton could not? But there was no time to figure it out; the men had brought out ropes. They pulled Stanton's hands back roughly, lashed his wrists tight behind his back. His face was pale with pain.

"You don't have to do this," Stanton said. In answer, one of the men hit him hard across the face with a balled fist and shoved him down to kneel in the dust.

"Thou shalt not suffer a Witch to live." Furness looked down

at him. "In New Bethel, we take the word serious. We whip whores, we hang thieves, and we burn sorcerers."

Stanton moved his jaw in a slow circle, then spat a mouthful of blood at Furness' feet.

"Do you deny that you are a sorcerer?" Furness asked.

"I am a Warlock." Stanton lifted his chin, his voice ringing clear in the stillness. "And this is the United States of America. Being a Warlock is not a crime."

"Not yet, servant of Baal," Furness said. "But God is not mocked. He calls the elect to vanquish sin and false powers."

"I am no minion of Satan, nor a servant of Baal." Stanton looked at the faces of the men around him. "The powers that witchcraft and sorcery harness are natural powers, legal powers. They are not—"

"All power is given by the Lord!" Furness roared. Without taking his eyes off Stanton, he spoke sidelong to a pair of his followers:

"Get kindling and good heavy oak logs. Wood that burns slow." He paused, lips curving with anticipation. "We'll send the sinner off screaming."

At that moment, Emily caught sight of something coming down the road. A buckboard loaded with marsh hay. Dag was in the driver's seat, craning his neck to get a better look at the brouhaha in front of the store.

"Dag!" Emily shrieked. *"Dag!"*

The man behind her clamped a callused hand over her mouth. She writhed under his grip, but he just pulled her back harder, drawing her tight and close.

But Dag had heard her. He reached down to the floor of the buckboard, and when he straightened, he had a rifle in his hand. Lashing his leads secure, he climbed down, squinting in her direction.

"Emily?" he called. Emily screamed affirmatively from behind the man's hand.

Dag levered his rifle. Grudgingly, the man holding her let his hand drop from her mouth.

"It's me, Dag!" she cried.

Dag raised the rifle. "Let her go."

"Hansen, this is New Bethel business," Furness barked. "You got no call to interfere!"

"What are you going to do with him?" Dag nodded his head toward Stanton.

"He's a sorcerer," Furness said. "You know what we do to sorcerers."

"Good," Dag said. Then he stepped forward, took Emily's wrist, and pulled her toward him with a jerk. She stumbled into his arms, and he lifted her easily over his shoulder like a bag of grain. With long strides he carried her back to the buckboard, dumping her into the pile of fragrant marsh hay.

"Wait, Hansen! The law wants her. You can't just . . ."

"The law can take it up with me," Dag said. "She's a Lost Pine girl."

Brushing hay from her face, Emily sat up and planted her hands on the buckboard's gate. "No!" she screamed. "Dag, please . . . you can't let them. You can't let them kill him!"

A badly controlled flare of jealousy darkened Dag's face. "Why not?"

"He hasn't done anything wrong!"

Leaping over the buckboard's gate, she snatched the rifle from his hand before he could speak. Pointing it at the sky, she fired. The sound echoed. Then she turned the rifle toward the men surrounding Stanton.

"Get away from him," she snarled, levering another cartridge. She lifted the weapon, centering her aim right between Furness' astonished eyes.

Furness took one step back, his face pale. He lifted his hands.

"Ensorcelled," he said, softly. *"Be sober, be vigilant; because your adversary the devil, as a roaring lion, walketh about, seeking whom he may devour."*

"That's me, the roaring lion," Emily said. "Now get away from him."

Slowly, Furness and his men moved to comply. Keeping the rifle up, Emily went to Stanton and reached inside his coat, feeling for the misprision blade. When she found it, she snicked it open. It gleamed in the high afternoon sunlight. She cut the ropes that bound him and handed him the blade.

"Get the horses," she said. Her eyes dropped only for a moment, but it was long enough for one of the men to bring up a pistol in a swift blur of silver. There was a puff of smoke and a pop; a bullet sliced like a red-hot knife across her upper arm.

Pain seared her. Her arm fell slack, though somehow she managed to keep hold of the rifle stock. Dag roared and rushed forward, grabbed a handful of the gunman's shirt, threw him like a bundle of sticks. Other men piled onto him; he lashed out at them, fists and elbows flying.

Emily clutched her arm, hot blood leaking through her fingers. Jumping to his feet, Stanton looked into her eyes.

"Can you ride?" he might have asked, but Emily's heart was thundering in her ears and her head was spinning. Stanton threw Emily's good arm around his shoulder, and dragged her toward Dag's buckboard. He lifted her into the back, then took the rifle from Emily's slack hand. He then turned back to where Dag was still brawling with the Scharfians.

"Hansen!" Stanton yelled, indicating Emily with a curt jerk of his head. Dag threw one last punch before rushing back to the buckboard and Emily.

Stanton, however, was not finished. Sighting down the rifle's barrel, he stormed toward the men, teeth bared.

"Get away from my horses!"

The men scattered quickly, leaving Furness to glare at Stanton, his gaze fixed and dark. As Stanton unhitched Romulus and Remus, his aim did not waver from the preacher's heart.

"The righteous will prevail," Furness murmured, as Stanton swung up onto Remus' back.

Emily felt the buckboard rock as Dag jumped into the driver's seat and slapped the leads, his near-panicked horses leaping forward almost out of their harness. Behind them, Stanton and his Morgans galloped in a cloud of dust, and Emily, looking at the brilliant red blood on her hand, lay back in the wonderfully soft marsh hay and passed out.

"What the hell have you done to her?"

The words swirled through Emily's head, like a dream

fading in morning light. But unlike a dream fading in morning light, these words kept getting louder.

"I haven't done anything. The situation got out of hand . . ."

"The situation got out of hand? Damn you, Stanton! Her hair's gone, she's dressed like a man . . . and there are Army officers all over Lost Pine looking for her!"

Emily was still in the back of the buckboard, the smell of hay filling her nostrils. The air had grown cooler, and the sun was considerably lower in the sky than she remembered it. The wagon was not moving. The raised voices were coming from a little ways off.

"Army officers?" Stanton's voice. "How many? Who is leading them?"

"A detachment of about thirty men, led by Captain John Caul." Dag's voice. "What in God's name have you gotten Emily into?"

Emily's arm ached. She brought fingers up to touch it. A cloth had been tied around it, and not particularly skillfully.

"We have to get her away from here as quickly as possible," Stanton said.

"*We* aren't doing anything," Dag growled. "You've gotten her into enough trouble. What were you thinking, taking her to New Bethel? Everyone knows that's a Witch-burning town! They would have burned her along with you, if they knew what she was! And they would have figured it out the minute they saw that rock in her hand."

"I didn't know what New Bethel was, or I never would have taken her there." Stanton's voice was low. "I don't want to see her hurt any more than you do."

"You're a goddamned liar," Dag snarled. "If you cared two pins about what's best for Emily, you'd want to see her back safe in Lost Pine, where she belongs—"

"If she goes back to Lost Pine she's as good as dead," Stanton broke in angrily. "You saw the stone in her hand. That's what Caul wants, and he won't stop at killing to get it!"

Emily sat up carefully, hand on her head. She still felt dizzy. There was blood on the hay around her—her own blood. She looked around. Stanton's horses were hitched nearby, switching their tails nervously.

The men did not notice her. Dag was staring at Stanton, fists clenched.

"That's not what Captain Caul says," Dag said. "He says the stone is a valuable magical artifact. He says you're just using Emily to get it for yourself. For your institute. He says that you're the criminal, hindering a servant of the public good . . ."

Stanton snorted. "He's lying. I have no doubt he's excellent at it."

"Caul says she's just an innocent victim. He says *you're* the only one who's in trouble." Dag's voice lowered a dangerous octave. " 'Seducement to treason,' he called it . . ."

"Oh, for God's sake," Stanton barked. "Caul will say anything to get his hands on the stone!"

"And I guess you'll do anything to *keep* your hands on it!" Dag seized a handful of Stanton's shirt, giving him a bone-rattling shake. "Why the hell should I take your word over his? He's a sworn lawman, and you're just some shifty, stuck-up, no-account traveling Warlock!"

Stanton sighed through clenched teeth, raising his hands in a placating gesture. When he spoke again, his words were slow and careful, with a note of assumed patience that wasn't at all successful.

"Mr. Hansen, I know how you feel about her. You want her to be safe. But I swear to you, Caul means her harm. And you can't protect her against him."

"Yeah, not like the bang-up job you did protecting her against the Witch burners in New Bethel," Dag sneered, releasing Stanton's shirt and shoving him backward. " 'Case you already forgot, Warlock, she was the one had to rescue you."

Emily saw Stanton's face disarrange briefly, and then, just as quickly, set with steely composure.

"That was a mistake," he said.

"You only get one."

"Dag . . . Mr. Stanton . . ." Emily said. "Stop it."

When Dag saw that she was sitting up, his face softened with concern and he hurried to her side.

"Emily," he murmured. "You shouldn't be up. You're hurt!"

She smiled sadly at the worry in his face.

"I'll be all right," she said.

"Good," Stanton said, straightening the front of his shirt angrily. "Then perhaps *you* can explain things to Mr. Hansen in language simple enough for him to understand."

The derisive sneer in his voice made her blood boil. He was a veritable prodigy at finding new ways to be insufferable! She bared her teeth at him.

"You!" she barked. "Why didn't you use magic against them?"

Answering anger kindled in Stanton's face.

"Maybe you didn't notice, but I did try to use magic against them—"

"Then why didn't it work? They would . . . they would have burned you!"

"And they would have burned you, too." Stanton's voice dropped. "Your lumberman has already been good enough to remind me of that fact." Throwing up a hand, he stalked off in the direction of his horses.

Emily sunk back into the hay, feeling suddenly very tired. The horses at the front of the buckboard whuffled and shifted. Dag stared after Stanton, frowning.

"I wouldn't mind giving him another black eye, if you'd like."

"I don't think so," she said. "This isn't his fault."

"Then whose fault is it?" Dag shook his head. "What's happened to you, Emily? What have you got yourself mixed up with?"

"I don't know, Dag." Emily exhaled the words. "But Mr. Stanton is right. I can't go back to Lost Pine. That's why we were trying to sell his horses in New Bethel . . . to get money for railroad tickets. We have to get to New York."

"New York?" Dag said it as if she'd revealed they were planning a trip to the moon.

"We have to go, Dag."

"Why?" Dag's eyes were hard, and he eyed the ring on her thumb, the one Stanton had given her back at the chophouse. She was fingering it absently. She noticed his gaze.

"It's nothing like that." She buried the hand under the hem

of her suit jacket quickly. "New York is where the Mirabilis Institute of the Credomantic Arts is. There is a man there, Professor Mirabilis, who can help me."

"Help you with this?" Dag took her right hand gently. For such a large man, his touch was surprisingly gentle. He looked at the faintly glowing stone that winked from her palm, mute and mysterious.

"Yes," Emily murmured.

Dag nodded silently.

"After you left, I went around to see your Pap a few times. I was so darn mad, I wanted to know why you'd gone . . ." Dag's face was quizzical, as if he were trying to remember an elusive dream. "He gave me things to drink. They made my head clear up a little. He told me something about the stone . . . told me that you and Stanton just went to have it looked at . . ." Dag paused. "I wanted to believe him, Emily."

"It's true," Emily said. "I only went to San Francisco with Mr. Stanton because the Mirabilis Institute has an extension office there. That's where Caul found us. He wants the stone, Dag. I think he'll do anything to get it."

"Caul does seem a pretty hard type." Dag's frown deepened. "His men have been poking around the Old China Mine. They shoot at anyone who comes near, no questions asked. But that's not the worst. Besim's disappeared. Folks swear they last saw him talking to Caul." He looked at Emily. "Caul's been asking about Pap, too."

Emily's whole body went cold. "Oh, Dag, no . . ."

"He's safe." Dag smoothed a hand over her arm. "Caul doesn't know where he is. I've got him hid in one of the timber camp buildings, and a dozen of my men with him. I won't stand for bullies harassing honest folk."

Emily said nothing, but her heart swelled with gratitude. She repressed the urge to hug him, for she knew it would only mean the wrong thing.

"Thank you, Dag." Tightness in her throat made her words small. "Thank you so much."

Dag was silent, chewing things over. When he spoke again, it was a petulant outburst.

"But why do you have to go to New York? Why couldn't they help you in San Francisco?"

"The professor who ran the San Francisco office was the one who double-crossed us," Emily said. Dag's nostrils flared.

"And so you're going to New York so they can double-cross you there?"

"Mr. Stanton has a lot of trust in Professor Mirabilis," Emily said.

"And you have a lot of trust in Mr. Stanton." Dag's voice was flat and strained.

"He has shown himself a decent and trustworthy individual," Emily said.

"Have you slept with him?"

Emily was so shocked that she jerked back, knocking her head against one of the high walls of the buckboard. She felt her face blazing red as she rubbed the smart.

"Dag!" she said, furiously. A wide smile broke over his face.

"I've got my answer." His voice was suddenly hopeful. "So it's true? There's really nothing between him and you? I've seen how he looks at you."

"What are you talking about?" Emily snapped, her cheeks flaming afresh. "He most certainly does not look at me."

Dag shrugged, scratching his jaw thoughtfully.

"When you ran off with him, I thought for sure . . ." He paused, checking himself. New hope glinted in his eyes. "But if I could believe . . . if I could believe that you were telling the truth, then maybe things could turn out all right after all."

Emily shook her head.

"Don't say it, Dag," she murmured, but he took both her hands in his.

"Why not?" he said. "I'll go with you to New York. I'll get you to this Mirabilis Institute place. We can be married and you can travel like an honest woman. And then, after this is all taken care of, we can come back home and put it all behind us."

Emily felt self-loathing soak through her.

"Dag . . . I have to tell you something. Remember when Besim did his Cassandra, and said that I was doing bad magic?

You thought it was bunk, but it wasn't. I *was* doing bad magic. The baddest magic I've ever done."

"What are you talking about?"

"I hexed you," Emily said miserably. "Put a love spell on you."

Dag stared at her for a moment. Behind his eyes, contemplation chased understanding.

"Did you do it . . . because you were in love with me?"

No, I just thought you'd make a good husband.

Emily couldn't bring herself to say the words, even though they were the truth.

"It was the most selfish thing I've ever done," she whispered. "The most selfish and thoughtless and . . ." She paused, taking a deep breath, trying to make the words come out right. "When I saw how bad it hit you, I was going to undo it right away. Honest. But the stone . . . I can't do magic with it in my hand, you see. So I went to San Francisco. I wanted to get the stone out so I could come back and take the spell off you."

Dag smiled sadly as he brushed a tear from her face.

"Probably wouldn't do any good," he said. "I've loved you for an awful long time, Emily. I can't remember when I didn't. You didn't need any love spell."

Emily stared at him. Was he telling the truth, or was it just his memory tainted by the spell? To her dismay, she saw that he was telling the truth. She saw it in the deepest part of his eyes. She'd cast a love spell on someone who was already in love. So that was why it had gone so wrong. She hadn't made one bad mistake, she'd made two.

"Dag, why didn't you ever tell me?"

"Every time I got up the courage, there was something else to do, something else to build. I wanted to be more, to be worth more." He shook his head. "I knew that if you loved me, we could have nothing and it would be enough. But I knew that if you didn't . . . well, I'd have to offer you the whole world. I guess I wasted too much time trying to cover both bets."

They sat in silence for a while.

"Could you . . ." Dag paused. "Could you be in love with me?"

Emily let out a long breath.

"I wouldn't have put the spell on you if I didn't think I could."

"I love you, Emily Edwards. I want you for my wife. Marry me and let me help you. I'll make everything better for you. I'll take care of everything. I promise."

Emily remembered the robin sitting on the windowsill. The omen of true love. Perhaps this was what it had meant all along. Right now, she felt very much as if she could love Dag Hansen. He was strong and safe and solid, and his promises of salvation were sweet as fresh honey. She could vanish into his arms and let him protect her from the world that was so much meaner and more complicated than she had ever imagined it. The thought of finding a place to hide from Witch burners and blood thieves, Warlocks and dead holy women suddenly had great appeal. Dag had plenty of money. He could pay for first-class tickets to New York and back. Besides, what kind of future did she have to look forward to without him? Even if she and Stanton did find a way to New York, and even if Professor Mirabilis was able to get the stone out of her hand, then what? Could she ever return to Lost Pine? And if not Lost Pine, where could she go?

But even as she thought these things, she knew the answer she had to give. Marrying Dag because she was afraid was as selfish as marrying him for his money. It was cowardly and unfair and cruel. She did not love him. Not the way he wanted her to, not the way he deserved to be loved. And even though she wished that Stanton hadn't said it, she knew that he was right. Dag could not protect her against Caul. Worse, she'd be plunging him into terrible danger right along with them. She bit her lip. She'd made two bad mistakes already. She would not make a third.

"I'm sorry, Dag."

"Why should you go into danger and not me?" Dag blazed. "Why should you risk your life alone?"

"I'm not alone."

"That's right, you have Stanton to help you. You'll let him help you, but not me?"

"It's Warlocks we face," Emily said. "He's a Warlock."

Dag was silent for a long, long time. His eyes scanned every inch of her face.

"Yeah, he's a Warlock. A great and powerful Warlock." Dag spat the words with disgust. "I'll take your kind of magic over the magic of Warlocks any day. Nice, homey magic. Fixing scraped knees and stuffing charm pouches and painting hexes. It was . . . nice. People didn't get hurt by it."

No one except you, Emily thought. *And now Besim, and maybe Pap . . . and all of Lost Pine . . .*

And in that instant, Emily realized that no matter what she did to mitigate her mistake, she could never repair all the damage it had caused. Perhaps she could return to Lost Pine someday . . . but she could never return to the place that she'd left.

"I'm sorry, Dag," she said. "I'm so sorry. For everything."

"Yeah," Dag said. "Me, too." He drew in a breath, let it out. Then he squared his shoulders, made a decisive gesture.

"Well then," he said. "You have to get to New York. So I'm going to get you to New York, even if it means I have to put you on a train with *that*." He gestured in the direction Stanton had gone. "I'll buy his horses. That'll give you the money you need for the train tickets."

Emily blinked at him.

"You'd do that?"

"It's just money," Dag said.

"Honor bright?"

"Honor bright." He smiled at the old words; when they were children, those were the words they had used to indicate absolute unquestionable truth. Then he took her in his arms and held her close, his nose buried in her hair. She clung to him tightly, closing her eyes. Just the feeling of being held by another human being was reassuring. She hadn't realized how much she craved it. After a long time like this, he let her go.

"I'll run the team back to Lost Pine and get cash-money out of the office safe. You and Stanton get up to Cutter's Rise. I'll meet you before the train gets there at half past ten."

He looked as if he was going to say something else, but he closed his mouth.

"Go on, now," he said. "There isn't much time."

*   *   *

Emily heard Stanton before she saw him. He was whistling something that managed to sound spry and despondent at the same time. She found him sitting on a rocky outcropping overlooking a deep valley that was colored golden with the rays of the sinking sun. He had his legs drawn up to his chest, his arms resting straight out over them. His long fingers were tearing apart a pinecone in a way that seemed to indicate a personal grudge against conifers.

Emily didn't go to him immediately. Instead she wandered around, gathering a handful of new green herbs. Popping the leaves into her mouth, she chewed them. Then she sat down next to Stanton, took one of his hands, and looked at the ugly rope burns on his wrist. Spitting the masticated herbs into her palm, she smeared them onto the raw scrapes.

"Ugh!" Stanton tried to jerk his hand away, but she held his wrist tight. "What are you doing?"

"Don't move," Emily said. She fished around in her pocket until she found Ruthless Mike's handkerchief. She tore it down the middle, then bandaged each of Stanton's wrists with the herbs and linen.

"You're the one who got shot." He looked at her blood-soaked sleeve.

Emily shrugged, unwrapping the dirty, badly tied bandage from around her arm. She looked critically at the wound. The bullet had raked the flesh deep, but it had long since stopped bleeding.

"It'll leave a right pretty scar," she said.

"Scars aren't pretty," he said.

Emily plastered the last of the chewed herbs onto the wound. She pressed clean dry moss over it and bound it all up with the last of the linen from the handkerchief. So much for Ruthless Mike.

"They could have killed you," Stanton said.

"But they didn't." Emily paused, stretching her legs in front of her. "Dag is gone."

Stanton's eyes flashed.

"You let him go?" he said. A silence. "I don't think that was a good idea."

"He's going to ride to Lost Pine. He's going to get money. He's going to buy the Morgans."

"Then shoot them for spite, I suppose."

"No," Emily said. "I explained everything to him. He understands that I have to go to New York. He's going to help."

Stanton looked at her. Emily wondered if this was one of the looks Dag had been referring to; if so, it didn't seem much different from the look one would give to an unimaginably simple child.

"You have a good heart, Miss Edwards," Stanton said softly. "He's not going back to get money to buy my horses. He's going back to find Captain Caul."

Emily shook her head violently. "He won't! I know he won't!"

"He loves you. He won't let you go. He doesn't understand what Caul is. He thinks he can bargain with him." Stanton was silent for a moment. "I've known men like that. They believe they can do anything."

"Dag's not like that," Emily said hotly. "He gave me his word, honor bright."

"That doesn't matter. You're not a man. You've never been in love. You don't understand."

"And you do?" Emily snapped.

Stanton said nothing, only gazed out over the rapidly darkening valley below. When he finally spoke, the words were bitten short.

"We need to do something that Caul doesn't expect. We'll ride south, to Stockton. I can get a good price for the horses there . . ."

"Dag will give us the money," Emily said. "Mr. Stanton, I've known Dag all my life. He's a good, honest man, Witched or not. If he makes a promise, he'll live by it. He will live by it if it kills him."

"If he does, it just might," Stanton muttered. His fingers resumed their methodical torment of the pinecone. "I should have known about New Bethel. The fact that I didn't . . ." he trailed off, shaking his head.

"Why couldn't you fight them?"

Stanton sighed.

"Too many of them, and not enough of me."

"You told me credomancy was the magic of faith," Emily said. "You never mentioned being in league with Satan."

"I am not currently in league with Satan, Baal, or any dark power in particular," Stanton said. "But the men in New Bethel believed that I was. They believed that I was damned, and that belief was focused and channeled through Brother Furness. I couldn't fight it. I'm not enough of a credomancer."

"So because Brother Furness believed you were damned, because he believed that you could not walk into a church, because he believed that the Bible would cripple you . . ."

"The power of his belief overcame my power to answer." Stanton tossed away the pinecone's now-denuded core. He flexed his fingers as if he longed for something else to take apart.

"What would have happened if you'd gone into his church?"

"If I had gone into his church, with those men despising me as a Warlock, I would have suffered the agonies of the damned they believed I should suffer. There are several gory descriptions of divine retribution in the Bible."

Emily shook her head. "So . . . really, even though they despise Warlocks, they're just like credomancers themselves, aren't they? Of a sort?"

Stanton looked at her and nodded with appreciation. "Precisely," he said.

"But what about Caul? Furness said he went into the church—"

"They didn't know what Caul was, and he was smart enough to make sure they didn't." Stanton was bitter. "But it is a great irony, isn't it? If the Scharfians are going to burn anyone, sangrimancers would be an excellent place to start. I wouldn't mind piling some tinder around Caul's feet myself." He snapped his fingers, muttered the familiar word, stared into the heart of the tiny flame that danced over his thumb.

Emily reached out, wrapped her hand around his, smothering the tiny flame.

"Never mind," she said firmly. "All's well that ends well."

He looked at her hand over his. Then his green eyes went to hers and held them. She flushed. So *this* was the look Dag had been talking about. Stanton put his other hand over hers, drew her toward him.

"Miss Edwards," he began softly. But then he fell silent. He took a deep breath. He gave her hand a very brotherly pat. "You have the makings of an excellent credomancer."

Climbing quickly to his feet, he brushed pine needles from his trousers. "Now, I take it you insist on this suicidal exercise with your lumberman?"

Emily felt slightly dizzy, and strangely cross. "He's not my lumberman," she snapped. "But if you're asking if I trust him—yes. I know he won't double-cross us. I'm certain of it."

"Let's just hope that's enough," Stanton said.

CHAPTER TWELVE

Hemacolludinatious

A few hours later, Emily was sitting high up in a fir tree, trying to keep quiet, and wondering for the hundredth time what Stanton was doing.

Cutter's Rise was little more than a wide flat spot where the dense pines had been hewn down, leaving thin churned earth salted with granite dust and covered with slick needles. It was not a passenger stop, but rather what the train men called a "jerkwater," where the engine could take on water from the tall tower before tackling the big climb just up the tracks.

The sun had set and heavy blue darkness had descended over the mountains, bringing with it the cold sounds of night. Train tracks stretched out in both directions, disappearing between the enfolding pines. Above them, the high passes of the Sierra loomed; from far below came the distant sound of a train whistle, thin and piercing.

It must be down in Gold Run right now. Emily listened hard to the lonely sound. *About a half hour out.*

She hoped Dag would hurry.

She looked back down at Stanton, who was making all sorts of strange and arcane preparations against what he believed was the eventuality of Dag's betrayal. In the middle of the clearing, in the light of a half dozen magically glowing brands, he was laying out tree branches in a large triangle.

"I thought you were a credomancer," she called down to him. "What are you doing pushing branches around?"

"I'm engineering a Trine," he said. "And you're supposed to

be hiding. Be quiet, and keep listening for Komé. She warned us before."

Emily fished the acorn out of her pouch and closed her fist around it, listening hard for the Maien's chanting. She didn't hear anything. In fact, the only thing that popped into her mind was the word "hemacolludinatious," a word that she didn't recognize but that seemed strangely familiar. She amused herself with trying to figure out what it might mean while she watched Stanton.

When he finished laying out branches in a triangle, he went to each side, speaking words over them in low rhythmic Latin. Then he sat in the center of the triangle, crossing his long legs and closing his eyes. He did not move, but sat still and silent, waiting. He looked as if he could sit there for a very long time. Emily wiggled, tried to get more comfortable.

"Mr. Stanton, can't it be argued that you're making it more likely that Dag will turn us over to Caul by *believing* he will?"

In the flickering light of one of the pine brands, she saw Stanton open one eye and look up at her.

"Now you're just splitting hairs." He closed his eyes again with a definitiveness that bespoke a resolve not to speak further. Apparently, however, holding his pedantic nature in check was too great a strain. He opened both eyes and looked up in her direction. "Credomancy is the conscious manipulation of the dynamic unfolding of reality through targeted and focused belief. It is a metaphysical system of great power. But it is not to be confused with trying to make unpleasant facts go away by believing them to be untrue. That's simply a childish denial of reality."

"And you think reality demands that Dag try to hand us over to Caul?" Emily bristled. "I don't think that's reality talking. I think that's you thinking you know something about someone who you really don't know anything about at all!"

"I hope you're right," Stanton said. He closed his eyes again, assumed an air of grave composure. "Now be quiet, Miss Edwards."

Emily leaned back against the tree trunk. The more Stanton told her about credomancy the more questions she itched to ask. How exactly could a credomancer use belief to manipulate reality when reality itself was so subjective? When everyone saw the same things so differently? When Dag looked at her, he saw a hometown Witch, an old friend—and recently, a bewildering heartbreaker. When Stanton looked at her he saw . . . well, perhaps it was better not to imagine what Stanton saw. So which was the truth? Which was reality? Which belief would prevail?

Give me good old-fashioned magic anytime, she thought. *I just have to know what plants to pick.*

The sound of a train whistle came again, closer this time. Emily was starting to really worry that Dag wasn't going to make it in time when the big man rode hell-for-leather into the clearing. He was atop one of the roans that had been hitched to the buckboard, and the poor animal shone from its extended effort.

Dag slid down from the saddle and looked at Stanton, still sitting in the middle of the triangle of pine branches. Dag looked around the clearing, breathing hard.

"Where's Emily?"

"She's safe." Stanton rose to his feet. Dag approached the triangle and tried to step across the border of branches. He was rebuffed by a force that glittered faintly as he struck it. Confusion swept over his face. He tried again, sticking a hand toward the barrier, hitting it with his fist; he pulled his hand back, rubbing the knuckles.

"What the hell is this, Warlock? Where's Emily?"

"I told you, she's safe," Stanton said. "Are you alone?"

"Of course I'm alone," Dag said. "I gave Emily my word, honor bright."

Stanton nodded. "All right." He took a step back. "You may enter."

Dag reached a tentative hand out toward the barrier, and this time there was no impediment. He stepped into the triangle, looking around.

"Did you bring the money?" Stanton asked curtly.

Dag pulled a purse of coins from his pocket. Stanton weighed it in his hand before tucking it away. Then he gestured toward the Morgans, which stood hitched under a tree a few feet away.

"You may take the horses and go," Stanton said.

"Just like that?" Dag's voice was high with outrage. "I wanted . . . goddamn it, I want to see Emily!"

"I've already made one mistake today," Stanton said. "And as you pointed out, one is all I get."

"She's in no danger from me, or from Caul, for that matter," Dag growled. "Caul's gone."

"What?"

"When I got back to Lost Pine, I found Caul and his men. Told them that there'd been trouble in New Bethel, that you were both still down there. They all tore off after you, Caul included. There's no way he can get back here before the train comes. Emily's safe."

Stanton looked at him and said nothing. Fury kindled on Dag's face.

"Damn you, Stanton . . . I want to see her!"

"I'm here, Dag," Emily called down to him. She had heard the honesty in Dag's voice. She knew in her bones that he was telling the truth, and maybe the force of her belief would overcome the force of Stanton's distrust.

She clambered down from the tree and ran to the edge of the clearing, just in range of the light from the pine branches. She didn't want the stone in her hand to disturb Stanton's carefully constructed Trine.

Stanton made a noise of protest, but Dag rushed over to Emily. He took her hands, looked at her face.

"You sure this is what you want?"

"It's not what I want," Emily said, "but it's what I have to do."

The sound of a train whistle coming closer made them both look down the tracks.

"Thank you, Dag," Emily said. "Thank you for watching Pap, and not telling Caul—"

"Maybe you don't want to thank him just yet."

The voice came from behind them, from down the tracks, beyond the perimeter of light cast by Stanton's glowing brands. Then there was the sound of horse's hooves crunching on the gravel beside the tracks. As the rider came into the circle of light, Emily's heart thudded behind her ribs, twice. Hard.

It was Caul.

He sat straight-backed on a horse that seemed too small for his bulk. He wore a long canvas riding coat, dark with wear, and a battered felt hat with frayed tassels and tarnished sabers. His white-streaked muttonchop whiskers gleamed in the werelight cast by Stanton's torches.

Dag stared at Caul. Confusion lined his brow. He took one step back. "No," he said. "You were supposed to go to New Bethel. That's what I told you." Dag looked at Emily, his eyes wild with anguish. "Em, I swear to you . . . I swear I didn't—"

"Sure you didn't," Stanton growled, not taking his eyes off Caul's hulking form.

"He didn't have to." Caul's voice was as strange as Emily remembered it: flat and uninflected. The big man slid down from the saddle, his weight threatening to drag the animal down sideways. He stood before Stanton briefly, regarding him with contempt. He flicked a fingernail against the magical barrier and was answered by a light recursive ringing, like the chime of a thousand small bells.

"A Trine. Delusion made physically manifest." He stared at Stanton with fish-dead eyes, gesturing vaguely at the tinkling echo as it faded into the night air. "What a waste. To throw away the rest of your life pulling rabbits out of a charlatan's hat. When you could have been and done so much more."

"Don't speak of my life as if you know anything about it." Stanton's voice was even and calm, as measured and emotionless as Caul's.

"I know more about it than you imagine," Caul said. "I know you could have served your country well, Stanton—if you hadn't squandered every opportunity that was presented to you."

"I have squandered nothing," Stanton said. "And I have seized every opportunity my conscience allowed."

"Conscience." Caul's mouth curved without humor. "Not

the word I'd use, though it does begin with the same letter."
Then he turned his eyes toward Dag and Emily. Quickly, Dag
pushed Emily behind himself, putting his body between her
and Caul.

"I've had better men than you try to throw me, Hansen,"
Caul said. He walked toward them slowly, his feet crunching
in the gravel. "I heard what happened in New Bethel long before you told me. I heard that you helped these two escape. And
I knew about the love charm Miss Edwards put on you—Besim
gave me an extended and detailed accounting before he died.
You wouldn't have come to tell me about New Bethel unless
you were trying to send me off in the wrong direction."

Dag looked desolate. His broad shoulders slumped with
guilt. Emily longed to reassure him, but she knew enough
about guilt to know that it wasn't that easy to dispel. She glared
at Caul. She had never hated anyone before, but suddenly she
felt its bitter blackness like a fist clenched around her heart.

"The stone in your hand is required for the public good."
Caul stared into her eyes as he walked toward her, seeming to
savor her hatred. "Surrender it now, Miss Edwards."

"And exactly how am I supposed to do that?" Emily flared,
lifting her hand challengingly and wiggling her fingers.

Caul pulled a long silver knife from his belt as he walked
toward her. It gleamed in the flickering light.

"During the war, I served General Grant as a battlefield surgeon. Sometimes he would visit the hospital tent. He would
try to comfort weak men with the idea that it would hurt less
if they didn't struggle." Caul continued to walk toward her
slowly, step by step. "As a good soldier, I let him believe it.
You can believe it, too, if you like."

"Stop."

Stanton's voice echoed through the forest, ringing off the
high slopes above. The booming, resonant force of it made
Caul freeze, his heavy booted foot halting in midair.

"Miss Edwards is not going to have her hand cut off,"
Stanton said.

Caul cocked his head, looking around himself. He struggled to move his leg, as if trying to pull his foot from deep
within sticky mud.

"Is this your best, Stanton?" he said. "I suppose I could hardly expect more, after New Bethel—"

"New Bethel was a miscalculation," Stanton said.

"A classically trained credomancer, a graduate of the prestigious Mirabilis Institute, without sufficient power to prevail over a handful of backwater Bible thumpers?" Caul shook his head. "That's not a miscalculation, that's a rout. The faith Mirabilis has invested in you must be pretty small indeed."

"Sophos Mirabilis," Stanton said, emphasizing each word, "is a fine man. His power is great, and I am his strong right arm."

Caul's lips pursed with distaste. "Such nauseating language you have to use. How can you live this way? How can you be satisfied with such mean scraps of power, so grudgingly bestowed from such unworthy men?" Caul jerked his foot hard, took another step forward. "Men who have no faith in you. Men who have no wish to see you succeed. Men, indeed, who wish to see you *fail*."

"Nonsense," Stanton said.

"Your placement in Lost Pine was a calculated humiliation. You can't deny that. Why does Mirabilis want to undercut your power, Stanton? Why does he want to make you a failure?"

"I know exactly who's trying to undercut me, sangrimancer," Stanton said with a contemptuous half-smile. "You'll hardly send me crying with a squink or two."

"Maybe not," Caul said. "But sangrimancers—men who practice *real* magic—have better weapons than squinks and Trines."

He moved quickly, his hand going to his throat and the two-chambered pendant that rested there. In one smooth movement he brought the alembic up and stretched the hand toward Emily, simultaneously speaking words that were dark, low, guttural. His hand was wreathed in brilliant shifting light, but he did not throw the magic; he just kept speaking, the power dancing around his fingertips growing brighter and brighter.

Emily's right hand shot up as if grabbed. She tried to set her feet, scramble for purchase on the slippery fir needles, but it was no use—she was pulled inexorably toward Caul and the magic gathering around his fist. Dag grabbed her, tried to hold her back, but Caul just spoke louder, and more quickly, and Dag was dragged along with her, skidding toward the chanting sangrimancer. When Emily was within Caul's reach, he shot up his other hand to grab her throat, his fingers nearly circling it. The magic that had drawn her to him evaporated into the stone with a loud pop; nausea billowed through her, mingling with pain and asphyxiation.

Dag threw himself at Caul, but Caul sidestepped, slamming a heavy elbow into Dag's back as the lumberman stumbled past. Before Dag even hit the ground, Caul kicked him square in the gut, hard. Dag crumpled, groaning.

Then Emily could see nothing but Caul's face as his huge hand squeezed more tightly around her throat. But she could hear Stanton's voice, booming cadent Latin. And she felt sudden little impacts coming from all around them. Little stones were whizzing through the air. Pebbles, cobbles, handsize rocks, sharp little chips of granite—all were flying with tremendous force right at Caul's head. The big sangrimancer winced, ducking, but the projectiles were battering him with the viciousness of a bee-swarm.

"Sometimes smaller weapons serve better," Stanton said, each word keen as the edge of a knife.

The stone was attracted to vast concentrations of power, like the one Caul had summoned, but less powerful spells—like the séance, or Stanton's ever-ready fingersnap flames—could still work if she was far enough away . . .

The storm of small missiles pelted Caul mercilessly, peppering his face and arms, leaving bloody cuts and welting bruises. Thrusting Emily roughly to the ground, he seized his alembic and stormed toward Stanton.

With a roar, he threw his body against the protective magic of Stanton's Trine. The alembic glowed in his hand as he slammed his shoulder against the Trine's magic again and again, as if he was trying to break down a heavy door.

Finally, drawing a deep breath, Caul gave a rumbling bellow from the deepest part of his gut—a roar that saturated the air with fury and hatred and terror. The sound echoed in the darkness, not fading but rather growing louder and more horrible. As it did, Emily saw the little projectiles fall away, dropping dead and still on the ground. Then, with a rush of massive power, Caul crashed against Stanton's Trine a final time.

With a screaming sound of shearing metal, the invisible walls broke, shattering in a shower of glittering gold. Stanton staggered, his long legs almost buckling beneath him. Pain contorted his features, but he managed to raise trembling hands in a posture of defense.

"Run," he whispered, so softly that Emily was surprised she could hear him. "Emily, *run*!"

Caul charged, brushing aside Stanton's defense and throwing him to the ground. Pinning him with one knee, Caul pressed the alembic hard against Stanton's chest, hissing guttural words of cursing. Stanton screamed, convulsing horribly as Caul's foul power tangled around him like red-hot wires.

Caul was going to kill him.

With a wild cry, Emily threw herself at Caul, leaping onto his back, scrabbling over his shoulder to grab the hand that held the alembic. When she finally got it, she pressed the stone in her palm against his monstrous fist. She felt the hugeness of the magic at his command, felt the stone struggling to absorb it. Her stomach roiled; the world spun. A piercing wave of fresh nausea knifed through her belly.

Caul lurched to his feet, leaving Stanton splayed like a blown-down scarecrow. Emily clung desperately as Caul wheeled, trying to throw her off. Finally, he got hold of her shoulder, and with a grunting heave, he sent her flying. She slammed into the ground hard, the breath punched from her body. The world spun in blackness, and when she could see again she saw that Caul was standing over her, his eyes calm and still.

"You troublesome *skycladdische* bitch," he said softly. He reached to his belt, pulled out the long silver knife. She stared up at him, unable to move.

Caul reached down. He bunched the collar of her shirt and jerked her upward. There was the sound of ripping fabric as her shirt tore away, leaving her throat exposed. The knife flashed down. Caul was going to kill *her*, she realized suddenly. Everything moved terribly slowly after she realized that.

And then, for no good reason, she opened her mouth and said the word "hemacolludinatious."

Caul's hand, in which the knife gleamed, slowed down even as the rest of the world sped up. Finally Caul stopped moving entirely and stood frozen, his knife trembling inches from her throat. He stared at her, his eyes glossy and unfocused. A smile broke out over his face, and a tear trembled in his eye, and his cheek flushed with rage. He gave a strangled cry—half a laugh, half a sob—and slowly sank to his knees, releasing his grip on the fabric of Emily's collar as he did.

The silver knife dropped to the ground, clinking against granite gravel. Caul bent his head, burying it in his hands for a moment, his shoulders shaking with sobs. Then he lifted his head to the sky and screamed, then he was seized with violent tremblings of laughter.

Emily stared at Caul, perplexed. From the corner of her eye she saw Stanton climb to his feet, unsteady on his legs as a newly foaled colt.

"What did you say to him?" Stanton rasped.

"A word," Emily said. "It popped into my head. I don't know what it means."

"What word?"

"Hemacolludinatious," she said.

Stanton blinked at her. He looked astonished and horrified all at once.

"That's not a word, that's a neologism." Stanton rubbed a hand over his mouth, and Emily saw that the hand was trembling. "You Sundered him."

"What do you mean, Sundered?"

"Military sangrimancers use a special magical technique to keep themselves under complete emotional control at all times." Stanton stared down at Caul. The man was clenched in a twitching ball, sobbing and snarling and clawing at the ground with dirty fingers. "They lock themselves up inside their own minds. Memory, emotion, everything. They keep just one key. A made-up word . . . a neologism. Speaking it when a man is unprepared is . . . horrible. It sends the sang-rimancer crashing back into himself, crushing him under his own betrayed humanity . . ." Stanton's voice trailed off into a mutter. "You Sundered him. My God."

The loud sound of a train whistle broke in sharply. The train was coming up the hill. It couldn't be more than five minutes away. She put her hand to her mouth.

"Dag!" she muttered, rushing back to where the big man lay. She knelt by him, touched his face. To her great relief he stirred, moaning, his hands pressed against his belly.

"Emily?" he said. "Emily . . . are you . . ."

"We're safe," Emily breathed, looking over at where Stanton was crouched beside Caul's crazily spasming form. Stanton had put a hand on each side of Caul's head and was muttering something in Latin.

Tears streamed down Caul's cheeks as he struggled ineffectually against Stanton's grip. "I won't f-f-forget forever!" He stumbled over the words as if his tongue were being jerked from his mouth. "I won't forget you or h-h-her either . . . I will f-f-find you . . ."

Teeth clenched, Stanton terminated the magical recitation with three loudly barked commands: *"Lacuna! Caesura! Oblivio!"*

He jerked his hands away from Caul's face. Caul slumped back, abruptly silent, his head lolling. Stanton reached down, taking the alembic from Caul's clasped hand. He stood, staring into the distance for a moment, as if he'd forgotten where he was.

"Is he dead?" Dag looked up at the Warlock with new respect. "Did you kill him?"

Stanton didn't answer, but threw the sangrimancer's alembic to the ground, crushing it under the heel of his boot. The glass shattered with a pop and hiss.

"I didn't kill him," Stanton said. "I'm not a murderer."

"Then what did you do to him?" Emily rose, putting a hand on Stanton's shoulder to steady herself.

"Put him to sleep, made him forget. Forget us . . ." Stanton's green eyes were strangely unfocused. "Forget everything. He'll wake up in a few days, but . . ." Stanton did not complete the sentence. Instead he stared off into the darkness, his eyes fixed and unseeing. Emily gave him a shake.

"Mr. Stanton?" she said. "Are you all right?"

"All right?" Stanton slurred the words like a drunkard. "No, I'm not, I'm fine . . ." Then he stopped speaking entirely.

The train was coming up the tracks, the beam of its headlamp a brilliant knife slicing the darkness. Emily found that she was no longer leaning on Stanton for support; rather, he was leaning on her. His eyes were sliding closed and then opening abruptly, as if he were trying to keep himself from falling asleep.

"Your train's here." Dag climbed to his feet slowly, straightening with a wince. "Let's get you both on it."

Emily looked at Dag, as if seeing him for the first time.

"Dag . . ." she whispered.

"I understand now, Emily," he said.

The huge black train pulled to a stop with a vast rushing of steam and a piercing squeal of hot brakes. Dag threaded an arm under Stanton's, shifting the weight of the Warlock from Emily's shoulders to his own. Stanton's eyes fluttered briefly; he looked up at Dag and mumbled, "Yes, I'd like coffee with the eggs, thank you . . ."

"Is he going to be all right?" Dag asked Emily as he dragged Stanton toward the passenger car. There was a loud hiss from the front of the train as the fire tenders jerked down the water pipe and sent cold mountain water gushing into the engine's tanks.

"I don't know," Emily said as they approached the closed door of the passenger car. The conductor leaned out the window, his face registering slight alarm. Emily could see her little group reflected in the man's eyes—three shabby men, torn and bloodstained, drunk, probably.

"Two for New York," Emily blurted, digging into Stanton's pocket for the purse of money Dag had brought. "The cheapest you got."

Emily dearly hoped the conductor couldn't see Caul's motionless form lying a few feet off. Apparently he couldn't, for while he hesitated a long moment, he finally took her money, tore off two tickets, and punched them slowly.

"I'll help you get him on," Dag muttered, and he lifted Stanton up the step into the car. With a bit of wrangling, he managed to get the lanky Warlock into one of the wooden bench seats.

The train whistle gave a curt blast; the conductor gestured impatiently to Dag.

"We're going!" he snapped. "Buy a ticket or get off!"

Dag turned to climb off the train. Emily stopped him in the vestibule, the little space between the cars.

"What about Caul? He'll wake up eventually, Mr. Stanton said—"

"I'll drag him way up one of the old timber roads. Easy to get lost up there, right?"

"And you'll watch out for Pap?" she said. The train gave another whistle; the conductor gave an impatient growl.

"We're goin', mister!"

"I'll see that he's safe," Dag said, ignoring the conductor.

The train began to move. It gave a jolting lurch forward and then began to rumble out of the clearing. Dag swung out of the open door, holding onto the side railing, but Emily caught his hand one last time.

"Thank you, Dag," she murmured. "Thank you for everything."

He pulled her close and kissed her with bright, brief intensity. Then he leapt from the train, disappearing into the darkness.

Emily stood in the vestibule for a long time. The conductor reached past her to close the door, making a sound of weary disapproval. She touched her lips where Dag had kissed them. They felt strange indeed. Then, shaking her head, she went back to Stanton.

The cheapest seats were in the emigrant cabin—a large drafty car with a coal stove at each end and hard wooden benches. Given the late hour, most of the seats had been folded down so that passengers could stretch out to sleep. The coal-oil lanterns that swung in gimbaled fittings in the ceilings were turned down low. The faint yellow light made everything seem dingy and mysterious at the same time.

Emily slid into the seat next to Stanton, elbowed him softly. "We've made it, Mr. Stanton," she whispered to him. "We've made it!"

But Stanton did not reply. His head lolled against the window. She shook him again. The train was gathering speed now, rattling and jolting.

"Mr. Stanton?" she said. He did not wake. She shook him harder, giving him little slaps on the cheek. He still did not wake.

He's just tired, Emily assured herself, swallowing hard. She laid a hand on his chest to feel if he was breathing. He was. Well, that was a good sign at least. Looking at her own hand on Stanton's chest made her remember the way Caul's hand had pressed the alembic there, just over where Stanton's heart was, and the sizzling wires of magic, blood red and rot black, that had surrounded him . . .

Just tired, she repeated to herself, letting her hand drop and closing her eyes.

CHAPTER THIRTEEN

Mother Roscoe's
Eye-Opener

Her own exhaustion made it easier for Emily to convince herself that there was nothing sinister about Stanton's abrupt slide into unconsciousness. Almost as soon as she closed her eyes the train's soothing clatter rocked her into a deep, dreamless sleep. She was jolted awake by words that seemed to be shouted directly into her ear:

"Fresh candy! Candy and cigars!"

Bolting upright from where she'd slumped against Stanton's shoulder, she found that the train had stopped. Brilliant sunshine streamed through the dusty windows of the car. A glance out the window at the name on the station indicated that they were someplace called Wadsworth. Young boys were walking up and down the aisle.

"Nice oranges from California, last you'll get!"

"Papers, getcher papers! Books just a dime! Full-color covers, gents! Thrilling exploits, madcap mayhem, wild adventure . . ."

"Can I see?"

The request came from a girl sitting in the seat across from them. She was plump and blond, with smooth skin and bright brown eyes. She wore a poke bonnet and a clean white apron over a cream-colored dress that was sprinkled with tiny pink rosebuds.

The newsboy lifted the flap on his battered canvas satchel so that she could paw through his assortment of brightly colored pulps.

"Have it . . . read it . . . thought it was awful dull . . ." she muttered to herself as she discarded one after another. Finally, she seized on one with a happy cry. "Oh! Haven't read this one before! I'll take it!"

Clutching the treasured find to her chest, the girl dug into a little woven purse and pulled out a dime. When the girl saw that Emily was watching, she blushed.

"It's a Jack Two-Fist," she said, as if Emily should know what that meant. Then the girl looked away shyly, but not before letting her eyes linger on Stanton with some concern.

Emily glanced at Stanton. She nudged him with her shoulder, hoping he'd stretch and groan. She laid a hand on his cheek; his skin, always quite warm, was now burning hot.

Her first impulse was to grab him by both shoulders and give him a really tooth-rattling shake, but the girl was right there. So, Emily went to address herself to more immediate concerns.

Being dressed as a man, she certainly couldn't use the "ladies' rest," so it was with great apprehension that she picked her way back to the "gentlemen's rest" at the rear of the car.

It was as disgusting as she expected. There was a dicey-looking chamber pot, and a trapdoor in the floor through which said pot was supposed to be emptied. Men being men, however, it seemed that most dispensed with the chamber pot altogether and opted for the more direct and inaccurate route.

Using the room's tiny cracked shaving mirror, Emily freshened her costume, brushing at the dirt on her suit and hastily smoothing her hair back up under her brown hat. Then she scrutinized herself. It was the first time she'd gotten a good look at herself in her masculine disguise. The hard traveling and meager accommodations had conspired to make her look more like a young man than she would have thought: grimy, angular, and . . . yes, ruthless. Her hand went up to her throat. The collar of her shirt was torn where Caul had grabbed her, the top two buttons missing from where they had been wrenched off. She clutched her collar, holding it closed. The last thing she needed was someone getting a look down her front.

On the way back to the seats she paused at the water spigot, where there was a dented tin cup for common use. She filled it and went back to where Stanton was sitting. She tried to force the water through his dried lips. Most of it ran out of the corner of his mouth.

Emily's hands trembled as she returned the cup to the spigot, balancing herself against seats to keep her footing on the rocking train.

Why wouldn't he wake up?

The train stopped in Mill City for lunch. Those who hoped to hit the lunch counters left at a flat run, for the train stopped only briefly for meals and sometimes pulled away without so much as a warning whistle. But Emily couldn't even think about eating, and wanted to take advantage of the empty car to employ more desperate means in her attempt to wake Stanton. Unfortunately, the blond girl stayed behind, too. She was using the coal stove at the end of the car to boil water for tea.

Emily swore under her breath as she laid a hand on Stanton's damp, pallid forehead. He was hot as a flatiron, and his face seemed thinner. His closed eyes seemed to be sinking backward into his skull. It was as if he were made of wax, and melting from the inside.

When the water boiled, the girl shook dried tea into a little china pot, and brought it back to the seats. Then the girl opened her basket and took out paper-wrapped items.

"Would you like a sandwich?" She offered one of the little bundles to Emily. "I made lots."

Emily didn't want it. Her heart was beating anxiously against her stomach, making her feel lightheaded and vaguely queasy. But the girl's face was kind, her look vaguely imploring. Emily took the sandwich, unwrapped it. The thick-sliced homemade bread was spread with farm butter and strawberry jam. It was very good. Emily found herself wolfing it down in three bites and wishing for more.

"I haven't seen you eat today." The girl produced a tin cup from her basket and offered Emily a cup of tea. Emily shook her head. "I guess you're down on your luck."

"Nah," Emily said. Having already become aware of her limitations in the field of masculine mimicry, Emily resolved to keep her utterances as syllabically limited as possible.

"My name's Rose," the girl said. "Rose Hibble."

"Elmer."

"Is your friend drunk?" Rose asked, nodding at Stanton.

"Uh-huh," Emily said. "Thanks for the sandwich."

"My uncle Sal was a drunk," Rose said thoughtfully. "You know how they say about people, 'drunk every night but Sunday'? Well, he was drunk on Sundays, too. Used to go into church to argue with God. Blamed if he didn't win nine times out of ten!"

"Hmmm," Emily murmured, hoping that the sound would indicate her lack of desire to hear more about Uncle Sal.

"I'm going to Chicago." Rose cocked her head. "Where are you going?"

"New York," Emily said, then immediately wished she hadn't. She shouldn't be talking at all. Why wouldn't Stanton wake up? She was no good at being cagey and secretive and sly. He was the credomancer, he was the one trained to manipulate the minds of men . . .

"New York!" The excitement in Rose's voice scattered Emily's thoughts. "How exciting. Me, I'm going to Chicago because my Aunt Kindy owns a hat shop. She employs a dozen girls, and she needs a clerk, and I've studied two years at the Nevada Women's College—mathematics and accounting and penmanship and bookkeeping—and so Mam said, 'Rose, you go on out to Chicago and put some of that education to good use.' Aunt Kindy is a good old soul, a godly woman, not too strong in the head, especially with her multiplication, and Heaven knows, you have to have your multiplication if you're going to run a business . . ."

The river of thought continued from this gushing fount of information. Rose exhaustively elaborated on the theme of Aunt Kindy's lack of mathematical skill before progressing through the life history of every member of her family, footnoted with her opinions on everything from the price of cornmeal to the proper way to iron sheets. Mostly, however, she talked about her dime novels.

"I brought some doozies with me!" She opened her heavy, lumpy carpetbag to reveal a rainbow galaxy of excitement and adventure. She showed them to Emily one after another, offering a precise and detailed description of each. Emily wondered why Rose didn't notice that they were all the same story, just with different names.

". . . and then Tom, the Straight-Shooting Outlaw, rides into the gulch and unties her, and pulls her up on his white horse, and they ride off into the sunset," Rose exhaled at the end of another one of these recountings, closing her eyes.

"And the corrupt Sheriff Black and his posse of thugs get killed in a rock slide, right?"

"No, they get scalped by redskins. There's this chief who owes Tom a favor because he saved his daughter, a beautiful Indian princess, from a raging grassfire." Rose gave Emily a scornful frown. "Rock slide, phooey!"

Emily chewed her lip as Rose pulled another book out of her bag and began describing it. So many of the books featured noble outlaws, flamboyant and reckless, the kind that signed their names in bullets but never really killed anyone.

Well, being an outlaw was nothing like that at all. It was frightening and uncomfortable. You didn't get to change your clothes, you had to use filthy bathrooms, you had to watch your friends die . . .

Emily's heart jumped and she had to swallow to shove it back down her throat. She glanced over at Stanton. He looked worse than ever. What on earth was she going to do?

The afternoon wore on. Rose kept talking. They entered the desert, cutting across the ghostly alkali plains that rolled out before and behind them, a smooth blank sheet. And Rose kept talking. At least she didn't seem to require much response. Her nonstop patter quickly became as much a part of the background hum of the train as the clack of the wheels.

As afternoon became evening and Stanton still hadn't woken up, Emily knew she had to do something. The other passengers were beginning to comment. There were murmurs about "the sick man in the corner." People held handkerchiefs over their mouths as they passed, and everyone gave Emily and Stanton a wide berth. Everyone except Rose.

"If you're going through to New York, you'll have to change

trains in Ogden," Rose observed. "I guess you'll have to carry him, huh?"

"Yep," Emily replied, as if she had to tote drunken associates all the time.

She had to wake him up before Ogden, before they had to switch trains. She couldn't drag a full-grown man around without attracting attention she couldn't afford to attract.

That night, when the conductor came by to fold the seats down into beds, Emily didn't know what to say.

"It's all right." Rose smiled at the conductor, nodding toward Stanton. "The poor man needs his rest. I can lay my head against the window."

Emily laid her head down and slept, hoping that Stanton would surprise her the next morning with one of his ill-tempered quips.

But he did not. He was still bleakly unconscious as they approached Promontory early the next morning.

She knew she was licked. She had to get him to a doctor. If he didn't wake up before Ogden, she'd drag him off the train and have him carried to one. And then . . . ?

And then, well, she'd get back on the train. She had to get to New York. That's what Stanton would want her to do, and she certainly owed it to him to make the right choice.

When the train stopped for breakfast, Rose got off. She was gone for quite some time—long enough, indeed, that Emily worried she might not make it back. But as the train gave its final whistle, Rose dropped into the seat across, her face flushed and her blond hair wisping around her face. She gave Emily a knowing grin.

"I figured it was time we got some help from Mother Roscoe!" she said. She showed Emily a small paper parcel that bore the stamp of the station's dry-goods store. Rose took out its contents one by one. Blackstrap molasses. Fluid extract of coca. Ground coffee beans, calomel, and brandy.

"What's all that for?" Emily said.

"It's for your friend. My mam used to stir some of this up whenever my Uncle Sal was having a bad time of it. She called it 'Mother Roscoe's Eye-Opener.' I don't know who Mother Roscoe was, but I'll wager she had lots of eyes to open in her time." Then, using the tin pan she'd boiled her tea water in, Rose began to mix the ingredients, using an alarmingly heavy hand with the coca extract. The girl swirled everything around, then put the pot on the coal stove.

"It has to boil for a bit," Rose said as the train lurched and got under way. In a bit, the smell of sickly sweet steam filled the cabin, and the girl took the pot off the boil and set it aside. When it was cool, she poured a little into a tin cup and showed it to Emily.

"Are you sure it's safe?" Emily said.

"Oh, yes, perfectly safe." Rose lifted it to her lips, drank deeply. Her eyes went wide and she hiccupped. "Tasty, too! You think you can make your friend drink it?"

Emily took the cup, sniffed it. She swallowed a mouthful. It was sweet and bitter at the same time, and there was an after-taste of metal filings and rust. It burned going down her throat, and even the small sip she'd taken made her heart thunder in her chest. It made her feel like she could leap out of the train and run all the way across the continent under her own steam. Yes, Mother Roscoe certainly knew how to open eyes! She lifted the cup to Stanton's lips, digging her fingers into the hinge of his jaw to make his mouth open.

"Come on," she whispered, massaging his throat, willing him to swallow. "This is your last chance, Dreadnought Stanton. Otherwise I'm going to New York without you."

She was answered with a little coughing choke from Stanton. A flicker of distaste passed across his face. He weakly lifted a hand as if to bat the cup away from his lips. Hope rose in Emily's chest. She tipped more of the liquid down his throat.

"Not too much," Rose admonished. "Just keep after him slow-like. Mam says too much Eye-Opener all at once can make a man's heart explode."

Emily kept administering small doses of the stimulant over the next couple of hours, happily noting its positive effects. Stanton even opened his eyes once, though they fell shut again abruptly after. Finally, as they were pulling into Ogden, he opened his eyes and they stayed open. He looked at Emily with slowly focusing recognition.

"All right," he croaked. "What's all this?"

Emily could have kissed him. Instead she explained the situation to him, speaking slowly, keeping her words small.

"We're pulling in to Ogden. We have to switch trains. You have to wake up."

"I'm very tired, Emily," he mumbled, tucking his head against her shoulder. "Just let me sleep awhile longer."

Emily glanced at Rose; the girl had her lower lip between her teeth and was making a great show of looking up at the ceiling.

"It's Elmer, remember?" she hissed, jerking her shoulder up. Then she put her mouth closer to his ear. "Caul attacked you with some kind of spell. You have to shake it off!" She tipped a large dose of the stimulant down his throat, and he gagged, spluttering. He sat forward in the seat, coughing loudly. Emily thumped him on the back.

The train was slowing as it pulled in to the station at Ogden. Stanton was still coughing as it lurched to a halt.

"We're here," Emily said. "Come on. We have to go."

With a great deal of effort, Stanton pulled himself to his feet.

"Food," he said. "I need food."

"Can you walk?" she said.

"Of course I can walk," he said, falling to the ground with a thundering crash. All eyes in the car turned to them. Emily lifted a reassuring hand.

"He's all right," she squeaked, forgetting entirely to keep her voice low. She reached down and helped Stanton up.

They climbed down off the train into the bright sunshine. Stanton squinted hard, lifting a shaking-weak hand to shade his eyes. There were dozens of farm women selling merchandise on the platform. Stanton walked dazedly past each one, pointing out what he wished Emily to purchase.

"Butter. Eggs. Sugar. Milk."

Emily purchased each of the items Stanton had indicated. Then, bundles in hand, they sat on a wooden bench on the platform. Emily watched in fascination and horror as Stanton (using his fingers) ate a tub of butter straight, in slow contemplative bites. This was followed by a dozen eggs broken directly down his throat and washed down with long gulps of milk from an earthenware jug. He took large bites from a cone of loaf sugar. After about ten minutes of this bizarre repast, he sat up straighter, taking a deep breath.

"Well, I'm in no shape to work any magic," he said, dusting crumbs of sugar from his clothes. He looked a little better; the waxy pallor was fading from his face, but the hollow purple shadows under his eyes were still deep and sickly looking. "But I think I can make it to the train."

"That's all I require," Emily sighed, feeling happier than she had in quite a while.

CHAPTER FOURTEEN

The Aberrancy Hunters

It was close to noon, and Ogden was flooded with warm spring sunshine. It was the biggest and nicest station they'd yet stopped at—an elaborate profusion of peaks and gables and awnings, with a high clock tower rising up from the middle. The paint was so fresh it still reeked of linseed oil. Ogden was a hub of transcontinental rail traffic, and the station teemed with feverish activity. Bags and trunks whizzed by on carts, salesboys hawked snacks and supplies, travelers crowded in a churning mass.

The Central Pacific line, on which they'd ridden since Cutter's Rise, ended at Ogden. Passengers continuing eastward had to transfer to the Union Pacific line, which would take them to Chicago. They arrived at the Union Pacific track with time to spare; trainmen were still swarming over the engine, loading fuel and putting on water.

They climbed onto a cramped car. Stanton sank into a seat with a groan. The carriage was smaller and older and shabbier than the Central Pacific cars had been, with lower ceilings and chipping varnish.

"No wonder I ache so badly, sleeping on a bench like this." He looked at Emily. "How long was I out, anyway? If we're already in Utah—"

"It's been a day and a half now."

"A day and a half?" Stanton eyed the yammering children, the women digging in baskets for treats to appease them. "And at least five more to look forward to. I wish I were still asleep."

She dug into her pocket, handed him the purse of money Dag had given her.

"They were your horses," she said. "I didn't feel right throwing your money away on a Silver Palace car."

He looked at the money, which must have seemed a damnably small amount. He tucked it into his pocket. "You're probably right. Discretion is the better part of valor."

"Oh, there you are!" The bright voice came from the aisle.

Rose was carrying all her things, struggling to keep the lumpy, overstuffed carpetbag from slipping out from under her arm. Her hair wisped around her face, and her cheeks were red with hurrying. She slid into the seat across from Emily, smiling happily.

"I almost didn't make it! I was in the mercantile, and you just can't tell one train whistle from another, can you?" She withdrew a crumpled paper candy bag from her pocket and reached into it.

"I got this for you, Mr. Elmer." She pulled out a bright silver safety pin. "For your collar. I thought you might like to stop having to hold it all the time. No, don't thank me, it wasn't anything. I went into the mercantile to buy some candy, and while I was standing there I got to talking with this old woman, she uses them for quilting, and I asked her could I have one. Didn't charge me anything, just said I could have one for free! Can you imagine?"

Emily smiled at Rose. She took the pin and fastened her torn collar.

Rose fixed her gaze on Stanton, looking at him with an abundance of sweet sympathy. "And how are you feeling? Would you like a piece of candy?"

Stanton gave her a look that encompassed his entire opinion of being spoken to like a sick kitten.

"This is Miss Rose Hibble," Emily hurried to explain. "She's from Reno. She's going to Chicago to work for her Aunt Kindy. It was her recipe for Mother Roscoe's Eye-Opener that helped revive you."

"Really." Stanton stared at Rose for a long moment, a moment that took on a menacing quality due to Stanton's general appearance of roughness. His face, usually clean-shaven, was stubbled and sunken, and there were still purple shadows around his eyes. Emily had the strangest apprehension that he was going to say something vile to her. But then he blinked, shook his head, and shrugged. "Well, thank you very much for your help, Miss Hibble."

"Miss Hibble, this is Mr. . . . Smith," Emily said. She remembered chiding Stanton for not making up a better name for her; now she found that it really wasn't as easy as it seemed.

"Oh, Mr. Smith? There's a Mr. Smith back in Reno, runs a blacksmith shop. I don't suppose you're related?" Rose tilted the bag of candy in Stanton's direction, giving it a little shake.

"It's highly unlikely," Stanton said. After a moment, he reached into the bag and took out a piece.

"Probably so. He's quite a strapping brute and you're rather on the spindly side, aren't you?"

"Indeed." Stanton popped the candy into his mouth and struggled to his feet. "Will you excuse us for a moment, Miss Hibble?"

Stanton gestured to Emily and they walked into the vestibule. It was enclosed with a flexible leather curtain and it was much louder, the rattling of the steel wheels on the tracks loud enough to make her teeth vibrate.

"How are you feeling?" Emily said, trying not to yell.

"My head is killing me," Stanton said, candy rattling in his mouth. "Caul got me with a *rigor rictus*. Lucky you were there to blunt it."

"Dag promised to ditch him somewhere nice and remote," Emily said. "I Sundered him, you scrambled him . . . will that take care of him long enough for us to get to New York?"

Stanton stroked his lower lip with his thumb. "Hansen told me Caul had about thirty men in Lost Pine. They'll be looking for him. And just like my Jefferson Chair ring lets Mirabilis keep track of me, Army Warlocks have their own ways of locating lost comrades. He won't quickly recover from the Sundering, but he only has to recover enough to order a general alert. There are dozens of Warlock units between here and New York. Soldiers could be waiting for us at any of the stations."

Emily leaned heavily against the wall of the vestibule, rubbing her upper arms with her hands.

"Why didn't you just kill him?" she muttered.

Stanton glared at her. "Why didn't *you*?" He crunched the candy in his mouth, a peculiar emphasis. "His knife was right there. He was unconscious. It would have been the work of an instant." He waited a long moment for an answer, his face painted with strange scorn. "Maybe, Miss Edwards, cutting throats isn't as easy as you think."

"I never said it was easy," Emily returned hotly. "But what the hell are we going to do? Sit back and enjoy the ride until a bunch of Army Warlocks swarm the train and put us in handcuffs?"

"First, you're going to listen for messages from Komé. She's warned us of trouble before, and forewarned is forearmed. Second, I think it's time to consider a change of disguise. If Caul doesn't remember anything else, he's certain to remember the fabric of that suit. And finally, this train must have a smoking car somewhere. I'm going to find it and see if there's any food to be had. Care to join me . . . Elmer?"

Emily wasn't quite ready to stop being mad, but after a moment she released her annoyance in a long breath. It *was* nice to have him back.

They exited the vestibule and went back through the car, past where Rose was sitting. The girl waved to them both.

"Save our seats?" Emily gave Rose a smile. Rose blushed prettily and looked coyly down at her Jack Two-Fist book.

"Come on," Stanton growled, giving Emily a pointed shove.

"You know," Emily said quietly, as they wended their way toward the back of the train, "I don't think I anticipated all the difficulties that this suit would present."

"Believe me," Stanton said, grasping at the overhead rails to keep his balance, "I will be pleased to provide you with a proper dress at the earliest possible opportunity."

Emily hoped no one had heard that comment.

They found the smoking car but they didn't find food until the train stopped for dinner. And even then there was little more to be had than thin, mingy sandwiches. Stanton bought two dozen of them and spent the afternoon eating, ignoring Rose's attempts to catch him up on the plots of all the dime novels in her carpetbag.

Later, as twilight painted the sky with delicious hues of pumpkin and lemon, someone pulled a violin from his luggage and began to play old tunes that resounded through the rattling compartment. The music was plaintive and sweet. It lulled Rose into a welcome reverie, and she drowsed against the glass, her little white finger holding her place in the Jack Two-Fist book.

The conductor strolled through the car, lighting lanterns and folding down seats. Stanton elbowed Emily.

"Come on, Elmer," he said. "It's the floor for us."

"Huh?"

"We shall allow Miss Hibble to sleep on the seats, of course." Stanton looked at Emily meaningfully. "It's the gentlemanly thing to do."

"Oh," Emily said. "Right."

They, along with a few other single men, hurried to find places on the floor. Emily and Stanton were stuck with a place up near the coal stove. Well, at least they would be warm, but it was a small comfort when weighed against the fact that they would be sleeping right next to the gent's saloon—near enough to smell the stench and be bothered all night by people climbing over them.

"Mind the spittoon," Stanton said, wadding up his coat for a pillow and tipping his hat down over his eyes. Emily stared up at the pressed-tin ceiling, the patterns shifting mysteriously in the half-light of the swinging lanterns. The fiddler was playing one last song. Emily felt a twinge when she recognized it.

"Sweet, Sweet Spring."

"Beg pardon," mumbled a man as he climbed over her.

Even though the next couple of days were uneventful, every day was more tension-charged than the last. Whenever they stopped, Emily scrutinized the passengers getting on, anxiously scanning the platform, playing a grim game of Guess the Maelstrom. It was an odd conundrum: putting miles of distance between themselves and Captain Caul should have made them safer—but with each mile, each moment that passed, the danger grew and grew.

Only while the train was under way could Emily relax, watch scraggy mountains dip and recede, and breathe the cool air that smelled of new-grown sage and rain.

Stanton spent most of his time in the smoking car, away from Rose's nonstop chatter. Emily was worried about him. He'd woken up from Caul's spell, but it didn't seem that he had entirely recovered. He was tense, constantly frowning, and the small muscles of his face jumped and spasmed at odd intervals. And while he wasn't the sweetest-tempered individual in the best of times, he was now positively snappish. She wondered if the attack hadn't done more damage than he wanted to admit. He wouldn't discuss it, of course. He just assured her curtly that everything was fine.

Insufferable.

But still, he didn't deserve any of this misery, just as Dag didn't deserve to have his heart broken, just as Pap didn't deserve to have to huddle in hiding from blood sorcerors tearing up Lost Pine to find her.

Three times what thou givest returns to thee . . .

Emily sighed, understanding for the first time the true seriousness of the rede.

It doesn't just return to you, she thought. *It returns to the people you care about. The people you love . . .*

". . . And his guns had pearl handles. Have you ever heard of such a thing, Mr. Elmer?"

Rose's words scattered Emily's thoughts. Emily shook herself.

"Pearl handles?" she said vaguely. She'd long since stopped listening to Rose's recap of some fictitious outlaw's exploits.

"Hand-carved mother-of-pearl handles on his revolvers, and with 'em he could shoot any walnut out of any walnut tree, just for the pointing! Can you imagine?"

"Whoever he is, I bet he doesn't carry those revolvers around to shoot walnuts with," Emily muttered. At the words, Rose's face became a picture of sweet pleading.

"Oh, but the Brushfork Bandito doesn't hurt people! When he held up that bank in Austin, he just tied everybody up. He even gave the doll back to the little girl who was crying! He's not mean, he's just . . . tormented."

"Tormented by not having enough of other people's money, I guess."

This made the girl smile, a pink blush creeping over her cheeks. She ducked her head and lowered her eyes.

"You seem tormented sometimes, too," Rose ventured, looking at Emily from under her eyelashes.

Emily couldn't help giving a loud laugh—a laugh that was entirely too high-pitched. She pressed her lips together quickly. From ruthless to tormented. It really was too amusing.

After a moment, Rose's smile faded. Her face clouded slightly. She chewed her lip.

"Your friend doesn't like me much," she said.

"Oh, don't mind him," Emily said. "He's got a lot on his mind."

Rose was silent for a long time. Lifting her heavy, lumpy carpetbag onto her lap, she wrapped her arms around it, hugging it to her chest.

"I don't like mean people," Rose said, finally. And then, surprisingly, she did not speak again for a long time.

It was later that day that they encountered the Aberrancy hunters.

Emily had wended her way to the back of the train, to the observation deck, and was watching the plains roll out behind them. She'd never seen anything as big and flat and queer. The plains were like looking at a huge body of water; it was hard to tell if the sky was being reflected by the land, or the land by the sky. The emptiness seemed to go on forever, bisected into two infinite halves by the scar of black track. The new green mist of the plains was dotted with blooming wildflowers; the air was thick with the smell of them.

The train gave a lurch, slowed, then stopped. Emily was seized with a sudden, inexplicable nervousness. What if they were trapped in the middle of all that emptiness? Who could ever find them? How could they ever find themselves? She went to look for Stanton, who was in the smoking car reading the papers.

Stanton was puffing contemplatively amid a sea of gentle-men. But while Stanton was casually perusing a copy of the *North Platte Sentinel,* the other men in the car were clustered around the windows on the right side, talking in excited tones.

"Do you see them?"

"Aberrancies, sure as shooting!"

Emily gave Stanton a questioning glance as she pushed her way through for a better look.

In the distance, three black, misshapen figures the size of oxcarts galloped over the plains. They had once been jackrab-bits. How three of them had encountered a black bolus at once, Emily couldn't guess.

They were being chased by a cavalry squadron; the soldiers were firing on them. Puffs of smoke issued from their rifles, and a second later came the sound of echoing pops.

Some of the men in the car dug into their pockets and brought out charms of protection and hung them around their necks, as if having them visible made them more effective. One man in a bright purple and yellow waistcoat saw this gen-eral action and laughed.

"Out come the charms!" he guffawed. "What a bunch of old women."

"What are you laughing at, mister?" someone replied hotly. "I been wearing this charm for thirty years, and I ain't ever been eaten by an Aberrancy yet."

This remark elicited approving chuckles. But the man in purple and yellow snorted dismissively as he leaned against the doorjamb, thumbs tucked into the armholes of his waistcoat.

"Aberrancies are nothing more than freaks of nature. Scien-tific explanations for them are easy to find. A gentleman by the name of Charles Darwin, in his book *Origin of the Species,* says that we all evolve. Aberrancies are just evolution gone haywire."

"Rubbish." Stanton did not look up from his paper.

"Excuse me?"

"Rubbish," Stanton repeated. "First of all, the correct title of the book you're referring to is *On the Origin of Species.* Second, Aberrancies are the result of toxic residuals exuded by the Mantic Anastamosis. That is the accepted understanding."

"That's what the Warlocks say, friend." The man laughed. "Either you been listening to Warlocks, or you are one!"

Stanton tapped ash from his cigar.

"No," he said. "Just a hobby of mine."

"Well, those Warlocks . . . they want you to believe that everything is bad magic. Part of the way they convince people into buying their services. But science can explain most things."

"Yes, *science*." Stanton's icily dismissive tone suggested the man in the purple and yellow waistcoat was the most dim-witted cretin it had ever been his misfortune to meet. "I fail to see why men who espouse the benefits of science so often advance their cause by dismissing the great natural power of magic."

"Oh, I ain't dismissing nothing, Mr. . . ."

". . . Smith," Stanton said.

"Mr. Smith. Science and magic can work together, I guess. Come from the same roots, some say."

"Precisely so," Stanton said. "Thus, it is foolish to scoff at men who take the perfectly sane and sensible precaution of wearing protective charms. I'm sure all these men have families, duties, responsibilities . . . I'm sure Mr. Darwin could offer little assistance if any one of them ever came face-to-face with a slavering, rampaging Aberrancy." Stanton fixed the man with a gimlet glare. "Could he?"

This comment brought sounds of loud agreement from around the compartment.

"As you say, sir, as you say . . ." The man in purple and yellow lifted his hands, stepped back. His face was flushed red to the ears. "I didn't mean nothing."

It was almost as if Emily could feel the mood in the car shift. The men who wore charms stood up a little straighter. They looked firmer, more resolute, and certainly happier. Stanton had defended them and made the man in purple and yellow seem a blowhard and bumbler. But the dissection had been unsettling to watch.

"Did you have to be so harsh?" she said under her breath.

"Uneducated idiots like that can wreak havoc with a credo-mancer's power unless they're brought up good and short." He sniffed distastefully. "Scientists."

At that moment, the conductor came into the car.

"Well, gents, they say it's a gusher," he announced, with a rueful glance at his watch. "They've sent Aberrancy hunters down the tracks to deal with the mess, but it could be hours before they let us pass."

"A gusher!" the words passed excitedly between the men in the car. Even the fellow in the purple and yellow waistcoat seemed awed by the announcement, but Emily had no idea what it meant.

"Let's have a look!" someone suggested.

"The train's not going anywhere!" came an answering voice. "I want to see the Aberrancy hunters at work!"

The young men were the first off, obviously glad for the opportunity to stretch their legs. They whooped their way toward the front of the train. Older men followed; even the man in purple and yellow went to have a look. Soon, the only ones left in the car were Emily, Stanton, and two elderly men whose faces were set in expressions that indicated they were far too old for such nonsense.

"A gusher?" Emily said to Stanton.

He looked at her tiredly, his eyes red rimmed.

"Must we? I have a headache."

"Fine." Emily threw up a hand. "I'll go alone. You stay here."

Stanton ground out his cigar.

"Oh, certainly not," he sighed. "Sit comfortably when I could be doing something dangerous instead? Perish the thought."

The scene of the commotion was about a mile up from where the train had stopped. Compared to the endless emptiness surrounding them, the group that had collected around the "gusher" seemed small and inconsequential. But as they drew closer, Emily saw that it was quite a large and active gathering.

And as they got closer still, she saw that the scene was actually one of barely controlled chaos. The crowd from the train was watching a crew of a dozen workers who milled about a dark, steaming mass. The workers wore globe-shaped helmets of silver, their features hidden behind green smoked-glass faceplates. Indeed, the workers did not display a single inch of skin; they were dressed in heavy suits of stiff material that glittered as they moved, as if their clothes were embroidered with diamonds.

"Are those the Aberrancy hunters?" Emily asked through a hand covering her mouth and nose; the smell was foul, like rotten eggs and decaying meat. "What's that they're wearing?"

"They're wearing protective suits of spun glass and silver," Stanton said. "Black Exunge will wick through most organic materials."

Emily and Stanton pressed through the crowd. On every side Emily heard the whispered word "gusher" again.

"What's a 'gusher'?" Emily asked.

"Sometimes large pockets of Exunge will collect under the ground, building pressure. Gushers are rare, and good thing, too, for their occurrence is nothing short of a natural disaster." Stanton looked up over the top of the crowd. "This isn't a gusher, though. If it was, they wouldn't be letting people push in so close to watch. Probably just a little upwell causing annoyances."

They finally came to a place where they could see the Aberrancy hunters at work. The men were using coal-oil flamethrowers to scorch the earth around a trickling black pool.

"They have to completely sterilize the area around the source of the flow," Stanton explained. "Notice that they're keeping the flames well away from the Exunge itself. It's indecently flammable, a property which can be either extremely dangerous or extremely useful."

As if to illustrate Stanton's somewhat oblique statement, a grasshopper leaping away from the heat of the flamethrower landed directly on the tarry mass. The insect began to grow at a frightful rate, expanding like a bubble in a pan of hot molasses. There were screams from the crowd; everyone pulled back in preparation for panicked flight. But the Abberancy hunters responded with practiced efficiency. One who'd been standing off to the side jumped directly into the path of the swelling Aberrancy, flapping a bright red handkerchief. The action drew the creature's attention, and it took one great hop toward the handkerchief-flapper, making a slurping sound as it landed. Once the grasshopper was a safe distance from the bubbling pool of Exunge, the hunter with the flamethrower touched the edge of the creature's wing with a thin stream of fire. It ignited in an eyeblink, exploding into a screaming, popping column of blue and gold flame. The crowd *ooh*ed and *aah*ed like children on the Fourth of July.

"I told you it was flammable," Stanton said, as if Emily had stubbornly refused to believe him. He scratched the back of his head. "Had no idea they were attracted to the color red, though."

Emily considered reminding him about his ill-considered red poncho, the one that she'd once coveted. But it seemed so long ago. So many things had happened since then, it wouldn't even be like teasing the same person. Instead, she watched the hunters douse the smoldering grasshopper with shovelfuls of prairie dirt. When the grasshopper excitement had passed, she pointed at a pair of hunters who were kneeling near the fountain, fitting a silver apparatus over it.

"What are they doing?"

"They're capping it, just like they'd cap a well of crude oil," Stanton said. "It will allow them to pump out the Exunge."

"And then what?"

"It will be stored in steel containers, like those . . ." Stanton pointed to a large supply of bullet-shaped containers lined up on the ground nearby. They were marked ominously with a skull-and-crossbones insignia.

"And what happens to the containers?"

"They are taken to government storage facilities," Stanton said.

"And what does the government do with it? Is there some way to neutralize it?"

"After a fashion," Stanton said. "When Exunge comes in contact with living matter, its destructive qualities are fixed and thus neutralized. So you can sacrifice living things to it, like goats or chickens, and render it harmless. How many goats or chickens depends on how much Exunge needs neutralizing."

Emily looked at the pile of containers. There had to be at least fifty of them.

"I'm guessing that's a lot of goats and chickens," she observed.

"I don't quite know what the government does with all the Exunge they store," Stanton admitted, "but I'm sure they have a rational plan for its disposal."

"Oh, sure. For the public good," Emily said. "Just like the Maelstroms."

The look in Stanton's eyes indicated that he hadn't ever quite made that connection before.

Two Aberrancy hunters were rolling a large, box-shaped cart over the ground. They came toward the crowd in an unswerving straight line; the crowd parted to let them through.

"What are they doing?"

"Following ley lines, looking for other weak spots where Exunge might be released," Stanton said. He pointed at the boxy cart. "That's a Potentiator. It measures the potential for—"

There was an extremely loud alarm from the box as it passed in front of Emily. She pulled back, startled. The hunters looked up. One of them jiggled the machinery.

"Get back!" one of the Aberrancy hunters cried loudly, his voice muffled behind the green glass of his visor. "There's a bolus right underneath!"

Emily and Stanton were swept back as the crowd retreated in one panicked mass, shrieks and shouts peppering the air. Once the area was cleared, however, the alarm stopped. The men moved the Potentiator over the spot again, but the alarm did not repeat.

Stanton seemed to find this failure of unfathomable interest. He watched the man with the Potentiator closely. He put a hand on Emily's shoulder.

"I want you to do something." He pointed to the man who was fiddling with the Potentiator. "Go ask him for the time."

"Are you insane?" Emily wrinkled her nose. "You think he's going to stop and pull out a pocket watch?"

"Just go ask." Stanton pushed her forward. She glared back at him, but went over to the hunter nonetheless. Before she could open her mouth to make Stanton's ridiculous request, the alarm on the Potentiator went off with an ear-piercing shriek. She clapped her hands over her ears and stepped back. She felt Stanton's hand wrap around her upper arm, and he pulled her back away from the crowd briskly, walking back toward the train. She heard the alarm stop again, and someone say, "Damn thing must be broken . . ."

They came to an abrupt halt when they were about fifty feet from the crowd. When she looked up at Stanton's face, she knew that something was very wrong. He was extremely pale, and he had a hand over his mouth—a gesture she associated with periods when he was lost in extreme thoughtfulness.

"Of course it would"—he muttered to himself—"and you absorbed all that magic that Caul attacked me with . . ." He let his hand drop, releasing a heavy breath.

"What's wrong?"

He seized her wrist, pulled the glove from her right hand. He looked at the stone, the muscles of his throat working anxiously.

"The color's changed," he said, turning her hand. "It used to be clear blue. It's almost yellow now. And look at all those little black inclusions . . ."

"It's been changing over time . . . I didn't think—"

"Don't you see? If this is a piece of the Mantic Anastomosis—and I now have no doubt that it is—it will behave like the Mantic Anastomosis. It will absorb and purify magic. And it will also segregate and excrete Black Exunge."

Emily's mouth went dry.

"That's why Komé was trying so hard to turn back the magic we were putting into the stone," Stanton said. "The more magic the stone absorbs, the larger it becomes . . ."

"The larger what becomes?" Emily said, softly. Stanton looked at her, his eyes holding hers.

"Komé was cradling something. Holding something black. I know what it is now." He paused. "There's a black bolus forming in the stone."

Emily said nothing, but the horror of it grew within her slowly.

"You mean . . . in my *hand*?"

"It is the nature of the stone to segregate and excrete Black Exunge," Stanton repeated carefully. "The stone is doing that. Those black inclusions—when there's enough of them, they'll become a bolus. When the bolus is large enough, the stone will expel it. There's no way you could avoid coming in contact with it."

Emily's heart thudded in her chest, and she thought of the grasshopper, shrieking and crackling as it burned to death. Or the Aberrant raccoon, dripping with black slime. She looked up at Stanton, and she saw the fear on her face reflected in his eyes. Hardly knowing what she was doing, she clutched his lapels and hid her face against his chest, squeezing her eyes shut tight. At first, Stanton pulled back imperceptibly. But then he placed a warm hand on her head, stroking her hair for a moment, a gentling touch.

"I'm sure that Komé is helping," he murmured. "I'm sure she'll do everything she can. But we can't let the stone absorb any more magic. If an actual bolus forms, she might not be able to control it . . ."

There was the sound of voices approaching—train passengers returning to the cars, chattering about flaming grasshoppers. Stanton seized her shoulders, put her at a manly arm's length, and gave her a bracing shake.

"Buck up," he said firmly. "It's only a few days to New York. Professor Mirabilis will know what to do. You'll be fine, Emily." He paused, giving her another little shake. "You'll be fine, I promise."

The Aberrancy hunters finished their work, leaving behind a neatly capped Exunge pit, and the train got under way a few hours later. Emily and Stanton were both very quiet for the rest of the day.

If she hadn't been "tormented" before, she certainly was now. She wished she could cut her hand off and run away. What had Stanton said about that man in Ohio? Fifty feet tall, he'd smashed up an entire township with his bare hands? And it took a whole detachment of military Warlocks to "put him down"?

She bit her lip hard and stared out the window. The sunshine of earlier in the day had vanished, replaced by brooding black clouds. In their depths, streaks of lightning flashed like distant signal flares. When the rain began, it came down in great gouty sheets that rattled against the windows like handfuls of pebbles. The temperature plummeted; passengers began pulling out shawls and coats against the cold. Emily just stared out the window, shivering.

Night came again, the lanterns were lit again, the conductor moved through the car to fold down the seats. Stanton and Emily took their now-accustomed places on the floor. But even with the coal stove on one side of her and Stanton on the other, she couldn't stop shivering. She wrapped her horrible plaid coat more tightly around herself, listening to the rain lashing against the roof.

The longing to run never left her, nor the nauseating understanding that there was nowhere she could run to. She tried to comfort herself; Komé had protected her, and would continue to protect her. But what if she couldn't? What if the Exunge in the stone was already on the verge of overwhelming the conscribed spirit's ability to control it?

"What will happen to me?" Emily asked quietly. Stanton, lying beside her, pushed up his hat.

"What?" he asked. It was clear that he hadn't been asleep; Emily guessed he was no more pleased to be sleeping next to a person who might at any moment become an Aberrancy than she was to be that person.

"If the stone expels the Exunge, what will happen to me? Specifically, I mean."

Stanton was silent for a long moment. When he finally did speak, his voice was matter-of-fact.

"There is a process of mutation that lasts about a minute. During that time, the Black Exunge works upon the physical system of the affected . . . creature. After that time, the Exunge is fully ingrained in the living spirit, and the transformation is complete."

"Back in Dutch Flat you said that Aberrancies were most vulnerable while they were mutating. Like the Aberrancy hunters burned that grasshopper while it was still growing."

"Yes," Stanton said.

"You have the misprision blade," Emily said. "Could you stop me with it?"

"Don't say such things," Stanton growled. "It's not going to happen."

"Now who's trying to believe unpleasant things into being untrue?" she murmured bitterly. "I suppose there's always your *flamma* trick, but that would hardly be fair to the other passengers."

There was a long silence.

"You will not become an Aberrancy, Emily." The finality in his voice was like a door slamming shut, but it did not make her feel better.

Emily turned her head, looked up at the shadows on the pressed-tin ceiling. They kept resolving themselves into giant loping jackrabbits, slavering raccoons, Aberrancy hunters with flamethrowers. The song of the rain snickered in her ears.

The next thing she knew, the cold apricot-colored light of dawn was threading through the windows of the car and there was a soft sound of metal grating against metal. It was the rattle of the stove door; the conductor was throwing in lumps of coal. In her sleep, she had curled close to Stanton, snuggled against his side. He'd draped an arm around her shoulder, and she'd pillowed her head on it. The rise and fall of his chest, the smell of stale cigar smoke in the fabric of his coat was reassuring. She let herself drowse that way for a moment, until a thought made her heart leap unpleasantly.

And what if the stone decided to expel the Exunge right now? What if you turned him into an Aberrancy right along with you?

She pushed herself away from him, cursing as she climbed to her feet. She staggered out of the car, wanting suddenly to put as much distance between herself and Stanton as she could. She decided she would go sit on the observation platform. For some reason, the idea of watching the plains' endless repetition appealed to her this morning.

The conductor nodded his head to her as she made her way back through the car.

"Mornin', son," he said. "We've passed the storms. Gonna be a nice day."

"I doubt it," Emily said.

CHAPTER FIFTEEN

Ososolyeh

Emily spent the early part of the morning alone on the observation platform at the rear of the train, thinking deep thoughts about life and death, until she finally got hold of herself, reclaimed her uncommon good sense, and scolded herself for being so tragic.

All right, you rotten mineral, she thought. *It's you or me. And it's going to be me. Because with all the power of my belief, I believe it's going to be me.*

Pulling herself up straight, she walked back to the seats, where Rose was regaling Stanton with another of her interminably winding tales. When she appeared, he stood, his eyes searching her face.

"Are you all right?"

"Yep." Emily flashed him her most confident smile.

"And where were you, Mr. Elmer?" Rose batted her eyelashes at Emily. "With all the Aberrancies running around, I couldn't think what might have become of you!"

Emily worked to keep her smile from dimming.

"I think we've left all the Aberrancies behind," she said.

"Horrible things," Rose said, confidingly. "You know, they say they're all the fault of Warlocks. That if godly people would finally take a stand and put their foot down against all these Warlocks and Witches running around . . . why, there wouldn't be any Aberrancies. They say that they're a punishment on godly people for allowing sin to walk the earth unanswered—"

"Who is this 'they' you're always referring to?" Stanton

glared at Rose, his eyes gleaming with unhidden malice. "Your mongoloid Aunt Kindy? Your drunken Uncle Sal? Or are you talking about the slack-jawed hacks who bang out those dime novels for a bottle of whiskey and the price of a flophouse?"

Rose stared at him, her mouth open in astonishment. But Stanton pressed on, his voice flat and awful.

"Or maybe you're just using the word 'they' as so many pea-brained idiots use it, as a cowardly rhetorical device, an excuse to say the things you really believe without giving anyone the chance to judge you for the narrow-minded, stupid creature you are."

Rose's lip trembled for a moment. Then she snatched up her carpetbag and ran out of the car. Emily stared at Stanton.

"What has gotten into you?" she asked. "That was awful. How could you—"

"That girl is an albatross." Stanton pressed his fingers to the bridge of his nose and rubbed his eyes. "Saying those things to you, after everything that's happened—"

"She didn't have any idea what she was saying," Emily said. "And if you were trying to protect me, at least you could have picked on someone your own size."

Rising abruptly, Emily went out in the direction Rose had gone. She found Rose sitting in the vestibule between cars, collapsed in a tearful heap. She was sobbing, clutching the carpetbag to her chest.

"Miss Rose?" Emily said softly.

"I'm sorry I bothered you." Rose dashed drops from her eyes. "I didn't mean to."

"Oh, him." Emily cast a scornful glance back toward the car where Stanton was. "He's a meaner varmint than Sheriff Black, the Skull Mountain Kid, and the Scabby Badger all rolled up into one."

Rose giggled, sniffling, at what was certainly quite a ridiculous combination.

"You're awful nice, Mr. Elmer," Rose said. "I have a brother like you. He's nice, too. Whenever anyone's mean to me, he knocks 'em down."

Emily sat down next to Rose, suddenly wishing that she

were Rose's brother. At that moment, she wouldn't mind a life spent taking care of a girl like Rose. A life spent protecting her from all the terrible things in the world. More than anything, she envied Rose's wide-eyed innocence, the cozy narrowness of her existence. She had no idea how vast the world could be, how many horrors and mysteries lurked in its dark places. Emily felt she had discovered far too much—far more than she'd ever wanted to, just as Lawa had promised.

Rose caught the faraway look in Emily's eyes, and something sly crept across her face. She leaned closer to Emily, whispered words in her ear.

"You're outlaws, aren't you?"

Emily pulled back a little, looked at her warily.

"What?"

"I know you're a woman," Rose said. "I knew it from the first time I saw you. That's why I was interested in you two. I thought . . . oh, never mind what I thought. I'm just a pea-brained idiot."

"No, you're not. Tell me what you thought."

Rose looked at her, her eyes sparkling with sudden excitement.

"I tried to guess what your story was," Rose said. "I do that sometimes. I just look at people and try to figure out their lives."

Rose hitched herself closer.

"Here's what I guessed. You can't have been outlaws long, because you sure don't do it very well. Maybe you robbed a bank or something. But you're madly in love, and you're on the run from the law. Is that it? You can tell me. I promise I'll keep the secret."

"That's not it." Emily felt herself blushing, but she didn't quite know why. "But that would make a good story, wouldn't it?"

"Things work out in stories," Rose said. "If this were a story, I wouldn't be going to Aunt Kindy's, I'd be going someplace . . . exciting." Her lip trembled. "I hate Aunt Kindy. All those things I told you about her weren't true. She's mean to me and she smells. I don't know what Mr. Smith called her, but I'm sure it meant that she's unpleasant. And she *is*. She's a spiteful woman who wants me around just so she can smoke cigarillos and drink gin on the sly."

Emily *tsk*ed sadly and put her arm around Rose.

"Maybe it won't be that bad," she said, aware of how useless the words were.

"Yes, it will be," Rose said. She was trying to hold back her tears, but they kept trickling down her cheeks. "She just wants me for a slave. And I have to go. What else can I do?"

"I'm sorry, Rose," Emily said softly. "It'll be all right. I'm sure it will."

Rose leaned against her, resting her head on Emily's shoulder, and Emily held her companionably. From behind them came the sound of a cleared throat. It was Stanton, looking down at them disapprovingly.

"Elmer," he said. "I need to speak with you. Now."

Emily glared at him. She gave Rose a strengthening squeeze before standing and following Stanton back to the seats.

"You've broken her poor heart," Emily said accusingly.

"Oh, please!" Stanton rolled his eyes. "You really *don't* know anything about being a man, do you?" Stanton gestured curtly to the seats, indicating Emily should sit; Emily shook her head furiously.

"I can't leave her like that. I'm going back."

"You'll do no such thing," Stanton growled. "You can't go putting your arm around a girl like that . . . you'll be facing her father down a shotgun. I have no doubt that her broken heart will heal before lunchtime. Now sit."

"Why are you being so horrible?" Emily hissed at him, sitting.

"Why are you being so naïve?" Stanton returned. "Of all the difficulties I thought we'd encounter on this trip, I must say a farm girl falling in love with you was one that never even crossed my mind."

"She's not in love with me," Emily snapped. "She knows I'm not a man."

Stanton's face hardened.

"You told her?" he said, in a low voice, leaning forward. "Damn it, Emily—"

"She figured it out herself," Emily said. "You said yourself that I'm unconvincing as a man."

"I had hoped you could at least convince someone like Rose," Stanton said. "The fact that she knows not only puts us in danger, but it puts her in danger right along with us."

That thought made Emily pause. Stanton saw the realization on her face, nodded soberly.

"Another one of the joys of being a fugitive." Stanton sighed. "It's high time we distanced ourselves from her. When we come into Omaha, I want you to get new clothes. We're going to get out of these damn Zulu cars and into a Pullman, where she can't follow us."

"Switch to a Pullman? Can we afford it?"

"We'll be in Chicago tomorrow night, and in New York a day after that. We're close enough that we can take the chance."

Emily sighed, chewing her lip. She thought of the tears on Rose's face, thought of how she was going to be sacrificed to the despised Aunt Kindy with little more than her good nature and her carpetbag full of half-baked heroes to keep her company. But then she thought of Rose at the hands of Captain Caul. Any loneliness the girl would suffer without them would be negligible compared to that.

"All right," Emily said finally, nodding her head in resigned agreement. "But it does seem a shame, she is so—"

Emily stopped speaking as Rose returned. Her eyes were red, and she did not meet Emily's gaze as she sat down, staring quietly out the window.

No more words were exchanged between the members of the sad little party. Rose looked out of the window dejectedly, sniffling at odd intervals. Stanton sat, arms crossed, staring at some invisible object in the middle distance that seemed, from his scrutiny, to be of incomparable interest. When they pulled into Omaha, Stanton rose stiffly.

"I'll go see to the arrangements we discussed," he said to Emily. "I believe you were going to find a general store?"

Emily murmured assent, made to follow him as he moved

quickly toward the exit. But before she could go, Rose seized
Emily's hand. She held it fast, looked up at Emily with red-
rimmed eyes.

"Don't go," she said. "Please don't go."

"I'm sorry, Rose. I have to."

"Something terrible is going to happen. I just know it," Rose
whispered. Her eyes were big with fear, and her hand, clutching Emily's, was trembling. "Something *terrible*."

"Once we're gone, you'll be safe," Emily said, under her
breath. She prayed it was true.

Rose said nothing.

"Good-bye, Rose."

Emily had to pull hard to remove her hand from Rose's
grasp. When she finally succeeded, Rose brought her hands up
to her face, covering her eyes.

"I hope we never see each other again," Rose said, her voice
husky. Then she turned her back on Emily, slumping over the
hard seat, her shoulders shuddering with a fresh flood of tears.

Emily turned, climbed off the train. She did not look back.

The train had only an hour's layover in Omaha, so Emily put
the sobbing girl out of her mind as best she could. She had a
specific errand, and a limited amount of time to accomplish it.
She couldn't be worrying about Rose.

She hurried through the crowds and ducked out of the station, spying a general store just across the street from the depot. Navigating the press of carriages and wagons that were
lined up to pick up or drop off train passengers, she made it inside, quickly scanning the selection of women's clothing available off-the-shelf.

On one hand, Emily thought it was rather a shame to spend
good money when her suit still had plenty of wear left in it. On
the other hand, Stanton was right about the excessive memo-
rability of the ugly plaid. Also, the thought of not having to use
the gentlemen's rest anymore appealed to her greatly.

It took very little deliberation to settle on a simple black
dress, for that was about all there was to be had. Even so, Emily
was able to bargain the clerk down considerably because it was
made of heavy wool and too warm for the coming spring. She

also bought a chemise and petticoat and pantalettes—all the things she'd left behind when assuming her disguise in San Francisco. It was a shame she couldn't afford different shoes; the heavy men's boots were bound to look odd under the skirt of a dress. She bought a hat, too, with a heavy dark veil.

Crossing back to the station, she was faced with a thorny dilemma: Where was she going to change? Should she enter the men's restroom and emerge as a woman, or risk the brouhaha that would certainly ensue if she were caught entering the ladies' restroom as a man?

She decided that both options were far too risky, and instead ducked into a small broom closet conveniently located between both restrooms. It was cramped, but she managed to effect the change without too much indignity. She very much appreciated the opportunity to remove the bandaging that flattened her chest; she'd forgotten how nice it was to take a deep breath.

While she was changing, she checked the injury on her arm. To her surprise, the bullet wound was completely healed, leaving behind only a faint pink scar where the laceration had been. She threw away the dirty bandage and crumbling moss, not bothering herself to wonder how it could have healed so quickly. Having encountered so many strange things that worked to her detriment, it was downright refreshing to run across a strangeness that behooved her.

She folded her men's clothes into a neat pile. Stepping out of the broom closet, Emily dropped them into the first garbage can she passed. The only thing she kept was the safety pin Rose had given her. One never knew when a safety pin would come in handy, and Emily felt like having a memento of the poor, sweet girl whose chatter she'd already begun to miss. She fastened the pin inside her sleeve and smoothed fabric over it.

When she returned to the platform, she searched the crowd for Stanton's lanky form. They hadn't thought to agree on a meeting place, and as they were switching to a Pullman she had no idea what car they would be getting on.

"Miss Edwards," a voice behind her said, making her jump. It was Stanton, his head low and his hat pulled well over his eyes. "Put your veil down. Word has finally caught up with us."

She followed Stanton's eyes to where two men in shiny gray suits stood side by side, scanning the platform. Emily put her veil down casually.

"Maelstroms?"

"Maelstroms, Pinkertons, undercover police . . . who knows. But they're not waiting for friends. Come on. We have to pass them to get to our car."

"How do I look?" she whispered to him.

"Better," he whispered back. "Who'll bother a man traveling with his widowed aunt?"

"The compliments just drip like honey from your lips, don't they?" she muttered as he extended his arm to her. She took it, keeping her head down and drawing herself against his body as if for support in a time of mourning. Taking the cue, Stanton bent his face close to hers and patted her arm tenderly.

"Walk slowly," Stanton murmured as he felt Emily's urge to run. They were passing directly in front of the men in gray. Emily could hear them breathing, feel their tense energy like big cats ready to spring, see the knives sheathed at their belts.

"Never give them cause to chase you." Emily spoke the words in an exhaled breath as they put the men behind them, neither one having given the poor man and his widowed aunt so much as a second glance.

They stayed hunched down in their seats until the train was well out of the station, after which time they could relax and enjoy the comfort of the Pullman. Once they were enfolded in its profusion of scrollwork and button tufting, it seemed as if nothing could ever go wrong again.

They had gotten into a parlor car, so they had their own little room and a porter in a white coat to see to their needs. Seats were dusted, pillows fluffed, ice water fetched. All around them, red velvet and burled wood shone, polished brass winked.

The atmosphere seemed to rejuvenate Stanton substantially. His eyes seemed brighter and clearer, his face ruddier, his mood noticeably more cheerful.

"I feel as if a weight has been lifted from my shoulders," he sighed pleasurably, stretching his long legs out before him. "Not to mention from my ears."

The train charged toward Chicago. Night came. The attendant laid a table for them with white linen and crystal, and served steaming bowls of terrapin soup and fat grilled steaks. Stanton bolted the food ravenously.

"You know, I've been thinking," he said, as he was working on his third plateful. "After our business is done, I must show you around New York. I hear Central Park is coming along quite nicely."

Emily, taking a deep swallow of red wine, smiled slightly.

"Mr. Stanton, I'd be overjoyed to see Central Park or any of the wonderful sights New York has to offer." The idea of sightseeing was so ludicrous as to be unimaginable. A free trip to see the wonders of New York, and all she had to do was stay one step ahead of military blood sorcerers, escort the spirit of a dead holy woman around her neck, and avoid becoming a rampaging Aberrancy. What a delightful bargain!

"You'll like New York," he said with a certainty she thought he had no claim to. "It's a wonderful city. Everything anyone could ever want is there."

"I'm sure you'll be glad to get back," she said. "And your family will be pleased to see you, I imagine."

He lifted an eyebrow at her, considering the statement.

"I hadn't thought of it," he said. "If bringing you back to the Mirabilis Institute contributes to the glory of the Stanton name, maybe they will be. Perhaps even tickled, though imagining my mother in that state is quite disturbing."

Emily stared at him. There was so much about the words that puzzled her, she didn't even know where to begin.

"But you're more than just a name." Emily looked at him. "A family's more than just a name."

"Not my family," Stanton said, stabbing a piece of steak with his fork.

"Then it doesn't sound much like a family," Emily said. "At least not my idea of a family."

Stanton shrugged. "I think we've already established that

your ideas and the ideas of civilized people are not always precisely aligned."

"I'm not talking about civilization," Emily snapped. "I'm talking about common decency."

"So then we're *not* talking about my family," he said.

"Any particular reason you're being so tedious? Or is it just a matter of general principle with you?"

Stanton tasted his wine, grimacing at some defect.

"Vile stuff, and halfway corked to boot," he said. He twisted the stem of the crystal between his long fingers, regarding the offending liquid with a frown. "My father is in politics, as you learned. He's an awful crook, but he's one of the most powerful men in the Republican party." He paused. "All the money's from my mother's side of the family. Her people are old Dutch, and she spends her time brutally enforcing the rock-ribbed ideals of propriety and decency that comprise 'the way things have always been done in New York.' " He looked at Emily. "I can't imagine you want to hear more."

"Try me," Emily said. She herself saw nothing wrong with the wine and was glad to pour herself another large glass.

"Three sisters—"

"Euphemia, Ophidia, and Hortense," Emily interjected.

"As unpleasant as their names suggest," Stanton continued. "Being the youngest, I was constantly subjected to their malformed mimicry of motherhood."

"They put your hair in curls and pushed you around in carriages, didn't they?"

"One prefers not to remember," Stanton said, taking up his glass, unsatisfactory as it was, and draining it swiftly.

When dinner was finished, the porter retrieved their plates and glasses, cleared the table, offered them a selection of reading materials, and volunteered to turn their lights up or down. He seemed on the verge of offering to get down on his hands and knees and provide them with a human footstool when Stanton waved him away.

Emily sat looking out the window, her chin cradled in her hand. The sunset was a beautiful shade of lavender, the clouds tinged with lime. Before the sun went down again, she realized, she would be in New York. The thought sent a nervous thrill through her entire body. Her throat was tight, her heart suddenly racing. She looked at Stanton.

"He will help us, won't he?" she blurted suddenly. Stanton, looking up from an evening edition of *The New York Times*, met her eyes quizzically. "Professor Mirabilis, I mean. He will help us. Everything's going to turn out all right, isn't it?"

"Professor Mirabilis is the most powerful credomancer in New York City," Stanton said. "He's the Sophos of the Institute—its leader. Its Heart. He'll know exactly what to do. Everything will be fine."

Each of Stanton's words fitted carefully against the last, building a comforting wall of syllabic certainty. But still, Emily rubbed her finger over the cool metal of the ring she still wore on her thumb—the ring Stanton had given her in San Francisco. She frowned, not looking at him.

"At Cutter's Rise, Caul said that Mirabilis had no faith in you." Emily spoke softly. "He said that he wanted to make you a failure."

"Caul was doing his best to squink me." Stanton's voice was dismissive, but his brow knit slightly. "For all Caul derides credomancy, he's not above using its tools."

"What exactly is a 'squink' anyway?"

"It's a minor credomantic tactic. It is an attempt to undermine the power of another by attacking his sense of self-worth. It's a contraction of the words 'squid ink,' because it's like a squid squirting ink to muddy the waters. A successful squink makes one question oneself, and questioning oneself leads to muddleheadedness and uncertainty."

"But what was he trying to make you question? What did he mean about squandered opportunities?"

"Speaking of Central Park," Stanton said, folding his paper and tilting his head to peer at her. "Did you know that it has a castle with enchanted swans?"

She blinked.

"A what?" Emily said.

"A castle," Stanton said. "With enchanted swans."

"But what does that have to do with—"

"It's called Belvedere Castle, and it's built on top of Vista Rock." Stanton's voice was low and rhythmic. "The second

highest natural elevation in Central Park. Before it stretches
a beautiful smooth lake dotted with irises and blue flags.
It's actually a reservoir full of Croton water, but they've done
a lovely job disguising that. Anyway, the enchanted swans
swim around on this lake, and on nights with a full moon,
they can talk. One of them has a very cultivated Afrikaner accent, though no one knows where he picked it up. He's called
Charlie."

Emily blinked at him again. His eyes held hers, and in their
green depths she felt, for a strange moment, that she could almost see the castle—a pile of white stone reflected in a rippling lake, blue flags and irises stirring in the wind.

"He can do what? In what kind of accent?"

"All of the swans have excellent conversational skills, but
Charlie is the most celebrated. Someone, though no one quite
knows who, has taught him to recite several cantos of Dante's
Inferno. Someone with an Afrikaner accent, it stands to reason. It's really quite a mystery."

Emily's head was suddenly a stew of castles and talking
swans and mysterious Afrikaners. She scratched a place behind
her ear as if that would bring her thoughts back into some kind
of logical arrangement.

"How did we get on enchanted swans?" she said with vague
irritation. "What were we talking about, anyway?"

"Sophos Mirabilis," Stanton said. "And how he's going to
help you."

Emily nodded, remembering.

"He'll know what to do? You're sure of it?"

"I'm absolutely certain of it," Stanton said. "I've never been
more certain of anything in my life. Don't lose heart now.
Everything's going to be fine."

Emily breathed out. The force and sureness of Stanton's
words made her feel warm and hopeful.

The feeling of pleasant optimism lingered for the rest of the
evening. The porter made up the beds, and Emily took the bottom berth, drawing the velvet curtain closed. Snuggling under
the blankets, looking forward to a good night's sleep, she
found that some of the excitement she'd felt at the beginning

of the trip had returned. They were almost to New York, and New York was sure to be a wonderful place.

"You know, Mr. Stanton," she said drowsily, as she heard him douse the lamp, "I find that I really am looking forward to seeing Central Park."

Rocking, swaying gently in that soft bed, Emily dreamed.

She dreamed that the whole world pulsed and throbbed around her like the heart of a giant beast.

She dreamed that she was standing in the middle of a wide stretching place, edges curving into the distance, the land reflecting the sky and the sky reflecting the land. The sound was all around her, as if she were a tiny grain of sand within a great thumping drum.

What if she lost herself in all that emptiness? How could anyone find her? How could she find herself?

She could see the veins of the earth, its sinews and structures. With the topsoil torn away, peeled back, she could see the shimmering traceries that lay hidden beneath, imagined but never seen—veins that glowed with orange and gold and yellow and red. Mirrorlike, the sky reflected the light, shimmering and shifting, cloudy and ethereal.

"It's so beautiful," Emily whispered in Miwok. Her words, spoken, sent light in a shimmering ripple along the glowing tracery, along thick broad veins and small feathery capillaries. To her surprise, Emily found that she could feel the movement of the light, feel it all through her body. It was ticklish and maddening all at once, like having her spine stroked by a velvet glove, like having her ears licked by a cat, like having her toes rubbed with ice by a warm hand. She gasped with delight, closing her eyes.

It is Ososolyeh, Komé said.

Opening her eyes, Emily saw that the old woman was before her, her naked old body withered and shrunken. Her body was entirely black, as if she were made of stretchy shining tar. She stood perfectly motionless, arms crossed over her sagging breasts, her head down.

Ososolyeh, ancient and vast, wanderer from the stars, the

great spirit of the earth. Komé's voice rose and fell counterpoint to the thrum of the earth around them.

"Then it does live," Emily whispered, feeling the certainty of it.

It lives, Komé exhaled. *It needs you, Basket of Secrets.*

"I don't understand what it wants," Emily said.

It has been trying to tell you. It has been trying desperately.

"I haven't heard it." Emily's despair made the light around her ripple with sad shades of blue and purple.

It speaks in the music of the wind. The shift of grass and branch. The shape of clouds. In all of these, Ososolyeh speaks. It has told you its will in every bird that has flown over your head, every mote of dust that has swirled before your eyes, every piece of earth that has turned from beneath your foot.

"I don't know the language of grasses and birds and dirt," Emily said. "Why can't you just tell me yourself?"

Ah, that would be a story that would take millions of years to tell in words, Komé said regretfully. *And the foulness binds me, and I am tired.*

"You have to help me understand," Emily begged.

The mind of Ososolyeh cannot be imagined. To hear Ososolyeh's voice, you must allow your mind to stretch to the size of the stars, for that is the size of Ososolyeh's dreams. You must forget that time exists. You must forget that you can die.

Emily didn't think she could forget that, looking at Komé's body, at the oily ugliness that bound her. She fell to her knees before the old woman, bending her head.

"I can't do it." She put her face in her hands. "Mother, I can't."

Yes, you can. Komé smiled and brought her hands down, placing them softly on Emily's head.

And Emily's head exploded.

Her tiny weak human skull inflated like an Aberrancy, a grotesque balloon, a cosmic ball of igniting gas. Memories flooded her, memories of a mind whose thoughts were too large and old to comprehend, memories that could only be felt and absorbed, memories of stars and infinite distances and eons of traveling, drifting, seeking. Her body exploded, too, becoming immense and spherical and bright, oh so bright, taking and returning the sweet force of life, cycling it back and forth in a beautiful complicated dance. The pleasure of it was unbearable.

Do you see? Komé asked finally, as eternity receded from Emily's mind.

Emily found that she didn't need to speak.

YES.

She saw that the heartbeat that surrounded her was her own. She saw that she could make the colors dance with the smallest impulse of thought. She made reds and blues shift, and discovered that she'd made them shift in the exact same way in one perfectly remembered moment a billion years earlier. She longed to remember more. She longed to stay here forever, now that she knew what forever was. But Komé gently lifted her hands from Emily's head, and the dream began to fade.

You cannot stay here, Basket of Secrets. You must go to them. They are waiting for you.

"Who is waiting?" Emily murmured sleepily, as dawn light seeped through her eyelids.

The Sons of the Earth.

Emily sat up with a gasp, knocking her head against the low ceiling. Groaning, she rubbed her forehead. Her arm felt like it was five hundred feet long.

She felt all out of proportion; everything around her was so narrow and close, but she felt so large and diffuse and rubbery. Tendrils of the dream spun away from her, and she felt a desperate desire to clutch at them. In that gleaming shimmering place, she had been so large. She had been Ososolyeh—a living thing with memories that stretched beyond the void of infinity. Now she was trapped, returned to the small sore breathing hungry confinement of a body that could die—circumscribed, imprisoned.

She jerked the curtain aside, desperate to escape the feeling of sudden, smothering enclosure.

The first thing she saw was Rose.

The girl sat on the seat directly across from Emily's berth. She was leaning forward, elbows resting on splayed knees.

Her eyes were wide and glittering, unfocused. Her dress was rumpled, her blond hair all askew.

The second thing Emily saw were Rose's guns.

A revolver was clutched in each of her dainty white hands. Pulling the hammers back, Rose lifted the guns and leveled them at Emily.

"*Buon giorno,* Miss Edwards," Rose said, her voice accented in lilting Italian. "Pleasant dreams?"

Rose's Thorns

Emily's eyes darted around the compartment. Stanton stood with his back to the door, as if he were holding it shut with the weight of his body. His head was drooped; he stared at the floor. His green eyes were narrowed slits.

"Mr. Stanton?" Emily ventured. She looked at the girl. "Rose?"

"Not at the moment," Rose drawled, the strange new accent making her words lazy. "I have her body for the time being."

Emily narrowed her eyes.

"This body belong to Rose Hibble. Indeed, most of the time it is inhabited by that silly little girl. Except when I need to use her."

Emily still stared.

"I see you are confuse. It is a common reaction." Rose stood, giving the courtliest bow possible in the limited space. "My name is Grimaldi. Antonio Pietro Grimaldi. Or at least, that was my name, when I have a body of my own. But that was many years ago, and there have been so many names and bodies since then." Rose—or Grimaldi—separated each word carefully, seeming to take pleasure in the act of speech. The girl touched a pendant that hung at her throat, a smooth brown nut that looked like a buckeye mounted in an ornate gold setting. "This, actually, is all there is of me. Here, in this uchawi pod, is where my spirit is remain attached. But I have learned to ride the bodies of humans. They are my mounts, my steeds. I use them to hunt."

"What do you hunt?" Emily said, knowing the answer but wishing she didn't.

"People." Grimaldi's voice caressed the word lovingly. "People for who other people will pay money."

Emily swallowed hard. She looked past Rose at Stanton. She watched desperately for any sign of a reaction, but he just stood, eyes fixed on the floor. Emily looked back to Rose. The cheerful spark in the girl's blue eyes had been replaced with distant coldness and a formless malice.

"You're a Manipulator." Emily suddenly remembered what Stanton had said about emancipated spirits who jumped from body to body, losing more of their moral compass with each transference. He'd said they were rare. Leave it to their luck to run into one.

"If you like to call me that," Grimaldi said. "But I prefer to be called what I am. Bounty hunter."

"What have you done to Mr. Stanton?"

"It is nothing. A minor compulsion. Compulsions, they are my specialty. It is so much easier to transport people when they don't even know they are being transported. When they are bind by chains they do not see or understand." Grimaldi paused. "You remember the Eye-Opener I give him? I hid in there a skeleton key that unlocks the will of the one who drinks it. Once I have him, I have you." Rose's lips curled into a sneer. "Because you will do whatever he tell you to do."

Emily pressed her lips together tightly.

"*Carissima mia,* how disapproving you look." Grimaldi laughed. "But I hear what you do to that man in Lost Pine. Forcing him to love you—what is this but a kind of compulsion?"

Rose's body shuddered from head to heel. She was fighting to regain control of herself, but it was futile. When she spoke again, it was still Grimaldi's smooth voice that came from her lips.

"Most Warlocks keep up a constant defense against such hostile magic." Grimaldi regarded Stanton with a lazy smirk. "But I am able to sneak it past him because he was asleep."

Then Grimaldi paused thoughtfully. "But it do not work on you. Very unusual. Very unusual *indeed*."

"So you work for Caul." Emily hurried to change the subject. That Grimaldi didn't know about the stone was something, at least.

"Caul hire me," Grimaldi said. "He offer me a thousand dollar for each of you. But I am not take you to Caul. There are others who want you. Others who will pay ten times more."

"Who?" Emily breathed.

"They are call the *Sini Mira*," Grimaldi said. "Sons of the Earth."

Sons of the Earth.

Something must have passed across Emily's face when she heard the words, for Grimaldi peered at her with close interest. "You know of these?"

"No." Emily lied. Komé had said the Sons of the Earth were waiting for her. That she must go to them. Surely the Holy Woman couldn't have meant this? That this body-jumping bounty hunter—this Manipulator—was to take her to them?

Emily noticed that Rose's body was shivering harder now. A miserable tear streaked a path down her dirty face.

"And are you going to let Rose go?" Emily demanded. "Once you've delivered us?"

"Oh, of course I will let Rose go!" Grimaldi's voice was slimy with pretended kindness. "Her body has amuse me, but I ride her since Promontory, and *carissima* Rosa, she grow so tired. Soon, her mind will be broken, and then she will be just a lump of meat. It does not do for a huntsman to ride a beaten horse. So I will take a new body." Grimaldi eyed Stanton. "His body."

Emily saw a shudder of revulsion pass over Stanton's entire frame.

"Like hell you will." Emily knew she had only one chance. She launched herself at Rose with a wildcat cry, knocking the girl's body to the floor of the compartment, grabbing for the uchawi pod at her throat. Stanton stared down at them from his position by the door, his eyes fixed and glazed, his hands clenched in fists.

"Bind her, Warlock!" Grimaldi screamed at Stanton. "Use your magic, hold her!"

Stanton did not move, just clenched his fists even tighter.

Rose had Emily's arms pinned at her side, but Emily worked one free, reaching up, fingers searching for the uchawi pod. The blond girl was heavier, her muscles strong from farm work, but Emily was strong, too. She grabbed a handful of Rose's now-loose hair, jerking her head down.

"Bind her, Warlock!" Grimaldi shrieked again. "I command you. Do it *now*!"

"No," Stanton choked. "No magic."

Rose rolled swiftly up over Emily's body, straddling her. With a ferocious cry, she brought her fist down hard into Emily's face—twice, three times. Emily fell back, stunned; the world spun and shuddered.

"Warlock, I command you!" Grimaldi's voice became vast and awful; Rose's hand clutched at the uchawi pod around her throat. Stanton winced, throwing his hands up over his head.

"No magic!" he screamed, his voice edged with agony.

Then, Emily saw it. Tucked underneath one of the seats was Rose's flowered carpetbag. Even ridden by a body-jumping bounty hunter, the girl wouldn't leave her treasured books behind. Emily reached for the heavy bag and grasped the rattan handles. She swung it up, smashing it against the side of Rose's head. Rose toppled. Emily swung herself over the girl's body, using the carpetbag like a bludgeon, bringing it down again and again. Blind, heart thrashing, she hardly knew what she was doing.

Finally, she stopped, and Rose lay still. Emily grabbed the revolvers from where they'd fallen, used the side of a seat to pull herself to her feet. She cocked the revolvers, pointed them down at Rose. Blood streamed from her nose; she wiped it away with the back of her hand.

"Kill her!" Stanton bellowed, his eyes shifting and churning with strange confusion. "Kill her, for God's sake!"

"It's not Rose's fault!"

With a roar, Stanton grabbed her and threw open the door, pulled her out of the compartment. They careened down the hall, into the vestibule. There was the thunder of clattering wheels, the hot inferno blast of steam rising up from the train's brakes.

Stanton wrapped his arms tightly around her body.

"Hold on to me," he said.

And then they jumped.

CHAPTER SEVENTEEN

The Cockatrice

They fell hard on the small gravel of the siding, crashing through scrub and dead weeds. They must have finally stopped, Emily supposed, for she could very clearly see the ground on which they had landed and it wasn't moving.

Stanton climbed to his feet, legs trembling. He swayed, holding his head, the heels of his palms pressing hard into his eyes.

"Knife," he muttered. "I need a knife." He reached into his pocket, pulled out the misprision blade, and slid it open with a hissing *snick.* Then he looked up at Emily, his face wild with fury.

"Get away from me!" he screamed at her, sweeping the air with his arm. "Far away!"

She scrambled away from him, turning to watch him sink to his knees on the train tracks. With swift brutality, he slashed the sharp edge of the misprision blade over each of his wrists. She watched with horror as he clenched and unclenched his hands, spurting arterial blood pooling around his knees. He barked a loud, resonant command and the bleeding stopped.

Rubbing his hands together, he drew strange glyphs in the spilled blood, chanting guttural magic in a language she had never heard him use before. The words were not clear clipped Latin but something else—something far older, harsh and cruel, rich with acrimony and malice.

As he chanted, power surged around him. The wind whipped the tall dry grass alongside the tracks. Emily drew back even farther, clutching her right hand to her chest as she watched a black thing rising from his spilled blood—a small black thing like a writhing leech. With bared teeth, Stanton seized a large piece of stone and began bashing the thing, crushing it into a pulp. The thing squealed.

"Bastard!" Stanton screamed, as he brought the rock down again and again. "Oily, stinking *bastard*!"

He beat at it until only a greasy stain remained, then threw the rock away from himself with an angry cry. He slumped over the smeared blood, breathing hard through clenched teeth.

Emily watched him for a long time. When she approached him, her steps were tentative crunches on the gravel. She touched his shoulder. There was a large rip in the shoulder of his coat through which torn and abraded skin showed.

"That . . . thing . . ." Stanton stammered. "In my own mind. Filthy, vicious . . . I would have used magic on you! I would have . . ."

"Are you all right?" she said.

He was silent for a long time. Breathing.

"I cleansed myself. I had to do it before Rose had a chance to wake up." He touched the blood around his knees, pressed his palms into it heavily. "It was the only way."

Emily looked at the crimson splashed all around him, at the garish blotches streaking his face and arms.

"What . . . kind of magic was that?" she asked, aware of the smallness of her own voice.

Stanton said nothing. His jaw was clenched.

"I've never seen you work that kind of magic before," Emily said.

"It's none of your business," he growled.

"But—"

"It's *nothing*," Stanton said, with a horrible force that made Emily shudder.

"We should get away from here, Mr. Stanton," she said quickly, not wanting to hear him speak in that voice ever again. "It's not safe here."

"It's not safe anywhere," Stanton said, closing his eyes. He made no move to stand.

The bleeding had slowed, but his wrists were still oozing, sticky crusting rivulets flowing over his fingers. Bending,

Emily tore fabric from the hem of her skirt, then knelt before him. Carefully, she took his hands, examining the cuts. They were not deep; they seemed to be healing even as she looked at him. She began bandaging them anyway. He took her hands midmovement. He took her by the arms and pulled her close. She felt his heart thrashing in his chest. He smelled of sweat and blood and creosote.

"Thank you." His voice resonated against her ear, his breath hot on her skin. The heat from his body beat against her in waves, but still she shivered.

"You only ever thank me when I save your life," she murmured.

He lifted his gory arms and took her face between his hands. With his thumbs, he smoothed the swelling places where Rose's fists had landed. Then he pressed his mouth hard against hers. His lips were hot and feverish; she felt the brush of his stubble against her cheek. She leaned into him, kissing him back, suddenly remembering all the times that she'd wanted desperately to kiss him but didn't know it. She felt light and translucent, like a paper lantern lit from within.

She felt his hands slide down over her waist. The touch made her breath tremble, blood rising to choke her. He pulled her closer, until the whole length of her body rested against his. The kisses became slower and softer. She could feel the ugly power of the blood magic fading from around him. Finally it was him she was kissing, not the anger and pain that had possessed him. But almost as soon as she realized this, he pushed her back gently and let his forehead rest against hers.

"No, don't stop," she said, her body flushed from crown to toe. "I mean . . . you don't have to."

"Yes, I do." He rolled to the side and climbed to his feet. He fumbled with the bandages hanging around his wrists, wrapping them tight. "I most certainly do."

"Mr. Stanton . . ."

"Come on," he said, not looking at her. "We have to go."

They struck out on a dusty frontage that soon veered from the tracks to cut arrow-straight through vast swaths of farmland—freshly plowed fields that showed the roots of turned-under winter cover crops. They walked in silence as the day grew hotter, the sun beating against their backs, the whirring shrieks of cicadas saturating the heavy air.

Emily hung back, walking well behind Stanton, staring fixedly into the clouds of dust that rose from her heavy boots with every step.

She was not sure what exactly had happened.

A Manipulator and strange sinister magic and . . . She touched a hand to her cheek. There were streaks of dried blood there, where his long fingers had touched her face.

No, she wasn't sure exactly what had happened at all.

Or why she felt safer with her hands on the revolvers she'd taken from Rose. They weighted her pockets and swayed against her legs. She kept stroking the hammers with her thumbs.

When they came to a crossroads where the road split off into four cardinal directions, Stanton stood squinting up at the signpost for a long time. If there had been signs on it at one point, they had long since been torn down.

"Cynic Mirror," he said. "Sini Mira."

"What?" Emily said.

"Your mother. You said she was looking for the Cynic Mirror. In Russian, *sin* means 'son.' *Mir* translates as 'earth.' Apply the plural possessive declension and you have 'Earth's Sons'—or as Grimaldi called them, the Sons of the Earth. The Cynic Mirror is not a thing . . . it's a group."

"You've heard of them?" Emily said.

"Yes." His tone made it sound as if he wished he hadn't. "They're a society of Russian scientists. Eradicationists."

"Eradicationists?"

"Eradicationists believe that the practice of magic should be stopped, but none of them agree on how that should be accomplished. The Scharfians, as you've discovered, advocate burning. The Sini Mira, on the other hand, believe that advancements in science will ultimately replace every advantage magic currently affords us. Their researchers are said to be working on a chemical method that will destroy the human body's ability to channel magic. It is said that all their experiments on human subjects have been fatal."

Emily absorbed this silently.

We must get to the Sini Mira. That's what her mother had really said that cold night in Lost Pine . . . but why would her mother have been going to Eradicationists?

"I'm supposed to go to them," Emily whispered. That's what Komé had said, that's what she'd seen in her dream.

"Ridiculous." Stanton turned east, began walking. "Your mother said that twenty years ago. I'm sure whatever business she might have had with them is long since passed."

But it wasn't just her mother's words that she was thinking of. Emily opened her mouth to tell Stanton about the strange dream she'd had on the train, what Komé had shown her, what she had said . . . but she drew the words back on a breath and pressed her lips together tightly.

She had trusted Stanton completely. His dismissive certainty had always made it easy to do so—hard to do otherwise, in fact. But self-sure as he was, even Dreadnought Stanton could be compromised. He could be brutalized, his mind taken hostage, his will bent or even broken . . .

The more he knew, the more danger he was in.

She looked up at his back. At the blood crusting on his palms.

And the more she knew about him . . .

She did not allow herself to complete the thought. Instead, she stopped suddenly, brow wrinkling, dust swirling up in front of her.

"I can't just *follow* you anymore," she said, the knowledge and the regret of it attacking her simultaneously. "I have to find a different way."

Stanton stopped, but did not turn. He stood staring down the dusty road that led east. He flexed his fingers, as if they were remembering something, then let his hands droop slack at his sides.

Emily caught up with him in a half dozen quick steps and placed her body in front of his. He did not look at her but rather past her, his eyes fixed on the road. She reached up and placed a hand on either side of his face. He flinched but did not pull away. She gently tilted his face down until his eyes met hers. She looked into those green eyes, trying to find something there that would reassure her, but there was nothing—only distance and formality. She let her hands drop quickly.

"I swear it won't happen again," he said.

"Which?" she said. "The blood magic, or—"

"Both are unforgivable."

Emily looked at him for a long time. There were so many things she wanted to know—but she wanted not to know them even more. She didn't want any more answers. He had been the one thing she could trust, the one person she could rely on. She wanted to beg him to be that way again. But it wasn't him who had changed. It was her. It was her own credulity she really wanted back. And credulity, like virtue, could be lost only once.

"Grimaldi will have gotten off at the next stop. He will have gotten a horse. He'll find us. And when he does—" Stanton stopped, and when he spoke again his voice was brilliant with despair. "You don't know what he's capable of. I know you don't trust me . . . I can't even trust myself. But I can't leave you. I won't."

Emily put her arms around him. She held onto him as if she were trying to keep him from floating away from the earth. He did not bend under her embrace, but rather stood with fists clenched at his sides. She held him more tightly.

"I do trust you," she whispered fiercely into the dirty, torn fabric of his shirt. "I have faith in you. We'll find a different way together."

Stanton was still for a long time. When he did finally put his arms around her, he clung to her like a drowning man, his hot breath stirring the hair on the top of her head. He held her like this for a long time. Finally, he straightened, drew in a deep breath. She looked up and saw that his face was set with familiar determination.

"Thank you, Miss Edwards," he said, releasing her.

There was a sound, like the dry chuckle of a very old woman. Emily turned slightly, trying to catch it, but it was already gone. But as she was turning her head, something else caught her eye: something back at the crossroads. For a moment, it

seemed that the dust took a shape, the shape of a woman pointing. Emily took a couple of steps away from Stanton, staring at
the dust as it blew away on a refreshing gust.

"What is it?" Stanton looked in the direction she was staring.

"Follow me," she said.

She walked back to the crossroad. Leaning against the
empty signpost, she pulled off her boots and her stockings.
She ground her bare feet into the hot dust, wiggling her toes.

Speak to me, she whispered. *Speak to me in a language I
can understand.*

Closing her eyes, she imagined Ososolyeh, its intricate
glowing traceries spreading out from beneath her feet. And as
she imagined it, she found that she could feel it pulsing and
throbbing beneath her bare soles. She let herself sink into that
vast place, let herself expand to become part of it.

She took a step.

And then another.

Energy threaded up around her feet, her ankles, her legs. A
hundred tiny filaments—like roots or streams or veins of
ore—traced the contours of her calves, her thighs. They gently
pulled her forward, and her steps became a drumbeat, rhythmic and cadent, step after step after step, in the direction
Ososolyeh wanted her to go.

"What are you doing?" Stanton hurried after her, grabbing
her boots and stockings out of the dust. "You're going *west!*"

Emily hardly heard him. The earth was singing in her ears.

Her body, a tiny pinprick on a vast terrain, moved through
eons of memory.

But she was no longer in her body, crawling like an insect
through dust and sun; rather, she slept in cool dark water flowing in deep channels. She remembered glaciers, great mountains of ice. She dreamed of oceans.

After an eternity and an instant, there was the sound of an
old woman's voice, speaking in Miwok:

Come back now, Basket of Secrets.

Her consciousness jerked back into her body, slamming
back into a hot tiny prison of thirst and exhaustion. She

stumbled and fell to the ground, groaning. She tried to pull her mind back together, but it was like trying to refold a map, she couldn't quite figure out how to do it. She felt Stanton kneeling beside her, a steadying hand resting on her back.

"Miss Edwards," he said softly.

She tried to move her mouth, tried to make words come out of it, but it was impossible. It was all she could do to open her eyes, to admit the piercing unwelcome brightness. Eyes were such ridiculous things, so limited, all they could see were reflections, never the truth itself . . .

"You're exhausted," Stanton said. "We've been walking for miles."

Emily sat up, coming back to herself bit by bit. Her mouth was bone dry and her head ached. She saw that they had left the road and had crested a little rise. She looked down on a field planted with a winter cover of hairy vetch that bloomed with pretty curves of tiny purple bells. In the center of the field there was a broad spreading tree in full leaf. The cool shade beneath it looked indecently inviting. But as she lifted a mute, trembling hand, it was not the tree that she pointed to.

"What is that?" Stanton said.

An odd machine rested a little ways off from the tree. It wasn't a farming machine. It was much larger, and unlike any farming machine it had long broad silver wings resting slack on either side. Helping her to her feet, Stanton took two steps forward and shaded his eyes with his hand.

"That looks like . . . but it can't be!"

"Can't be what?"

"If that's not a Cecil Carpenter, I'll eat my hat." Stanton started running down the hill through the field of purple flowers and tangled foliage.

"What's a Cecil Carpenter?" Emily called after him. Her legs were sore and her feet ached and she wasn't about to do any running.

"Cecil Carpenter is a designer of biomechanical flying machines," Stanton began, only to fall into awed silence as he came upon the machine. The thing was even more imposing up close. Its body was as broad as a railcar. Each wing was as long as a hundred-year fir and as wide as a wagon.

"Tail of a serpent, body of a rooster . . . this is one of his Cockatrices!"

The creature was made of a softish silver metal, dull from oxidation and battered from wear. Its rooster head and sinuous tail had been intricately decorated with smooth hard-fired enamel—now chipped and cracked—in deep shades of lapis lazuli, cherry-heart crimson, and pollen yellow. There was a deep-set passenger compartment scooped out of the back between the wings, which contained a half dozen wide banquettes upholstered in red plush. These also showed signs of hard use; the nap was rubbed off the seats and backs and there were several patches.

Stanton ran his hands over the individually molded wing feathers, each one delicately engraved to look like a real feather.

"All aluminum! That must have set him back a pretty penny."

"So what's it doing here?"

Stanton pointed to a place on the Cockatrice's side, just below the wing. An ornate cartouche bearing the words "Myers & Shorb's Traveling Carnival of Novelties" had been half painted over.

"It must have been a carnival attraction," Stanton said. "But why anyone would just leave it sitting out in the middle of a cornfield—"

There was the sound of something clacking shut. Emily and Stanton looked up quickly, found themselves looking down the twin blued-steel barrels of a shotgun.

"Ain't no one just left nothing sitting nowhere," said the old man holding the shotgun. "Now get your gol'durn hands off my Cockatrice."

Emily and Stanton lifted their hands slowly.

"Just who th' hell are you two?" The old man wore tobacco-stained overalls and a straw hat. He was as thin and hard-tanned as a piece of jerky; the deep wrinkles on his face were lined with grime. "Coupla nice-dressed young people, pokin' around where you're not wanted . . . you two from the *guv'mint*?"

"Certainly not!" Emily responded to the question with the same vehemence. "We were just . . ." She paused. Telling him that the great spirit of the earth had led her here probably wouldn't cut much ice. "We were just out walking. It's so hot, and I saw the tree, and . . . and then we saw this beautiful machine."

"Ha. Fifty miles from the nearest town. You're not out on any lover's stroll. You're a couple bummers, that's what you are." The man made a menacing movement with his shotgun. "Now git off my land. I got important business, and this ain't no carnival ride no more."

"Couldn't we just rest in the shade for a little while?" Emily put as much sweet supplication into her voice as she could reasonably muster. "I'm so tired, and it's so hot."

The old man frowned at her thoughtfully. Then he looked over at Stanton, stared at him for a long time, up and down. When he saw the blood on Stanton's hands, his eyes narrowed.

"What about him?" The old man clutched the shotgun more tightly. "Don't he talk?"

"I talk," Stanton said. "I do all kinds of things."

"I'll bet you do," the old man said, still looking at Stanton's hands. He paused. "I heard you talking about this here contraption like you know something about it."

"As I was telling Miss . . . Smith," Stanton began, "it's a Cecil Carpenter Cockatrice. One of his older models. Looks like it's been used hard and not particularly well kept. You said it's yours?"

"Yep," the old man said. "Bought it off a traveling carnival show."

"You intend to fly it?"

" 'Course I intend to fly it. Matter o' fact, I'm gonna fly it out of here tomorrow morning."

"Ah," Stanton said. He threw Emily a look that was precisely equal in meaning to an index finger twirled alongside his temple. "Well, I guess it's still every American man's right to throw away his life if he chooses." He took Emily's arm and turned to go. She made small noises in protest, but he squeezed her elbow and she fell silent.

"Wait!" the old man called after them. "What are you talking about? I don't aim to throw my life away!"

"You fly in that thing and you will," Stanton called back without turning. "The men who sold it to you are crooks. You might get it up in the air, but you won't be able to keep it there. Unless . . ."

"Unless?"

Stanton smiled, turned slowly.

"Unless you put down that shotgun and let Miss Smith sit in the shade for a while," he said. "And a drink of water would be nice, too."

"Name's Hembry," the old man said, squatting down some distance from them with the shotgun across his knees. "Ebenezer Hembry."

Emily and Stanton were sitting under the shade of the big oak tree, and Hembry was watching them closely. Unslinging a canteen from around his shoulder, he tossed it over to Emily. After she'd drunk deep of the warm, stale-tasting water, Hembry fixed his gaze on Stanton.

"Now, Mr. . . ."

". . . Jones," Stanton said, and Hembry gave a little chuckle.

"Yeah. Sure. Well, Mr. *Jones* . . . what exactly did you mean about my Cockatrice?"

"It's a death trap," Stanton said. "Muscles are probably half rotted away by now."

"Muscles?" Hembry chuckled louder this time, and slapped a knee, too. "Well, that shows what you know, friend. This thing here, it's a machine. Machines ain't got muscles."

"Biomechanical flying machines do," Stanton said.

He spoke these words in a tone that Emily had learned to associate with an impending lecture, so she leaned her head back against the tree trunk and considered taking a nap. Hembry, on the other hand, leaned forward.

"What the hell does that mean?" he said. "Biomechanical who-what?"

"Carpenter's contribution to the world of engineering is his ability to interweave living flesh and machine to exploit the unique advantages of each. By using the long muscles of elephants and blue whales to provide motive power, the system can be fueled with a simple glucose solution as opposed to . . ."

"Glucose? You mean like sugar?" Hembry said. "The carnies told me I had to fill up the tank with sugar water."

"Sugar water is all wrong." Stanton sounded aggrieved. "You need a much richer solution. Pure corn syrup for a preference, barley syrup if you've got nothing else."

Hembry clenched his lips, but said nothing.

"But the syrup is really the least of your problems. To get that Cockatrice into the air, you're going to need a Warlock."

Emily opened her eyes.

"A Warlock?" Hembry's bleat made it sound as if Stanton had said he needed sixteen albino pygmies and a mule.

"The muscles on a Cockatrice have been specially treated to keep them in a state of suspended animation, but even so, they have to be fed and tended and kept limber. The muscles on your Cockatrice haven't been properly cared for in weeks, maybe months. A Warlock could revive them and repair the damage. Refresh their life force. Then, and only then, you'd be able to fly out of here."

Hembry let out a long breath. Reaching into his back pocket, he took out a thick green glass-topped jar. Emily recognized it as the kind she used to put up huckleberry preserves. Hembry unlatched the lid, spat tobacco juice into it, then capped the jar again and stuck it back into his pocket.

"Weevils in your bean plants?" Emily asked. Hembry looked at her, a slow smile spreading across his face.

"Yes'm, I have the misfortune of that blight," he said. "Ain't nothing better to get after 'em with than 'baccy-juice. I guess you ain't from the guv'mint after all."

"Mr. Jones." Emily looked at Stanton. "If Mr. Hembry were able to find a Warlock . . . which would be an utterly astonishing discovery out here in the middle of nowhere . . . how far could he fly in his Cockatrice?"

"Why, Miss Smith, he could fly all the way to New York City if he had a mind to," Stanton said.

"Don't need to git to New York City." Hembry's mouth twisted in distaste. "Need to git to Philadelphia."

"Philadelphia?" both Stanton and Emily said at once. Hembry sighed, reached inside his tea-colored shirt, pulled out a many-times-refolded broadsheet.

"It opens tomorrow," he said, as Emily smoothed the paper out over her lap.

Philadelphia Centennial Exposition.

Emily's eyes scanned the highlights. *Opening May 10, 1876 . . . President Ulysses S. Grant . . . the Emperor and Empress of Brazil . . .*

Something on the broadsheet caught Emily's eye. Looking at Stanton, she laid a finger next to a small line of type at the bottom of the poster.

"Look who's going to be at the opening of the Mantic Pavilion," she breathed.

"Sophos Mirabilis, of the Mirabilis Institute of the Credomantic Arts," Stanton said.

They both looked up at Hembry in unison.

"Mr. Hembry," Emily said. "I believe we can help."

Stanton jumped to his feet and took Hembry by the arm. The old man made a protesting sound, but Stanton gave him no time to reach for his shotgun; he pulled the man several feet away from where Emily was sitting. Even at that distance she heard the finger-snap and the word: *flamma.*

She certainly heard Hembry's ringing cry of astonishment: "You? A Warlock? What the hell is a Warlock doing out here in the middle of nowhere?"

"Never mind about that," Stanton said as they walked back to where Emily was. "You need a Warlock. Here I am. I can get your Cockatrice flying again, on one condition. We go with you."

"What?" Hembry's voice was a betrayed bray. Frowning, he snatched the straw hat from his head, threw it on the ground for emphasis. "No sir! I ain't taking passengers. This ain't a pleasure trip!"

"It isn't going to be any kind of a trip," Stanton said, "unless you take us."

Hembry snorted. He crossed his arms and pressed his lips

together as if he was done with conversation entirely. But he did speak again, and when he did, his voice was hushed and his eyes kept darting back and forth as if spies might be hiding in the hairy vetch.

"Listen, you folks don't know what I'm aiming at," he said. "Like I say, this ain't a pleasure trip. This is a rebellion."

"Rebellion?"

"Yeah," Hembry said. He reached into his other back pocket, pulled out a plug of tobacco, and took an angry chaw. "I got me a little message for President Ulysses S. Grant and all them thievin' fat-cat Replug-uglican cronies 'a his. And I aim to deliver that message right there at the opening of that grand goddamn centennial they'all spent so much of my tax money on."

"What kind of message?" Stanton asked. Hembry lifted his chin.

"A message that honest folk won't stand for it no more!" he shouted. He gestured around himself broadly. "Look at my land! Used'ta all be planted in corn—corn I used in my own still, for my own customers, just like my pappy did, and his pappy 'afore him. But Grant's crooked whiskey-ring boys took it all away from me. Busted up my business, sent thugs to skeer my wife and young'uns . . . I haven't dared plant so much as a pea for the past five years. So I took my last thousand dollars . . . the whole of my life's savings . . . and I bought this here machine. I'm gonna fly into that exposition, and I'm gonna stand in front of President Ulysses S. Grant, and I'm gonna spit in his eye! If that ain't my right as an American, I don't know what is!"

A smile broadened over Stanton's face with every word Hembry spoke. When the old man fell silent, he clapped Hembry on the shoulder.

"Ebenezer Hembry," he said, "that has to be the most wonderful plan I've ever heard."

The complete sincerity with which Stanton said it surprised Emily. Hembry heard it, too. The excitement of finding a kindred spirit brightened his features. He seized Stanton's hand in a grimy clasp.

"No foolin'?" he said.

"No foolin'," Stanton said. "Now look, how much corn syrup can you get your hands on?"

Stanton and Hembry worked all afternoon and well into the night. After the sun went down and the shade of the oak tree was no longer quite so necessary to her comfort, Emily wandered back up to the top of the rise so she could be far away from whatever magic Stanton would have to work to revitalize the Cockatrice's muscles. Stretching out on a mattress of soft vetch, she pillowed her head on her arms and looked up at the stars for a long time, dreaming of infinite spaces and ancient memories.

When she felt a hand on her arm many hours later, she thought she must be dreaming, for everything was so still and dark. The only light came from a low-hanging sliver of parchment-colored moon on the eastern horizon. From somewhere came the acrid smell of burning tobacco.

It took her a moment to realize that someone was straddling her, pinning her body to the ground, fingering the silver safety pin that she'd hidden inside her sleeve.

The someone was a girl.

A blond girl.

Emily lifted her hands in defense, found that they were bound with a stout leather cord. Rose pressed a revolver hard against her temple.

"You think you can play the games, eh?" Grimaldi hissed through clenched teeth. "This time, you will not escape."

CHAPTER EIGHTEEN

The Cynic Mirror

"Come, *carissima mia*." Rose jerked Emily to her feet. "Come and meet the gentlemen who have bought you."

Down the hill, beneath the oak tree, stood a half dozen men. They had suspended their lanterns from the tree's broad limbs, and the light illuminated a strange process.

"What are they doing?" Emily stumbled as Rose shoved her forward down the hill.

"I do not know the scientific term," Grimaldi said. "But in Italian, it is *avvolgendo nel bozzolo*. Wrapping things up."

Each of the strangers had a large cylindrical object strapped to his back that was connected by a flexible rubber hose to a handheld nozzle. They were using these devices to wrap a glistening cocoon around the struggling Hembry, spinning silk around him like cotton candy. The old man's astonished eyes peeked out over the top of his confining wrappings.

When Emily came into the circle of lantern light, she saw that Stanton was already bound tightly. His eyes, gleaming green, found Emily's and held them. But Emily had no time to read the warning there as a man stepped forward to greet her.

He was a well-preserved man of advanced age, as white-blond as the moonlight. He wore a suit and waistcoat of a foreign cut. An acrid cigarette burned between his fingers.

"I am sorry we must be introduced in this fashion." The man's voice was thickly accented in Russian. "I am called Perun."

"You hide behind an alias," Stanton barked. "Perun is the name of the Russian god of thunder. What is your real name?"

"Real names are not important, Mr. Stanton." Perun lifted his cigarette to his lips, not looking at him.

"These are the Sini Mira, Emily," Stanton said. "Eradicationists. You can't—"

Perun made a small gesture, and one of the large men who had just finished mummifying Hembry raised his wand and wound sticky threads around Stanton's head and mouth. Stanton struggled furiously against the confinement, sounds of anger muffled by the silk wrappings.

"Behave, Mr. Stanton, or I will direct him to cover your nose, as well."

Stanton subsided slightly, glaring at the Russian.

"Mr. Stanton is correct, I do represent a group called the Sini Mira. However, his opinion of us is colored by many prejudices which are neither fair nor accurate. We are scientists." Perun took a deep drag off his stinking cigarette, tapped ash. "I cannot tell you more until we can reach a place of safety. You will come with us now."

"What are you going to do with Mr. Stanton?" she said.

"Oh, *please*!" Grimaldi rolled Rose's eyes. "Really, it becomes quite annoying, Miss Edwards!"

"If you do not resist, Miss Edwards," Perun said, "we will not hurt anyone."

"And if I resist?"

Perun shook his head. He sighed. "We are not brutal, nor are we unkind. But you do not understand how important the stone in your hand is. If you did, you would know that any stubbornness will put you and your friends in grave danger."

"We've already been in grave danger from this body-jumping bounty hunter you hired to catch us." Emily gestured toward Rose, and the vicious Manipulator who possessed her. Rose's body looked even worse for wear now; her eyes were desperate as a trapped animal's and there were swollen, painful scrapes on her face where Emily had beaten her with the carpetbag. Emily shifted her eyes back to the white-blond Russian. "You see how he hunts, don't you? The girl he's riding right now . . . he's killing her. You hired a monster like that, and I'm supposed to believe you have my best interests at heart?"

"We could not allow him to hand you over to the Maelstroms. As I have said, you do not understand how important the stone in your hand is."

"Tell me, then," Emily said. "Make me understand."

"Ah." Perun exhaled a curl of blue smoke that glowed in the very first light of dawn. "That would be a story that would take millions of years to tell in words."

The echo sent a chill down Emily's spine. Those were Komé's words. The words the Holy Woman had spoken in her dream.

Perun saw the recognition on her face and nodded with satisfaction.

"You have experienced the consciousness of the earth. We call her *mat syra zemlya*, the Great Mother. She has bestowed a rare gift upon you, Miss Edwards, and an even rarer duty—a duty you share with the Holy Woman. A duty she has surrendered her physical existence to serve. We, too, have come to serve, and you will find us no less dedicated."

"How do you know all this?" Emily's throat was dry.

"I will tell you all about it when we reach a place of safety. I will tell you everything you wish to know."

Perun bent his head closer to hers.

"And I can tell you even more than that," he murmured in her ear. "You have heard the name Lyakhov, have you not?"

Emily trembled, the sound of the name sending little explosions through her brain.

"That's not my name," she said softly.

"You are correct, it is not," Perun said. "A daughter would be more properly called *Lyakhova*."

Emily's eyes flashed up.

"You knew my mother?"

Perun seemed to choose his next words carefully. "I can tell you where you came from, Miss Lyakhova. Who you really are. These are things you have always wished to know. The service of *mat syra zemlya* is not without reward."

Emily looked over at Stanton. His eyes gleamed warning;

he shook his head as violently as his restraints would allow. In the rising light of dawn, the Cockatrice shone dull gray.

"All right." Emily quickly shifted her gaze back to Perun to avoid Stanton's eyes. "I'll go with you. But you have to let Mr. Hembry and Mr. Stanton leave. Let them take the Cockatrice. I want to know that they're safe."

"You will go with us in any case." Perun's voice was cool and firm. "I have no need to bargain with you."

"You want me to trust you? There's nothing you can say in a million words that will speak louder than a single action." Her voice became softer. "Please."

Perun looked at her. He breathed smoke in and out. Finally, he gave a curt nod.

"For you, Miss Lyakhova, I will do this," he said.

Reaching inside his coat, Perun retrieved a small vial. Tucking the cigarette between his lips, he squinted against the rising smoke as he unscrewed the top. Stepping over to where the men lay captive, he dripped liquid from the bottle on each of them. The silk floss sizzled and hissed, individual strands becoming a gleaming, brittle mass that crumbled easily. Stanton jumped to his feet but Rose's revolvers swung up, staying his movements.

"It'll be all right, Mr. Stanton," Emily said.

"If she's going, I'm going," Stanton said.

"You arrogant, stubborn, troublesome *Warlock*!" Grimaldi spat furiously, advancing on Stanton. Rose shoved the revolvers into Stanton's belly, teeth bared. "Who do you think you are? Who do you think holds the guns? If you do not do as you are told, I will blow your guts through your body and give to Miss Edwards the heart she has become so silly over."

"Stop, Grimaldi." Perun's voice rang out. "The Warlock may leave. I have given my word on it." He paused. "But under no circumstances will he be allowed to come with us. The secrets we possess are too deep, too vital, too closely held to risk allowing a Warlock—particularly a Warlock like Mr. Stanton—to learn of them."

"And what do you mean by that?" Stanton growled.

"You think we don't know about your background?" Perun exhaled a thin stream of smoke. "Your years at the Erebus

Academy? You may call yourself a credomancer now, but that's not what you were *then*." Perun's jaw rippled with distaste. "There is an old Russian saying. 'A serpent changes his skin, but not his fangs.' "

"You're worried about my fangs, but you're going to let me leave in a twenty-ton biomechanical flying machine?" Stanton balled his fists. "What's to stop me from flying it right back at you?"

"You are free to do whatever you like, Mr. Stanton. The spider silk we used to bind you can just as easily be used to snarl the wings of that machine and bring you down. Or I will just shoot you between the eyes. I am a very good shot."

Perun and Stanton looked at each other for a long time.

"Go, Mr. Stanton." The words caught in Emily's throat. "I told you, I have to find a different way."

"No, that's *not* what you said . . ." Stanton took a reluctant step backward, prodded by Rose's revolvers. He looked at Emily, shaking his head. Hembry was already gone, having scrambled into the Cockatrice and taken refuge within its deep passenger compartment.

"Come on," Hembry called. "Get in, you durn fool!"

"Emily . . ." Stanton said.

Emily clenched her fists, the tight leather bindings cutting into her wrists. She stared at the ground.

"Go," she whispered.

She didn't see Stanton climb into the Cockatrice; she did not lift her head again until she heard the sound of metal sliding against metal. Then she looked up and saw the Cockatrice beginning to move, silver wings lifting like a glittering sheet, each feather ringing and chiming. The gleaming snakelike tail uncurled sinuously, slithering along the ground. The proud enameled head rose, the beak opened slightly. Red eyes, set deep under a jutting brow, began to glow.

The Cockatrice gathered its two legs under it, lifted its wings high, then brought them down with a mighty flap as it sprang up from the ground in a powerful rush. The smell of hot oil and metal and sweet burning sugar filled the air. The machine soared upward, rising into the pink mist of dawn. Perun watched it go, drew in a deep breath.

"Men," he sighed. "Prepare yourselves. He will be back."

"No!" Emily whirled on the Russian, but Rose held her fast, an arm looped through Emily's bound arms, a gun pressed to the side of her head.

"I have given him the chance for your sake, Miss Edwards." His tone made Emily's chest turn to lead. "But I am afraid he will not take it."

Around them, men began to scramble. They went to where their horses stood waiting, fastened their barrel-shaped weapons tightly to their animals' saddles with clips and buckles. They drew rifles from saddle holsters, chambered rounds. Perun and Emily watched the Cockatrice swoop up sharply, then bank like a swooping eagle, swinging back in a graceful arc.

"Goddamn it, Mr. Stanton," Emily whispered through clenched teeth. "No."

One of the men handed Perun a rifle. The Russian lifted it to his shoulder, sliding the bolt home with a loud clack, and drew a bead on the approaching Cockatrice with its blued-steel barrel.

"No!" Emily screamed, at Stanton and the Russian both. She struggled furiously against Rose's grip.

"Make another move, Miss Edwards," Grimaldi whispered in her ear, "and you won't live to see him die."

Licked you once, Emily thought, ferocity charging her. *Guess I can lick you again.*

She dropped to the ground; the pistol blasted by her ear. Bouncing back to her feet, she brought her bound hands down over Rose's head, jerking the leather tight around the girl's throat. Rose's hands flailed, revolvers shining. Emily pulled tighter.

The Cockatrice dived toward them, metal feathers ringing. Emily could see Stanton, leaning out over the edge of the open passenger compartment, his hands outstretched. The men of the Sini Mira dropped to the ground as the Cockatrice plowed over them. Only Emily and Rose remained standing . . . and Perun, training his rifle on Stanton.

Stanton's hands came down, clutching at the fabric of Emily's dress. Emily lurched, her shoulders screaming with pain as her feet left the ground. The leather bindings around her wrists burned as Rose was pulled up with her; there was the sound of tearing fabric.

Then another sound—the crack of Perun's rifle. Stanton faltered, grunted. Emily felt one of his hands go limp and slack, and she slid down, her heart and stomach tumbling with the drop. Stanton had her by one hand.

There was a high whistling noise. The stringy silk floss of the Sini Mira devices fluttered around them, whisper-soft. The strands slapped against the side of the Cockatrice, hundreds of them, making a pitter-pat sound like rain. The silk tangled around wings, legs, tail . . . around Emily, around Rose, pulling them down . . .

Stanton was halfway out over the side of the passenger compartment now, his hands clutching at Emily's skirt. He got two good handfuls and pulled up hard, his face wrenched with pain. Emily could see blood spreading over Stanton's shirt, staining his breast red. Warm gory drops spun in the rushing wind, splattering against her face.

There was a screech of metal, and several jolting shocks. The sticky string was taut and glossy and shiny as twisted steel. The horses below scrambled for purchase, struggling to keep themselves from being lifted along with the Cockatrice.

With one large heave, Stanton managed to get Emily into the passenger compartment, dragging Rose behind her. The girl was limp, her face reddish-purple; she did not move.

"I'll bust us loose!" Hembry, at the controls, felt around in the space under his feet. "Packed these just in case!" He pulled out a small crate that was packed with egg-shaped items cradled in wood shavings. The crate bore the familiar Baugh's Patent Magicks logo on the side and an advertisement of the contents: *Explosive Exterminating Egg. Extreme Mantic Potency Against Gophers, Moles, and Sundry Burrowing Vermin Guaranteed.*

He pulled out one of the brass eggs and depressed a button on the top.

When Stanton saw what Hembry was holding, his eyes went wide.

"No!" he screamed, his hand scrambling for Hembry's. "Don't! No magic!"

But Hembry had already dropped the egg over the side.

"Emily, get down!" Stanton cried. But it was too late. The egg exploded with a white flash of light. The explosion corresponded with a sudden upward lurch of the Cockatrice as the bulk of the restraining ties were severed; the rest tore free with a twinging noise. But even as the Cockatrice was freed and began to gain altitude, the explosive magic that had freed it veered upward as well. A dense, pearly cloud of magical power buffeted the Cockatrice, and Emily's hands, still bound by leather, were roughly seized by the force of the stone's attraction to it.

Stanton wrapped his arms around her waist and braced his feet.

Her hands were drawn out of the open passenger compartment to meet the rush of luminescent magic. The flood of power corkscrewed into the stone like a twister in reverse, and her whole being glowed with such a dazzle of light and heat that she wondered if she wasn't exploding right along with everything around her.

"Higher!" Stanton yelled at Hembry, straining to keep Emily from being pulled from him. His voice sounded strangely thin and distorted, as if her eardrums had ruptured. "Get us *higher*!"

The Cockatrice was flying straight up now, wings pumping powerfully. As they broke through the first layer of clouds, the flood of magic subsided, then finally broke off entirely with a loud snap. Emily tumbled backward.

Stanton was over her in an instant, holding her down. With one hand he pressed her wrists above her head; the other hand disappeared inside his coat for the misprision blade.

But moments passed. They stared into each other's eyes, breathing hard. Emily's body tingled as if it was full of bees, buzzing and stinging. Her hand ached and burned. But she did not become an Aberrancy.

"Damn it, Mr. Stanton," she said finally, her voice a trembling whisper. "If it *had* happened, the Exunge would have gotten you, too."

Stanton took his hand from inside his coat. He pushed himself off of her, throwing himself backward, cursing under his breath.

It was a while before Emily could sit up. Her shoulders ached, her head was splitting, and her hand felt as though it had been plunged into boiling water.

Stanton was watching her. He sat propped against one of the passenger banquettes, a hand pressed over his bleeding shoulder. His cuff and sleeve were soaked brilliant red; his face was corpse pale. She put her hand over her mouth and willed herself not to cry.

"It's all right, I think the bullet went clean through." His voice was gentle, as if he was speaking to a frightened animal. "Come here, Emily."

Emily crawled to where he sat, put her body alongside his. He smelled of blood and sugar; his breathing was shallow and ragged. She put her forehead against his good shoulder, squeezing her eyes shut tight.

Stanton took Emily's hands. With trembling, blood slick fingers, he untied the leather that bound her wrists. Then he took her right hand and pulled the glove off of it. Together, they looked at the stone.

The yellowish color was gone. The stone was now completely clear, clear as glass. And in the center of it, like a foul yolk in a bizarre egg, was a perfectly round black blob that pulsed with every beat of Emily's hard-pounding heart.

Emily did what she could to stop Stanton's bleeding, using wadded cloth torn from the hem of her petticoat. When she was done, she went to kneel over Rose's motionless form. Letting her hand rest on Rose's belly, she was overjoyed to feel breath stirring there.

Grimaldi's revolvers were still clutched in the girl's hands; Emily took them and tucked them away. She touched the bruised places on the girl's face, and the garish welts where the leather had cut into the white flesh of her throat.

"I didn't mean to hurt you, Rose," Emily said, voice breaking. "Honest I didn't."

Stanton was silent for a long time.

"Hembry," he said finally, "give me your jar."

"What fer?" Hembry took the jar from his back pocket, rolled it toward Stanton. "Got weevils?"

"Of a sort," Stanton said.

He came to kneel beside Emily. Emily watched as he pushed Rose's collar aside, revealing the uchawi pod nestled in the dip between her collarbones. Using the lid of the jar as a scoop, he tipped the uchawi pod into the jar and captured the pendant's chain between the lid and lip. Clamping the lid down tight, Stanton jerked the chain from around Rose's throat.

The girl gasped, every muscle in her body contracting to board-stiffness. After a moment, she exhaled, her body melting and softening like honey spreading out on a plate.

"Rose Hibble," Stanton said in her ear, loudly. "Now you are free."

Then, sitting back, Stanton lifted the jar and watched the uchawi pod settle into the foul brown muck at the bottom.

"Serves him just about right," Stanton said.

"That's all it takes?" Emily said.

"If she'd been awake, Grimaldi would have made her claw my eyes out." He gave the jar an angry shake. "He would have used her until she was dead. Vicious bastard."

Emily stared at the jar. All that cruelty, all that malice . . . trapped inside a fragile shell of green glass.

"You're sure that will hold him?"

"Glass is one of the most powerful magical insulators known," Stanton said. "He's in there until he can be released into custody."

"Or until we kill him," Emily was aware of a brutal note in her voice. She looked at Stanton. "We could crush the uchawi pod."

Stanton stared at the jar, his jaw clenched tightly, eyes narrowed with despising. Finally, though, he put the jar down and did not look at it again.

"This is still the United States of America," he said. "Even Grimaldi is entitled to a trial by jury." Stanton's voice became soft. "We are not murderers."

At that moment, Rose began to stir. She sat up slowly, her

hand against her head. Emily helped her sit up, murmuring comfort. Rose looked at Emily, but not for long. Her eyes searched wildly until they found Stanton. She reached for his hands, pressing her lips to them fervently.

"Thank you, Mr. Stanton," she mumbled against his fingers. "Thank you for setting me free. He was so terrible. So . . . *mean*. The things he said to me . . . in my head, where I couldn't get away . . ." Squeezing her eyes shut, she broke down in horrible racking sobs, curling up against him, limp and shuddering.

"I know, Miss Hibble," Stanton murmured. "I know."

They came over Philadelphia a little after midday. A wild whoop from Hembry alerted them to their arrival.

"We're coming up on the exposition grounds . . . there!" Hembry pointed. Perched on the bank of a slow shining river, the grounds were dominated by two long, low buildings, massive warehouselike structures of cast iron and brick and glass, their cupolaed roofs surmounted by hundreds of gold-edged pennants snapping in the afternoon breeze. Broad flagstone causeways gleamed white, lined with saplings and dotted with pavilions. A rail line encircled the whole conurbation like a border drawn around a child's picture.

Before the larger of the two buildings stretched a smooth flat green. It was packed with people listening to a speech that was being delivered from a bunting-draped platform at the far end.

Hembry locked the wings out flat and glided down over the crowd. Running to the back of the Cockatrice, he fumbled with some canvas ties, unfurling a long hand-lettered banner:

"HANG BABCOCK! HANG THE WHISKEY-RING SCOUNDRELS! JUSTICE FOR ALL!!!"

Cackling to himself, he returned to the pilot's seat.

"Now let's really get their attention," he said. "Hang on!"

He pushed a button. The Cockatrice opened its beak and let out an ear-splitting shriek. The people on the green looked up, scattered, parasols and top hats parting like a fluffy and overdecorated Red Sea. By the time the Cockatrice had swooped back around, the center of the green had cleared. The Cockatrice touched down gently, sleek snake's tail curling neatly around its long body.

Hembry's face was triumphant as he popped his head out of the passenger's compartment, punching a fist in the air.

"Death to tyrants!" he hollered. "Hang the crooks!"

The crowds, which had clustered on either side of the green, were silent. Then there was the sound of a lone cheer. The cry was taken up by dozens, then hundreds, then thousands of people. A huge roar of approval swept over the crowd, punctuated by whoops and whistles. On the distant podium, the man who had been delivering his speech goggled at them, his dark brow unhappily furrowed.

"President Ulysses S. Grant." Stanton gestured toward the faraway notable. "Congratulations, Hembry. I'd say you're the only man ever to spit in a president's eye from five hundred feet away."

All around the Cockatrice, the crowd pressed in.

Emily was already halfway out of the passenger compartment when she saw that Stanton wasn't following her. He was speaking to Rose, looking down seriously into her flushed and eager face. The girl beamed up at him, her eyes liquid with adoration.

". . . You know, more than anyone, how important this is," he said as he handed her the glass jar with the uchawi pod in it. She trembled as she took it from him, but once it was in her hands she clutched it to her chest savagely, knuckles white.

"Good girl," Stanton said. "Hold on to it tight. When the police arrive, you tell them to summon special officers from the Warlock division to take a Manipulator into custody. You don't let that jar out of your hands until they do. Can you remember that?"

Rose nodded.

"I'll see to it, I promise." Rose's voice was husky. "You can count on me, Mr. Stanton."

Emily took Stanton's good arm somewhat impatiently.

"Come on," she said, pulling him away. "Let's go find the man we've come three thousand miles to see."

* * *

They were hard-pressed to wade through the throng; people were smothering them with pats on the back and congratulations. But as they made their way farther back they came to a place in the crowd where no one had seen them emerge from the Cockatrice and so were able to move more quickly.

"And here I was getting lectured about farm girls falling in love with *me*!" Emily muttered as she jogged to keep up with Stanton's long strides.

"Our timing couldn't be better," Stanton said. "The President is scheduled to open each of the pavilions individually after his speech, which means Professor Mirabilis must be waiting for his arrival at the Mantic Pavilion. So all we have to do"— Stanton slid a map out of the back pocket of a man who was rushing past them to get closer to the Cockatrice —"is find it."

"Disgraceful!" Emily whispered, casting a guilty glance backward. Stanton unfolded the map as they walked.

"Mantic Pavilion." Stanton pointed up a wide flagstone boulevard lined with ornate gas streetlamps. "There."

Emily slowed to a halt, awestruck, gaping.

In the dazzling midday sunlight, the Mantic Pavilion gleamed, a fantasy of gold leaf and red paint and black enameled latticework. It was an eye-popping vision, an exotic grotto of power and majesty. The roof, cobalt tiled, put the springtime sky to shame. The roof pillars had ends carved like spitting dragons. Trees of red orchids in huge, glossy black pots lined the way to the two tall doors.

"Yes, it's designed to make you feel that way." Stanton placed a finger under her chin to close her mouth. "I think it's pretty tawdry myself, but there's no accounting for taste."

They entered through the tall doors, which were carved of ebony and bound with brass. They strode into the darkness of the cool main hall, the click of their heels on the slick black marble floor echoing as they walked toward a small platform that was decorated with red, white, and blue bunting. Several men were gathered around the platform. They all wore silk top hats and dark frock coats with red orchids in their lapels. They all turned as Emily and Stanton approached, each man's eyes narrowing by a different degree.

"We must see Professor Mirabilis," Stanton said breathlessly.

No one said anything. The men stared at Stanton and Emily with knit brows and slack jaws. Emily was suddenly aware of how awful they both looked. She was dusty and tattered and wispy with spider silk, and Stanton was worse, pale and trembling, sleeves and shirt soaked in blood both fresh and dried.

"What's going on here?" The voice came from within the cluster of dignitaries, and from it stepped a compact young man with a neatly clipped red mustache and a ferret on his shoulder. He was wearing a trim charcoal suit and a green silk tie, and there were many gold rings on his fingers. He was carrying a leather notebook and a stub of pencil. When he saw Stanton, his civil servant's look of incipient dismissiveness mutated into amusement and surprise.

"Aren't you . . . why you *are*! Dreadnought Stanton!" The young man had an undulating southern accent, heavy as honey. He cast a long lazy look over Stanton's bloodsoaked form. "Gone back to your true calling?"

"We must see Professor Mirabilis," Stanton repeated, louder.

"He's getting ready for the ceremony to open the pavilion. And then . . . why, he's ever so busy. Really, I don't think he'll be available at all during the exposition. Maybe you can call on him back at the Institute next week—"

"Next week?" Stanton roared. "Tarnham, you idiot, we have to see Mirabilis *now*! It's a matter of life and death."

"Life and death?" Tarnham smirked.

"Life and death," Emily snarled. She pulled Rose's revolvers from her pockets and cocked back the hammers. She leveled the guns at Tarnham's gut, and the smile on his face became brittle.

"Life and death?" It was a rich, robust voice, and it rang bell clear. The clot of dignitaries parted, and a man with longish white hair and a white goatee stepped forward. He wore an exquisitely tailored suit of plum-colored silk and a vivid red waistcoat, across which draped a gold watch chain sparkling with a variety of strange fobs. His keen, appraising eyes made three precise movements: first to Emily's revolvers, then to her face, then to Stanton's bloody hands.

"Well, never let it be said that I don't make myself available when it's a matter of life and death."

"Professor Mirabilis," Stanton sighed. He motioned for Emily to lower the guns, then strode forward and clasped the old man's hand gratefully, his green eyes brilliant. "You don't know how good it is to see you."

CHAPTER NINETEEN

Senator Stanton

Mirabilis led them into an antechamber, a room designed to serve as the office of the Mantic Pavilion. It was decorated somewhat more simply than the rest of the structure; what was a riot of exotic color outside was kept to a mild commotion within. The walls were a deep rich red, and the pressed-tin ceiling gleamed with gold leaf.

"Have a seat. You both look . . . overwrought." Mirabilis reached into his pocket for a handkerchief and wiped away the bloody smear Stanton's handshake had left on his palm. He gestured to two black leather chairs positioned in front of a black lacquered desk. Emily and Stanton sat gratefully. Mirabilis went to a sideboard where a bottle of liqueur and a platterful of small glasses sat. He poured two glasses of the liqueur and handed one to each of them. Stanton put his liqueur on the desk without a second look, but Emily bolted hers, the sweet taste of oranges and spices trickling down the back of her throat.

"Another?" he asked her. "Perhaps we can trade." He looked meaningfully at her guns, and Emily felt suddenly embarrassed. Sheepishly, she slid the revolvers over the polished desk. Nodding like a grandparent who'd heard a clever recitation, Mirabilis poured her another glass.

"Now, Mr. Stanton, what's this all about?" Mirabilis took a seat behind the desk. He carefully retrieved the guns and placed them in a drawer. "You'll make it quickish, I trust? The President's due to arrive in fifteen minutes."

Stanton drew a deep breath, as if to launch into a lengthy explanation. Then he released the breath and shook his head.

"Look at her hand," Stanton said.

Emily pulled the glove from her right hand and stretched it toward Mirabilis, palm forward. Squinting at the stone, he reached into his waistcoat pocket for his pince-nez. He perched the eyeglasses on his nose and leaned forward to peer more closely.

"Extraordinary," he said.

"A piece of Native Star," Stanton said. "A fragment of the Mantic Anastomosis."

Mirabilis removed the glasses and let them dangle between his fingers. He looked between the two of them.

"Tell me everything," he said.

Fifteen minutes later, Emily and Stanton had told him just enough to make it obvious that they needed more than fifteen minutes. They had not, however, gotten around to telling him about their ride in the Cockatrice when Tarnham thrust his head in through the door, his face harried and harassed. From its perch on his shoulder, the ferret peeked through the door as well, beady eyes glimmering.

"Sir, things are terribly unsettled out here!" It was clear that Tarnham was being jostled from without. "Everyone's in an uproar about this Cockatrice nonsense."

"Cockatrice?" Mirabilis looked at Stanton, lifting a bushy white eyebrow. "What Cockatrice?"

Stanton opened his mouth to explain, but Tarnham broke in, exasperated.

"These two set down a Cecil Carpenter Cockatrice on the main green just as neat as you please. Disrupted the whole proceedings! Police everywhere . . . the whole place is about to come to blows."

"Mr. Stanton?"

"I simply helped an American citizen exercise his right of free speech." A smirk lifted the corner of Stanton's mouth.

But Tarnham, whose head was still poked through the door, assumed a far sourer expression.

"That's not all, sir. There's folks outside positively demanding to be let in, not the least of whom is—"

"Senator Argus Stanton!" came a bellowed roar from just outside the door. Tarnham's face disappeared for a moment, but apparently whatever stalling tactic he'd attempted had failed miserably. A large man pushed through the door, trailing four magnificently upholstered women in his wake.

The senator looked exactly like Stanton would look if he were thirty years older and weighed a hundred pounds more. His large bones were covered with sturdy flesh, and he seemed the sort of fellow that had a tooth-rattling handshake. The women behind him sidled in nervously, as if they were afraid that something might touch them. The one Emily supposed was Euphemia was nearly as tall as Stanton. The oldest woman, certainly Stanton's mother, was small and sleek as a pit bull.

"Dreadnought!" the big man boomed.

Stanton winced, then turned slowly, his hands clasped behind his back. His face was set in an odd kind of sneer, like a boy resigned to be beaten for doing something admirable.

"Hello, Senator," Stanton said, and then, inclining his head toward the women: "Mother."

The sneer on Stanton's face became blank astonishment when his father stormed forward, clasping him in a bear hug and slapping him on the back.

"Wonderful, wonderful!" the senator roared. "Dreadnought, my dear boy! You saved his life! You saved the life of the President of these United States!"

"What?" Stanton winced away from his father's embrace, outrage overcoming agony. "What in God's name are you talking about?"

"You brought down that backwoods nutcracker! That half-baked hick! I hear that Cockatrice was filled with enough bombs and ammunition and hell knows what else to blow up the President, the first lady, and every other fine Republican servant of the people on that platform! That goddamn atheist wanted the life of our duly elected leader, and you kept him from fulfilling that fatal intent—"

"I did no such thing!" Stanton bellowed. "Hembry's a harmless Illinois moonshiner . . . He wouldn't hurt a fly!"

"Everyone's been howling about how corrupt our boys are . . . Well, I guess this gives those atheists and bomb-throwing anarchists a black eye right back!" The senator positively glimmered with glee. "There'll be a big trial. You'll testify of course . . . and meanwhile there's so many places I can take you around . . ." The senator smoothed a big hand through the air, as if painting the headlines on the sky: "Dreadnought Stanton, Son of the Senior Senator from New York, Spirit of the Next Hundred Years of the Republic!"

"I don't want to be the spirit of the next hundred years of the republic!"

"Goddamn it, boy, if I say you're going to be the spirit of the next hundred years of the republic, then you'll be the spirit of the next hundred years of the republic!" The senator balled a fist, looking for something he could pound for emphasis. Finding nothing, he chopped the air brusquely. "You're a protector of the common American, an upholder of justice! Do you know what this means to me?"

"In an *election year.*" The words came from Stanton's mother, low and intense. They seemed to be spoken through clenched teeth, and they made everything in the room seem very quiet by comparison. Emily had a sudden terror that the woman would speak again, and was thankful when it became apparent that the words would be her only offering. She drew back among her daughters, who wrapped around her like a brocaded asbestos shawl.

"Now listen, you can't stay holed up in here with this pack of mumbo jumbo men." Senator Stanton began shoving his son toward the door. "The police need to speak with you, and there are more newspapermen outside than you can shake a stick at! Come on with me and we'll—"

"Impossible," Stanton sidestepped his father's shovings. "There are things I need to attend to here."

Senator Stanton's eyes swept over Mirabilis and Emily as if they were paper cutouts; his look indicated clearly that no conceivable dealings with either of them could be worth keeping newspapermen waiting.

"By God, boy, the presses won't wait!" the senator bellowed. "They want this in the morning editions!"

"Go on, Mr. Stanton," Mirabilis interrupted him mildly. "I will see to the business you have brought me."

Stanton stared at Mirabilis, stunned.

"You can't be serious!" Stanton pointed at Emily. "She has possibly the greatest magical discovery of the past millennium in the palm of her hand, and you want me to leave? Do you know how much I went through to bring her . . . to bring this matter to your attention?"

"Of course I do," Mirabilis said. "But I am serious. Go out and give the press a full recounting. Tell them how you rescued the life of our beloved President from the hands of this . . . bomb-throwing anarchist, whoever he is."

"I didn't come three thousand miles to *electioneer*." Stanton spat out the final word as if it tasted bad.

"Nonetheless, you are still a Jefferson Chair. I am still your employer. Unless you choose to resign your position, you will do as I request." His voice dropped an octave, his tone becoming quite disapproving. "And for heaven's sake, find a doctor! Have that shoulder seen to."

A look of surprise came over the senator's face. He looked at Stanton, as if just at that moment noticing that his son was paper-pale and covered with blood.

"Shoulder?" he barked, as if shouting might make the injury rethink its impudence. "Something wrong with your shoulder, boy?"

"Professor Mirabilis." Stanton's voice was low and imploring. Mirabilis gestured to him and spoke harsh, quiet words in his ear. When Stanton straightened, there was a look of resignation on his face. He set his jaw, inflated himself with a deep breath.

"All right, then." Stanton straightened his collar and brushed an insignificant speck of dirt from his frayed and blood-soaked sleeve. He nodded to Emily, dipping his head low by her ear as he passed.

"I'll send someone to help you," he murmured.

Then he lifted his chin, followed his father out the door, and was gone.

CHAPTER TWENTY

The Otherwhere Marble

After the senator left, it took a few moments for the thundering to subside. It was as if a freight train were receding into the distance, pulling all sound and energy after it, leaving a vacuum of disorienting silence in its wake. Into this vacuum Tarnham peeked gingerly; Mirabilis gestured him to enter.

"We'll have to cancel the opening ceremony." Mirabilis spoke with the brusque offhandedness of one used to command. "Have the railcar readied for our departure. Miss Edwards and I are returning to the Institute at once."

"Opening ceremony is canceled at any rate," Tarnham pouted, glaring at Emily for some reason known only to himself. "The President has canceled all the openings due to the so-called 'assassination attempt' that Stanton thwarted."

"Good. Finish things up here. I want you back on the four o'clock train. We've got a lot of work ahead of us."

Tarnham sighed his way out, and Mirabilis took Emily's hand in his. He brought his eye down close to it, scrutinizing the black blob in its center.

"No one's ever actually seen the process by which the Mantic Anastomosis segregates Exunge," Mirabilis said. "You say there was a color shift? Correlated to the amount of magic it absorbed?"

Emily nodded. "It went from a dark cobalt blue, through a milky yellowish, and then . . . this."

"Very intriguing," Mirabilis said, tapping the stone with a fingernail.

"And you can study it to your heart's content once it's out." Emily pulled her hand away.

"Of course," Mirabilis said, watching her hand as she tucked it behind herself. "Your troubles are at an end, Miss Edwards. Come with me, and we'll get you taken care of immediately."

Mirabilis opened the office door and gestured her through.

The interior of the Mantic Pavilion was no longer the echoing empty space she'd entered earlier. The place was now packed with hundreds of exposition attendees, apparently drawn by Stanton's fresh notoriety. Word must have spread that it was a Warlock who'd thwarted the assassination attempt (Emily frowned at herself—even she was thinking of poor Hembry as an assassin now?) and suddenly the Mantic Pavilion had become an exceptionally popular attraction.

"Well, well." Mirabilis appraised the crowd with the canniness of a cardsharp. "This is quite promising."

Tarnham oozed out from somewhere unseen, his pencil hovering over his leather pad.

"Your carriage is outside," he began. "I've sent word to the station to have the railcar hooked up. With all the commotion, there might be some trouble getting out, but—"

Mirabilis waved him silent, his eyes narrow with calculation. "Listen, Tarnham . . . keep track of the reporters who are writing up this story. I want their names forwarded over to Mystic Truth. Tell the editors—tell Barclay, he's got a flair for the melodramatic—tell him to work this up into a serial. I want a draft on my desk in two days."

Tarnham's face disarranged unpleasantly.

"A serial, sir?" he said. "About *Dreadnought Stanton*?"

"Can't you feel the power in the room?" Mirabilis closed his eyes and breathed deep, as if he were standing in a field of springtime flowers. "It's invigorating!"

"Professor, Mr. Stanton won't want a serial written about him," Emily said, as Tarnham muttered off.

"Oh, he'll loathe the idea." Mirabilis led her past a cluster of women who were *ooh*ing and *aah*ing over three neatly shrunken heads arrayed on red velvet under glass. "But I don't care what Dreadnought Stanton loathes or does not loathe. It's the interests of credomancy that I'm concerned with."

They came to a grand-looking door in the center of the hall; it seemed to have been beaten of solid gold. Mirabilis pulled a large ring of keys out of his pocket and began sorting through them.

"Mystic Truth needs stories like this to build the power of credomancers all over the country." Mirabilis opened the door to reveal a large room, lit by softly glowing orbs of blown glass. He stretched out a polite arm. "After you."

Emily peered into the room, holding her hand behind her back as if hiding crossed fingers. The glowing orbs sat in circlets of worked gold, each circlet hanging from the ceiling by three slender chains. They certainly looked as if they might be powered by magic, and she didn't want to test it empirically. Seeing her hesitation, Mirabilis chuckled.

"I assure you, there is no free magic in the room. There are quite a few objects in here that would interact badly with it."

Stepping into the room, Emily found that it was unexpectedly large. Displays ringed the room, each one lit by its own cluster of glowing orbs.

"This room is not open to the public. It contains exhibits the Institute reserves for its most honored and distinguished guests," Mirabilis said. "These are advancements that must not be widely promoted . . . at least, not yet."

But Emily had no time to see any of the advancements, for Mirabilis led her directly to a carved mahogany pillar on which stood a medium-size ivory statue of a headless Venus, lit by a glowing shaft of light. The Venus had something clasped around her throat—some kind of silver collar—and really, she wasn't entirely headless. While the statue was completely solid beneath the collar, above the collar the statue's head was vague and semitransparent—ectoplasmic.

Mirabilis picked up a black marble, about the size of a robin's egg, from where it sat on a blue silk cushion at Venus' pretty little feet. He held it up against the light.

"Look inside."

Emily squinted into the black marble. The light shining through it revealed the head of the statue, floating in a void, clear and distinct.

"It's called an Otherwhere Marble," Mirabilis said. He

closed his hand around the marble and made a flourish; unfolding his fingers, the marble was gone. Emily half expected him to pull it out of her ear. "It contains an entire collapsed dimension. The Boundary Cuff around Venus' neck is a transporting device. It sends whatever it clasps into the dimension inside the marble."

Emily blinked once or twice, trying to wrap her head around the concept.

"What do you mean, 'another dimension'? Like another country? Like . . . Belgium?"

"Another dimension is nowhere on this earth, or even in this universe," Mirabilis said breezily. "It's a place outside of this reality and inside another."

Emily touched a tentative finger to the ghostlike head of the statue, then passed her hand back and forth through it. There was nothing there.

"Now watch." Mirabilis rolled his fingers to make the marble reappear. Using it, he tapped a precise rhythm against the metal of the Boundary Cuff. Then he unclamped it from around the statue's throat. Abruptly, Venus' head resolidified. Emily reached up and flicked a fingernail against the solid ivory.

"The Boundary Cuff is the most compact portational device ever devised. More important, it is a product of science, not magic, which should be of additional reassurance to you." Mirabilis eyed her wrist, judging it for size. "Now, let's have your hand, my dear . . ."

Emily pulled back, hugging her arm against her chest. "Now, hold on just a second!" This Mirabilis person certainly had a way of moving quickly. "Another dimension?"

"It's perfectly safe," Mirabilis soothed. "We cannot remove the stone until we get back to the Institute. This will keep you safe in the meantime. If the stone does excrete the black bolus, the foulness will be contained away from where it can do you harm. I'm putting a whole reality between you and death."

Emily looked at him, but did not move her hand toward him.

A note of impatience crept into Mirabilis' tone. "Miss Edwards, it's really the best I can do at the moment."

Emily took the old man's measure through narrowed eyes.

Stanton trusted him absolutely, and indeed, he seemed the picture of integrity and wisdom. All right, then. She let out a long breath and extended her hand. "Will it hurt?"

"Not in the least." Mirabilis snapped the Boundary Cuff around her wrist. Her hand faded to smokelike insubstantiality.

And indeed, her hand didn't feel any different. She looked at the place where the Boundary Cuff separated her living flesh from the ectoplasm of her ghost hand. She could see her blood and muscles and bone in vivid cross section, as clearly as if they'd been pressed against glass. The gruesome view made her shudder, and she let her hand drop quickly.

Mirabilis held the marble up to the light, and Emily could see her hand floating within it. She wiggled her fingers, and the hand wiggled in response.

"You say this isn't magic?" Emily breathed. "My goodness, if science can do this, why do we need magic at all?"

Mirabilis rubbed the marble delicately between two palms. He spread his hands, and suddenly a white dove was perched on his finger, looking rather dazed and disoriented. Emily knew how it felt. Another small movement, a wave and a pinch, and the dove was gone, replaced by a fragrant red orchid that Mirabilis tucked behind Emily's ear.

"Science still can't do that," he said. "Come along. The carriage is waiting."

Emily had thought the Pullman car with which she'd had such a brief acquaintance was luxurious, but it was nothing compared to the Mirabilis Institute's private railcar. It was carpeted in thick soft wool, paneled in polished rosewood, and fitted everywhere with gilt ornamentation.

Settling himself in a comfortable wing chair of sorrel-colored leather, Mirabilis snapped his fingers at a porter in a white jacket who was poised at steel-spring attention.

"A brandy for me. And for Miss Edwards . . . ?" He looked at her expectantly. Well, she certainly wasn't expected to order a brandy, though she wouldn't mind one right about now. What on earth would they have on hand? An imp of the perverse overtook her.

"I'll take a nice cold glass of pineapple juice. No ice." She narrowed her eyes at the porter, daring him to clear his throat regretfully. But the man just gave a tiny bow, and when he returned a moment later, he placed a glass of thin, sweet yellow juice at her elbow. Beads of condensation affirmed that it was perfectly chilled.

Warlocks.

There was a lurch and a clatter of iron wheels as the train got under way. Not the *train,* Emily corrected herself, for that word implied a multiplicity of cars following an engine. In this case, the engine existed solely for their benefit. Stanton hadn't been kidding when he'd said the Institute was well funded.

"Now that we have averted the worst, I want to hear your story again . . . and leave nothing out." Mirabilis settled himself deeper in the deep leather chair, swirling his brandy in its large bubble-shaped glass. He was obviously expecting the story to be a long one.

It was. Over the next two hours, Emily recounted every detail, from their encounters at the Miwok camp to the duplicity of Mrs. Quincy to the battle in which she'd Sundered Captain Caul. She described their struggles with the bounty hunter, the strange arrival of the Sini Mira, and their ride in the Cockatrice. Then she stopped.

"And you know the rest." She let out a long breath. Mirabilis nodded gravely.

"Quite an adventure for a timber-camp Witch," he said. His eyes once again became distant with thought. There was a long silence.

"What did you say to Mr. Stanton, anyway?" Emily said finally.

"Eh?" Mirabilis' eyes focused, and his face took on a look of extreme irritation. "What?"

"Why did you make him go away?"

"Well, for one thing, he was the victim of what sounds like an extremely nasty compulsion," Mirabilis said. "Compulsions remain in the body and can reemerge—or be reactivated."

"But he cleansed himself," Emily said. "I saw him do it."

"So you explained. It sounds like it was quite a *display*."

Mirabilis' mouth twisted with distaste. "But no man can cleanse himself dependably, no matter what kind of magic he uses. There is an excellent Witch Doctor of my acquaintance in Philadelphia. I told Mr. Stanton he should visit the man immediately."

"Couldn't you help him?"

"Of course I could," Mirabilis said, "but even I must choose my battles. And you, Miss Edwards, are the battle I choose. You have the Maelstroms and the Sini Mira after you. Keeping you safe from them will be more than work enough, without inviting a Warlock of questionable dependability into the mix."

"Mr. Stanton has always been completely dependable," Emily snapped, more sharply than she intended to. "He did a very good job. Without him, I wouldn't have made it here."

"I am sure Mr. Stanton did a very competent job," Mirabilis said, as if he were speaking of a bank clerk or a gardener.

Emily narrowed her eyes. "You don't like him much, do you?"

Mirabilis flashed her an abrupt, brilliant smile. "Why, Miss Edwards! Whatever gives you such a ridiculous idea? I treasure all my subordinates. Mr. Stanton is no exception."

"Then why did you send him to Lost Pine?"

"Well, why not? What's wrong with Lost Pine?"

"I heard you sent him there to get him out of the way. To humiliate him." Emily didn't mention that the words had been Caul's.

"Humiliate him?" Mirabilis bellowed. "Young woman, are you humiliated to come from Lost Pine?"

"Of course not." Emily lifted her chin. "It's a good place, with good people." She spoke with rising heat. "Good, ordinary people who help each other!"

"There you have it." Mirabilis shrugged conclusively.

Emily wrinkled her nose, trying to figure out exactly what conclusion he'd offered her. Finally, she gave it up and spoke a bit more calmly, her cheeks pink with embarrassment.

"It's just that it seems a shame that he can't . . . be here. After all he did."

"Mr. Stanton will be amply rewarded for his participation."

Mirabilis' voice was velvety with condescension. "Gaining public recognition as the man who saved the life of a president could boost his power substantially. But he cannot harvest that power unless he seizes the opportunity and promotes himself. And he has the press at his feet to do it!" Mirabilis shook his head wonderingly. "He's always had the most unfathomable distaste for the practice of propaganda."

"But it's not the truth, Mr. Hembry wasn't an assassin!" Emily said. "And besides that, it's . . . undignified."

"Dignity is like morality," Mirabilis barked. "Too much is as bad as too little. And as for truth . . . too much of that is even worse, as I hope you never have to find out."

Emily pressed her lips shut, pressed herself back against the seat. She felt as if her knuckles had been rapped with a cane.

"Besides, by forcing Mr. Stanton to face the press, I kill two birds with one stone." Mirabilis' voice was gentler now. "He harvests the power he has earned, and his father is propitiated."

"Propitiated?"

"Credomancers propitiate the powerful," Mirabilis said. "And Senator Argus Stanton is a formidable politician. He has been in Washington for years and there's no sign that the legislature of New York will ask him to come home anytime soon, no matter how many scandals he gets himself involved in. He must be propitiated so that he, in turn, can propitiate the powerful people above him." Mirabilis frowned, shook his head. "Unfortunately, Mr. Stanton has never been willing to fully exploit the . . . *opportunities* . . . that his close association makes possible."

"Surely you're not saying he should use his father's connections to get ahead?" Emily lifted her eyebrows. "That's . . . well, that's just dishonest! He wouldn't stoop to that. I know *that* much about him."

Mirabilis looked at her for a long time without speaking. He blinked, then stared at her some more. Finally, he drew in a deep breath.

"You know, Miss Edwards," he said finally, "you really must see Central Park while you're in our fair city. It's got some amazing attractions."

But Emily didn't have a chance to voice her opinion on the attractions of Central Park, because at that moment the train gave a lurch and slowed to a stop. Emily glanced out the window, glimpsed the marble colonnades of a soaring train station rising up around them. Mirabilis smiled.

"Ah," he said. "Here we are. Welcome to New York."

They arrived at the Institute at that peculiar moment of afternoon when sunlight is soft and heavy as beaten gold, and Emily found herself wondering if perhaps the professor hadn't planned it that way. She couldn't imagine a more spectacular or awe-inspiring sight than the palatial Mirabilis Institute.

Fired by the diffuse golden sunlight, the rambling four-story mansion of frosted white marble looked as if it had been poured rather than constructed. The windows were dazzling sheets of magma; the colonnade of slender pillars sentinels of flame. As Emily stepped out of the carriage into the broad porte cochere, she steeled herself against expected heat, but the air was cool and spring sweet, heady with the perfume of fat, grapelike clusters of exuberant wisteria.

Astonishingly, the inside of the Institute was even grander than the outside. Everything glimmered with high polish: gold, black, red. Masses of crimson orchids nodded in jewel-toned pots cradled in frothy ormolu. Embroidered silk shone against ghostlike marble walls. And everywhere, mirrors winked oblique reflections, like eyes furtively watching one's back.

But despite all the grandeur, Emily could not stop looking at Mirabilis. Within the Institute's walls, he seemed to expand, the edges of him becoming softer yet more powerfully distinct. It was as if he'd grown six inches and shed twenty years. She could imagine him belonging nowhere else.

In the exact center of the high-ceilinged foyer, an elderly serving man waited to receive them. He wore a gray coat that bore the Institute's ornate shield.

"The Institute is pleased at your return, Sophos." The old man recited the words with grave formality.

Brusquely, Mirabilis handed off his coat, hat, and gloves. The serving man bowed respectfully as he took them. He seemed about to say something, but Mirabilis stopped the words in his mouth with a lifted hand.

"Thank you, Ben." His eyes shone keenly, his voice rich and resonant as polished amber. "Miss Edwards, you deserve a rest. But first, there is an experiment I'd like to perform. Will you come with—"

"Japheth Mirabilis!" A loud female voice echoed against the high ceiling.

Both Emily and Mirabilis turned. A large woman was storming toward them, her heels clicking on the polished marble floor. She was block shaped, with shining black hair and wide-set eyes. She wore a rustling dress of dark green silk, elaborately draped and extravagantly bustled. Her little hat had a frothy black ostrich feather that cuddled against her forehead.

"What is she doing here?" Mirabilis muttered sidelong to Ben.

"She arrived before I received the message not to admit anyone," Ben replied softly. "And after the message came, she refused to leave."

"The Witches' Friendly Society has jurisdiction here!" the woman brayed, pointing an accusing finger at Emily. "You have no right to hold her!"

"What is she talking about?" Emily asked.

"My name is Penelope Pendennis," the woman said briskly, handing Emily a card but not taking her eyes off Mirabilis. "Witches' Friendly Society. I'm here to serve as your representative."

"My what?" Emily asked, looking at the card. It featured three female hands clasped together.

"The Witches' Friendly Society is a national trade union," Mirabilis said wearily. "For the protection of American Witches."

"As resolved at the United States Mantic Conference in Cincinnati in 1874, we have the right to be involved in all matters concerning the protection of the rights of—"

"Yes, yes," Mirabilis barked. "I don't dispute your claim. I just don't know how on earth you . . . females . . . find out about these things!"

"What is this all about?" Emily asked.

"I am here to protect you." The woman's eyes were pyroclastic in their intensity. "We have heard about your situation. As your representative, I can offer you independent advice."

"Independent!" Mirabilis snorted.

"Independent of the prejudice and favoritism of *Warlocks*." She looked at Emily. "At the very least, I hope to serve as an unbiased observer of whatever Mirabilis intends to do with you."

Do with me? Emily knitted her brow. "Then you're a . . . a *sorcière*?"

"No, I'm a *Witch*. It's only the Warlocks who insist on that finicky *sorcière* nonsense. They like to reserve the term 'Witch' for their dirty jokes." She glared at Mirabilis for the sins of his gender before continuing. "I'm a specialist in Federalist Earth Magic. Large-scale agricultural blessings, enlightened empire building, destiny manifestation."

"And your society does what exactly?"

"Our society was formed at the beginning of the century as a way for Witches to help other Witches. To protect ourselves from prejudice, and especially to protest the treatment Witches have always received at the hands of Warlocks."

Emily was aware of an extravagant sigh from Mirabilis' direction.

"Treatment?" Emily raised an eyebrow. "What do you mean?"

"My dear, if you have to ask, you obviously haven't been paying attention." Miss Pendennis leaned forward, putting her mouth close to Emily's ear. "Dreadnought contacted me from Philadelphia," she whispered. "I'm a great friend of his sister Hortense. He thought you could use someone to help you navigate. And I don't blame him . . . it's all hidden knives and squinks and mumbo jumbo around here!"

Emily nodded slightly, then straightened and looked at Mirabilis.

"I shouldn't mind having Miss Pendennis observe, at least."

Mirabilis threw up his hands—a gesture of complete hopelessness. His whole body indicated his utter disapproval. Finally, though, he let out a breath.

"As you like." Mirabilis shook his head. "Females!"

Miss Pendennis elbowed Emily in the ribs and gave her a wink.

"Now that we've got that sorted out, can we get on with business?" Mirabilis said. "I wish to perform an experiment. Please come along."

It was more a command than an invitation, for Mirabilis turned on his heel and began walking, not even looking back to see if Emily and Miss Pendennis were following.

They followed.

He led them into the main hall, above which soared a large rotunda. Two broad marble staircases curved up to the second floor. A shining circle of red and gold had been tiled into the marble at their feet, and in the center of the circle stood a statue of a wise-looking goddess. She had one slender arm upstretched, and in her hand she held a torch that burned with a low blue flame.

"The Veneficus Flame," said Professor Mirabilis. "It monitors the mantic energy stored in the earth and serves as a gauge of its vitality."

"It's so low!" Miss Pendennis said.

Indeed, the flame was hardly higher than the nail on Emily's thumb. It looked fragile, as if the smallest gust of wind could extinguish it.

Mirabilis nodded. "It has never burned so low before." He snapped his fingers at Ben, who emerged silently. "Bring me a ladder and the measuring stick."

The old man returned a moment later with a tall oak ladder and a stick on which lines had been neatly painted in white. Ben leaned the ladder against the statue's back.

"Miss Pendennis, Miss Edwards will have to climb that ladder," Mirabilis said. "You are such a sturdy young woman . . . would you mind steadying the bottom so she does not fall?"

"Right," Miss Pendennis said briskly, moving to take her position. As she did, Mirabilis leaned close to Emily.

"Your hand must be reclaimed from the marble for this experiment. May I?"

Emily extended the stump of her hand. Mirabilis gestured

subtly, seeming to pull the marble from thin air. Furtively glancing to make sure Miss Pendennis wasn't watching, he tapped it against the Boundary Cuff three times in a precise rhythm.

Emily found it reassuring to watch her hand resolidify, whole and unharmed. Despite all the trouble it had given her, she'd hate to lose it in some other dimension somewhere.

Mirabilis gestured Emily toward the ladder; she climbed to a level with the flame.

"Now what am I . . ." She looked down to speak to Professor Mirabilis, only to find that he was right next to her, hovering in midair, the tall measuring pole in one hand. She recoiled. Below her Miss Pendennis tensed.

"Steady now!" the woman called up.

"What are you doing?" Emily glared at Mirabilis, clutching her hand to her chest. "I'll be killed if the stone absorbs any more magic!"

"Don't worry, my dear," Professor Mirabilis said. "I am the supreme master of the Institute. The Sophos. Within these walls, I have access to a variety of useful powers that do not require the exercise of free magic. I won't let any harm come to you. Trust me."

Tentatively, Emily brought her hand back out.

"I don't think I'll ever learn all the ins and outs of this credomancy nonsense," she muttered.

Mirabilis continued as if she had not spoken. "On April the 23rd, the flame was at this level." He held the tall measuring stick next to the flame and pointed to a place on the stick that was at least eight inches higher than where the flame currently guttered. "On April the 24th, a little more than two weeks ago, the flame dipped to the level you see it today. For such a dramatic reduction to occur, fully seventy-eight percent of the magic potential in the Mantic Anastomosis would have to simply . . . vanish."

"Vanish?" Miss Pendennis called up to them. "Power cannot vanish!"

"April the 24th," Emily said softly. "That's the day the stone went into my hand."

"So you told me earlier," Mirabilis said. "Which leads us to the experiment." He took her hand and drew it close to the flame.

"Don't worry," he whispered tenderly. "It's quite cool. You won't feel a thing."

He had such a reasonable tone, such a soothing way of talking. She hardly knew why she didn't struggle more as he put her hand over the flame, putting the gem right in the tongue of blue fire. In a brilliant whoosh, the flame flared through the stone.

Emily blinked, staring at the blue flame as it danced and twisted like a gas jet. It was on a level with the mark for April the 23rd.

"We've found our missing magic," Mirabilis said.

"Do you mean that seventy-eight percent of all the magic in the world is in the rock in my hand?" Emily looked at the stone, at the black blob within it that seemed to pulse faintly with every beat of her heart.

"Poppycock!" Miss Pendennis barked. "Mirabilis, that's impossible."

Mirabilis shook his head and smiled down brightly at her. "Nothing is impossible."

Mirabilis gestured for Emily to climb down, and she did, slowly and carefully, head spinning. Seventy-eight percent of the world's magic? Well, no wonder everyone had been so all-fired anxious to get ahold of it!

"But magic is still working fine." Emily looked at Mirabilis. "If all that magic is in my hand, then why are you still able to float around like a hot-air balloon?"

"Think of a lamp, Miss Edwards." Mirabilis drifted thoughtfully to the ground. "Whether it has an inch of oil or is full, it will burn just as brightly. It will only sputter and fade when it is empty."

"So . . . unless there's some way to get the magic back out of the stone, then magic will . . . dry up?" She blinked. "But it's part of everything that lives!"

Professor Mirabilis said nothing for a long moment. And when he opened his mouth to speak again, his words were lost in the sound of a shuddering, booming explosion.

The entire room went brilliantly, blindingly white. The first boom was followed hard by a second; the sound resonated through Emily's entire body, making her teeth rattle. Miss Pendennis put both hands on Emily's shoulders, and for a moment, Emily felt certain that the large woman was going to throw her to the ground.

"Merciful goddess," Miss Pendennis barked, looking around. "We're under attack!"

"Of course we are." Though Mirabilis' voice was mild, he did take Emily's hand rather quickly, clasping the Boundary Cuff around her wrist. Her hand faded back into insubstantiality.

"Well? Who's attacking us?" Miss Pendennis said. Another flash and explosion, and a fine dusting of flaking gilt shimmered down from the ceiling.

"I thought the Witches' Friendly Society knew everything," Mirabilis said derisively. "Were you not aware that this girl has both the Maelstroms and the Sini Mira after her?" He paused, anticipating the next flash and rumble; it rattled the glass of the windows obligingly. "Given that we are under attack from magic, and military magic at that, my guess is that it's the Maelstroms."

B-b-b-bring her out, Mirabilis.

The strangely stuttered words were a rumbling in the air, a command vibrated rather than spoken. They shook the walls of the Institute with their resounding volume. Emily recognized the voice.

Captain Caul.

"Oh, the nerve of him!" Mirabilis said. "That bloodletting scoundrel thinks he can give me orders in my Institute, does he?" Mirabilis stormed up one of the curving staircases, taking the steps two at a time, Emily and Miss Pendennis hot on his heels. Walking quickly to a pair of glass doors that led onto the terrace of the curved portico, Mirabilis threw them open. He moved with such directness and assurance that Emily felt safe enough to peer out from behind him at the scene below.

Two dozen soldiers on horseback were ranged in the Institute's bluestone courtyard, and at their head was Captain Caul atop a sleekly groomed chestnut stallion. But Emily had to stare at him for a long moment before her eyes could accept that it was the same man she'd last seen at Cutter's Rise. There, he'd been an implacable monolith, menacing in his stillness. Now he was like a giant marionette in the hands of a deranged puppeteer—every muscle of his body jerked and twitched, moving without meaning or purpose. His head bobbed strangely, down and to the left, as if an invisible string threaded through his shoulder was tugging on his ear.

"Dreadnought told me you Sundered the beast," Miss Pendennis whispered in Emily's ear with gruesome relish. "Ravaged every nerve in his body, by the look of it. Serves him right!"

Explosions shuddered all around them. The Maelstrom soldiers were a picture of intense focus. Each time one lifted his alembic, another booming retort shook the air. Heedless, Mirabilis strode out onto the portico. Planting his hands on his hips, he thrust out his chest and looked down at Caul from within a shimmering sphere of power; the soldiers' attacks glittered around him, falling away in bright harmless showers of sparks.

"Come on out, Miss Edwards," Mirabilis said loudly, gesturing to Emily. "There's nothing to fear from this pack of little tin soldiers."

Caul stared up as Emily emerged. First, he lifted a trembling fist—a silent signal to the soldiers surrounding him. They lowered their alembics, and the explosions subsided. With a sharp wrench of his head, Caul managed to tip his hat, his uncontrolled shaking making the crossed sabers glint.

"H-h-hello again, Miss Edwards." He spoke slowly, laboring over each word. "What has h-h-happened to your hand?"

"I've got it locked away where you will never get it," Mirabilis jabbed a triumphant finger at him. "It is mine, and it will remain so."

"I have c-c-come to claim it, Mirabilis. For the p-p-public—"

"For the public good," Emily cut him off. "I didn't believe it when you could say it straight, and I don't believe it now."

A spasm of fury kindled on Caul's face, but did not stop there; it spread through his whole body, twisting him in his saddle. His poor confused horse shifted nervously beneath him, Caul's heels tapping against its sides at odds with the big hands pulling on the reins as if they were a drummer boy's sticks.

"Insolent t-t-tramp," he muttered into his own chest. When he spoke again, it was to one of the men standing behind him. "S-S-Sergeant Booth. I n-n-need your help to speak to these s-s-subversives."

An ardent-looking young man presented himself at the captain's side, giving Mirabilis a proud glare before quickly shedding his blue coat, revealing pale bare arms. He reached up and clasped the captain's hand in a firm, steadying grip. Caul gave the young man a barely perceptible nod. Then he drew the silver knife from his belt and slashed the sergeant's inner arm from elbow to wrist. The young man flinched slightly, but squeezed his commander's hand so his blood would flow more quickly. This was not necessary; his blood was already spurting in great arcing gouts, dripping through Caul's fingers as he clutched the sergeant's forearm in his fists. Caul closed his eyes and spoke low jagged words. Power massed around his fingers. The young man doubled over as if punched in the gut.

Mirabilis looked away, his face a mask of disgust. But Emily watched; she could not tear her eyes from the horrifying display. She watched the young man's face twist in agony as magic enveloped him. She watched as his knees buckled, until finally it was only the strength in Caul's grip that kept him upright. All the while, power whipped around them both—power the color of bruises and clots and contusions. Finally, Caul opened his hands, and Sergeant Booth slid to the ground, twitching like a butchered chicken.

Caul took a deep breath and released it slowly. He now looked more like Emily remembered him. Only a lazily spasming eyelid hinted at his previous debility.

"How many enlisted men do you go through a day?" Mirabilis asked when he could finally bring himself to speak again. By that time, Sergeant Booth had stopped twitching, his body contorted in a painfully unnatural position.

"My men understand the importance of this mission," Caul said. "As should you, if you've discovered the power that stone contains."

"I have," Mirabilis said. "And if you think I'm going to hand it over to a bunch of sangrimancers—sanctioned by the President or not—you're sorely mistaken."

"If I imagined you would hand it over, I wouldn't have to waste time and men on you, you filthy anarchist!" The sudden intensity of Caul's rage made his horse sidestep nervously. Clenching his teeth, Caul paused and took a deep breath before continuing. "We have the same enemy, Mirabilis. *Temamauhti,* the greatest foreign threat this nation has ever faced. The emergence of the stone can only mean that the time is near."

"Temam-what?" Emily said to Miss Pendennis.

"Temamauhti?" Mirabilis' voice rose with amused astonishment. "Are you serious? A half-baked doomsday prediction served up by a bunch of Aztec goddess fanatics?"

"Itztlacoliuhqui is gathering strength," Caul said, leaning forward on his horse. His eyes were terrifying in their mad intensity. "Even if she lays waste to the rest of the world, with the power in that stone, we can keep her from crossing *our* borders . . ."

"Let all the nations of the world collapse in wretched misery, as long as Americans get to keep their apple pie." Mirabilis winked at the women behind him. "Sangrimancer patriotism," he stage-whispered.

"Clearly, appealing to *your* patriotism is a waste of my time, *Herr* Mirabilis," Caul growled. "I'm sure you'd love to see the United States destroyed. Because you're like all refugees. You are welcomed as guests, but the fact that you can never be more than that drives you mad. You steep in your bitterness, malcontents collecting like pus in an infected wound . . . You plot revenge. You foment anarchy."

"All while paying taxes and supporting a number of charitable causes," Mirabilis said. "I don't know where I find the time."

"Even the President has taken note of your institute's mongrel admissions policy," Caul continued. "Jews, Arabs, women . . . even a Chinaman or two. You may pay taxes, Mirabilis, but you're no American."

"I'd ask you to forego the jingoistic claptrap, but it's terrifyingly obvious you truly believe it." Mirabilis' voice was cold.

"At least spare me the name-dropping. I may not have the President's ear, but I have connections of my own."

"Like Senator Stanton? The man who's sold his own soul so many times that no one can figure out who actually owns it?"

"I own his son," Mirabilis said.

"Who is still half a sangrimancer, despite your finest efforts to recast him in your own shoddy mold."

"He is no such thing." Mirabilis lifted his chin and spoke with great dignity. "He is a Jefferson Chair of the Mirabilis Institute, and I have great faith in him."

"F-faith?" The twitch around Caul's eye was spreading to his neck and shoulders, making him wriggle as if someone had dropped ice down his back. Whatever relief Sergeant Booth's blood had given him, it was obviously only temporary. "Faith in his m-m-mediocrity, I suppose. He's a rotten credomancer, Mirabilis. And that's just how you like it, isn't it?"

Mirabilis pressed his lips together in a thin white line.

Caul fixed glittering eyes on Emily. "Speaking of Dread-nought Stanton . . . where is he? There's so much I'd like to d-discuss with him."

Emily swallowed hard, her heart thumping alarm. She looked at Mirabilis, but the expression on his face did not change. Instead, he clasped his hands behind his back and strolled to the edge of the portico terrace. On the wide railing stood several delicate marble urns, each planted with bright flowers. He ran a negligent finger along the rim of one of the urns, bent slowly, and sniffed appreciatively. When he straightened, his lips were curved in a lazy, self-satisfied smirk that even Emily found incredibly provoking.

"I confess, I find it difficult to feel very worried about Mr. Stanton's welfare," he drawled, "given that you and your boys can't even knock down my dainty little pansies."

"P-p-pansies?" Caul bared his teeth in a horrible grimace, his body clenching in on itself with rage. It took him some time to master himself, long enough that Emily worried that he might call for another sergeant. But finally he straightened. Emily could hear him breathing fast and hard, as if in pain.

"I'm well aware you've spent the past decade making your

institute strong. S-strong on that mountebank trash you sh-shovel down the throats of gullible Americans. But I will *crack* you, Mirabilis. I will *shatter* you. The attacks will continue until we have what we want. Whether that's b-b-before your institute is reduced to a pile of smoking rubble is up to you."

"You're not dealing with a small-town Witch anymore, someone you can bully with blood magic and loud noises. I have the stone and you don't. Really, is there anything more to say?"

Caul broke into sudden, incomprehensible laughter. It was a low jagged laugh, threaded with genuinely deranged glee, that made Emily's skin crawl. It was a long time before he could speak again, and when he did, Emily saw that he was twitching again, as bad as ever. "W-w-words are your weapons, Mirabilis. Not mine. If you've r-r-run out of them, that's your misfortune."

Then Caul looked at Emily, still smiling broadly, eyes glimmering with malice. His fingers trembled against the brim of his hat, and his gaze lingered on the stump of her hand.

"Good day, Miss Edwards," he said. "I'll s-s-see you again soon."

CHAPTER TWENTY-ONE

Hidden Knives

Back inside, Mirabilis closed the rattling glass doors against the bangs and flashes of the sangrimancers' resumed onslaught.

"Don't let it worry you, my dear," Mirabilis said to Emily, over a piercing squeal that terminated in a wall-shaking concussion. "The Institute is my fortress, and this is a minor annoyance at most. I shall see to it that these ridiculous attacks are stopped and that Caul is sent to peel a mountain of potatoes somewhere."

The absurdity of the image made Emily smile wanly. Seeing the spark of a smile, Mirabilis stoked it by taking her hand and giving it a warm, fortifying squeeze.

"You should rest. We'll talk in the morning. Ben will see you to your room."

"And me?" Miss Pendennis pushed forward. "I'm not running that gauntlet out there, so you'd better have a place for me to sleep, too."

"Of course, Miss Pendennis," Mirabilis said, as a particularly dazzling and earsplitting blast made the floor under his feet rock slightly. "Nothing is more important than ensuring the complete comfort of our guests."

Emily and Miss Pendennis followed old Ben upstairs to the third floor. Ben gestured to the room that would be Miss Pendennis', and the large woman paused on the threshold, looking Emily up and down briskly.

"You'll be all right? You're not scared?"

Emily raised an eyebrow. Outside, the attacks were intensifying, escalating to foundation-rattling blasts. Goddamn right she was scared. But just what Miss Pendennis thought she could do about it, Emily couldn't imagine.

"I'll be fine," Emily said finally.

"Don't you worry. Mirabilis will get these attacks stopped. In the meantime, if you need me, just sing out."

Ben opened the door to Emily's room and showed her in. He spent a little time shuffling around, turning up the gas in the ornate gilt fixtures. The increase in light revealed something to Emily. She stifled a shriek, hand over her mouth.

Thin trickles of blood were streaming down the wall, fresh and bright red.

Ben *tsk-tsk*ed mildly when he saw the gory streams. He went over to the wall, laid his hand against it, and said something in soft clear Latin. The blood did not disappear, but at least it stopped trickling.

"Sangrimancer mischief," he said.

"I thought the Institute was a fortress!" Emily's voice was thin. Was there going to be blood running down the walls all night? Maybe finding Miss Pendennis wouldn't be such a bad idea after all.

"A roof will shelter you from the rain, but the damp may get through," Ben said. It was the most he had said in her presence, and she was surprised by how kind and comforting his voice was. "Don't worry, Miss Edwards, you'll be completely safe. I promise."

She looked at him. He looked strangely familiar, but she could not think why. Perhaps it was because he reminded her of Pap, gentle and mild and soft-spoken. He possessed an unstrained quality of solidity and dependability—a quality entirely different from Mirabilis' maneuvering and calculation.

"You'll find clean night things in that cupboard, and there's hot water in the ewer." He bent his head respectfully. "If there's nothing more you require?"

"No . . . no, thank you."

"Good night, miss."

It wasn't until Emily was folded into bed with the covers up well over her chin that Ben's soothing influence evaporated, and she began to tremble again, anxious thoughts and ugly memories spinning between her ears. Images of the eager young sergeant, blood spurting from his arm—sacrificing his life without a second thought. And Caul's hideous madness, the thinly veiled threat . . . *So much I'd like to discuss with him,* he had said.

She, at least, was inside the Institute, even if there was blood on the walls. But Mirabilis had sent Stanton away, alone and unprotected. What if Caul found him?

That thought alone was disturbing enough. But then a different thought, slanting at an odd angle to the first, disturbed her even more.

What if Caul meant something different?

What if the words weren't a threat?

A Warlock of questionable dependability, half a sangrimancer . . .

Emily closed her eyes, shuddering at the memory of the magic Stanton had worked to cleanse Grimaldi from his blood . . . acrid words, hot swirling winds, long fingers making gruesome patterns in the dust. Of course it had been sangrimancy. She'd known it the moment she'd seen it. Any fool would have. But she'd pretended blindness. Not out of ignorance or naïveté, but because she . . .

Because there was nothing else she could do, that's why. She'd pushed it out of her mind because it could not be considered at the time. Unless she'd been willing to follow the consideration through to its logical conclusion and leave him, walk away right then and there . . . and how could she leave him, after everything? After all they'd been through?

Half a sangrimancer . . .

What if Mirabilis had sent Stanton away because he didn't trust him?

A sudden coruscation of light illuminated the room through the heavy silk curtains, followed by an echoing explosion that made Emily's ears hurt. She buried her head deeper in the soft pillow. It smelled of honeysuckle and starch.

Well, I *trust him,* she thought fiercely. After all, she owed him that much. Maybe he did know blood magic, but that didn't mean he was a *sangrimancer,* not even half of one.

He'd been shot and almost burned at the stake . . . and there had been so many opportunities to redirect the situation to his advantage, if that was his true aim. To think him untrustworthy was ludicrous.

These attempts to construct a bulwark of certainty kept Emily's brain feverishly active for a long time. But just when she thought there was no way she would be able to catch a wink of sleep that night, sleep reached up and caught her, folding her in blackness, dragging her deep.

Night. Low swinging lamplight.

She dreamed she was on the train, curled close to someone warm. She breathed pleasantly, until she realized that she was really alone after all.

She sat up, looking around herself. There was no other living creature on the train, just murky yellow light and the sound of a fiddle playing.

"Sweet, Sweet Spring."

Moonlight through the train's shutters sliced her white nightgown into strips. She looked out the windows at the rolling landscape. Aberrant jackrabbits were easily loping alongside, their long ears laid back flat, their eyes red and glowing.

There was a voice muttering around her . . . through her . . . in her . . .

But I try before!

It was a strange voice. Familiar. Unfamiliar. Masculine when she remembered it as feminine. Looping and perfumed.

That rock in her hand, it interfere. It did no work . . .

T-T-TRY AGAIN.

The voice that broke in was different. Hard, harsh, and edged with insanity, it filled the compartment, echoing off the walls. It went upward, like a bubble of gas released from beneath viscous mud. Emily looked up, watching it go, and saw that the train had no roof. Above, the sky was velvet black, seeded with stars.

God, her head ached.

I tell you, it will no work!

AND I T-T-TOLD YOU TO T-T-TRY AGAIN.

At the far end of the compartment, a dark figure was stand-ing, a huge man. He moved toward her in a hobbling shuffle. He looked lumpy, malformed. Emily wanted to run, but she could not. She could not speak. She could not scream.

The jackrabbits laughed.

The man was not a man.

Rather, it was two men pushed together into one. It was as if each man had been made of clay and a child had wadded them up together. Half a face was squashed up against a flat-tened skull; one old brown eye leered at her and one insane red one appraised her.

The thing lifted a hand. Its hand was strong and large. The fingers sank into the soft part of her throat, finding the edges of her windpipe. It squeezed.

Carissima mia.

It held her for a long time, each vastly different eye boring into her in its own way. Her head pounded as if it would ex-plode. She writhed under the tightening grip, whimpering. Light sparkled at the corners of her eyes, flashes of suffoca-tion. They resolved themselves into horrific images, knives in brutal hands, honed razors, hollow sharp silver needles. They were coming at her with them, coming for her . . .

LEAVE HER FOR N-N-NOW, the red-eye commanded. WE H-H-HAVE WHAT WE NEED.

Blackness swallowed her at the same moment Emily woke, thrashing wildly under the white sheets.

She leapt from the bed as if it were on fire. Her heart was racing as she sucked in great gulps of air. Coming for her . . . razors and needles and knives . . .

She rushed to the door, fumbled at the bolt with a shaking, weak hand. When she'd released the lock, she threw the door open. She looked down the hall.

She had to find someone, tell them . . . tell them that . . .

. . . that . . .

. . . that *what*?

She looked up and down the hall, blinking. What had she dreamed? Suddenly, she could not remember, and the harder she tried, the more the memory retreated from her.

Rabbits.

There were huge rabbits with red eyes, and a train . . .

A flash of light, followed by a rattling boom, threw the room into stark relief. The brightness and noise startled her, making thoughts fly from her head like frightened birds.

The beating of her heart was subsiding now. She blinked, holding the nightgown tightly around herself. Why on earth was she standing out in the hall? She didn't remember coming here.

Letting out her breath, she softly closed the door of her room and went back to bed.

And when she woke the next morning, she'd forgotten that she'd dreamed at all.

In fact, all she knew was that she had slept deeply, and for a long time, and that she felt a great deal better for having done so. The next thing she realized was that the sound of explosions had ceased. She went to the window and peeked through the curtains. The sun was high in a clear blue sky. Birds darted over the trees, chirping merrily.

From behind her came the sound of a cleared throat, followed by mock thoughtful, soft-drawled words:

"All the way from California with a succulent little *skycladdische*. How very nice for our dear Dreadnought! I wonder if they'll put that in the serial."

Emily whirled, frowning. Tarnham, Mirabilis' red-haired secretary, stood leaning against the doorjamb. In his arms he had a package wrapped in paper. Her hand flew to the neck of her nightgown.

"What the devil!" she spluttered.

"Oh, I'm sorry. Did I say that out loud?" Tarnham's voice was oily with assumed innocence. On his shoulder, the ferret watched her with beady eyes, climbing across the back of Tarnham's neck to get to his other shoulder. "My mouth, it has a mind of its own sometimes."

"I couldn't care less the kind of mind your mouth has!" Emily blazed, lifting a finger to point at the door. "Get out of here!"

"Now, now. Don't get all huffy. I was asked to bring you this. It's a clean dress."

"Well, you can leave it on the table," Emily said. Tarnham complied, but didn't stop grinning. He paused at the door on his way out.

"The Sophos and that Friendly Society person are downstairs waiting for you. I suppose you've got a lot of practice throwing clothes on quickly. I'll tell them you'll be down soon."

Then, chuckling to himself, he pushed himself away from the doorjamb and vanished, not even bothering to close the door.

Cheeks burning, she crossed the room and slammed the door shut, locking it. How had the door gotten unlocked, anyway? She remembered locking it before going to bed.

No, she must have forgotten. But she certainly wouldn't forget after this.

She took her time unwrapping the package Tarnham had brought; in fact, she took a good long time. What exactly did he mean, a lot of practice throwing clothes on quickly? And that word again, "skycladdische" . . . She didn't know what it meant, but she'd only heard it out of the mouths of men like Tarnham and Caul, which meant that it couldn't be anything nice.

The dress he'd brought her, while clean, was coarse and gray and looked like a servant's uniform. Emily pulled it on with the resignation of one who'd become accustomed to being dressed like a moron, a pauper, or both. It was overlarge and overshort, which meant that her ugly men's boots would be on full display. The one piece of luck was that the dress buttoned up the front, but even so, it was hard to get the buttons done up using just one hand.

When she was finally ready, she walked downstairs slowly. She hardly looked in Tarnham's direction as she noticed him waiting for her at the bottom of the stairs, stroking the ferret tucked under his arm.

He grinned. "Decided to teach me a lesson?"

"You did not enter my thoughts in the smallest degree," Emily said frostily. Tarnham gave a mellifluous, rippling laugh.

"Oh, so you're one of those." He sidled up to her, uncomfortably close. "The kind who take themselves seriously.

Like the burlesque dancers who think they're *artistes*. How cute." He paused, waving a dramatic hand. "Well, never mind then. I won't josh with you anymore. Though I must say, it's too bad when a girl can't have a sense of humor about herself."

Tarnham showed her to Professor Mirabilis' office—a spacious, book-lined room that smelled of leather and beeswax. There was a large stained-glass window directly behind the enormous desk, red-velvet draperies, and heavy carvings of black walnut. The ceiling was a trompe l'oeil of a sky at the precise moment of sunset.

Professor Mirabilis and Miss Pendennis were sitting together in leather chairs arranged before a large fireplace of black marble veined with gold. Miss Pendennis looked up as Emily came in, her face pursing sourly as she looked Emily up and down. Mirabilis rose, crossed the room, and took Emily's hand in his. He smiled broadly.

"Good morning, Miss Edwards. I trust your rest was refreshing?"

"I slept well," she said. She glared at Tarnham's retreating back but said nothing. "I'm glad the attacks have stopped."

"I promised you would be safe," Mirabilis said. "As I told you, I have friends in high places."

"None of them women, obviously." Miss Pendennis eyed Emily's gray dress with outrage. "Or else you wouldn't have dared to send this . . . this . . . *squink* of a dress! What's your game, Mirabilis? Humble her and keep her off balance? What exactly are you softening her up for?"

"Miss Pendennis, I won't stand to be spoken to like that," Mirabilis growled. The words made Emily cringe; his voice echoed in the same way Stanton's had up at Cutter's Rise, but it was filled with an entirely different kind of menace and threat.

"Wrathfulness," Miss Pendennis said knowingly, discomfited not in the least. "It's no use, Mirabilis, I know all the credomantic tricks. Anger will not disarm and bewilder me. And I won't let you use it, or any other tactic, to control Miss Edwards."

A look of grudging respect crept over Mirabilis' face.

"Miss Pendennis, you really are something. I can honestly say I've never met your equal."

"Flattery," Miss Pendennis said. "Skip it."

Mirabilis smiled to himself as he struck a dignified pose by the fireplace. "I have been thinking things over carefully," he said. "And I have come to the conclusion that there is only one course of action."

"Take the rock out of my hand?" Emily said.

"No," Mirabilis said. "We must create a Precedent."

"A what?" Emily looked at Miss Pendennis, but all the woman's glaring attention was focused on Mirabilis.

"In credomancy," Mirabilis continued, "power is built by setting Precedents. For example, you've heard of the defeat of the Spanish Armada?"

Emily stared at him. "What does the defeat of the Spanish Armada have to do with my hand?"

"Who is the greatest naval power in the world?"

"Britain?" Emily felt it was probably the answer he was fishing for. She was rewarded with a smile.

"Correct. Before the defeat of the Spanish Armada, were the British known for their naval power?"

"How should I know?"

"Well, they weren't. And they wouldn't have been if it hadn't been for that one historic action." Mirabilis made a conclusive gesture. "That is a Precedent. An action so decisive and unanswerable that it sends ripples outward throughout the rest of history, alters the fundamental fabric of reality. From that moment, the world believed that Britain was a great sea power, and so it became a great sea power."

"Are you going to make Miss Edwards into a sea power?"

Mirabilis smiled frostily at Miss Pendennis' impertinence, then looked back at Emily. There was a look on his face that reminded Emily of a salesman, waiting for just the right moment to bring up the matter of price.

"This is my proposal. With that stone, I will set the boldest Precedent ever," Mirabilis said. "I have called a Grand Symposium for this evening. Credomancers, animancers, and, yes, sangrimancers will help decide on the disposition of the stone together."

"You can't be serious!" Miss Pendennis was on her feet. "You can't trust sangrimancers!"

"It is by trusting them that I will make them trustworthy."

"But they are depraved!"

"The worse we believe them to be, the worse they will become."

"How much worse can they get? They murder people and steal their blood!"

"What is to say that they might not be changed? If we do not believe they can change, they never will."

"Believe them into being good?" Miss Pendennis snorted. "I tell you, Mirabilis. I've heard my fair share of credomantic bunkum over the years, but this takes the cake. It's impossible."

"Nothing's impossible," Mirabilis said.

There was a long pause. Emily was acutely aware of her own breathing.

"That stone contains vast magical potential," Mirabilis said finally, "the heritage of every Warlock and Witch who has ever lived or will live. Can you not see, Miss Edwards, that it is only fair, and it is only right, that representatives from every magical tradition have a say in its disposition?"

"Don't answer that!" Miss Pendennis barked. "He's trying to trick you into agreeing!"

"Miss Pendennis, please." Mirabilis' words were an attenuated sigh. His gaze remained fixed on Emily. "It's not a trick, Miss Edwards. It's simply a question. Will you attend the Grand Symposium tonight?"

"What if I refuse?" Emily said.

"Then you are free to leave," Mirabilis said.

"Leave?"

"And walk right into the arms of the Maelstroms, or the Sini Mira?" Miss Pendennis blazed. "Let whoever grabs her first take the stone and use it however they like?"

"Don't be idiotic, Miss Pendennis. It does not suit you. Whatever Miss Edwards' decision, her hand will remain here, under my protection."

"What?" Emily leaned forward in her chair, outraged. "You're just going to . . . *commandeer* my hand?"

"What else would you have me do?" Mirabilis asked. "Do you not see the almost impossible responsibility you have placed upon me, Miss Edwards? The knife's edge I must negotiate to save you, the Institute—even the future of magic?" He paused. "Your participation in the symposium—specifically your connection with Komé—will be of great help in navigating that treacherous edge. I would be most grateful for your cooperation. But if I cannot have it, I must do without."

There was a long silence, broken finally when Miss Pendennis slapped the arm of her chair.

"Well, isn't this a fine kettle of fish," she bleated. "And folks wonder why Witches need a Friendly Society!"

"Oh, that's *right,*" Mirabilis narrowed his eyes at Miss Pendennis, his voice taking on a tone of inspiration. "I've forgotten all about the Witches' Friendly Society. Why, your troubles are at an end, Miss Edwards! I'm sure the members will be delighted to open their homes to you—a kind of underground railroad of one. Of course, they'll be putting their husbands and children in the path of the Maelstroms, but that's just a minor detail. Go on, then. You *females* work it out among yourselves. I've clearly wasted my time trying to come up with a solution when one was staring us in the face all the time."

Emily glanced at the woman for her reaction. Even Miss Pendennis' seemingly unflappable brusqueness had transmuted into obvious consternation. Emily felt suddenly trapped and alone.

You are *alone, carissima mia.*

Emily winced at the sudden slight pain, but it faded quickly, and in an instant she had forgotten it. She drew in a deep breath, let it out.

"Well, what's in it for me?" she said, with more petulance than she had intended. Mirabilis' eyes widened, but Emily pressed on. "Mr. Stanton promised me payment. Will you honor that arrangement?"

"Of course, Miss Edwards," Mirabilis said. "If that is what you want."

"I want twenty thousand dollars," Emily said. It was, of

course, an impossible sum. It was the kind of money that people talked about in hushed and respectful tones. No one really had twenty thousand dollars; it was a number with far too many zeros to be believed. But it was the amount of the bounty that had been offered for her and Stanton. They were worth that to someone.

To her surprise, Mirabilis grinned broadly and clapped his hands together. "Done," he said.

Emily gaped at him with all the astonishment of one who had been expecting "truth" and had gotten "dare."

"You can't really mean it . . ." Emily sputtered. She wondered, suddenly, if she hadn't been trapped in some exquisitely cunning fashion.

"Of course I do!" Mirabilis said. "I'll have a contract drafted immediately."

"And if some harm should come to Miss Edwards during this suicidal adventure?" Miss Pendennis asked.

"I will add a codicil that the money shall be paid regardless. It could pass to your adoptive father."

Emily knew that she would never again have the chance to make such money—a fortune! It would fix her for life . . . and even if the worst happened, she'd know that Pap was provided for. It was an opportunity she could not pass up.

Firmly, she extended her good hand to Mirabilis. But just as she was about to shake on it, she abruptly pulled her hand back.

"One more thing," she said. "Miss Pendennis must be allowed to participate in the Grand Symposium and advise me as need be."

Mirabilis sighed.

"As you wish," he said, reaching for her hand, but again she held it away from him. She watched his face closely as she spoke the next words.

"And Mr. Stanton, too."

Mirabilis' eyes widened, then narrowed again, calculation shifting behind them. He was silent for a long time. His hand hung in the air. He made no move to take hers.

"Impossible," he said.

"I've heard you say several times that nothing is impossible."

Mirabilis continued to stare at her. She began to feel quite uncomfortable under that gaze, so she blurted out: "Mr. Stanton's attendance is a condition of my participation."

Mirabilis smiled gently at the force of her statement, but there was no pleasure on his face. He reached for her hand with a sigh. He gave it three firm shakes.

"Agreed," he said.

"Well, that was infinitely worse than I expected," Miss Pendennis said, not very encouragingly, as they left the office and headed back upstairs.

"Do you think he really believes that setting some kind of 'Precedent' is going to work?" Emily puzzled. "Or was it all just eyewash to get me to participate?"

"Well if it was, he sure wasted his fine breath, didn't he?" Miss Pendennis said wryly. "Given that all he had to do was offer you a little money."

"I don't know what kind of sums you're used to," Emily looked at her, "but twenty thousand dollars is hardly a little money."

"It is if someone's asking you to cut your own throat to get it," Miss Pendennis mused, but then said no more. "Anyway, I have no idea what Mirabilis really has up his sleeve. But one thing's for sure. If it's a credomancer's plan, it's sure to have a half dozen double-reverses, with some curlicues and manipulative filigree tacked on for good measure." She lifted her hands in a gesture of plaint to the pitiless heavens. "Oh, give me good old earth magic anytime!"

Emily nodded in agreement as they reached Miss Pendennis' door.

"Well, we've got a lot of work to do, and less than fifteen hours to do it." Miss Pendennis' face brightened when she saw that there were two large steamer trunks sitting in the center of the floor of her room. "Thank the goddess! They've arrived."

The big woman knelt before one of the chests, unlocked it, and threw up the lid. A large square leather case bound in steel and fastened with two heavy steel hasps was nestled into the top of the trunk. Miss Pendennis took this case out,

straining against its weight, and laid it aside. She pulled out
the wooden shelf insert that had supported it. When the
drawer was removed, a compacted foam of silk and lace billowed out extravagantly.

"It's the best I could do on short notice," Miss Pendennis
said as she looked through the trunk. "Have a seat, I'll be
with you in a moment."

There was a little table in the corner of the room; on it was
a pot of coffee and the morning newspapers. Emily sat,
glimpsing a picture of something snakelike.

Pulling the newspaper closer, she saw that the front page
featured a hastily composed engraving of the Cockatrice.
The picture was surrounded by smaller cartouches in which
were depicted some familiar faces: there was Stanton—the
expression on his face somewhere between dauntless and
displeased—and his father right next to him, the pair of them
surrounded by illustrated swags of bunting. Farther down was
a menacing-looking picture of poor old Hembry, and below,
in a pretty flowered cartouche, a dreamy-eyed Rose Hibble.

"Credomancer Thwarts Attempt on President's Life!" the
headline screamed in black blocky text. "Warlock Son of
Senator Argus Stanton Subdues Wild-Eyed Anarchist Mis-
creant!" the subhead exclaimed. "Extreme Excitement at the
Philadelphia Exposition!" the sub-subhead added rather tire-
somely.

Emily scanned the thrilling account. She noted with interest
how the story had been altered to avoid any mention of the
Manipulator, or of her own presence on the scene. In fact, the
stories mostly focused on Stanton's superhuman heroics, his
forthright desire to uphold the principles of Justice and Lib-
erty upon which American Democratic Ideals were based, and
the admirable modesty of his assertion that he "really didn't do
anything."

Miss Pendennis straightened, a dress in her hand. When
she saw Emily reading the paper, she snatched it away and
tossed it aside.

"Don't bother with that garbage," Miss Pendennis said,
shaking out the dress. "You can't expect the truth from any of
the metropolitan newspapers. They're all credomantic tools

nowadays." As a replacement, she handed Emily a copy of *Practitioners' Daily*.

"Journal of record for the American magic user," Miss Pendennis said. "Generally trustworthy. Can't go wrong with it."

Practitioners' Daily had far fewer engravings than the other papers, and far more printing. One headline, however, was very large:

"Antonio Pietro Grimaldi, Notorious Manipulator, Taken into Custody by Philadelphia Police."

"That Grimaldi's a loathsome scoundrel," Miss Pendennis offered. She had laid the dress across the bed, and was back on her knees, digging through the trunk. "There are a lot of people in the magical community who will be pleased to see him brought to justice!"

"Mr. Stanton was under a compulsion from Grimaldi," Emily said.

"So I heard. One of the few pieces of information I was able to drag out of Mirabilis this morning. Dreadnought was furious at being sent off. He thought he was safe, with Grimaldi in custody and all . . . but I suppose Mirabilis was taking no chances."

"Taking no chances?"

"Can you imagine the damage that might have been done if Dreadnought had come back to the Institute while the compulsion was still active?" Miss Pendennis clucked absently as she compared two equally uncomfortable-looking corsets.

"But the Institute is Mirabilis' fortress," Emily said quietly. Her head was beginning to ache. "Surely a compulsion would not work within the Institute."

"Direct cellular subjugation to a hostile Warlock must never be taken lightly," Miss Pendennis said gravely, as if she'd just delivered a common aphorism. Then she stood, her arms overflowing with petticoats and other silken things. She dropped these on the bed with an airy *floof*.

"All right. First off, if you're going to go through with this 'Precedent' Mirabilis intends to set, you must at all costs avoid being seen as someone the Warlocks can trifle with."

Miss Pendennis pointed to the dress she'd laid out on the bed. It was a shimmering fantasy of heavy shot silk, its folds gleaming every shade of purple from dark aubergine to brilliant violet. There was enough fabric in the skirt alone to make Emily three dresses. "That dress is a Worth. From Paris. That dress they will not trifle with."

"Why should anyone want to trifle with me?" Emily regarded the garment. "I'm a practitioner, just like them."

"Oh, Miss Edwards! You do have something to learn!" Miss Pendennis chuckled grimly. "Modern magic is a gentleman's game, like playing the stock market, or smoking cigars, or driving fast little carriages. Men do. Women don't."

"What are you talking about? Women have always been Witches!"

"Women have always been whores, too," Miss Pendennis said pointedly. "Warlocks tolerate nice women of good family and independent means who dabble in the supernatural arts. When it's a lady like me or that awful Mrs. Quincy you encountered in San Francisco, they dismiss it as an eccentricity, like writing poems or keeping two dozen cats. But honest working women who practice Witchcraft for a living? For money? That's a whole different kettle of fish. Strictly *skycladdische*."

Emily narrowed her eyes.

"I've been called that," Emily said, her throat dry. "*Skycladdische*."

"Of course you have," Miss Pendennis frowned. "Though I hope Dreadnought wasn't crass enough . . ."

"No," Emily said quickly. "Caul. And Tarnham."

"Tarnham? That rotten little worm!" Miss Pendennis pursed her lips disapprovingly. "So conflicted he has to carry around a familiar. Pathetic."

"I didn't know credomancers kept familiars," Emily said. "Do you mean the ferret?"

"Practitioners who can't resolve deep emotional conflicts about their mantic powers use familiars as a crutch," Miss Pendennis explained. "Tarnham's family is hellfire-and-brimstone Baptist. Tough to escape an upbringing like that.

Deep down, he believes he should burn at the stake. So the ferret is his partner in crime. By bonding his power to the animal, he can believe that it's the animal that's evil, not him. It keeps him sane . . . though in his case, that's a relative term."

Emily pondered this. Then she looked at Miss Pendennis warily.

"So, what does it mean? Skycladdische?"

"It's German. It translates simply as skyclad-one. Skyclad is an old term for nakedness—the state in which many common spells are performed. Of course, it's not the nakedness *per se* that's the problem, it's what the nakedness leads to."

"What it leads to?"

"Licentiousness and lust! Depravity! The Witch as seducer of men and eater of their organs of generation! The Witch as unprincipled opportunist who will not scruple at sacrificing her very virtue for the power she has no right to wield!" Miss Pendennis waved a fist in the air, spoke the words in a declamatory voice, as if she were up on a podium making a speech. Then she regarded Emily closely.

"You're blushing," Miss Pendennis said. "I'm sure you're a nice, decent girl. But don't ever forget this—there is not one Warlock in the world who will give you credit for being anything better than a brazen hussy."

Emily's eyes flashed up rebelliously. That wasn't true! Certainly Stanton didn't think . . .

. . . but then Emily's cheeks burned even hotter. Why on earth wouldn't he? What reason had she ever given him to think otherwise? How about the time he'd seen her dancing naked under an oak tree, trying to bewitch a man into marrying her so that she could get her hands on his money? She pressed her hands to her face, suddenly wishing she could sink through the floor.

"To summarize the sad state of the world," Miss Pendennis said, lifting a finger. "Ladies: respected and revered. Skycladdische: despised and discarded. And that's why the Witches' Friendly Society exists. Of Witches, by Witches, for Witches! Simple enough?"

Emily said nothing.

"So, we transform you into the very picture of propriety and respectability. At least until Mirabilis' Grand Symposium is finished."

"If you say so," Emily said softly.

"All right then," Miss Pendennis barked, like a drillmaster. "Down to your chemise!"

"The thing to remember is that clothes are like armor." Miss Pendennis pulled out a steel-boned corset and held it up, eyeing Emily's waist critically. "You don't normally wear corsets, I presume?"

"I always found it hard to climb mountains in them," Emily said.

"Women who don't wear corsets are called loose. Yet another euphemism for whore." Miss Pendennis fastened the obnoxious garment around Emily's waist, pulling the laces to an extreme tightness.

"The more clothes you wear, the more protected you are." Miss Pendennis continued her previous lecture as she pulled and tugged, grunting. "Clothes deflect reproach." She didn't stop tugging until the laces had been drawn so tight that Emily despaired of her ability to draw enough breath to walk across the room. Miss Pendennis nodded fiercely. "With practice you could go as small as any lady of fashion, but that's enough to fit into the dress."

"How do the ladies of fashion manage?" Emily panted.

"They manage because they have to," Miss Pendennis said, tying the corset. "Now, I'm an advocate of dress reform myself. I despise the thought of what this barbaric truss is doing to your innards. But we must choose our battles and that's one I'm sure I won't win for a long time, if ever."

The purple silk ballgown from Worth had been laid carefully across a chair to wait for the Grand Symposium. For daytime wear, Miss Pendennis pulled out a fawn-colored cashmere embroidered in black floss and declared it just the thing.

"Warm and soft, delicate and vulnerable." Miss Pendennis pulled the dress down over Emily's head, her fingers flying up Emily's back to fasten the multitude of little pearl buttons. "Fuzzy, too. The symbolism just gets cruder from there."

"But I thought I was supposed to be *armored,*" Emily said.

"That's the paradoxical thing about a woman's armor," Miss Pendennis said as she fluffed the dress in a few places. "The softer it is, the better it serves."

"You're not making any sense! I thought the idea was to keep men from getting ideas. Men get ideas about soft, fuzzy, vulnerable girls!"

"Of course they do," Miss Pendennis said. "But they feel *guilty* about them."

The woman stood back at arm's length, pinching her chin between her thumb and forefinger critically. She seized a little black hat and perched it atop Emily's head, cocking her head to scrutinize the effect. As she was pinning it on, there was a soft knock at the door.

"Right on schedule," Miss Pendennis murmured. "That'll be Ben, coming with some plan to distract us. Mirabilis will have arranged it, because it won't do to have us sitting up here thinking all day. He'll have a lecture for us to go to or something . . . somewhere we can't really talk. Which is exactly why I put you into this lovely walking outfit. Follow my lead."

There was another knock, gentle but insistent.

"Enter!" Miss Pendennis barked, angling Emily's hat attractively.

Ben appeared in the doorway, hands clasped behind his back.

"Excuse me, Miss Pendennis, Miss Edwards . . . but since the symposium will not commence until later this evening, Sophos Mirabilis thought you might enjoy attending a presentation by one of our senior professors. He is speaking to a group of advanced students on the topic of—"

"Oh, thank you so much for the offer," Miss Pendennis said, "but Miss Edwards is simply withering for want of fresh air. We're on our way for a walk in your institute's lovely gardens. You needn't trouble yourself on our account."

Ben looked at Emily's walking dress. He smiled gently.

"Of course," he said. "The weather is quite fine, and I will be happy to show you the Institute's conservatory."

Miss Pendennis frowned slightly. "We hate to put you to

the trouble," she said. "I'm sure preparing for the Grand Symposium will require all of your attention."

"The arrangements will be seen to," Ben said. "The Sophos has asked that I allow nothing to interfere with my attendance upon the Institute's two most important guests."

"I'm sure he did," Miss Pendennis muttered, giving Emily's shoulder a final brush and handing her a parasol as if it were a club.

"All right, walk fast and see if we can't give him the slip," Miss Pendennis whispered to Emily as they emerged into the sunshine. Ben, for his part, was quite obliging. He lingered behind, giving the two women a wide berth for their private conversation.

"Now listen. We obviously won't have much time to go over this in depth, but we need to have a plan of attack for tonight. The one thing you have to remember is that you have as much say in this symposium as anyone else. More, in fact, because you're the one with the rock in your hand. So have you given any thought to what you think should be done with it?"

Emily drew her brows together but said nothing. She reached up and felt for the hardness of the acorn around her throat. But as she did, she knew that Komé couldn't give her an answer . . . just as Miss Pendennis couldn't, nor Mirabilis, nor even Stanton. She knew, suddenly, that this question was for her, and it always had been.

"Do you think we should recommend that the power be returned somehow?" Miss Pendennis prompted softly. "Or maybe it was accreted and shed by some poorly understood geological mechanism—in which case, returning it might be ill-advised."

Miss Pendennis' words faded as Emily stopped, placing her hand on the rough bark of a large tree. She could feel life thrumming through it. She felt her eyes unfocus as she re-membered Komé's words . . .

You must allow your mind to stretch to the size of the stars, for that is the size of Ososolyeh's dreams.

You must forget that time exists.

You must forget that you can die.

"The Sini Mira," Emily said distantly. "The Sons of the Earth."

Miss Pendennis whistled. The sound of it brought Emily back to consciousness. She focused on the woman's face.

"Hand it over to a bunch of Russian Eradicationists?" Miss Pendennis shook her head. "Caul's paranoid enough about a bunch of extinct Aztecs. Thank goodness he's not here to hear you say *that*."

"Miss Edwards is perhaps referring to the Sini Mira's well-known research correlating the exponential increase in the human use of magic over the past two hundred years with the increased production of Black Exunge," Ben's voice broke in softly. Emily and Miss Pendennis turned, both unaware that the man had come up close behind them. "The same research suggests that the Mantic Anastomosis possesses a consciousness—an utterly alien, nonhuman consciousness, but a consciousness nonetheless. Taking those findings together, perhaps it is possible that the appearance of the stone was not merely a geologic accident."

"A consciousness?" Miss Pendennis snorted. "The Mantic Anastomosis is nothing but a huge web of rock."

Emily looked at Ben. There was a soft challenge in his eyes, as if he was waiting for her to say something. After a long moment of silence, he looked over at Miss Pendennis.

"I'm sure you know better than me, miss," he said.

The conservatory was a large, ornate white building with vast panes of glass that gleamed in the late morning sunshine. As they walked up the path approaching it, Emily saw men in servant gray sweeping broken glass from the slate flagstones. It was the first tangible evidence Emily had seen of the attacks of the previous night.

Inside the conservatory it was close and sweltering. The air was heavy with the rich perfume of a hundred kinds of brilliant blooming orchids. The orchids seemed to be Ben's special passion. As they moved along the smooth pebbled walks he showed them dozens of varieties in all colors: deep luxurious oranges, vibrant ceruleans, gentle shell pinks.

Ben stopped in front of one particular orchid vine that sat at the center of the conservatory. It was huge. At its base it was as thick as a man's waist, and its long curling tendrils easily overtopped the hundred-foot pillar of cork that was the vine's support. It sported hundreds of deliciously fragrant blossoms that were a somewhat bilious shade of chartreuse veined with chocolate brown.

"This is the one everyone comes to see." Ben reached out a finger to almost touch one of the nodding blooms. "The Dragon's Eye Orchid. The largest in the world. Its roots go well underground into the limestone gravel underneath the conservatory."

Emily nodded appreciatively, fanning herself with her hand.

"I hope it's not too warm for you, Miss Edwards?" Ben murmured.

"Hot as Hades," Emily said. Having grown up in the mountains, Emily had never experienced such a humid place. Sweat beaded on her brow; she wiped it away with three fingers. "Now I know how Mr. Stanton must have felt!"

Was it her imagination, or did she see a shadow of a smile pass over Ben's face?

"Huh?" Miss Pendennis had stopped by a bed of vegetables and was looking at a purple cabbage that was the size of an ottoman. "What's that?"

"Mr. Stanton. He is always so warm. You never noticed?" Emily said. "The first time he ever gave me his arm, I thought he was ill with a fever. But he said it was some kind of an impairment."

"Impairment?" Miss Pendennis' brow furrowed. "Nonsense. Dreadnought is healthy as a horse. Has a fantastic appetite."

"Well, the appetite is part of it," Emily said. "It's why he has to eat all the time. He called it something in Latin . . . *Exussum cruorsis* . . ."

"Burned?" Miss Pendennis' voice dropped to a murmur. Her eyes went wide, and she stared at Emily with sudden horror.

"Well . . . yes. Burned. He said that was a rude way of putting it."

Miss Pendennis put a hand over her mouth.

"Hortense never told me," she said. "Oh, my. I never knew. That's . . . tragic."

"Tragic?" Emily drew her brows together. "I don't see what's so tragic about it, unless you have to pay his grocery bills."

Miss Pendennis stared at Emily.

"You don't know what being burned is, do you?" She paused. "He didn't tell you?"

Emily felt suddenly apprehensive. "Tell me what?"

"Calling someone 'burned' is imprecise. What they are is 'burning,' as in 'burning up.' What is he, almost thirty?" Miss Pendennis did a swift calculation. "Oh, mercy. The poor boy can't have more than ten years left. At *most*."

A sudden chill danced over Emily's skin, as if the sun had gone behind a cloud. But the day remained as clear and blue as before and the conservatory remained just as sweltering.

"Ten years? You mean ten years to . . . practice magic?"

"Ten years to live," Ben broke in softly. His words were formed with delicacy and precision. "*Exussum cruorsis* is a degenerative magical blight. Within a few years, Mr. Stanton won't be able to keep weight on at all, no matter how much he eats. He will starve to death."

Emily's head spun. The words rattled around in her head like lead shot dropped in a silver bowl.

Burning up.

She remembered the conversation she'd had with him in the chophouse in San Francisco . . . *Training as a Warlock aggravates it substantially* . . . he'd made it sound like such a little thing!

Sudden fury made all her muscles tense and shake.

Emily was suddenly aware of the fact that Ben was watching her closely. She brushed past him toward the door.

. . . *Professor Mirabilis perceived profound advantages in having me attend the Institute* . . .

Oh, the stupidity! Emily clenched her fists tightly. How could he have done it? And how . . . how could he not have told her?

"Miss Edwards . . . hold on!" Miss Pendennis called after her.

But Emily didn't hear the rest of what Miss Pendennis said, for she was running back toward the Institute, as quickly as her silk-shod feet would carry her.

CHAPTER TWENTY-TWO

Cupid's Bludgeon

Emily raced through the gardens, stormed up the stairs, slammed a door behind her as she entered the cool darkness of the Institute. Stalking toward the broad marble stairs in the main hall, she did not notice Professor Mirabilis until she had torn past him, wisping rage.

"Miss Edwards."

The words were low and not spoken with any particular urgency, but Professor Mirabilis' voice stopped her as surely as if the old man had seized her arm. Clearly, one did not ignore the Sophos of the Mirabilis Institute.

Emily froze, stock-still and trembling, staring at the floor. She did not look up as Mirabilis strode casually toward her.

"My, don't you look nice!" Mirabilis smiled. "And you've managed to give the strident Miss Pendennis the slip. You have excellent judgment." His voice lowered an octave. "Miss Pendennis is an . . . *exceptional* woman. But your native common sense is more than equal to the challenges that face you. I do hate to see women swayed by advisers who may not have their best interests at heart."

Emily curled her lips back from her teeth, but said nothing.

"Now," Mirabilis continued, "tonight's Grand Symposium will be preceded by a small dinner for the colleagues. If you could be downstairs by eleven to meet—"

"Fine," Emily said curtly.

"Additionally, please understand that this Grand Symposium shall be a dangerous gathering. No great thing can be accomplished without a correspondingly great measure of risk. For your safety, I have not told all to all. Answer questions honestly if I ask them, but volunteer nothing. Allow me to do all the talking."

"It's your money," Emily said, aware that her voice was trembling slightly. "You're paying for my time."

Mirabilis knit his brow. His face was inscribed with annoyance, as if her petulance was a personal affront.

"Miss Edwards, is there something wrong?"

She tried to say nothing. She tried to keep her mouth shut, but words burst from her lips in a sudden molten gush.

"Profound advantages?" She lifted her eyes, fixed Mirabilis with accusing venom. "How could you let him do it? How could you let him discard his life so stupidly? And then you added insult to injury by making it all meaningless. Subverting him. Undercutting him. Sending him to Lost Pine. You never wanted him to succeed. All you cared about was his father's connections! You never had any faith in him. You wanted to make him a failure. I don't know why . . . but it's horrible. It's horrible and it's vicious and I despise you for it!"

Mirabilis was silent for a moment, obviously sorting through the particulars of the wild flood of accusation.

"I don't know what Mr. Stanton has told you," Mirabilis began.

"He told me . . ." She searched her memory, her voice breaking with despair. "He told me it was a *defect*. He told me it was an *impairment*. He made it seem like such a small thing."

"All credomancers are liars," Mirabilis interjected, smiling at what was probably a very old chestnut within these walls.

"Mr. Stanton isn't a liar," she spat, refusing to be jollied. Mirabilis frowned.

"Miss Edwards, get ahold of yourself," he rumbled, and the words were like a hundred strong hands seizing her and giving her a shake. She lowered her head, breathing hard. Mirabilis was silent a moment before continuing.

"Mr. Stanton was burned long before he came to the Institute," Mirabilis said. "He continued his studies here with full awareness of the implications it would have for his health. It was his decision, and he made it for good reasons."

"There are no good reasons for suicide," she hissed.

"That, Miss Edwards, is where you are wrong."

Emily stared at him. His eyes glittered dangerously.

"What the hell do you mean by that?" Emily whispered.

"Credomancy isn't the only thing he's studied," Mirabilis said. "And this isn't the only place he trained."

"The Erebus Academy," she said, remembering Perun's words in Chicago. Mirabilis nodded.

"It is an elite institution, the West Point of the Army's magical divisions," Mirabilis said. "Mr. Stanton was there for three years. That is where he studied sangrimancy, with the intention of becoming a Maelstrom."

Emily felt as if the floor were falling from beneath her feet, but she stood stock-still.

"He did very well there, I understand." Mirabilis clipped each word; it almost seemed that he took perverse pleasure in them. "Indeed, he was, by all accounts, exceptionally well suited to the practice of blood magic. His snobbishness, his impatience with human frailty, his rigid worldview . . ."

"Then how did he end up here?" Emily's throat was dry.

"I approached him at a . . . fortuitous moment. I made arguments that helped him understand that studying at my Institute would be beneficial. That greater goals could be served."

"What greater goals?"

"That's really none of your business, is it?" Mirabilis said. "But you are correct in one regard. I never thought he'd amount to much as a credomancer. It is simply not his area of natural proficiency."

"So you did subvert him. You did want him to be a failure," Emily said, suddenly understanding, "because he was too dangerous any other way."

Mirabilis looked at her for a long time.

"Don't you think the world is better served by Dreadnought Stanton the mediocre credomancer than Dreadnought Stanton the very talented sangrimancer?" Mirabilis said at last.

"Don't you think there are enough Captain Cauls in the world as it is?"

"He couldn't ever be like that," Emily said.

"People can surprise you," Mirabilis said. "And not always pleasantly."

Emily stared at him, her eyes wells of horror. Mirabilis did not smile at her.

"The fact that you have developed a fondness for Mr. Stanton is abundantly clear. I wish to make it similarly clear that nurturing such fondness is a grave error. The blight he labors under is powerful. What is done cannot be undone. He is not for you, and he never can be." Mirabilis frowned more deeply. "And if the boy had an ounce of decency, he would have made you understand that from the beginning."

He clasped her solid hand, made a little bow over it. "Until tonight, then?"

And he walked off briskly, his footsteps echoing in the tall empty hall.

Damn him!

When Emily got to her room, she slammed the door behind her and began removing every single article of clothing Miss Pendennis had so carefully put her into. Her immaterial hand made this a tortuous process; buttons scattered and fabric ripped as she pulled at her garments angrily.

Damn Dreadnought Stanton!

She threw the dress in a heap on the floor, and piled the corset and the petticoats and the bustle and the chemise and all the other nonsensical pieces of effluvium on top. When she was finished, she climbed into bed stark naked but for the silk pouch she always wore. She curled herself up into a ball and pulled the blankets over her head.

Damn all Warlocks anyway!

She lay curled in the still whiteness of the bed, listening to her heart pounding against her ribs. Despite her best efforts to maintain a comforting shield of anger, it was crumbling beneath pain and confusion.

Why hadn't he told her?

All those days and nights . . . everything that had passed

between them. Everything they'd been through. And he'd never told her. Never told her he'd studied blood magic . . . never told her he'd planned to become a Maelstrom, just like that monster Caul . . . never told her he was dying . . . never told her anything about who he really was. And after all, why would he? One didn't go around telling such personal and important things to the *luggage*.

Emily buried her head in her pillow, feeling acutely disappointed and embarrassed.

. . . if the boy had an ounce of decency, he would have made you understand that from the beginning . . .

How could she have let herself go and grow feelings for him? She was furious with her own stupidity. As if a few kisses meant anything. It was just a meaningless encounter, a by-product of the madness of sangrimancy. He didn't want her. If he did, he would have told her. He wouldn't have left such horrible explanations to strangers. He would have trusted her. Goddamn it, she had trusted him! She had trusted him, and he had trusted her with nothing.

Three times what thou givest.

So there it was, then. The final and most crushing of the retributions she'd earned. A silly, stupid broken heart. How perfectly appropriate. And to think that she'd done this to Dag, good, kind Dag . . . .

She wished for Dag, suddenly. If she hadn't felt close to him before, she certainly did now. She understood him, understood the agony of loving someone who didn't love you back. She wanted to crawl into his arms and be soothed, and soothe him in return, and forget all the grand ideas she'd ever had about true love, and the necessity for it. Because true love was a load of baloney. Finding a good friend . . . a good friend who trusted you . . . was more than enough.

Mirabilis had said that everything would be all right after the Grand Symposium. With a little luck, she could start for home in a day or two. With a little luck, she'd never have to look at Dreadnought Stanton's face again. She buried her face deeper in the pillow, trying to reconcile herself to the thought.

There was a soft knock at her door. Emily huddled deeper under the covers as the door opened.

"Miss Edwards?" Miss Pendennis' voice from the door was puzzled. "My goodness, your clothes are all in a heap! Are you all right?"

"I have a terrible headache," Emily said. "I'd appreciate it if you'd—"

"Certainly," Miss Pendennis said. "I've got something that will fix you right up."

Emily had been planning to say "leave me alone," but never mind.

The strange thing was that the pretending of a headache actually preceded the onset of one. A heavy bilious headache that came on abruptly. Within moments, Emily's head was throbbing.

CARISSIMA MIA.

Emily pressed fingers to her temple, trying to remember what she'd just been thinking about. Something that had made her angry and upset all at once. But though she tried hard to remember what it was, all she could come up with was a memory of huge rabbits. Huge black rabbits with red eyes.

"Here we are," Miss Pendennis said, bustling in. Emily pulled the covers down just far enough to expose her eyes and watch Miss Pendennis approach. The woman was carrying the large leather case Emily had seen her unpack earlier that morning, the one that was bound in steel. Pulling a chair to the side of the bed, Miss Pendennis sat down. She laid the case on the bedside table and snapped it open, revealing an exotic assortment of items nestled in a blue velvet lining: bright iridescent bottles, long quills and parchment, candles of many colors.

Miss Pendennis lifted out the top drawer of the case, laying it aside, momentarily revealing another layer of larger items underneath. There was a chalice, a bowl, and . . . Emily felt a strange thrill go through her . . . an athame. A gleaming Witch's blade, small and slim, a single piece of exquisitely sharpened steel with a handle wrapped in thin black velvet cording. It was neatly fitted into the bottom of the case. Emily's gaze lingered on it for a long time. It hummed softly to her. She longed to touch it.

PERFECT.

Sudden panic gripped Emily as images of spurting blood flashed at the corners of her eyes.

"No!" She sat up, sheet clutched to her chest, eyes squeezed shut against the sudden burning pain in her temples. She looked at Miss Pendennis, opened her mouth to say something, but the minute she did, the words evaporated.

Miss Pendennis looked at her, astonished.

"Miss Edwards?" she asked. "Were you going to say something?"

NO.

"No," Emily said quickly, the word sounding before she even knew her lips had formed it.

Miss Pendennis put her hand on Emily's forehead, held it there for a long time. Her eyes took on a canny quality.

"You said Dreadnought drank a compulsion potion, didn't you?" Miss Pendennis said. "But of course, when you drank the potion, nothing happened. Because of the stone in your hand."

Emily opened her mouth to say, "That's right." But before the words could be spoken, she closed her mouth abruptly.

AH, IT IS A TRICKY WITCH! BRAVA!

"I never drank the potion," Emily said, finally, laboring over the words.

Miss Pendennis looked at her.

"So you didn't touch or taste any of it?"

Yes, Emily struggled to speak. *I tasted it to make sure that Mr. Stanton wouldn't be hurt . . .*

NO, CARISSIMA MIA, YOU NEVER TOUCH IT

Yes, I . . .

NO.

"No," Emily said, haltingly. "Rose . . . Grimaldi . . . made it. She . . . fed it to Mr. Stanton. I never touched it."

Miss Pendennis scrutinized Emily's face. She knew that the woman did not believe her. She also knew that the woman could not be allowed to disbelieve her.

WE WILL MAKE HER BELIEVE.

Emily felt hot, unbidden tears well up in her eyes, all the tears she'd been meaning to cry a moment ago. Her heart ached; she curled herself forward over her knees, sobbing wretchedly.

"Miss Edwards! Emily! My dear, what is the matter?"

"Mr. Stanton," Emily said simply, through the hand that covered her face. "Why didn't he tell me? Why didn't he . . . tell me?"

OR WILL THIS MANNISH FEMALE NO UNDERSTAND THE BRO-KEN HEART?

But understanding did dawn on Miss Pendennis slowly. She clucked her tongue, laid a heavy hand on Emily's shoulder, sighing heavily.

"Oh, dear," she said ruefully. "Oh, dear. I'm so sorry. I didn't know."

Emily sobbed harder. She was acutely aware of Miss Pendennis' hand patting her back soothingly.

"Now, now," Miss Pendennis said. "I was so surprised myself, I didn't mean to go on and on about it. How stupid of me. I'm so sorry. You mustn't worry yourself about it. We have so much to do."

YES, CARISSIMA MIA, SO MUCH TO DO!

The thought struck Emily between the eyes. It made her sit up stock-straight and dash her tears away.

"You're right," she said. "So much to do."

Throwing the sheet off herself she leaped out of bed and rushed to the pile of discarded clothing. She pulled on her undergarments and threw the chemise over her head, then held up the corset.

"I want to get dressed again."

Miss Pendennis rose from the bed slowly, regarding Emily. Emily could see her own madness, her frantic incoherence reflected in Miss Pendennis' eyes. But there was nothing she could do. Nothing she could do.

Without a word, Miss Pendennis positioned the corset around Emily's waist and tied her into it. When the woman reached down to retrieve the fawn-colored cashmere, Emily growled petulantly.

"No, not that one," she said. "I never want to see that horrible dress again as long as I live." She let her lips form into a sweet, soubrettish smile. "Isn't there another? You have ever so many . . ."

"Of course, I'm sure I can find something . . ."

Miss Pendennis closed the door behind herself silently, and when the woman was gone, Emily found her fingers playing quickly over the clasps of the leather case that was bound with steel. Perhaps she snapped it open. Perhaps she ran her fingers over the beautiful blue velvet lining. If she did, each action was immediately forgotten.

GOOD.

GOOD, CARISSIMA MIA.

REST NOW.

REST UNTIL IT IS TIME.

The next thing Emily knew, Miss Pendennis was shaking her. Emily opened her eyes and found herself staring at the brightly colored carpet on which her head rested. She was entirely at a loss to explain how her head had come to rest on said carpet.

"Miss Edwards!" the woman was saying. "Miss Edwards!"

Emily blinked confusion.

"Miss Pendennis?" she said.

Fragmented memories tumbled through her head: the conservatory, steamy heat, a stalk through the park. She had been angry, terribly angry about something . . .

Stanton.

That was it, Dreadnought Stanton, his checkered past and his circumscribed future. The memory closed around her oppressively, bitterness rising afresh. But a broken heart didn't explain how she'd ended up facedown on the carpet.

"Come on, up with you." Miss Pendennis put her hands under Emily's arms and lifted. "I must say, for a robust California girl you're as vaporous as any eastern female I've met. You can put on a new dress later. Now you're getting back into bed."

Back into bed? New dress? Emily looked down at herself, clad only in corset and chemise. When precisely had her clothing gone missing? She climbed into bed, confused, and Miss Pendennis tucked her under the covers.

"Now, does your head really hurt? Or did I simply fail to catch your clever way of indicating you wanted a good cry?"

"My head feels fine," Emily said finally.

Miss Pendennis nodded briskly. She took the case from the bedside table.

"Unfortunately, I can't mix up a nostrum that will help the real problem," Miss Pendennis said. "Look, I'm terribly sorry about Dreadnought and all those careless things I said earlier. I had no way of knowing that you two . . ." She paused awkwardly. "I'm just never good at figuring those kinds of things out, I'm afraid."

Emily felt a blush creep up her neck. There was only one thing worse than having a broken heart. It was a broken heart laid out on the table for everyone to cluck over. She gritted her teeth. "Mr. Stanton is the least of my worries."

Miss Pendennis smiled wanly.

"Good girl," she said. "Keep your chin up."

Emily spent the rest of the day in bed—an occupation that was apparently ladylike, but that gave her far too much time to think about things she'd rather not have thought about. She was glad when Miss Pendennis came in with the purple moiré silk over her arm and said it was time to dress for the Grand Symposium.

Emily stared into the mirror as Miss Pendennis fussed around her, making the final touches to her costume. Swathed in shimmering silk, Emily looked as rich and unapproachable as a plate of gilded truffles. The dress had a tight bodice, cut low to reveal her shoulders and arms. The skirt billowed extravagantly from the waist, then twisted and looped and puffed in innumerable, fascinating ways. Her hair had been knotted at the back of her head and secured with the hair sticks; Miss Pendennis had secured a fluffy spray of ostrich feathers to camouflage the sparseness of the bun.

Emily extracted her mother's amethyst earrings from her silk pouch and hung them in her ears.

"Those suit the dress perfectly!" Miss Pendennis touched one of the drops with a finger. "You are full of surprises, Miss Edwards."

"A lady is supposed to be, isn't she?" Emily said softly as she tucked her silk pouch down the side of the dress, nestling it next to her left breast.

CHAPTER TWENTY-THREE

The Skycladdische and the Sangrimancer

The Grand Symposium was to be held at midnight, and was to be preceded by a late supper. Emily and Miss Pendennis went downstairs together, walking briskly to the mezzanine that overlooked the Institute's magnificent great hall.

"Stay close to me," Miss Pendennis whispered, looking side to side, as if they were going together into a jungle. "I'll tell you everything you need to know."

They paused at the top of the wide marble staircase that led down to the floor of the hall. The room blazed with light reflected from dozens of mirrors and innumerable cut crystal prisms that dangled from the gilded gas fixtures. The ceiling was a series of stained-glass domes, their vivid colors muted against the dark evening sky. The air was rich with the scent of orchids—an exotic perfume wafting from masses of deep-red blooms arranged in huge ormolu vases.

At the far end of the room were two enormous black doors, highly polished, inlaid with channels of hammered gold as wide as Emily's forearm. These channels outlined a large triangle. At each point of the triangle was an arcane symbol, and in the center of the triangle, where the doors met, was the sigil of a closed fist. Inscribed in gold beneath the triangle's base, words in Latin: *Ex Fide Fortis*.

Miss Pendennis noticed the direction of Emily's gaze. "Never mind the Great Trine Room—look over by the fireplace."

Emily's eyes found the fireplace, which was carved of white marble and had to be at least ten feet tall. Around it, a small group of men stood smoking and drinking brandy from large bubble-shaped snifters. Three of the faces were familiar: Mirabilis and Tarnham, with old Ben hovering nearby in formal pressed whites. The fourth man was of medium build, with a very self-satisfied air about him.

"That's Addison Rocheblave," Miss Pendennis said. "President of Rocheblave Consolidated Industries. Surely you've heard of him?"

Emily shook her head.

"He's the richest sangrimancer in America, if not the world. He built his fortune on other people's blood, operating asylums, poorhouses, whorehouses, orphanages, opium dens, gambling pits . . . anyplace where easily forgotten unfortunates could be lured and bled. By doing this, he's addressed the greatest difficulty any sangrimancer faces—maintaining a ready supply of blood for their ghastly rites. Not that they usually mind harvesting it themselves, mind you. For them that's part of the fun. But it's rather hard to maintain a decent lifestyle if you have to wander from town to town, murdering randomly and hoping not to get caught."

Miss Pendennis drew a deep breath.

"Anyway, he's leveraged that blood money to cement business alliances with everyone who is anyone . . . the Astors, Rockefeller, Morgan, Gould, you name it."

"A big bug," Emily summarized.

"I'll bet he paid Mirabilis a pretty penny for the privilege of attending," Miss Pendennis mused. "I wouldn't be surprised if your twenty thousand is coming out of his pocket."

Emily fought a wave of revulsion at the idea. Then motion at the other end of the room drew her attention. At first, Emily had the strange impression that a tramp had found his way into the Institute. But the man, in a high-collared black suit with frayed cuffs, was being respectfully escorted by Institute guards toward the fireplace. The man was so hugely fat that Emily wondered how he could stand up, much less walk—but he moved across the floor with surprising briskness.

"I don't believe it!" Miss Pendennis grinned wolfishly. "This just gets better and better. If Caul could see this, he'd rip himself to bits."

"Who is it?"

"Selig Heusler. The High Priest of the Temple of Itztlacoli-uhqui." She lifted an eyebrow. "A pretty shabby specimen, if you ask me."

"Itztlacoliuhqui?" Emily remembered Caul speaking the strange word. "The goddess with the half-baked doomsday?"

"*Temamauhti.*" Miss Pendennis nodded. "I don't know anyone who takes it seriously, except that lunatic Caul. Put two sangrimancers in a room and they'll come up with some kind of harebrained scheme to take over the world, or destroy it. Temamauhti is a harebrained scheme of the latter sort. A blood apocalypse of unimaginable proportions." She paused. "Mirabilis probably invited him just to tweak Caul's ear. Oh, the old boy has brass, I'll give him that!"

"Ah, Miss Edwards, Miss Pendennis!" Professor Mirabilis' cheerful voice echoed in the hall's vastness. "Gentlemen, please!"

Glasses of brandy were put down and cigars were hastily extinguished. Mirabilis gestured the women down the stairs. "Come, join us!"

When they had descended, Mirabilis took Emily's arm and escorted her toward the fireplace. "Not everyone is here yet, but they shall be arriving shortly."

"Who else is coming?" Emily asked warily.

"I have invited three representatives from each of the grand traditions," Mirabilis said, not really answering.

"Credomancers and their trines," Miss Pendennis, walking behind them, muttered. Mirabilis did not look back, but bent his head close to Emily's to whisper. "Remember what I told you earlier."

"Eyes open and mouth shut," Emily whispered back, now understanding the reason Mirabilis had emphasized it. "Don't worry, I got it."

When they reached the group, Mirabilis stepped back and presented Emily with a flourishing bow, as if she were a life-size doll of his own design.

"Gentlemen, this is Miss Emily Edwards, of whom you have heard so much." Mirabilis looked at each of the sangri-mancers in turn. "Mr. Heusler. Mr. Rocheblave."

Emily stared into the middle distance, trying to ignore the fact that the men were looking at her like a cupcake on a plate. Her carefully cultivated composure was rattled when Heusler grabbed her arm. He lifted the truncated appendage to his face so he could examine it with his small paste-diamond eyes. As he turned her arm this way and that, Emily caught a glimpse of dark patterns showing under his grimy cuffs. Black inked tattoos, the kind sailors wore, but heavier of line and strangely unsettling.

"Where's the stone?" Heusler finally asked, after having apparently committed the exact lineaments of her arm to memory. "I didn't come all this way to look at a stump."

Mirabilis disengaged Emily's arm from Heusler's grasp, put his body between hers and the High Priest's.

"Your questions will be answered when the Grand Symposium commences," Mirabilis said.

"He's got it locked up somehow," Rocheblave said to Heusler. He had a high, querulous voice. "And here I thought credomancers put more store by trust."

Mirabilis smiled noncommittally and gestured toward the end of the room where a table had been laid.

"The remaining colleagues will join us soon," Mirabilis said cheerfully. "Shall we eat?"

At the table, which shone with silver and prismatic cut crystal, Emily was seated between Mirabilis and Miss Pendennis. She picked at a plate of something exotic that probably contained lobster. Miss Pendennis leaned across her, speaking to Mirabilis under her breath.

"So I'm dying to know—who have you invited from the animantic tradition? I know Mr. Saladin Buck is off in Europe somewhere, but surely you got ahold of Mrs. Amanda Haynes Reader . . . or maybe Townley Newgate? This symposium sure could use a little Townley Newgate right about now."

Mirabilis buttered a small piece of bread with extravagant casualness, but said nothing.

"Well?" Miss Pendennis demanded.

"Miss Edwards and the Indian Holy Woman will serve as the other two animantic representatives," Mirabilis said smoothly.

"Are you *insane*?" Miss Pendennis' voice carried across the table, as did the sound of her fist pounding the damask. Mirabilis smiled apologetically as the gentlemen around the table looked up. Heusler seemed glad for the opportunity to let his piggy little eyes linger on Emily. "You're telling me that spirit workers will be represented by—excuse me, Miss Edwards—a backcountry Witch with no experience of magical society and an *Indian in a nut*?"

"And a very pushy women's reform crusader," Mirabilis said mildly, sipping his wine. "You've summarized it perfectly, Miss Pendennis."

Emily looked down at her plate, trying to ignore that horrible High Priest. He just kept looking at her, his tiny eyes appraising and disgustingly suggestive. To make matters worse, he was seated next to Tarnham; when the fat man leaned his head over and said something under his breath, Tarnham laughed in not a nice way and reached up to stroke his ferret. Emily thought of black knives and blood. The images made her flush suddenly.

"I'm going for some air," Emily murmured.

But Miss Pendennis didn't seem to hear. She was leaning toward Mirabilis again, her cheeks pink with indignation.

"Come to mention it, you've hardly outdone yourself in your selection of credomantic talent either. *Tarnham,* for mercy's sake? Your *secretary*? Why not Rex Fortissimus, or one of your own magisters? And where's Dreadnought, anyway? You promised Miss Edwards that you'd allow him to participate!"

Emily pushed herself away from the table without waiting to hear Mirabilis' response.

Along one side of the great hall was a line of tall French glass doors that opened onto a broad veranda overlooking the Institute's gardens. One of the doors had been left ajar to admit fresh air. She snuck out through it, her skirts rustling. She came to stand by the mossy stone railing, looking down over it at the smooth green grass below.

She shivered a little; the night air was cold, and the veranda was dark. She had only been away from the table for a few minutes when she heard footsteps coming up behind her.

"Well," a voice drawled lazily. "If it isn't the guest of honor."

Emily didn't need to turn to know that it was Tarnham. She pretended as if she hadn't heard him, but it didn't help. He sidled up to her, a greasy grin on his face. His ferret peered at her.

"Parted from the stalwart protector of her virtue?" Tarnham smirked as he rolled the last word around in his mouth. "Don't tell me you've already been routed! Dinner isn't even over yet."

"I haven't been 'routed' Mr. Tarnham," Emily said flatly. "I came out for some air."

"Yes, I suppose girls like you need cooling off every now and again," Tarnham said. "By the way, Heusler is quite taken with you. Says he'll pay good money. I could hardly discourage him, since I hear money's what you're mostly interested in."

He stared down at her décolletage and made a little reproachful *tsk tsk*.

"Why, you've got a loose thread, just there." His hand came up to where her dress dipped to reveal the cleft of her breasts. "Why don't you let me . . ."

Without a second thought, Emily hauled back and slapped him across the face, putting her whole shoulder into it. Tarnham went reeling, staggering a step. He rubbed his cheek and stared at her with wide eyes.

"I won't be squinked, Mr. Tarnham," she said. "I don't care what kind of woman you think I am, but skycladdische or not, I'm someone you'd better not trifle with!"

Tarnham stared at her. "You struck me!"

"I'll do it again, you slimy, smirking hoodlum," she hissed, balling her hand into a fist. "I don't know how women do things in New York, but in California we settle matters like this with six-shooters. Now take that ugly rat of yours and leave me alone."

Tarnham drew himself up, tugged his coat down, and retreated in a hurry. Emily turned away. Anger and indignation burned in her cheeks. Yes, she would be heartily glad to never see another Warlock again!

She was surprised by a soft ripple of laughter drifting up

from the shadows, where the stairs led down to the garden. Someone thought that was funny, did they? She stormed over to see who it was.

It was Stanton.

"Well done." He grinned. He was wearing dark evening clothes and an overcoat, and he looked well. Better than he had a right to. "I have always wanted to see Tarnham get the kind of female attention he deserves."

"I'm glad I could oblige," Emily said coolly, turning away.

"Emily? Are you all right?" Miss Pendennis ducked her head out of the door. "I heard a blow, and then that Tarnham came scurrying through ever so . . ."

When Stanton saw Miss Pendennis, he gave her a little salute. "Hello, Pen."

"Hello, Dreadnought." She smiled at him. "Thank the goddess you made it. It's downright ugly in there!"

Miss Pendennis looked between Emily and Stanton. She scratched the back of her head, cleared her throat.

"Yes. Well. I'll just go back in, then." She looked at Emily. "As long as you're . . . all right?"

"I'm fine." Emily bit the words. "I shall be in momentarily."

When Miss Pendennis was gone, Stanton said, "She's a great friend . . ."

". . . of your sister Hortense. Yes, I've heard." Emily didn't look at him. "I've heard a great many things." She paused. "How's your shoulder?"

He shrugged the shoulder in question. "Better."

"And I expect you've gotten yourself cleansed?"

"Quite a disgusting process, really," Stanton said. "It involves bone rattles and live chickens. You would have found it fascinating."

"Oh, I've found more than enough to fascinate me," Emily said. "I'm getting pretty tired of being fascinated by things, actually."

Stanton said nothing. He was looking at her, his green eyes traveling from her face to her feet.

"You look wonderful," he said.

Emily shrugged as if the subject bored her, letting her hand smooth over the purple silk of her skirt. Then she turned away from him abruptly and went back to the railing. He followed, coming to stand next to her. They looked out over the darkened gardens, the smell of distant daffodils rising on the gentle breeze.

"Ready for the Grand Symposium?" he asked.

"No, given that it has no chance of success and Mirabilis' true motivations for holding it are clouded with intrigue."

Stanton nodded, leaned forward on the stone railing, supporting himself on his elbows. He looked at her sidelong. "I'm glad you asked for me," he said. "I'll do everything I can to help, I promise."

"You always have," Emily murmured. *Except tell me the truth about anything.*

The act of speaking with Stanton made her feel cross and lonely. Never mind. By this time tomorrow she'd be on a train back to California with twenty thousand dollars in her pocket, and that was all she cared about.

Without a word, Stanton reached over, took the stump of her ghost hand, and lifted it gently. He looked at it like a jeweler inspecting a broken watch.

"Professor Mirabilis didn't tell me about this," he said. "Where exactly is your hand?"

"It's in another dimension," Emily said. Stanton's fingers were warm on her arm.

"I guessed as much," he said. "The Institute has a world-renowned extradimensional research program. I might have applied for it if I hadn't taken the Jefferson Chair—"

Emily jerked her arm away abruptly. "I'm sorry you didn't," she said. "I'm sorry you wasted so much of your precious time in Lost Pine. I'll give everyone your regards when I get back."

"You're leaving?"

"Just as soon as this is over with. I'm going home."

"To marry your lumberman, no doubt."

"Yes," Emily spat. "To marry my lumberman."

Stanton blinked at her. "What?"

Emily didn't reply. Nervously, she ran her index finger over the gold ring she wore on her thumb. When she realized what she was doing, she stopped abruptly. She lifted her hand to him, fighting to hold it steady.

"Mr. Stanton, will you please remove the ring from my thumb?" she asked. "I doubt we'll be seeing much of each other after tonight, so it's best that I return it now."

Stanton made no move to take the ring.

"Are you really going to marry the lumberman?"

"Yes," Emily said. "I've got a great future ahead of me, just like you've got a great future ahead of you." She paused, letting her hand drop angrily. "Of course, your future will be far shorter than my future, but that hardly matters. Because our two futures won't have anything to do with each other, given that I'm a skycladdische and you're half a sangrimancer!"

Stanton stared at her, obviously absorbing the specifics of the outburst. He lifted a hand and rubbed his broad forehead with his thumb and forefinger.

"Well, I must say. I thought you said you wouldn't stand to be squinked, but they've obviously been squinking you from here to next Sunday!"

"It's not a squink if it's the truth," Emily hissed. "Is it?"

"What? That you're a skycladdische, or that I'm half a sangrimancer?"

"That you're dying." Emily's voice was low and resonant.

Stanton was silent for a long moment.

"We're all dying," he said eventually. "I'm just doing so at a more rapid pace than most."

"Why didn't you tell me?"

"Because it wasn't your business to know," Stanton said.

Emily looked at him and was silent for a long time, her eyes searching his face.

"I figured that would be your answer," she said. "That's your answer when it comes to anything about yourself that's real."

Stanton let out a long sigh, his brow contracting darkly.

"I didn't tell you because . . . because what's done is done. You make a choice, and it seems right at the time, and . . ." He shook his head in frustration. "It just doesn't matter, that's all."

"It does matter," she whispered. "It matters because—" Emily stopped short. She shook her head. "You should just be more careful, that's all."

"More careful?"

Some words were like smoke; if exhaled carelessly, they

could never be reclaimed. Emily knew such words were dangerous, but she did not care.

"Not to let people fall in love with you," she said.

He said nothing, just stared at her face. The moment hung for a long time, longer than it should have. Longer than it would if Stanton was going to say something in return. She turned away, cheeks burning.

"I know you don't want me. You made that clear when you kissed me . . . or stopped kissing me." Emily's jaw ached with humiliation. "Anyway, don't stand there trying to figure out some credomancer's dodge to make me feel better about it."

"Of course I want you," he growled, leaning closer to her. "I've wanted you ever since I saw you dancing naked under that damn oak tree, botching up that preposterous love spell."

Emily jabbed an accusing finger at him. "So you did see me!"

"It was an appalling spectacle," he said. "I enjoyed it tremendously."

"So why didn't you tell me? Why didn't you do anything about it? Were you afraid I'd expect something from you? From the scion of the Stanton dynasty?" Her voice became bitter. "I don't want anything from you, Mr. Stanton."

"You know, there's one thing about you that always astonishes me. The longer you talk, the wronger you get." His voice rose in intensity if not in volume. "Have you thought, for one instant, that perhaps I didn't do anything because I respect you? Because I don't think of you like some cheap hussy who can be bought with a hot meal and a little clever persuasion?" He paused, frowning. "If you don't think I care about you more than that, then you really don't know anything about love."

Then he saw the tears rising in her eyes, and he took her in his arms and gathered her close. She buried her face in the fabric of his shirt; he brought up a hand to stroke her hair.

"I'm sorry, Emily," he said. "Really I am."

"Why didn't you tell me?" she said again.

There was a long silence. When he finally spoke again, she felt his voice rumbling in his chest.

"Because I liked having you believe I was someone I wasn't. When you looked at me, you didn't see all the mistakes I'd made, and I could pretend I'd never made them." He paused. "But I did make them. And pretending I didn't is . . . indecent."

She squeezed her eyes shut. "I don't care," she whispered.

"Ten years ago I was a cadet at the Erebus Academy, I'm sure they told you that." His voice was flat. "I studied sangrimancy and I would have become a Maelstrom. I told you how military sangrimancers protect themselves with neologisms. I had one of my own once, just like Caul. But a neologism cannot be maintained forever. The horrors it represses must be released sometime. The first time is always the worst, it is said." He was quiet for a long time, and she felt him shudder. "After the first time, I couldn't continue."

"Conscience," Emily said.

"Or cowardice," Stanton murmured. "It doesn't matter which. Neither is an excuse."

She held him tighter, as if physical closeness could hold him to her. But already, she could feel his distance, feel him moving further and further away.

"I wish I could be someone you should love," he said, and there was terrible finality in his voice. "But I'm not. I wish I could say you should love me, but I can't. Because it's not fair. Three times what thou givest, remember?" He paused. "I haven't even begun to pay for what I've done. Being burned is my price, and there will be others. I won't ask you to pay my debts with me."

Emily grabbed the fabric of his coat in her good hand, clasped it, and shook Stanton furiously.

"It doesn't matter," she cried desperately, fighting tears. "You've told me a hundred times that I don't know anything about love, but you're the one who doesn't know anything. You don't know anything at all about love!"

"You think I don't?"

"You don't!"

"Certain of that, are you?"

"Reasonably," Emily said, her voice quivering.

He pulled her closer, brought his face to hers, close enough that she could feel his hot breath against her lips. But then he stopped, their skin a feather's distance apart. He turned his head.

"Maybe you're right," he said, pushing her away.

She pressed her hand to her mouth, stepping backward. Stanton drew a breath to say something, but before he could speak, Mirabilis' voice rang from the doorway.

"Miss Edwards," he said, "we're ready for you."

Emily turned, ran toward the door, skirts swishing.

"Emily," Stanton called after her in a low voice, but she pretended not to hear, stepping quickly into the brilliant room beyond.

CHAPTER TWENTY-FOUR

The Grand Symposium

When she reentered the great hall, the clock was just striking midnight. She saw that the colleagues had been joined by two burly manservants in Institute gray who had positioned themselves, arms crossed, in front of the two huge black doors.

Miss Pendennis came to her side, took Emily's arm.

"Everything all right?"

"Fine," Emily said. Quickly, she dashed tears from her cheeks. As Stanton came into the room, pausing on the threshold to take in the faces of the participants, she looked away.

"Dreadnought Stanton!" said Heusler with a slimy smirk. "The spirit of the next hundred years of the republic!"

Stanton narrowed his eyes at the sangrimancer.

"High Priest," he said in a strained voice. His eyes flicked from the fat man to Mirabilis, who frowned, gesturing impatiently for Stanton to join the group. When they were all assembled, he lifted his hands in welcome.

"Ladies and gentlemen," Mirabilis said. "For the actual proceedings, we shall repair to the Great Trine Room. For the safety of all, I must insist that everyone leave all weapons, magical or otherwise, with these gentlemen." He nodded toward the thickset guards in gray. "They will be kept safe during the symposium."

"Just a minute, Mirabilis," Rocheblave said. "I want to know where the third sangrimancer is. I see animancers and now"—he nodded meaningfully at Stanton—"a veritable superfluousness of credomancers. But I see only two sangrimancers."

"The third sangrimancer awaits us in the Great Trine Room," Mirabilis said. "For reasons of safety, I insisted that he submit to a more intensive physical search."

"Showy charlatan's tricks," Heusler grumbled. He lifted a bloated finger and pointed at Mirabilis, Tarnham, Ben, and Stanton in turn. "Why four credomancers?"

"Ben is my personal servant," Mirabilis said. "He will not be participating as a colleague. As my secretary, Mr. Tarnham will be otherwise occupied, so I have asked Ben to record the events as they unfold."

"Then he's not a credomancer?"

"I serve the Sophos," Ben said, and dipped his head meekly. Strangely enough, the answer seemed to satisfy them, though Emily wondered if any of the sangrimancers noticed that it wasn't actually an answer at all.

"Please, gentlemen, let us proceed. The hour grows late." Mirabilis gestured toward the gray-uniformed men who were standing at the doors.

"Going unarmed into Japheth Mirabilis' center of power. I must be mad!" Rocheblave said as he surrendered his alembic and a large curved blade that was intricately chased in gold. He laid these on a tray covered with red velvet; the gray-uniformed guard holding the tray was careful not to touch the objects as he covered them with a piece of red silk.

"No one is required to participate, Mr. Rocheblave," Mirabilis said.

Rocheblave snorted, shrugging off his expensive-looking jacket. One of the large gray men patted his arms and legs.

All the men were searched in turn. Heusler surrendered a glittering blade of black obsidian that he placed on the tray with delicate reverence. When Stanton's turn came, he showed the contents of his pockets: a handkerchief and the misprision blade, which he removed from inside his coat and laid on the tray.

"Why, Mr. Stanton," Heusler said drily, "you still carry a bleeding blade. Perhaps I was too quick when I assumed we sangrimancers would be outnumbered."

"I also carry a handkerchief," Stanton said, as he tucked the square of fabric back into his pocket. "It does not mean that I am consumptive."

When all the men had been searched, the guards looked nervously at Emily and Miss Pendennis.

"Surely the women don't need to be searched," Ben ventured. Heusler pounced on the words like a cat on a cockroach.

"Of course they must be searched. I won't volunteer my instruments of power and have some Witch slide through on the disingenuous pretense that she can't stand to have a man touch her." His eyes grazed the rest of the assembly, stopping on Stanton for a moment before coming to rest on Emily. "Miss Pendennis is not the only one with reservations about the caliber of individuals you've invited, Mirabilis."

Mirabilis gestured to Miss Pendennis. "Fine. Let's get it over with."

Miss Pendennis stood stalwartly, chin up, arms stretched out to her side, while an embarrassed man in gray ran quick hands over her waist, hips, and the bottoms of her legs.

"Miss Edwards?" Mirabilis gestured her forward.

Emily stepped up, and the guard repeated the perfunctory search, nodding approval. Heusler crossed his arms like a petulant toddler.

"No! Her I don't trust. I want to see her legs."

"Heusler, really," Mirabilis snapped. "That's entirely uncalled for!"

"I'm sure the straightforward Miss Pendennis lacks the imagination or inclination for subterfuge. But her . . ." Heusler shook a finger at Emily. "I want to see what the skycladdische has tucked into the tops of her stockings."

"How dare you," Stanton growled, but Emily had just about all she could stand of the insolent High Priest. Furiously, she reached down and grabbed handfuls of purple silk.

"Look all you want, you filthy bloodletter!" Emily hiked her skirts over her knees, revealing legs modestly stockinged in white. "Shall I strip naked and dance a mazurka?"

Heusler stared at her legs for a moment, then smirked disdainfully.

"That won't be necessary," he said. "I've seen what I need."

Emily threw her skirts down and crossed her arms, looking

away angrily. Miss Pendennis came up to her side, placing a comforting hand on her shoulder.

"There's the end to our carefully crafted illusion of reticence and delicacy."

"I don't care," Emily whispered fiercely. "It doesn't matter. They all think they know exactly what I am. Let them go on thinking it, if it makes them so happy. This time tomorrow I'll be a hundred miles away!"

"Let's get through tonight first," Miss Pendennis said.

"Now, if we're finished with ungentlemanly insults," Mirabilis glared at Heusler, "we can proceed about our business."

Turning, he laid a hand on each of the tall black doors. He spoke words in Latin, and there was a loud scraping sound as the tumblers of a great lock fell backward. When the noise finally stopped, Mirabilis gestured diffidently, and the huge doors swung open, silently, as easily as if they were spun of sea foam. When they had all passed through, Mirabilis closed the doors, locking them with an echoing *chunk*.

The vast room was murky—a gloom that even hundreds of tall white candles could not entirely dispel. In the center of the room was a circle of high-backed mahogany chairs, each upholstered in gold brocade.

The third sangrimancer was seated in the chair farthest from the door. In the low light, it was impossible to see his face. Emily smelled him before she could see him; he was smoking a stinking cigar. As she got closer, she saw that it was held in a twitching hand.

"It's about t-t-time." The stuttered words washed over Emily like ice water. She clutched abruptly at Miss Pendennis' arm.

"Captain John Caul." Mirabilis extended a hand toward the man sitting in the shadows.

"I don't believe it!" Stanton stared at Mirabilis. "Sophos, you can't allow him to participate. You know what he—"

"One doesn't set a Precedent of this magnitude by bringing together friends," Mirabilis said firmly. "Captain Caul has been relieved of all of his magical implements and he has been extensively searched. I am completely certain that he carries nothing on his person that can harm anyone in this room. He

called off the Maelstrom attacks on the Institute. In reciproca-
tion, I invited him to join us."

"He blackmailed you," Stanton snarled.

"Enough, Mr. Stanton!" Mirabilis barked. "Your lack of faith
in my judgment is as unhelpful and annoying as I knew it
would be. Need I remind you that if it were up to me, you
would not be here?"

"Doubtless Mr. Stanton is afraid. It w-w-wouldn't be the
first time." Caul drew deeply on his cigar, as if the smoke
would help calm his shaking. "We're in the heart of Mirabilis'
p-p-power, Stanton. What c-c-could I possibly do against
that?"

There was a threat and a menace and a promise in his voice
that made Emily shudder.

"Take your seats," Mirabilis said firmly. "Let us begin."

Emily sat next to Miss Pendennis, in the chair farthest from
Caul. Without a word, Stanton claimed the chair next to her,
glaring pointedly at Caul and then, with more bemusement, at
Mirabilis. Flanked by Miss Pendennis and Stanton, Emily felt
well defended. But she didn't relax in the least.

Mirabilis stood in the center of the circle, hands clasped behind his back. He looked like a ringmaster, polished and
suave.

"Colleagues, first I want to thank you all for agreeing to participate in the creation of what I am sure will be the most powerful Precedent ever. This represents a turning point in the
history of magic, the birth of a new spirit of collegiality
between—"

"For God's s-s-sake, *stop it*." Caul roared, bringing a hand to
his head as if in horrible pain. The big muscles of his arms and
legs spasmed in sympathy with his annoyance. "I won't have
you w-w-wasting my time with credomancers' games. Drop
the pretense of this being a 'collegial' gathering and call it
what it is . . . a n-n-negotiation for the survival of your institute."

"I agree that it is more correctly called a negotiation, Captain Caul," Rocheblave said. "But don't make the mistake of
thinking you're the only one at the table."

"I'll be d-d-damned before I let Mirabilis hand the stone to either one of you," Caul said, glaring at Rocheblave. His eyes then went to Heusler, mad hate flaring in them like a match touched to Black Exunge. "*Especially* you, High Priest. I know *exactly* w-w-what you'd use it for."

"Maybe *you* don't like us, *Captain* Caul," Heusler examined his ragged fingernails casually, "but surely you're aware that your sentiments are not shared by everyone in the military."

"You mean conciliatory turncoats like General Blotgate? S-s-slaves your outlander goddess has gotten her black claws into?"

"Gentlemen, *enough*." Mirabilis' voice rose above the din. "The aim of this gathering is to dispose of the stone in a manner most beneficial to all the magical traditions. It is not a forum for rehashing your internecine squabbles."

"Fine," Heusler said. "Then let's have a look at the goddamn stone. That's what we came for."

"Fair enough." Mirabilis reached into his pocket and withdrew the Otherwhere Marble, holding it up to glint softly in the half-light. "Gentlemen, Miss Edwards' hand—with the stone embedded in the palm—is within this marble, safely protected."

"What is that, some kind of magical orb?" Rocheblave asked.

"Never you mind," Mirabilis said, as he motioned Emily to a place outside the circle of chairs, where they were out of sight of the group.

"The sangrimancers have no understanding of the technology involved," he whispered. "It's the only thing that protects you. Understand?" He tapped the marble against the Boundary Cuff three times, in the same particular rhythm he'd used before. Then he tucked the marble into his pocket and took her elbow, guiding her back into the circle.

Emily extended her hand to the sangrimancers. Rocheblave and Heusler examined it closely, then Caul stepped forward. She'd forgotten how big he was; he towered over her like a mountain, solid and menacing. Taking her hand, he squeezed it until she almost cried out.

"S-s-skycladdische," he whispered.

"Hemacolludinatious," she hissed back.

Caul put his head close to her ear, close enough that she wondered if he was going to bite it. "I'm going to enjoy b-b-bleeding you," he said. "S-s-sooner than you think . . ."

"Captain Caul!" Mirabilis barked. Caul straightened and let Emily's hand drop. Quickly, Mirabilis clasped the Boundary Cuff around Emily's wrist again.

"Now. You have all been briefed on how the stone came into the possession of Miss Edwards, the strange properties it has exhibited, and the vast quantity of power it contains. It is my belief that the Mantic Anastomosis has shed this power for a reason," Mirabilis said. "That the appearance of the stone is the result of greater depredations—depredations hidden and unseen." Mirabilis' eyes roamed each of the three sangrimancers in turn.

"That theory supposes that the Mantic Anastomosis is capable of conscious action," Rocheblave sneered coolly. "I'd expect that kind of crackpot baloney from a dirt Witch, but from you, Mirabilis?"

"I cultivate an open mind, Mr. Rocheblave," Mirabilis said. "I am sure you'll agree that there is much about the Mantic Anastomosis we do not understand."

"There's nothing *to* understand," Rocheblave countered. "It's a pile of rock. Nothing more."

"You're wrong," Emily snapped at him. "It's alive. It thinks, it dreams. I know. I've seen it."

Heusler and Rocheblave exchanged scornful smiles.

"Like I said," Rocheblave said. "Crackpot baloney from a dirt Witch."

"Why, you . . ." Miss Pendennis looked on the verge of charging the self-satisfied sangrimancer, captain of industry or no. But Mirabilis' next words stayed her.

"Regardless of your prejudices, Mr. Rocheblave, I would like us all to hear the testimony of the third animantic colleague—Komé, a Miwok Indian Holy Woman."

"Yes, I've been meaning to ask about that," Heusler said. "Where exactly is this third animantic colleague, this Indian Holy Woman?"

"She is in Miss Edwards' possession," Mirabilis said. "Her spirit is currently encapsulated within an acorn. The woman performed a spiritual transfer so that she could stay with the stone. She claims to serve as an interpreter for it."

"An interpreter? For a *rock*?" Rocheblave barked a humorless laugh. "Is this a joke? Do you really think you're going to sell me on a fraud so obviously self-serving? Your redskin squaw will say whatever that dirt Witch—or *you*, more likely—has told her to say." Rocheblave leapt to his feet. "I can't believe I wasted my time with this nonsense."

"How do you propose we contact this Holy Woman?" Heusler asked, bringing his hand down to rest on his leg. His thumb stroked the fabric of his trousers lazily.

"We will contact her through a group séance," Mirabilis said. "You will each be in direct contact with her. You will each be able to perceive, for yourselves, the genuineness of her claims."

There was a challenging silence. With a grumble, Rocheblave settled back into his chair, and Heusler shrugged with resignation, the kind of shrug a skeptic would give before a game of three-card monte. "It's your Grand Symposium, Mirabilis."

Mirabilis gestured to Emily.

"Miss Edwards, will you bring out the nut?"

Emily reached down inside her dress and pulled the silk pouch from where it was nestled. She ignored Heusler's snide stage-mutter: "And I was worried about her stockings. I wonder what else she has down that dress!"

Emily retrieved the acorn and held it loosely in the palm of her hand, showing it around to the participants.

"You'll also need this," Mirabilis said, withdrawing the Otherwhere Marble from his pocket and placing it in her hand. Marble and nut clicked gently against each other in her fist. "I don't think I need to remind you to handle it with great care."

Mirabilis gestured to the center of the circle. "Miss Edwards, please kneel here." Emily arranged herself carefully, her tightly clenched hand resting on her knee. She breathed deeply, trying to calm her thudding heart.

She remembered how she and Stanton had performed the séance before; they had sat with their hands close but not touching. It appeared that a group séance required the same proximate distance. The colleagues gathered around her, letting their hands hover over her without actually touching. Strangely enough, she could feel each hand as clearly as if it were touching her. She felt the sangrimancers' hands floating over her back, exuding an aura of rot. Caul's hand hovered an inch from her throat, and she had to fight the urge to shy away from it. Tarnham's hand was suspended over her upper arm, but it didn't feel like a hand, it felt like myriad scurrying paws, making her flesh crawl. Miss Pendennis' hand, smooth and firm as wax, trembled alongside her ankle. Stanton knelt beside her, his hand cupped an inch above the hand that lay on her knee. Mirabilis stood over her, his hand stretched out flat across the top of her head.

"Miss Edwards," Mirabilis said, "please summon Komé's spirit."

Taking a deep breath, Emily closed her eyes.

Ososolyeh, she thought, letting herself tumble toward it.

Emily concentrated as she had at the séance before. But instead of concentrating on Komé, Emily remembered the place she had seen in her dream, the vast beautiful landscape that stretched into infinity. The place where the light was her plaything, where she was Ososolyeh—ancient and vast, wanderer from the stars, the great spirit of the earth.

The sound of a great heart beating.

Basket of Secrets. Basket of Secrets. Basket of Secrets.

Miwok words floated around her, darting about her head like fireflies.

She felt herself spreading out, becoming huge and eternal and deep, felt the threads of her human consciousness stretching unimaginably thin over a tessellation of incomprehensible intricacy. She stretched and spread until she was no longer anyone human at all. The Warlocks called her the Mantic Anastomosis, Komé called her Ososolyeh, but she had no name. She was only what she was. She was only memories—an infinity of memories.

The memory of traveling through endless reaches of empty blackness, measuring each moment by the unique smell of the star-seeded clouds as they drifted by, borne on thin winds of

old power that vibrated like a current. A million smaller inde-
cipherable sense memories: The sense of darkness. The sense
of never. The sense of the vibrations of things infinitely small.
The sense of the eternity within every single fraction of every
single moment.

Komé's voice surrounded her. *This is where you come from.
From the stars, never born, never dying.*

Then, another flash of memory—a treasured memory of a
beautiful sphere of fire, shimmering like a droplet of molten
steel on a bed of powdered coal. A young sphere, churning
with fire and energy, not yet painted in the greens and blues
that would come. She wrapped herself around the flaming
sphere, the young tender planet, taking its molten warmth into
her core. She wrapped herself around it tight and snug, threading herself into the tiniest places, wicking the energy into herself. Keeping the hot secret core safe within, a yolk on which
to feed. She cooled, cracked, smoothed. Became a web. A web
that breathed in and out, taking and receiving, radiating power
and bringing it back in a sweet respiration.

Home, sweet home.

A billion years passed. She felt them all pass, felt the exact
detail of each second with complete clarity. Each eon, each
year, each day, each moment was a miracle of separation, a
brilliance of meaning, a richness of experience. She savored
them all.

And then . . .

Pain.

Ososolyeh had never known pain, had never known of the
existence or concept of pain. It could only be understood in
human terms, animal terms, the terms of the tiny crawling
creatures. It was agony. It was wretched misery. It was deep
needles plunged into her, sucking at her greedily, bleeding her,
emptying her. Unbalancing the delicate dance, the eternal respiration, taking and receiving . . . making her hollow. The
pools of filth grew ever larger, welling and pooling and bubbling. She was a lake being drained, mud congealing at the
bottom, cracking and thick . . .

And then, she began to expand. To transform. Her entire
body, her entire existence inflated like an exploding sun,

blossoming with pustulant black eruptions. She churned into a foul froth. She was engulfing herself, transformed by the waste she could not excrete fast enough, green and blue gone now, transmogrified into an unending blackness—roiling, stinking foulness . . .

An Abberancy. The tiny, insignificant part of her mind that was still Emily Edwards screamed out in panic. She was turning into an Aberrancy.

It can be stopped, Komé's voice susurrated urgently. *It can be stopped, Basket of Secrets.*

Black and roiling, bubbling and hissing. An Aberrancy that engulfed the entire world, a planet of pestilence, a whole world of blackness and filth and rot and death . . .

The poison, the Maien said. *The poison hidden by the god of oaths. It did not die with him.*

Komé's words were lost in the torrential garble that was her, that was everything. She could hear nothing, only blackness. She could see nothing, only blackness. She was frothing and tumbling and dying. She was dying.

Osoolyeh desires it.

Then, in the Grand Trine Room, someone screamed. The piercing, tortured shriek tore Emily's mind from the grasp of Ososolyeh's consciousness, one reality cracking to reveal glimpses of another . . .

And she fell, and she bubbled, and she died.

In the Grand Trine Room, someone screamed—a high lingering warbling scream rent from the core of the creature that gave it voice.

Emily opened her eyes, gasping, fumbling around herself like a drowning victim. She felt Stanton falling to his knees beside her, reaching for her arms; she looked at the place where her hand should be. She looked for the bubbling blackness, for the foulness that would engulf her . . .

. . . but her hand was still just a ghost-image floating above a cuff of silver, and her arm was smooth and white.

"It's all right," Stanton murmured, holding her to still her violent trembling. He smelled of blood, but maybe that was just another part of the horror. "It's all right, Emily. It was just a vision. A Cassandra."

The screaming continued, like a man being torn to pieces. Emily looked to see where the soul-wrenching sound was coming from.

It was coming from Tarnham.

The scene was ghastly. Tarnham was soaked in blood, bound by lashing tendrils of power. He struggled in wild terror. In his teeth, clenched like a bit, was the Otherwhere Marble. He screamed against it like a man gagged. Emily looked down into her palm. Only the acorn remained there.

"He's got it!" Emily screamed. "He's got my *hand*!"

"Stop him!" Mirabilis roared. But it was too late. In a flash, Tarnham was gone, leaving behind only a smell of brimstone and burning hair.

"His ferret!" Miss Pendennis pointed. "Look there!"

Tarnham's ferret had been slaughtered, torn to pieces by someone's hand, and the bloody remains of the creature used to inscribe a magical sigil on the floor of the Grand Trine Room.

"Blood magic," Stanton barked, jumping to his feet and storming forward. He looked at each of the sangrimancers in turn. "Which of you did it? And how . . . in Mirabilis' own Grand Trine Room?"

Heusler and Rocheblave looked at each other suspiciously, each scrutinizing the hands of the other for traces of blood. It wasn't until that moment that Emily noticed that Caul wasn't with them. Rising quickly, Emily felt a hand wrap around her arm. She looked up, into Caul's twitching face. He smiled.

"Carissima mia," he whispered. "It is t-t-time."

She winced, sudden pain bending her almost double. It was as if acid had been poured into the twisting channels of her cerebellum. *No,* she thought. *No . . . she would not . . .*

It is time, the voices in her head commanded her.

Hardly knowing what she was doing, Emily leaned forward. Her hands moved on their own. She squeezed her breasts together from the sides to slacken her corset front. Reaching down between the corset and her chemise, she felt for the black-handled knife that she had hidden there, the sharp athame that she had stolen from Miss Pendennis' traveling case. The muscles of her arms spasmed as she struggled against the compulsion, but the magic was too strong. She withdrew the knife, holding it loosely in a shaking hand.

Caul snatched it. And then everything that had been moving so quickly moved even faster.

The huge man crossed the Grand Trine Room in two strides, toward Mirabilis. Before anyone even saw his movement, Caul had a hand buried in the Sophos' white hair. He jerked the old man's head back sharply, and with a swift, easy movement, Caul slashed Mirabilis' throat. Blood sprayed dark in the murky half-light.

Mirabilis gurgled, choking, scrabbling at the air for a moment before dropping to his knees. Caul threw him backward, and the knife came down again with swift efficiency. Emily saw Stanton and Miss Pendennis throwing themselves at Caul, grabbing at him to make him stop, but Caul was too huge, too strong. Even as they hung off him, trying to pull him away, Caul butchered the old man. The knife in his hand tore open Mirabilis' chest from throat to belly. A foul odor rose. Caul plunged his hand into Mirabilis' chest, pulled out the old man's shuddering heart, slashed it free with a short movement from the knife. Arterial blood sprayed black in the dim flickering light. Caul raised the heart high.

I claim this place!

Caul's voice boomed against the walls of the Great Trine Room, echoing and thundering.

I claim mastery of the Great Trine!

The explosion of light that came from Caul's gory upstretched fist was blinding; it outlined each of the colleagues in white-hot brilliance, sending them staggering, then spinning away from him on the blood-streaked marble floor. Caul stood wreathed in brilliance, restored and rejuvenated as if he'd bathed in the blood of a whole regiment of Sergeant Booths. He threw his head back and laughed—a rich Italian-scented laugh, high and fluty.

Then, another voice.

"No."

Resounding, old, powerful, the voice shook the walls to their foundations, cutting Caul's horrible laughter short.

The word came from Ben. He stepped out from behind his desk. He came to stand before Caul. His hands were held in front of his chest, his fingers almost touching. He did not look like old Ben anymore, though; he looked like someone much greater. Emily realized suddenly that she had seen his face before.

"Benedictus Zeno." Caul broke the silence, making the air vibrate cruelly. His voice was touched with recognition and surprise. "I had no idea you were still alive. And working as a servant for the Institute. Is that how old credomancers are put out to pasture?"

"Leave this place!" Ben commanded, taking two menacing steps toward Caul.

Caul thrust Mirabilis' heart out before him, squeezing it so that gory drops splashed onto the marble at his feet. Ben winced, faltered. His shoulders sagged slightly.

"You transferred the power of the Institute to Mirabilis a long time ago. You cannot take it back that easily." Lifting his knife, Caul slashed out at Zeno. With a great deal of effort, old Ben was able to tear himself free of whatever magic bound him; he moved, but not quickly enough to avoid Caul's knife, which slashed across his upper arm. With a strangled cry, he bent, blood seeping through his fingers.

"I have taken the heart of the Heart!" Caul lifted the gory trophy high over his head once again. "I have claimed the Trinc from within. Mirabilis' power, the power of the Institute, is now mine." He gestured to Rocheblave, who was watching him with consternation and awe.

"Mr. Rocheblave, I require your assistance in the name of the United States Army. If you want to live to see the sun rise, you're going to help me. Tie them all up." He gestured to Miss Pendennis. "The fabric in her petticoat should be sufficient to your needs. Zeno first, and make sure you gag him. He's still the father of modern credomancy, after all. Then the High Priest. Don't worry about retribution, neither he nor that whore goddess he serves will be a threat after I'm done with them."

Rocheblave moved to comply. Miss Pendennis surrendered

her petticoat rather than have it taken from her, and
Rocheblave quickly tore it into long strips. As he was doing
this, Emily noticed Zeno whispering something furiously to
Stanton and reaching toward him with a bloody hand.

"You must!" Zeno said, clasping Stanton's hand weakly as
Rocheblave came up behind him and pulled the two of them
apart.

"Stanton!" Caul barked, lifting a hand. "I am your Sophos
now. Sit down and don't make another move." Stanton gri-
maced, but sat quickly and did not move again.

Rocheblave moved behind Heusler now, pulling his arms
back and wrapping cloth around his wrists.

"You're making a bad mistake, Caul," Heusler said, his
voice taking on a new quality of menace. "If you kill me, Her
retribution will be unimaginable. Give the stone to me now,
swear your allegiance to Her, and perhaps I will intercede on
your behalf."

But Caul showed no signs of hearing Heusler's words. His
attention was otherwise. He reached into Mirabilis' blood-
soaked pocket and withdrew a black marble. He held it up to
the light, looked in it.

"What a pretty little hand!" he said, his voice softly accented in Italian.

"Grimaldi!" Stanton spat. "But you were taken into custody
in Philadelphia . . ."

"The Philadelphia police were most obliging to the Army's
request to remand a hostile foreign Warlock," Caul said. "And
despite the errors of his birth, Grimaldi has done good work
for us in the past."

"And you've given your body to that . . . thing?" Stanton
spoke with revulsion. "My God, Caul."

Caul patted his stomach, grinning like the cat who'd swallowed the uchawi pod. When he spoke again, it was Grimaldi's
drawl that flowed from his lips. "It is the necessity, Mr. Stanton. You can search the hands, you can search the clothes . . .
But you can no search the *stomach*!"

"But . . . Tarnham . . . he had the marble!" Miss Pendennis
said.

"Tarnham never had a goddamn thing," Caul said. "It was

just a credomancer's sleight of hand. Mirabilis was trying to set us sangrimancers against one another. Trying to get us to believe one of the others took it. With us chasing after one another, he could keep the real stone for himself."

"But . . . it was blood magic . . ." Miss Pendennis said.

"If it *was* one of us tearing up that ferret, wouldn't have Zeno raised the alarm?" Caul said scornfully. "Misdirection, Miss Pendennis. While everyone's attention was on that sham of a séance, Stanton did some first-year blood work with Tarnham's rat. I knew Mirabilis had to have some kind of plan up his sleeve."

"A plan that provided you with a perfect distraction." Stanton spoke through clenched teeth.

"I knew an opportunity would present itself—it always does, for a good soldier. Thank you for your help, Stanton. I doubt any of my own men could have done better."

With a furious cry, Stanton sprang to his feet, fists clenched. He made it only two steps toward Caul before the hulking sangrimancer stopped him with a dismissive gesture. "I told you to sit *down*."

Stumbling as if Caul had thrown a rope around his ankles, Stanton fell to the floor, next to Mirabilis' butchered body. He buried his face in his hands, still smeared with Zeno's blood.

"Now," Caul said, "we finish this."

Caul lifted Mirabilis' heart before him. Making bold, angular swipes through the air, he used the bloody organ to trace a large rectangle. When he'd completed this action, he barked three loud commands, and the rectangle began to glow faintly. A dark room could be seen through it.

Go through, carissima mia.

The compulsion was irresistible. Emily walked toward the portal.

As her feet moved of their own accord, a sudden flurry of activity caught Emily's eye. Stanton had risen to kneel by Mirabilis' body. He smeared his already-bloody hands through the ocean of Mirabilis' thickening blood with quick, sinuous movements, muttering low bitter words as he did. Radiance grew around his fingertips. He cupped it in his hands as he rose to his feet. His presence seemed to expand to fill the entire room, though he was no taller than he'd been before. With a loud sound, he clapped his hands together, and the magic arced and sizzled between them.

Then, through clenched teeth, he uttered words that made the earth shudder:

"By the blood of my Sophos and the Sophos before him, I *reclaim*."

Caul whirled—too late. It was as if the words themselves attacked him. They collapsed him inward and pinned his arms, wrenched his head back, and forced him to his knees. His massive form struggled mightily against them; he screamed with pain and frustration. Stanton braced his feet, gritted his teeth, holding Caul like a fisherman fighting a whale.

Emily didn't want to go through the portal. But the command had been given.

Go through, carissima mia.

And so Emily went through.

CHAPTER TWENTY-FIVE

Blood and Bile

It was like stepping off a cliff into a churning ocean of blood and screaming. After tossing nauseatingly for what seemed a very long time, Emily landed hard in another room.

The room was well lit—an abrupt change from the gloom of the Great Trine Room.

Carissima mia, the call echoed to her, but it was growing fainter and fainter, until it was hardly there at all. She blinked, the ache in her head subsiding.

She looked up, her eyes adjusting to the brightness. She was in a business office, small and rather cramped; there was a calendar on the wall that was out of date. There was a desk. And behind the desk, watching her, sat an elderly man with a crisp Vandyke beard, white threaded with black. He was sitting perfectly still. When he saw that she had finally noticed him, he smiled slightly.

She stared at him. While his face was normal, almost kindly, his staring eyes were totally black from lid to lid.

He wore a strange machine on his body. His arms and hands were encased to just above the elbow in metal plating that was ingeniously crafted to fit together as precisely as the scales of a snake. Flexible rubber tubes ran backward from the wrists of the gauntlets to two glass bottles that were fastened to his back by thick leather straps. Emily could not see what was in the bottles, but whatever it was glowed, illuminating the back of the chair in which he sat.

The man sat forward slowly. His chair creaked, and the

armoring around his hands and arms clanked faintly. He looked Emily up and down.

"Where am I?" Emily's voice caught on the words.

"You're in Charleston, South Carolina," the man answered, his words lightly accented in French. "And you are in the offices of a company called Baugh's Patent Magicks."

Baugh's Patent Magicks? The establishment that had almost run her and Pap out of business in Lost Pine? Emily's apprehension was buried momentarily under astonishment.

"Are you Baugh?"

The old man looked at her quizzically. Then comprehension dawned on his face and he chuckled.

"Oh, yes. Baugh. I'm afraid there never really was a Baugh. Or rather, there was, but I only had the pleasure of his acquaintance for a very short time. He met with an accident. He bled to death." The old man's black eyes narrowed. "I am Rene, Comte d'Artaud."

"All right, that's *who* you are," she breathed, "but *what* are you? A sangrimancer, like Caul?"

Artaud made a face.

"No, I am not a *Warlock*," he said. "I am a *consultant*. An expert. I happen to have a large contract with the United States Government." He gestured toward her arm. "The stone in your hand is going to help me fulfill it."

"What kind of expert are you?"

"I am an expert in power," Artaud said. "The finding of it, the refinement of it, and the extraction of it. The stone has so very much power locked inside it, and Captain Caul felt I was just the man to get it out." He cocked his head. "Where is Captain Caul, anyway?"

The question seemed easy, but Emily had to think about it, sorting through her jumbled memories one by one. They were horrible images, edged with steel . . .

The Great Trine Room. A black-handled knife. Blood.

Caul and Stanton, battling for ownership of the Great Trine over Mirabilis' gory corpse. The memory made Emily breathe in sharply. Stanton had to win, she thought. He had to. She looked up at Artaud, teeth clenched.

"Caul is dead," Emily spat, putting all the force of her belief into the words.

"Oh, I doubt that," Artaud said. "But I was counting on him to retrieve that Otherwhere Marble device."

"Well, he didn't." Emily lifted her ghost hand and waved it in his face spitefully. "That means you'll never get the stone."

Artaud shook his head and sighed extravagantly. Lifting a hand, he leveled one of his metal-scaled fingers at her. Light massed around his metal-clad hand, nacreous and pale, and flashed in a bright bolt toward her. Flames engulfed her body, scalding along every nerve ending with brilliant agony. Emily shrieked and writhed, her fists clenching involuntarily, her muscles spasming in torturous unison.

The pain subsided after an eternity. Emily lay on the floor, breathing hard, her muscles twitching. She moaned, fighting the humiliating urge to sob like a child.

"You see, *ma petite,* that's where you're wrong." Artaud was standing over her, looking down at her, his black eyes flat as scuffed obsidian. "It just means it will take longer and hurt more."

Artaud pushed her down a hall that was hung with advertising posters for Baugh products. His metal-sheathed hand was clamped around the back of her neck, its strength obviously reinforced by whatever strange power the gauntlets possessed. The little shoves he gave her were made painfully insistent by the shocking jolts he delivered with them. Every time his cold metallic hand pressed against her flesh, she winced, cringing.

"It's really too annoying, leaving me in the lurch like this," Artaud muttered as they walked, punctuating angry words with twinging shocks. "All this dirty business simply isn't in my scope of work. Well, if I must, I must. Warlocks!"

They passed rooms where hundreds of women in shapeless brown dresses worked at long low tables, assembling brightly colored patent magic charms. Fingers flying, heads down, they were monitored by strolling, sour-faced supervisors. The air hummed with tedium and exhaustion.

"The late shift," Artaud said when he saw Emily looking.

"Lazy sluts, all of them. Paid by the piece, and they still won't apply themselves." His fingers flexed. "Perhaps I just haven't found the right means of motivating them."

"I suspect you're doing quite well for yourself regardless," Emily growled.

"Oh, yes, quite well," Artaud said. "The mail-order operation is simply a front, you understand. But one must never pass up an opportunity to make a profit, *n'est-ce pas?*"

They paused before a large iron door. A sign on the door showed an engraving of a rampant eagle, sheaves of spears clutched in its claws; black block letters read: *Restricted. No Trespassing for Any Reason Whatsoever. By Order of the United States Army, President Ulysses S. Grant, Commander in Chief.*

As Artaud fiddled with a ring of keys, Emily had a sudden urge to make a break for it. As if intuiting this, Artaud took an even firmer grasp on her neck.

"Don't be foolish," he said. "You're about to see something amazing."

The doors opened on a cavernous factory space. From wall to far-distant wall were hundreds of giant silver and black machines, thumping and clattering. Pistons pounded, flywheels whizzed, canvas drive-belts stuttered. Emily stared, the thunderous din of it all pounding in her ears.

"This is the Extraction Room." Even though the words were spoken close to her head, Artaud had to yell to be heard.

"What *is* this?" she murmured, assuming that he could not hear her. But he answered nonetheless, as he shoved her toward a set of stairs; she had to catch herself on the railing to keep from falling down them.

"These machines extract pure raw power from the Mantic Anastomosis," Artaud cried, spreading his gauntleted hands. "*Chrysohaeme,* the ancients called it. The golden blood of the earth. You are standing inside the first successful terramantic extraction plant ever built on such a large scale."

Emily said nothing, her eyes darting from side to side. There had to be some avenue of escape. Artaud had the gauntlets, but if she was quick enough . . .

Artaud's face fell in a frown. He'd obviously been expecting some expression of awe. With a small hiss of annoyance, he grabbed her upper arm and held it tight. Fiery pain seized her, drove her almost to her knees.

"What do you think, Miss Edwards?" he hissed, bringing his face close to hers again. "Is it not phenomenal?"

She nodded quickly, flinching away from him.

Artaud grunted satisfaction as he pushed her forward again, down a broad walkway between two lines of machines. The floor was constructed of heavy metal grating, underneath which a viscous black fluid swirled and bubbled. Emily recognized the foul smell of rot and decay. Black Exunge.

"Those machines over there are called needle borers." Artaud gestured to a bank of tall machines with large pistonlike attachments that drove slender silver poles up and down in metal-ringed holes in the floor. "The pistons you see aboveground aren't the actual drills; the drills themselves are sunk deep underground."

"Fascinating," Emily said quickly, hoping to avoid another painful rebuke. But even as she spoke, she was remembering something even more painful . . . the feeling of needles plunging into her, sucking at her . . . The memory that had been Ososolyeh's.

This was what Ososolyeh had shown her.

"The needle borers extract the power in its raw form, which then goes through those machines for processing . . ." Artaud pointed to another bank of machines, squat and dome shaped, which rattled as they worked. "Then, it is processed further, distilled and refined until it reaches this state." He pointed toward a large area built up high with heavy wood shelves. On the shelves rested row upon gleaming row of bottles, filled with a glowing golden fluid—the same glowing fluid that Artaud carried in the bottles on his back.

Chrysohaeme.

Earth's blood.

"It is the pure extraction of magical power," Artaud said, watching Emily as she stared at the bottles. There were thousands of them. "Of course, this isn't one hundredth of what we've extracted over the past two decades. The rest is in military storage facilities in Virginia, I believe. Caul says they're storing it up to defend against some kind of foreign threat." Artaud's voice was scornful. "If Caul wasn't always so busy worrying about foreigners in woodpiles, he would see the incredible potential of the applications I have developed. He wants to protect America just as it is—but with my devices, America could rule the world!" Artaud lifted his hands, wiggled his fingers. "These gauntlets, for example. I've designed them to give an untrained individual the ability to exercise powers greater even than a fully trained Warlock. Warlocks are limited in the amount of magic they can channel. But with these gauntlets there is no such limitation."

Artaud paused, regarding his metal-sheathed fingers.

"Of course, I still have to work on the rate at which they use the chrysohaeme . . . they drain the tanks far too quickly. Haven't quite figured out how to regulate the flow properly . . ."

"What's the Black Exunge for?" Emily lifted a hand, pointing in the direction of a group of men who were using a steel chute to pour the stinking tarlike fluid into a large tank. They were wearing protective suits of spun silver and glass—the same suits the Aberrancy hunters had worn.

"Very good, Miss Edwards." Artaud sounded genuinely pleased. "That is indeed geochole—or Black Exunge, as you call it. You see, when we started this operation over ten years ago, we had no trouble finding large chrysohaeme pockets to extract. Over the years, however, they became harder to find— in fact, they began to move from day to day. Very frustrating. So we adopted what we've come to call the Exunge extraction method."

Artaud pointed to another row of racks, on which rested a different kind of container—bullet-shaped steel containers stenciled with a skull-and-crossbone design. The exact kind of containers she'd seen the Aberrancy hunters putting Black Exunge into.

"In the early days, geochole was difficult to obtain," Artaud said. "Now it is wonderfully plentiful, making our job that much easier."

A goose-pimply chill chased over Emily's flesh. More magic being used . . . more Black Exunge being created, overwhelming the Mantic Anastomosis' natural ability to process and purify it . . .

"What is the Exunge extraction method?" she asked, but something in the back of her mind told her she knew already.

"Black Exunge is heavier than chrysohaeme, just as water is heavier than oil. We pump Black Exunge deep into the Mantic Anastomosis to get at fragmented pockets of chrysohaeme. It's quite an effective technique."

The back of Emily's throat went dry and tight.

This was what Ososolyeh had shown her.

A lake drained, leaving nothing but foulness behind. But these fools weren't just sucking the sweet water from the lake, they were pumping poison back into it, container upon container, clogging it with filth and venom.

A world engulfed by roiling blackness.

The Mantic Anastomosis was a living thing.

A living thing that could become an Aberrancy.

The Mantic Anastomosis purges itself of Black Exunge for a reason, Emily realized. *Black Exunge is as toxic to the Mantic Anastomosis as it is to any living thing. If Ososolyeh's ability to purge itself is overwhelmed, it will become an Aberrancy. Everything that lives on earth will be consumed. Everything— everything—will die.*

Emily held her hand over her mouth, not trusting herself even to breathe. Artaud watched her, and when he spoke he sounded even more pleased than before.

"You really are taking an interest!" he said, wonderingly. Then he shook his head. "What a shame."

Artaud brought her to a room on the far side of the Extraction Room, which was small and cold and dark. As Artaud pushed her over the threshold, Emily realized that he did not intend that she would ever come back over it. Not on her own two feet, anyway.

As Artaud moved around the room, raising the gas jets, Emily could see white enameled medical implements. In the middle of the room there was a large, flat dissecting table, with deep channels designed to direct the runoff of blood into a bucket. The dominant feature of the room, however, was another of Artaud's machines. This one was a girdered archway of steel, surrounded by smaller tubelike chambers, haloed by an intricately wired nest of cloth-wrapped cords.

"Sit." Artaud gestured to a wooden chair in the middle of the room as he moved toward the machine. Emily stood stock-still.

Anything would be better than being locked in this room with this man, she realized, gut trembling. Anything.

She sprang for the door, her fingers wrapping around the knob just long enough to feel that it was already locked.

Teeth bared, Artaud spread all five gauntleted fingers at her, driving her to her knees. She bent over double, one arm flying up protectively over her head, the other frozen on the locked doorknob. Involuntary tears flooded her eyes.

"Haven't we already discussed motivation," he said, "or did I not ask politely enough? My apologies. I will try again. Will you please sit?"

Slowly, Emily dragged herself to the chair, breath coming in whimpers. She pulled herself onto it, wrapping her arms around her body, bending double to ease the lingering, cramping aches.

Artaud nodded with satisfaction as he went back to his machine. He flipped switches one by one, and a universe of little lights began to glow like bugs on a summer night. Emily watched him, teeth clenched.

Now what?

Suddenly, Emily noticed that there was something warm touching her. She flinched away, wondering if it was another of Artaud's attacks—but then she realized that the warmth was coming from her own hand. From the Jefferson Chair ring around her thumb, where it was resting against the bare skin of her upper arm . . . it was warm. Warm as the hand of a friend.

Stanton was looking for her.

Sudden hope sang in her sore, twitching body. She pressed the ring against her lips, closed her eyes. He was looking for her. It was something, at least.

"After Caul retrieved Grimaldi from the custody of the Philadelphia Police, I had them search your unconscious mind for information about the Otherwhere Marble." Artaud did not look at her as he went to a metal rack on which dozens of bottles of chrysohaeme sat arranged like colossal, glowing ant eggs. "Thus, I know that it's a transdimensional portational device of some kind. Mirabilis must have believed that no one could possibly gain access to the dimension in which your hand was stored. But with enough power, it's possible to open a gateway to any dimension necessary." Artaud began loading the bottles into the huge machine, like bullets in the chamber of a revolver.

Emily clenched her fist hard around the warmth of the ring. There wasn't going to be time for him to find her. Artaud was going to tear open the dimension where her hand was . . . and probably tear her open along with it. Her pulse raced in her temples. She had to do something. Her eyes darted around the room. If only she had a weapon, one she could reach before he could get his hand up to stop her . . .

A weapon.

The idea came to her in a flash, with such force that it made her hand rise abruptly to her throat.

Of course. A weapon. She did have a weapon. A terrible, beautiful weapon.

Emily fumbled for the silk pouch that was still tucked down the side of her dress. She pulled out the blue and red calico pouch she had carried with her since she'd left Lost Pine. She palmed the little bundle of ashes.

She raised the pouch to her mouth, using her teeth to bite through the thread. When it was open, she spilled the powder into her hand, and whispered the spell over it to recharge the magic:

"My decision is firm,
My will is strong,
Let this spell bind him
All his life long."

Then she closed her fist around the powder and waited until Artaud was finished. He seized the fat handle of a knife-switch, pulled it down. The portal blazed with sudden light, coruscating with wereflames of brilliant dancing plasma.

"Now, be a brave girl." He laid a heavy, sizzling hand on her shoulder, fingers digging hard into her flesh. "I'm afraid this is going to hurt quite a lot."

Emily blew the powder at him in a billowing cloud. The smell of lavender filled the room.

Artaud gasped, choking and waving his hand in front of his face.

"What the . . . !" he bellowed, taking two alarmed steps backward. And then he stopped, blinking, his black eyes flat and unreadable.

"My God," he said softly. "What have I done?"

CHAPTER TWENTY-SIX

Skycladdische's Revenge

There was a long silence. Artaud stared at her, unblinking, unmoving. Then, abruptly, he dropped to one knee before her, grasping at the hem of her dress.

"Behold, a god stronger than I that is come to bear rule over me," he whispered as he pressed the purple silk against his face, making a sound of pleasure in his throat. One of his metal-cased hands snaked out to caress her ankle. She tried to move her leg away, but Artaud's cold hand rose to stroke her calf. She pushed it away angrily.

He smiled up at her, a mean, hungry smile.

"Now, you little *connasse*, is that nice?" he asked, biting the last word. Wrapping his arms around her ankles, he tipped her backward. She fell hard, banging the back of her head against the wooden chair. In an instant Artaud was over her, his body pressing down on hers.

"Don't be coy," he growled at her, and she was suddenly very aware that his teeth were rotted brown stumps. She tried to turn away, but he mashed his mouth down over hers, pinning her arms by her sides. She screamed in her throat and tried to push him away. But Artaud worked one steel-clad hand up to the neck of her dress, and there was the sound of tearing fabric.

Then, another sound. A loud, abrupt humming.

A sudden flash of light came from the machine's glowing archway, from the activated dimensional portal. Artaud looked back, frowning; the momentary distraction gave Emily the chance she needed to her free her hand from where the old

man had it pinned. She reached up to where her silver hair
sticks were. Seizing one, she drove it toward Artaud's face.

The stick missed the old man's eye, but delivered a sharp,
painful smart just under it. Artaud drew back, bellowing with
rage and surprise. As he did, a hand clamped down on Artaud's shoulder, pulling him up and pushing him back roughly
across the floor.

Emily scrambled backward, holding the hair stick like a
dagger in her hand. But when she saw who had thrown Artaud off of her, she let it drop to her side.

"Mr. Stanton!" she breathed.

With two long strides, Stanton went to the portal and
punched buttons in a rapid sequence. There was the sound of
pounding from the other side—heavy hard pounding. Someone was trying to follow . . .

"Behind you!" Emily screamed.

Stanton spun, but it was too late. Artaud's hand came up,
intense radiance exploding from his fingertips, so bright that
it made Emily's eyes water. The outpouring of energy crackled and seared the air.

Stanton leaned into the blast, rhythmic Latin streaming
from his lips. He twisted one hand over the other, small mo-
tions summoning larger forces—a cold blasting whirlwind,
whistling angry and harsh. Emily was spun across the floor by
the sudden gusting force; she grabbed at the legs of a heavy
table to hold herself in place. Stanton stood before Artaud, feet
planted firmly. With curt movements, he spun Artaud around
and around, lifting him from the ground, battering him against
walls.

Then, Artaud's other hand came up, his fists clenched thumb
against thumb. And with a bark that echoed even over the
whistling cyclonic din, he sent a tremendous blast of concentrated brilliance against Stanton's chest. Stanton flew backward,
his body slamming hard against the far wall. The spinning gale
he had summoned vanished abruptly, dissolving into small
sighs, dusty whorls, gasps. Stanton slid to the ground.

And then, the only sound in the room was the pounding
coming from the other side of the portal.

Emily scrambled to Stanton's side, grabbing him by the shoulders. His blood-streaked face was gray and slack; his chest was still.

"Mr. Stanton?" Emily touched his face. His skin was ice cold.

The pounding on the door intensified. Sudden, familiar, searing pain sliced through her skull.

Carissima mia.

Emily's whole body contracted with loathing and anguish. No, not that. It couldn't be. It was too much. Grabbing handfuls of Stanton's jacket, she hid her face against his chest.

Open the door.

Emily was not aware that Artaud had come up behind her until he reached down and grabbed her, hauling her to her feet.

Open the door.

The pounding on the door had become rhythmic, like the beating of drums. An ancient command, burning in her blood, a throbbing like the beating of her heart.

"Do you see what happens?" Artaud raised a fist; Emily watched it coming toward her slowly. "Faithless whore!"

Open the door.

Now.

The compulsion was too powerful to resist.

Emily ducked Artaud's blow easily, then brought up a fist and struck him hard across the face. What the blow lacked in strength it made up in precision; Artaud staggered backward. Emily went to the portal and touched the buttons in the exact order in which they were flashing through her mind.

The portal cracked open and Caul staggered through. His face was pale with exertion and lined with strain; his body and hands were covered with cracked, dried blood.

"Finally," Caul said. He placed a hand on her head. *"Dormiente."*

Emily melted, suddenly exhausted, unable to keep her legs underneath her anymore. Caul held up the Otherwhere Marble, rolling it between his thumb and forefinger.

"Stanton remembered some tricks from his days at the

Academy." Caul looked down at Stanton's body, and then at
Artaud's tanks. "But not enough of them, it seems."

Caul threaded his fingers through Emily's hair and pulled
her to her knees. She hung limply in his grasp.

"Don't you dare hurt her!" Artaud cried. "She is mine,
Caul, do you hear me? Mine!"

Caul regarded him curiously. Then he looked down sideways at Emily, and gave her a vicious little shake. "I guess
I underestimated *your* capacity for playing tricks, skycladdische."

"You know what these can do, Caul," Artaud growled,
holding his gauntlets out before him. "Let her go this instant!"

Caul raised an eyebrow. He did not let Emily go.

"Go ahead, Artaud," he said.

Artaud clenched his teeth, balled his hands into fists, put
them together thumb to thumb.

"You think I won't?"

"I think you *can't*. Your bottles. They're bone dry."

There was a moment of silence. Then, with a cry, Artaud
scurried toward the racks, fumbling for another glowing
bottle. Caul followed him, dragging Emily by the hair. With
his other hand, Caul seized the harness on Artaud's back and
threw him backward. Artaud thudded heavily to the floor, his
sundry appliances clanking and squeaking. Caul came to
stand over the black-eyed man. Artaud looked up at him,
pleadingly.

"John, don't. Please, don't do it. You mustn't hurt her. I beg
you . . ."

"It's for your own good," Caul said. Lifting his heavily
booted foot, he delivered one sharp blow to the Frenchman's
chin, sending him crashing backward into unconsciousness.

Emily, her hair still clutched tightly in Caul's fist, made a
small unintentional sound in her throat—despair and fear
mixed in equal parts. Caul looked down at her as if he'd forgotten that she was there.

"Dormiente," he said again. Fresh languor crept through
her. She felt suddenly as soft as butter that had sat in the sun.

Then he stretched her out on the floor.

Her body was limp and transfixed. All she could do was stare up at the ceiling, her head filled with pain and the distant sound of clanking machines.

He went over to the dissecting table, where a gleaming array of surgical implements lay arranged on a tray. He touched each one of them. Finally, he selected a heavy silver cleaver.

Then he knelt beside her, placing the marble between her limp fingers.

"Open the cuff," he said. "You know how Mirabilis did it."

There was nothing strong left in her at all. Her body was soft as water, and her hand moved on its own. Emily tapped the marble against the Boundary Cuff in the same rhythm Mirabilis had used. Her hand rematerialized. Caul tossed the cuff aside. It spun away, clattering.

Caul held her hand for a moment, stroking the stone gently with his thumb. Then he stretched her arm out away from her body. He held her arm down hard against the cold stone floor. He brought the cleaver up. And then he brought it down.

The ring of steel and the abrupt, metallic smell of spurting blood were the last things she knew.

CHAPTER TWENTY-SEVEN

Heavy Weather

Smells.

Acrid burning flesh and cold congealed blood and aromatic spirits of ammonia.

"Wake up." A voice resonating in the far distance. A hand waving something under her nose, something cold and bitter and sharp. "Wake up, Miss Edwards."

Pain woke as she did, stirring like a provoked beast, diffused through all parts of her body but concentrating in agony at her wrist. She turned her head to look at her arm. A bloody tourniquet was tied tightly around it, halfway between elbow and wrist.

"My . . . hand," she said.

"Not anymore." Caul's voice. He laid the smelling salts aside, next to a field surgeon's case of brightly polished mahogany. Inside the case, large silver needles shone. "You do present me with the most interesting challenges. Removing clumsy skycladdische love spells is hardly my area of expertise. Comforting brokenhearted Frenchmen even less so. And yet I will be called upon to do both, if Artaud is to be in any condition to extract the power from this stone."

"You can't remove the love spell," Emily rasped. "Only I . . . only I can. And I *won't*."

"Your blood will do as I bid it do," Caul growled. "Your blood is all that you are, every fragment of your will, every moment of your life. And it's going to be mine."

Caul began taking needles out of the case, one by one. He

showed one to her. It was the size of a pencil, delicately engraved, with a razor-sharp tip.

"One for your *carotis communis* . . . here, on your throat." He touched the place gently. "One for each of the brachial arteries that run along the insides of your arms, and one for each of the large femoral arteries that run along the insides of your legs." He spoke as if reciting from a book. "You'll be dry within five minutes, *carissima mia*."

The last words were spoken in Grimaldi's cruelly perfumed Italian accent. A shadow of distaste passed over Caul's face. He clenched his teeth, spoke in an undertone.

"Perhaps the most useful aspect of your blood is that I'll be able to use it to exorcise this greasy Wop from my body."

She was so cold.

It was the coldness of her hand that made her notice how hot the ring around her thumb had grown. She clenched her hand into a loose fist, ignoring the prick of tears in her eyes.

She closed her eyes, waiting for the needles to slide under her skin, to pierce her, to empty her

"Stop, sangrimancer."

Emily's eyes opened slowly. It was Stanton's voice, low and shuddering. She turned her head a little, and she could see him standing on shaking legs, pulling himself up against the shelf that held the bottles of chrysohaeme. His skin was the color of plaster; the streaks of dried blood on his cheeks stood out in gruesome relief.

"Stanton." Caul's voice was lazy. "And we thought you were dead."

"There are very few advantages to being burned," Stanton said. "But there is one. You can't stop me with raw magic. You might as well try to drown a fish."

"I'll remember that," Caul said. He tilted his head. "You're just in time to watch me bleed this little tramp. You do remember how they're bled, don't you?"

"I'm not going to watch you bleed anyone," Stanton said. "I'm going to stop you."

Caul lifted his eyebrows in amusement.

"Stop me? You can hardly stand up." Caul lifted the large

silver cleaver, its edge crusted with Emily's drying blood. He took a step toward Stanton. "Reclaiming Mirabilis' power was a dirty trick, but that's easily reversed. Once you're dead, I'll have the stone and the power of the Institute—and even that Aztec High Priest Mirabilis was good enough to obtain for me. In one day, I will have amassed enough power to crush any goddamn foreign subversive who turns an ugly eye on my United States. It's a great day to be a patriot."

"Not so much as you'd think." Stanton pulled one of the glowing glass containers from the shelf beside him. He knocked it against the side of the heavy shelf, cracking it open. He plunged his hand into the shifting, shimmering chrysohaeme.

The transformation was immediate and complete. Stanton lit up like a magnesium torch. His face and eyes and tongue went black as a photographic negative. Around him, a blinding aura of multicolored light flashed and swirled. He raised a hand toward Caul, magic burning in traceries around his fingertips.

"That won't do you any good." Caul reached into his pocket and pulled out Emily's limp, severed hand. It was loosely wrapped in a blood-sodden handkerchief. "You can throw as much power as you like, the stone will absorb it all."

"I know," Stanton said.

And he threw power—a flood of brilliance that illuminated the white walls with violently shifting shadows of color. Caul stood, legs spread defiantly, holding up Emily's gory hand like a shield. He grasped the severed hand with both of his own, straining against the force of Stanton's magic.

"You could have stood with me, Stanton!" Caul screamed, a high gleeful scream, tortured by the power surging around it. "You could have used your powers for *good* instead of throwing them away. You called it principles, but it was nothing more than cowardice. I know what you are! You're nothing more than a goddamn . . . yellow . . . coward."

"I know what I am." Stanton's voice resonated. "And I know what I'm not."

And then it happened.

The stone blossomed. Exploded. It happened so fast that Emily's blurry eyes could hardly follow it. A black dripping ball of slime wrapped itself around Caul's hand. The big man looked down in blank astonishment, screaming.

The black mass slithered up his arm like a hundred tiny snakes. His body began to expand. He threw his head back and screamed again—a loud long scream that became high and otherworldly as the rivulets of black slime reached his throat and plunged into it like grubbing maggots.

"Don't let him touch you," Stanton said to Emily, his voice echoing as if it were amplified by a million bullhorns. "Get away from him!"

Emily sat up slowly. She could not move very fast. She swung her legs off the table, and the world spun around her. Caul's shrieks rang in her ears. The brilliance of the air around her, shifting and distorted with magic, made the floor difficult to locate. But she found it.

Stanton's face glowed stark white, his body burning like the sun.

"Get away!" he screamed.

Caul was expanding to such a size now . . . bigger and bigger, blacker and blacker, exuding the smell of a field of rotting corpses under a hot summer sun. He was reaching for her, black slimy paws fumbling to grab her. Dodging him unsteadily, she threw herself against a far wall, where one of the gas fixtures glowed softly. She waited as he got closer, until he was almost on her, reaching for her throat . . .

Then she turned up the gas full blast, the sudden high flame catching a corner of his sleeve.

She dove for safety as he exploded in an inferno of light and color and heat, white and blue and red. Heat battered at her as she rolled behind the dissecting table. The smell became that of fat blood-fed flies roasting in the flames of Hell.

Caul stopped screaming; instead, he crumpled, a slow collapse punctuated by sprays of sparks. Finally he stilled, and then there was just the sound of whistles and bubbles and pops, and flames licking the ceiling and smoke filling the room.

Then, there was a loud *crack*.

From the center of the flaming mass a huge fountain of silver light shot up to the sky, blasting the roof outward in a hail of wood and plaster and tar paper. Looking up through the destroyed ceiling, Emily saw that the night was velvety black, salted with stars.

The fountain of light shot up, expanding like a reversed funnel as it rose, broad and thin and shimmering like the clouds of luminous stellar gas Emily remembered from the memories of Ososolyeh. The colors of it were so beautiful: resonant basso reds, deep echoing blues, shimmering, soaring yellows. The multihued light cloaked the sky in heartbreaking radiance.

Then it began to rain.

Coruscating drops of power sizzled down like tiny comets, phosphorescent glitters like dying fireflies that made the ground glow where they hit. The brilliant shower quickly doused the flames, clearing the smoke from the air, revealing Caul's charred corpse. Kneeling, his fists were pressed against his forehead.

Emily did not realize how silent it had become until the hollow clank of the empty chrysohaeme container resounded through the room. Emily's eyes found Stanton's. No longer wreathed in power, he looked thin and tired. He swayed, gave her a nod, then collapsed heavily to the floor.

She went to him, falling to the ground beside him. Pain jolted through her as she reached to touch him with a hand that was no longer there.

"Mr. Stanton," she said. The raindrops of iridescent silver brilliance fell all around them, making the air glow with released power. The whole world around them shone like an illuminated manuscript, brilliant colors made precious with bright nacreous gems. The raindrops glowed in Stanton's hair, leaving marks of light where they fell on his pale, upturned face.

"Mr. Stanton?" she whispered, brushing drops of brilliance from his face. "Dreadnought?"

He opened his eyes. They were entirely black, from lid to lid.

"I like it better with the 'dear' after it," he said, distantly.

"Are you all right?" she breathed. "Please say you'll be all right!"

"Of course I'll be all right," he said. "Though I am a bit hungry."

CHAPTER TWENTY-EIGHT

The Man
Who Saved Magic

Dreadnought Stanton stood proudly over the infamous sangrimancer, the blood fiend who clutched and scrabbled miserably at his feet—a wretched spectacle.

"I die . . . yes, I die! For you have defeated me in all truth, and the great engines of evil that were at my command! And you have defeated me twice over, for you battled fairly against my methods, which were deceitful and dishonorable! Truly I lose to a better Warlock, and a better man!"

And letting out a final, foul breath, the blood fiend reclined, expiring.

"Such terrible dangers shall never again threaten our great nation!" Dreadnought Stanton said firmly, regarding the formidable enemy who lay dead at his feet. "The great goals of credomancy shall uphold the virtues of this land, the honor of its women, and the innocence of its youth!"

Emily closed the book, repressing an almost unbearable urge to salute.

The book was fresh from the presses of Mystic Truth Publishers. It had an eye-popping chromolithographed cover that featured Dreadnought Stanton boldly fending off rotting zombies, fearsome sangrimancers with blood dripping from the corners of their mouths, and leaping lions. Emily wasn't sure where the lions had come in, but they certainly added excitement.

The Man Who Saved Magic was the title, inscribed in powerful red letters. Emily made a mental note to send a copy to Rose. It would give the girl palpitations.

She glanced at her new hand sitting on the book. It was so strange and yet so pretty; she often felt her eyes sneaking toward it. The prosthetic was made of ivory and silver. The fingers were long and slim, articulated with silver joints that bore elaborate scrolls of machine engraving. There were even sweetly carved pink nails. A smoothly molded cuff of silver, also scrolled with engraving and lined with peach-colored velvet, reached halfway up to her elbow.

"Presented by the Witches' Friendly Society, this First of June, 1876," was scrolled along the edge of the cuff. "To Miss Emily Edwards, in honor of her signal accomplishment."

Next to it, her real hand seemed large and clumsy. But then again, her real hand was alive. She placed this living hand on a small golden ball that rested beside her on the windowsill. It was somewhat smaller than a croquet ball, decoratively engraved. It was called a rooting ball. Hermetically sealed, it contained a special nutrient fluid in which Komé's acorn was suspended—it was hoped that the acorn would sprout and root so that it could be planted. Emily closed her eyes and felt for the spirit of Komé; the Holy Woman shifted comfortingly beneath Emily's touch.

"Dreaming the afternoon away, I see." The loud voice came from the door. It was Miss Pendennis, dressed in visiting clothes: a dark dress with gloves and hat and reticule.

"Just doing some improving reading." Emily held up the book. "It's quite thrilling. I had no idea Mr. Stanton did all those things! And I had no idea that I swooned quite so much, or that my name was 'Faith Trueheart.'"

Miss Pendennis raised an eyebrow.

"Certainly you didn't think they'd put Emily Edwards in the book," she said. Then she sat down in a chair with a weary sigh.

"Well, I've got news, since you obviously prefer reading trash to picking up a copy of *Practitioners' Daily*." Miss Pendennis settled herself, putting her large feet up on an ottoman. "They've finished tearing down the terramantic extraction plant in Charleston. Baugh's Patent Magicks is no more. The threat to Ososolyeh, the great consciousness of the earth, is ended."

Emily liked the grand finality of Miss Pendennis' statement. And while she was highly pleased that the threat to the great consciousness of the earth was ended, the first thing that crossed her mind was Lost Pine. Now that Baugh's Patent Magicks was out of business for good, there was sure to be plenty of work waiting for her there.

Miss Pendennis sighed with satisfaction. "All's well that ends well."

"Didn't end too well for Mirabilis," Emily said.

"Poor arrogant fool." Miss Pendennis shook her head. "A victim of his own hubris, really. He was so supremely confident of his abilities. That's a credomancer for you!"

So confident of his abilities, he was willing to risk the lives of everyone around him to see his plans fulfilled, Emily thought. "How's Mr. Tarnham?" she asked quietly.

"Home in the bosom of his family, never to practice magic again." Miss Pendennis shook her head. "They like him a whole lot better now that all he can do is stare at the wall and drool. Poor boy. He was so attached to that ferret." She sighed heavily. "Maybe if they pray hard enough over him, he'll be able to speak again someday."

Emily looked at her ivory hand. "I guess Caul wasn't the only one with a ready supply of Sergeant Booths."

Miss Pendennis shook her head, letting the dark sentiment linger for a moment before dispelling it with a falsely bright tone.

"Speaking of arrogant fools, I dropped in on the Stantons the other day."

Emily inclined her head. She did not look at Miss Pendennis.

It had been nearly a month since Emily had seen Stanton last, on the pier in Charleston, the world around them drenched with the light of Ososolyeh's released power. Before she'd stirred from the drowsy drugs they'd given her to relieve the pain of her amputation, Stanton had vanished from the hospital, whisked back to New York by Benedictus

Zeno and a coterie of senior professors from the Institute. Emily was left to recuperate in the hot, muggy hospital in Charleston. A well-trained staff of efficient Witch Doctors had accelerated the healing of her amputated limb, and had cleansed her of the compulsion the Manipulator had hidden in her blood. She had written Stanton a letter to tell him that, as a matter of fact, she had found the live chickens and bone rattles very fascinating indeed. There had been no reply. After she'd left the hospital, she'd returned to New York to collect her twenty-thousand-dollar payment from the Institute. Emeritus Zeno—as he was respectfully called now—was extravagantly hospitable, drafting her a check with extreme haste, providing her the use of the Institute's most lavish and uncomfortable suite, and offering to help her with any travel arrangements she might wish to make. It all left Emily feeling distinctly that she was not wanted. So she'd gone to the Grand Central Depot and bought her train ticket back to San Francisco.

"How is Mr. Stanton?" Emily asked softly.

"Looking well, I guess." Miss Pendennis shrugged. "Up and about. The senator has reporters and political cronies in at all hours to meet him. He's a veritable attraction at the brownstone on Thirty-fourth; the senator might have to start selling tickets." She paused, pulling off her gloves and reaching into her reticule. "Listen, Em. He asked me to give you this."

It was a slender envelope, inscribed with Stanton's firm angular hand. It did not look promising.

"Do you want me to—" Miss Pendennis started to rise.

"No, don't bother," Emily said, unfolding it. "It's short."

Dear Miss Edwards:

Emeritus Zeno tells me that you are returning to California. I suppose you are going back to marry Mr. Hansen. I am glad for you. You are a brave and wonderful woman, and you deserve the joy and security of a long, settled marriage.

I wish you every happiness,
Dreadnought Stanton

Insufferable.

She folded the letter and put it back into the envelope. Emily didn't know her hand was trembling until Miss Pendennis laid a hand over it and stilled it.

"Em, may I speak bluntly?"

"I would be shocked if you didn't."

"You wouldn't make a good credomancer's wife. You know it as well as I do. You'd be squinking him from noon to night. A credomancer can't have a wife who's always squinking him." She paused. "If he were going to marry at all, which he wouldn't because . . . Well, anyway, if he were going to marry, Stanton would require a wife who worshipped the ground he walked on, that's all."

"That certainly does seem to leave me out of the running," Emily said.

"Never mind," Miss Pendennis said briskly. "I've got something to get your mind off Warlocks. The Witches' Friendly Society would like to book you on our upcoming lecture tour. I'm leaving next week, going all around the world. Why don't you come with me? There are hundreds of women in the magical community who are dying to meet you."

"I don't think so," Emily said. "I'm going home."

There wasn't much to pack for her trip, and when it came time to go, Emily went to find Benedictus Zeno to say good-bye. She knocked softly at the door of Mirabilis' old office.

A low-toned voice mumbled something that might have been "come in"; she opened the door.

"Emeritus Zeno, the carriage is waiting, I just wanted to say—"

She stopped abruptly, silenced by the look on Zeno's face— a look of strange annoyance, as if the very act of her walking through the door was an affront.

She'd never seen his face arranged in any manner other than smiling pleasantness. But, frowning, his face looked terrible and old and unsettling. It was so strange and unexpected that it took Emily a moment to recover. In that moment, she noticed that there was another man in the office with him.

It was Stanton.

The men were standing together; Stanton had his coat on and his hat in his hands.

Emily and Stanton looked at each other. The last time she'd seen him in Charleston, his eyes and tongue had been black as a photographic negative. Now he looked neatly tailored and pressed, as if he'd just been unwrapped. He regarded her from what seemed a far greater distance than the few feet that separated them.

"I'm terribly sorry," she said, flushing. She turned quickly to go.

"No, Miss Edwards, wait a moment," Zeno said. The look of annoyance had vanished quickly, but his voice bore a faint hint of exasperation. "Mr. Stanton is just leaving."

Emily studied the floor while Zeno and Stanton moved toward the door. It seemed to Emily that Stanton hesitated for a moment. At the hesitation, Zeno extended a hand and said firmly: "Good day, Mr. Stanton."

Stanton took Zeno's hand and shook it resolutely.

"Good day," he said. Emily looked up in time to see his back as he hurried through the door, closing it behind himself softly.

When he was gone, Zeno came to Emily, took both her hands, looked at her traveling costume.

"Well, Miss Edwards," he said softly. "All ready to go, I see."

"I'm sorry, Emeritus," she said, uncertain why she felt so compelled to apologize. "I'm terribly sorry."

Zeno nodded toward the door through which Stanton had left.

"Mr. Stanton will be taking the position of Sophos, director of the Institute. He's the only one who *can,* given the . . . unorthodox circumstances." Zeno paused, regarding Emily with steady, calm eyes. "The role of Sophos will occupy every moment of his day, and every ounce of his energy. The Institute is perhaps the most influential credomantic establishment in the world, and he will serve as its Heart."

"He will do a wonderful job," Emily said.

"Yes. He will." Zeno stared hard at Emily. Then he relaxed, a small benevolent smile creeping back over his lips. "Now then, when does your train leave?"

"In a couple of hours," Emily said. She felt suddenly despondent and out of place. The magnificence of Zeno's office—the office that would be Stanton's—was suddenly oppressive and horrible. She tucked her reticule tight under her arm, the impulse to flee strong and strange. "I suppose I should go."

Zeno took her hand, her living hand, and gave it a strengthening squeeze. The gesture had an immediate impact; she felt invigorated, brighter. She lifted her chin, drew a deep breath. She longed suddenly for the smell of pine.

"Thank you for everything, my dear," Zeno said. "You have done the world a great service. These troubling matters no longer concern you. Go home now. Go home and flourish."

Emily walked into the empty hall and took a deep breath. The sun came through the windows; the day was beautiful for traveling. She let the breath out. The carriage was waiting. She walked away from the office quickly, her heels clicking on the marble floor.

She paused only a moment beneath the statue of the wise-looking goddess that held up the Veneficus Flame. She looked up. The flame was high and strong. Emily placed her hand on the statue and closed her eyes; she could feel the power of Ososolyeh thrumming beneath her fingertips.

Forgive him.

Emily's heart fluttered. The words were as clear and sharp as if they had been spoken in her ear.

"Miss Edwards?"

It was Stanton's voice.

Emily opened her eyes slowly. She considered walking away until she could not hear his voice anymore. But she turned, looking at him. He was standing some distance from her, pinching the edge of his hat between his fingers.

"Hello, Mr. Stanton."

He opened his mouth, then closed it abruptly, as if he'd forgotten what he was going to say.

"How is your hand?" he said finally.

She lifted her arm. "Still gone."

Silence.

"Penelope tells me you're going back to Lost Pine," he said. "Congratulations."

"On what?"

"On making a wise choice."

She drew herself up and tried to look down her nose at him, but found it impossible given their difference in height.

"You're a very smart man, Mr. Stanton," she said, "but you're not as smart as you think you are."

He blinked at her.

"Good-bye," she said, turning to go.

"Emily," his voice mingled hesitancy and urgency in equal measure. "Wait."

She turned back, breathing out a little impatience.

"Yes?"

"Do you remember? On the train? I . . . made you a promise."

"You never promised me anything," Emily said.

"But I did," Stanton said. "I promised I'd show you Central Park."

"Leave it to a New Yorker to put a bunch of trees in one place and call it wonderful," she said, as they looked over the huge expanse of open land dotted with swaying saplings. "I grew up in California, Mr. Stanton. I've seen plenty of trees."

"Those were California trees." He lifted an eyebrow. "These are New York trees." He offered her his arm. "Would you like to walk?"

She took his arm. He was warm as always. Burning up from the inside. The last time she'd been this close to him, he'd been as cold as ice. The memory made her shudder.

They went down a path that led under a long avenue of pink-blooming cherry trees. Little petals like flakes of fragrant snow drifted down around them with every stirring of wind.

"Why are we here, Mr. Stanton?" she asked tiredly. "Must we continue this torture?"

"I find the day rather pleasant," he said.

"Walking arm in arm with somebody you've got a deep affection for is pleasant," Emily said. "Walking arm in arm with somebody you've got a deep *unrequited* affection for is torture."

"Your affection is not unrequited," he said softly.

"Really?" She bit the word. "You leave without saying good-bye. I send you a letter, and you don't write back. And when you finally do write, it's to congratulate me on going home to marry another man. How could I have failed to recognize such a bold and heartfelt declaration?"

Stanton was silent, then he took a deep breath.

"What do I have to offer you, Emily?" he said. "Ten years— or less? The fact that I'll leave you young enough to make a pretty widow? You'll be better off this way."

"Which way is that?"

"Going back to Lost Pine. Going back to your lumber—to Mr. Hansen."

"I'm not going to marry Dag," Emily said. "I don't love him. If I did, I wouldn't care if he was going to die tomorrow. I'd marry him and be glad for every moment. But I don't love him. I love you."

"And I love you," he said. "More than anything I've ever loved or could imagine loving. And that's why I won't let you be hurt."

She lifted her ivory hand. "That hurt," she said. She touched her chest, the place where her heart beat. "This doesn't."

Stanton said nothing, but reached up to pluck a petal from where it had lodged in her hair. He let it drop. "You won't even be out of your thirties," he mused softly.

"Why must you always make things so complicated?" She stomped a petulant foot. "You're alive now. I'm alive now. Forget the rest! Didn't Ososolyeh teach you anything?" She dropped to one knee and clasped his hand earnestly. She looked up at him, making her eyes big and cowlike. "Dreadnought Stanton, will you marry me?"

"For heaven's sake!" Stanton said, looking around. "Get up! You can't do that. It's not . . ."

"Proper. I know. But I'm not expected to be proper, I'm a skycladdische, remember?" Emily said.

"And I'm still half a sangrimancer," Stanton said, softly.

He crouched down to look into her face, resting his elbow on his knee. "Remember?"

She looked into his eyes. They had changed color, she noticed. They used to be bright green, but the blackness had not left them entirely. Perhaps it never would. Perhaps they would always remain as dark as polished serpentine, veined with deep rills of ebony.

"I know what you are," she said. "And I know what you're not."

He did not say anything for a long time, and Emily began to feel annoyed. She stood and brushed off her dress.

"Of course, if you'd rather not marry me, I suppose we could come to some other arrangement," she snapped. "I'm a woman of independent means now. I don't have to marry anyone."

Stanton caught her arm, rose. He took both her hands, living and dead, and held them tightly. He looked down into her face. A sudden breath of warm wind rustled the trees, sending showers of blossoms swirling around them.

"Miss Edwards, I would be proud and honored if you would marry me and be my wife."

Emily shrugged diffidently. "I'll think about it."

He blinked at her, face falling; then he smiled. "You're insufferable," he said.

"Yes, we're well matched that way. Shall we keep walking? I want to see the castle you told me about. And Charlie, the enchanted swan who can recite Dante."

"The moon's not full," Stanton said. "Besides, I just made Charlie up. I'm sorry."

Emily heard the echo of Mirabilis' words. *All credomancers are liars.*

"But there is a castle," Stanton hurried to add. "And a reservoir with Croton water. And irises and blue flags. Honestly."

"Then we'll just have to do without Charlie." Emily tucked herself in close to him. He was so warm, so wonderfully warm. They walked down the avenue of blossoming trees, and Emily was astonished when she saw that the shifting leaves, for one indefinable moment, spelled out a word.

Yes.

She blinked, lifting a hand to point, but in a breath of wind, the word was gone.

New York trees really were different from California trees, she realized with sudden amusement.

Stanton looked down at her. "Do you remember when we first came to the Miwok camp? When Komé kept rattling on at me? You thought it was about the stone, but she was really saying something entirely different."

"You said she congratulated you," Emily said.

"She did. On finding such a suitable wife. I told her I wasn't married, that I did not intend to be married, and that I certainly wasn't going to marry you." He grinned. "That was when she hit me."

Emily laughed and looked up at the sky. It was the most beautiful shade of blue. They strolled thoughtfully for a while, the late afternoon sun slanting low and golden across their path.

"She also predicted that our home would be filled with the happy thunder of robust boy-children," Stanton remembered, offering it up as if it were an exceptionally tempting treat.

Emily frowned. "As the one who will presumably be called upon to produce the robust boy-children in question, I must say that it sounds like an awful lot of work."

"There are elements of the process that can be somewhat enjoyable, I'm told." Stanton stopped her in the middle of the path. He put his hands on her waist and drew her very close. His hot breath tickled the little hairs on her forehead.

"Now see here," he said, his voice so quiet it rumbled in his throat. "I am very much aware of the fact that you haven't said yes yet."

"To which, the marriage or the boy-children?"

"Well, I thought you might object to one without the other, but . . ."

Emily silenced him with one finger pressed against his warm lips. White and pink petals drifted all around them.

"Yes," she said.

Epilogue

Benedictus Zeno closed his eyes and breathed in the air.

He'd forgotten the particular smell of Russian spring: high and thin and green, rich with the fragrance of black earth and cold water and mushrooms. There was still snow in patches, but a warming wind from the Caspian Sea stirred the tops of the birches.

He was sitting on the ivy-draped terrace of a dacha outside of Saint Petersburg, next to a man whose hair and beard were white-blond and whose eyes were intensely blue. The man was called Perun, but that was not his real name. Few in the Sini Mira used their real names. For decades, Zeno had called him only by the name he used within the Sini Mira, the name of the heavenly smith, the god of thunder.

They sipped tea sweetened with raspberry jam from glasses set in silver holders. On a table beside them, a brightly enameled samovar steamed pleasantly.

"Well," Zeno grumbled in Russian. "*That* didn't go very well, did it?"

"Certainly didn't," Perun said. "Not at all." He paused. "Such is life in the service of the Great Mother."

"Your most revered Ososolyeh," Zeno said, "can be a fickle, whimsical, opaque *bitch*."

Perun frowned deeply. "Mind your manners in my house, *credomancer*," he growled. "She is mother of us all, and her wisdom is great."

"The whole point of allowing *sangrimancers* into my Institute was to learn from them, to use the earth's consciousness during the séance to gain insight into the Temple's plans for Temamauhti. To learn how the power in the stone should be used for our defense. And here we are, power gone, Mirabilis dead, and my Institute fallen into the hands of *Dreadnought Stanton*. And you're going to sit there and tell me to mind my manners?"

"Peace, Benedictus. The power has been returned to the earth where it belongs. The terramantic extraction plant in Charleston has been destroyed. Do not make the best the enemy of the good."

But Zeno was not mollified. In fact, his next words were even louder. "But Ososolyeh *must* have felt the compulsion working on Miss Edwards! Komé must have known . . . why didn't she warn us?"

Perun shrugged, spread his hands.

"You cannot expect the Mother to think as we humans do," he said. "Though I grant it would be more convenient."

"The way things turned out, it might have been better if we'd let Caul have the stone," Zeno muttered bitterly. "At least he was fighting the right enemy."

"Do you really believe a narrow-minded bigot like Caul could have defeated the Black Glass Goddess?" Perun lifted an eyebrow. "His masters were happy to let him stockpile power, but they would never have let him use it. Putting the stone in his hands would have been as good as handing it to Itztlacoliuhqui herself." He reached for an engraved silver case, snapped it open. He withdrew a brown cigarette, lit it, then exhaled smoke with great pleasure. "I think Captain Caul was lucky to have died with his illusions intact."

"I wish I'd been allowed to keep a few more of mine," Zeno said, waving a hand to dispell the acrid stink. "Stanton! Master of my Institute! The thought turns my stomach. And on top of that, he's in *love*." Zeno spoke the word with mincing distaste. "As if a Sophos doesn't have enough to worry about without being in *love*."

"They're going to be married, then?" Perun asked. Zeno snorted disapproving assent.

"After Charleston, I had Stanton utterly resolved to give her up—for her own good, of course." Zeno shook his head.

"But all she had to do was show her face at the wrong place at the wrong time, and . . ." Zeno threw up a hand. "Love!"

Perun smiled. "We can't all be priests, Benedictus."

Zeno slapped a hand on the table with remembered indignation. "Do you know what he said to me when I reminded him that there were still larger goals to be considered?"

"I can't imagine."

"He said, 'the board has changed, and our strategy must change as well.' And in the most *insolent* manner!" Zeno frowned at his own boots. "Without a doubt the board has changed—it has changed for the worse. We have been pushed a dozen moves closer to checkmate, and the one man who has even the remotest hope of forestalling it is picking out china and deciding what to put on the wedding invitations."

"Claiming Mirabilis' power with blood magic . . ." Perun sighed, shook his head, watched the smoke rising between his fingers. "Well, I suppose there wasn't anything else to be done. But really, you brought it on yourself. Letting Mirabilis go through with that ridiculous symposium in the first place. If you'd just handed the stone over to us . . ."

"Caul would have reduced the Institute to rubble," Zeno growled.

"Every man has something he wishes to protect," Perun mused, lifting the cigarette to his lips. "But to save the world, he may be asked to sacrifice that which he holds most dear."

The men contemplated this in silence for a long time. Perun smoked his cigarette down to a scant nub, flicked it onto the flagstones, and watched it burn itself out.

"We will look for the poison that Komé spoke of," he said finally. "The poison hidden by the god of oaths. She could only have meant Volos' Anodyne. If we can find it and implement it quickly, perhaps no one will be required to sacrifice anything."

Volos' Anodyne, the unripened fruit of the Sini Mira's profoundest scientific mind. It was always thought lost, uncompleted . . . but if Komé spoke the truth, it existed—somewhere. This was hope, great and brilliant, and all too fragile.

"The High Priest was at the symposium," Zeno said. "Yet another instance in which I find myself questioning your

Great Mother's boundless wisdom. I don't suppose she might have told us about the poison *without* Heusler being there? Now we have to raze the Temple to find it. You know they will stop at nothing to destroy it."

"The Temple does not know Volos' true identity. They won't even know where to begin to look."

"And we do?"

"Surely Miss Edwards—"

Zeno shook his head curtly, breaking off the words. "The less she knows, the less trouble she can cause us," he said. "That woman has a positive *knack* for getting into trouble with sangrimancers. And if they manage to discover that Lyakhov was—"

"Please," Perun interjected, lifting a hand. "Call him by his nom de guerre. Call him Volos, after the god of oaths. It honors his memory better."

"It may well be the only honor his memory receives," Zeno snapped. "Miss Edwards says her mother left nothing behind when she died in Lost Pine; a few minor female ornaments. Certainly no notes or papers. She assured me of this—she said that her 'Pap' told her everything he knew."

"And she is telling the truth?"

"Do you think she could lie to me?" Zeno asked. Perun drew in smoke, closed his eyes, exhaled peacefully.

"We will find it," he said. "The Great Mother will not let us fail. *Ex fide fortis,* yes?"

Zeno took a deep breath—of good clean Russian air, instead of smoke, and released a sigh. "Yes," he said. *"Ex fide fortis."* Then he stood, shrugging on his coat and clapping on his hat. "Now, if you'll excuse me, I have to go teach a lovestruck sangrimancer how to run my Institute." He opened his mouth as if to say something more, but then pressed his lips together and shook his head. He lifted a hand in mute farewell as he vanished into the twilight.

Perun sat alone on the terrace for a long time after he was gone, smoking and thinking. He watched the sun go down, listened to the sounds of darkness closing in. Finally, when the last cigarette in his case was gone, he barked a laugh that resounded off the inkstroke trees. He lifted a glass of now-cold tea in a salute to the rising moon.

"To the only thing that can civilize a skycladdische, redeem a sangrimancer, and leave a poor old credomancer at a loss for words!" He poured the liquid on the ground for luck, then rose to fetch more cigarettes.